The Horror Omnibus

Ruskin Bond has been writing for over sixty years, and now has over 120 titles in print—novels, collections of short stories, poetry, essays, anthologies and books for children. His first novel, *The Room on the Roof*, received the prestigious John Llewellyn Rhys Prize in 1957. He has also received the Padma Shri (1999), the Padma Bhushan (2014) and two awards from Sahitya Akademi—one for his short stories and another for his writings for children. In 2012, the Delhi government gave him its Lifetime Achievement Award.

Born in 1934, Ruskin Bond grew up in Jamnagar, Shimla, New Delhi and Dehradun. Apart from three years in the UK, he has spent all his life in India, and now lives in Mussoorie with his adopted family.

Other Ruskin Bond Titles

Angry River
A Little Night Music
A Long Walk for Bina
Hanuman to the Rescue
Ghost Stories from the Raj
Strange Men Strange Places
The India I Love
Tales and Legends from India
The Blue Umbrella
Ruskin Bond's Children's Omnibus
The Ruskin Bond Omnibus-I
The Ruskin Bond Omnibus-II
The Ruskin Bond Omnibus-III
The Ruskin Bond Omnibus-IV
The Ruskin Bond Omnibus-V
Rupa's Supernatural Omnibus
The Rupa Book of Great Animal Stories
The Rupa Book of True Tales of Mystery and Adventure
The Rupa Book of Ruskin Bond's Himalayan Tales
The Rupa Book of Great Suspense Stories
The Rupa Laughter Omnibus
The Rupa Book of Scary Stories
The Rupa Book of Haunted Houses
The Rupa Book of Travellers' Tales
The Rupa Book of Great Crime Stories
The Rupa Book of Nightmare Tales
The Rupa Book of Shikar Stories
The Rupa Book of Love Stories
The Rupa Book of Wicked Stories
The Rupa Book of Heartwarming Stories
The Rupa Book of Thrills and Spills
The Rupa Book of Spooky Encounters
Rendezvous with Horror
Shudders in the Dark
The Rupa Book of Eerie Stories
All Roads Lead to Ganga

RUSKIN BOND
The Horror Omnibus

RUPA

Published by
Rupa Publications India Pvt. Ltd 2007
7/16, Ansari Road, Daryaganj
New Delhi 110002

Sales centres:
Bengaluru Chennai
Hyderabad Jaipur Kathmandu
Kolkata Mumbai Prayagraj

Edition Copyright © Rupa Publications India 2007
Selection and Introduction Copyright © Ruskin Bond 2007

All rights reserved.
No part of this publication may be reproduced, transmitted,
or stored in a retrieval system, in any form or by any means, electronic, mechanical,
photocopying, recording or otherwise, without the prior permission of the publisher.

P-ISBN: 978-81-291-1255-2
E-ISBN: 978-81-291-4466-9

Twenty-second impression 2025

25 24 23 22

Typeset by Mindways Design, New Delhi

Printed in India

This book is sold subject to the condition that it shall not, by way of trade or otherwise,
be lent, resold, hired out, or otherwise circulated, without the publisher's prior consent, in
any form of binding or cover other than that in which it is published.

Contents

Introduction	ix
The Squaw BRAM STOKER	1
The Tiger A.E. COPPARD	18
The Doll's Ghost F. MARION CRAWFORD	33
The Skeleton JEROME K. JEROME	49
The Staircase HUGH WALPOLE	57
The Haunted Doll's House M.R. JAMES	78
The Ghost BY WALTER DE LA MARE	94

Mrs Amworth   96
    E.F. BENSON

The White Wolf of the Hartz Mountains   116
    FREDERICK MARRYAT

Dracula's Guest   143
    BRAM STOKER

Carnival on the Downs   159
    GERALD KERSH

The House of Strange Stories   177
    ANDREW LANG

The Overcoat   188
    RUSKIN BOND

The Mirror   192
    REETA DUTTA GUPTA

The Werewolf   203
    C.A. KINCAID

At the Pit's Mouth   219
    RUDYARD KIPLING

Boomerang   227
    OSCAR COOK

The Hollow Man   239
    THOMAS BURKE

The Beast with Five Fingers   257
    W.F. HARVEY

The Lodger   292
    MARIE BELLOC LOWNDES

The Last Match EDWARD FITZ-GERALD FRIPP	333
Haunted Villages LT. COL. W.H. SLEEMAN	363
The Vampire SYDNEY HORLER	370
The Bordeaux Diligence LORD HALIFAX	378
The Doctor's Ghost DR NORMAN MACLEOD	382
All Souls' EDITH WHARTON	388
The Phantom 'Rickshaw RUDYARD KIPLING	419

Introduction

All those who enjoyed shuddering their way through my earlier volumes of scary stories will find a satisfying spooky sequel in the collection of horror stories. With a repertoire of ghostly themes, claustrophobic settings, and threatening situations, the grisly tales in this volumes will not disappoint young horror addicts.

What is real and what is imaginary? Do ghosts really exist? Over the years, story-tellers have given substance to our worst fears. Here, too, readers are invited to let their imagination run amok. These are some of the spookiest tales ever written by masters of the macabre. Terror and adventure lurk in the pages of these varied horror stories.

Included in this collection are some classic tales, the period chillers, written by undisputed masters of the genre—Bram Stoker, Rudyard Kipling, A. E. Coppard, Hugh Walpole, and others—as well as numerous lesser-known hair-raisers from across the world. While Bram Stoker's 'The Squaw' retells the story of a cat that will have her revenge, Edith Wharton's 'All Souls'' transports us to the eerie world of black magic. Other masters of the art featured here are F. Marryat, who takes us on a terrifying journey through the Hartz Mountains; E. F. Benson, who discovers a vampire in a sleepy village; and M. R. James, whose haunted doll's house will scare you out of your wits. From phantom rickshaws to haunted houses, werewolves to vampires, prepare to encounter dangerous elements and explore uncharted territories.

So watch your step. Look around. These hair-raising stories are guaranteed to make your flesh creep. This is a perfect book for long winter evenings of drawn curtains and dim lights. Or summer nights with the moonlight streaming in at the window and a jackal howling outside the door?

Ruskin Bond

The Squaw

Bram Stoker

Nurnberg at the time was not so much exploited as it has been since then. Irving had not been playing *Faust*, and the very name of the old town was hardly known to the great bulk of the travelling public. My wife and I being in the second week of our honeymoon naturally wanted someone else to join our party, so that when the cheery stranger, Elias P. Hutcheson, hailing from Isthmian City, Bleeding Gulch, Maple Tree County, Neb., turned up at the station at Frankfort, and casually remarked that he was going on to see the most all-fired old Methusaleh of a town in Yurrup, and that he guessed that so much travelling alone was enough to send an intelligent, active citizen into the melancholy ward of a daft house, we took the pretty broad hint and suggested that we should join forces. We found, on comparing notes afterwards, that we had each intended to speak with some diffidence or hesitation so as not to appear too eager, such not being a good compliment to the success of our married life; but the effect was entirely marred by both of us beginning to speak at the same instant—stopping simultaneously and then going on together again. Anyhow, no matter how, it was done; and Elias P. Hutcheson became one of our party. Straightaway Amelia and I found the pleasant benefit; instead of quarrelling, as we had been doing, we found that the restraining influence of a third party was such that we now took every opportunity of spooning in odd corners. Amelia declares that ever since she has, as a result of that experience, advised all her friends to take a friend on the honeymoon. Well, we 'did' Nurnberg together, and much enjoyed the racy remarks of our Transatlantic friend, who, from his quaint speech and his wonderful stock of adventures, might have stepped out of a novel. We kept for the last object of interest in the city to be visited, the Burg, and on the day appointed for the visit strolled round the outer wall of the city by the eastern side.

The Burg is seated on a rock dominating the town, and an immensely deep fosse guards it on the northern side. Nurnberg has been happy in that it was never sacked; had it been it would certainly not be so spick and span perfect as it is at present. The ditch has not been used for centuries, and now its base is spread with tea-gardens and orchards, of which some of the trees are of quite respectable growth. As we wandered round the wall, dawdling in the hot July sunshine, we often paused to admire the views spread before us, and in especial the great plain covered with towns and villages and bounded with a blue line of hills, like a landscape of Claude Lorraine. From this we always turned with new delight to the city itself, with its myriad of quaint old gables and acre-wide red roofs dotted with dormer windows, tier upon tier. A little to our right rose the towers of the Burg, and nearer still, standing grim, the Torture Tower, which was, and is, perhaps, the most interesting place in the city. For centuries the tradition of the Iron Virgin of Nurnberg has been handed down as an instance of the horrors of cruelty of which man is capable; we had long looked forward to seeing it; and here at last was its home.

In one of our pauses we leaned over the wall of the moat and looked down. The garden seemed quite fifty or sixty feet below us, and the sun pouring into it with an intense, moveless heat like that of an oven. Beyond rose the grey, grim wall seemingly of endless height, and losing itself right and left in the angles of bastion and counterscarp. Trees and bushes crowned the wall, and above again towered the lofty houses on whose massive beauty Time has only set the hand of approval. The sun was hot and we were lazy; time was our own, and we lingered, leaning on the wall. Just below us was a pretty sight—a great black cat lying stretched in the sun, whilst round her gambolled prettily a tiny black kitten. The mother would wave her tail for the kitten to play with, or would raise her feet and push away the little one as an encouragement to further play. They were just at the foot of the wall, and Elias P. Hutcheson, in order to help the play, stooped and took from the walk a moderate-sized pebble.

'See!' he said, 'I will drop it near the kitten, and they will both wonder where it came from.'

'Oh, be careful,' said my wife; 'you might hit the dear little thing!'

'Not me, ma'am,' said Elias P. 'Why, I'm as tender as a Maine cherry tree. Lor, bless ye, I wouldn't hurt the poor pooty little critter more'n I'd scalp a baby. An' you may bet your variegated socks on that! See, I'll drop it fur away on the outside so's not to go near her!' Thus saying, he leaned over and held his arm out at full length and dropped the stone. It may be that there is some attractive force which draws lesser matters to greater; or more probably that the wall was not plumb but sloped to its base—we not noticing the inclination from above; but the stone fell with a sickening thud that came up to us through the hot air, right on the kitten's head, and shattered out its little brains then and there. The black cat cast a swift upward glance, and we saw her eyes like green fire fixed an instant on Elias P. Hutcheson; and then her attention was given to the kitten, which lay still with just a quiver of her tiny limbs, whilst a thin red stream trickled from a gaping wound. With a muffled cry, such as a human being might give, she bent over the kitten licking its wound and moaning. Suddenly she seemed to realise that it was dead, and again threw her eyes up at us. I shall never forget the sight, for she looked the perfect incarnation of hate. Her green eyes blazed with lurid fire, and the white, sharp teeth seemed to almost shine through the blood which dabbled her mouth and whiskers. She gnashed her teeth, and her claws stood out stark and at full length on every paw. Then she made a wild rush up the wall as if to reach us, but when the momentum ended fell back and further added to her horrible appearance, for she fell on the kitten and rose with her black fur smeared with its brains and blood. Amelia turned quite faint, and I had to lift her back from the wall. There was a seat close by in shade of a spreading plane tree, and here I placed her whilst she composed herself. Then I went back to Hutcheson, who stood without moving, looking down on the angry cat below.

As I joined him, he said:

'Wall, I guess that air the savagest beast I ever see—'cept once when an Apache squaw had an edge on a half-breed what they nicknamed "Splinters" 'cos of the way he fixed up her papoose which he stole on a raid just to show that he appreciated the way they had given his mother the fire torture. She got that kinder look so set on her face that it jest seemed to grow there. She followed Splinters more'n three year till at last the braves got him and handed him over to her. They did say that no man, white or Injun, had ever been so long a-dying under the tortures of the Apaches. The only time I ever see her smile was when I wiped her out. I kem on the camp just in time to see Splinters pass in his checks, and he wasn't sorry to go either. He was a hard citizen, and though I never could shake with him after that papoose business—for it was bitter bad, and he should have been a white man, for he looked like one—I see he had got paid out in full. Durn me, but I took a piece of his hide from one of his skinnin' posts an' had it made into a pocket-book. It's here now!' and he slapped the breast pocket of his coast.

Whilst he was speaking, the cat was continuing her frantic efforts to get up the wall. She would take a run back and then charge up, sometimes reaching an incredible height. She did not seem to mind the heavy fall which she got each time but started with renewed vigour; and at every tumble her appearance became more horrible. Hutcheson was a kind-hearted man—my wife and I had both noticed little acts of kindness to animals as well as to persons—and he seemed concerned at the state of fury to which the cat had wrought herself.

'Wall, now!' he said, 'I du declare that that poor critter seems quite desperate. There! there! poor thing, it was all an accident—though that won't bring back your little one to you. Say! I wouldn't have had such a thing happen for a thousand! Just shows what a clumsy fool of a man can do when he tries to play! Seems I'm too darned slipper-handed to even play with a cat. Say, Colonel!'—it was a pleasant way he had to bestow titles freely—'I hope your wife don't hold no grudge against me on account of this unpleasantness. Why, I wouldn't have had it occur on no account.'

He came over to Amelia and apologised profusely, and she with her usual kindness of heart hastened to assure him that she quite understood that it was an accident. Then we all went again to the wall and looked over.

The cat missing Hutcheson's face had drawn back across the moat, and was sitting on her haunches as though ready to spring. Indeed, the very instant she saw him she did spring, and with a blind, unreasoning fury, which would have been grotesque, only that it was so frightfully real. She did not try to run up the wall, but simply launched herself at him as though hate and fury could lend her wings to pass straight through the great distance between them. Amelia, womanlike, got quite concerned and said to Elias P. in a warning voice:

'Oh! you must be very careful. That animal would try to kill you if she were here; her eyes look like positive murder.'

He laughed out jovially. 'Excuse me, ma'am,' he said, 'but I can't help laughin'. Fancy a man that has fought grizzlies an' Injuns bein' careful of bein' murdered by a cat!'

When the cat heard him laugh, her whole demeanour seemed to change. She no longer tried to jump or run up the wall, but went quietly over, and sitting again beside the dead kitten, began to lick and fondle it as though it were alive.

'See!' said I, 'the effect of a really strong man. Even that animal in the midst of her fury recognises the voice of a master, and bows to him!'

'Like a squaw!' was the only comment of Elias P. Hutcheson, as we moved on our way round the city fosse. Every now and then we looked over the wall and each time saw the cat following us. At first she had kept going back to the dead kitten, and then as the distance grew greater, she took it in her mouth and so followed. After a while, however, she abandoned this, for we saw her following all alone; she had evidently hidden the body somewhere. Amelia's alarm grew at the cat's persistence, and more than once she repeated her warning; but the American always laughed with amusement, till finally, seeing that she was beginning to be worried, he said:

'I say, ma'am, you needn't be skeered over that cat. I go heeled, I du!' Here he slapped his pistol pocket at the back of his lumbar region. 'Why, sooner'n have you worried, I'll shoot the critter, right here, an' risk the police interferin' with a citizen of the United States for carryin' arms contrary to reg'lations!' As he spoke he looked over the wall, but the cat, on seeing him, retreated with a growl into a bed of tall flowers and was hidden. He went on: 'Blest if that ar critter ain't got more sense of what's good for her than most Christians. I guess we've seen the last of her! You bet, she'll go back now to that busted kitten and have a private funeral of it, all to herself!'

Amelia did not like to say more, lest he might, in mistaken kindness to her, fulfil his threat of shooting the cat: and so we went on and crossed the little wooden bridge leading to the gateway whence ran the steep paved roadway between the Burg and the pentagonal Torture Tower. As we crossed the bridge we saw the cat again down below us. When she saw us, her fury seemed to return and she made frantic efforts to get up the steep wall. Hutcheson laughed as he looked down at her, and said:

'Good-bye, old girl. Sorry I in-jured your feelin's, but you'll get over it in time! So long!' And then we passed through the long, dim archway and came to the gate of the Burg.

When we came out again after our survey of this most beautiful old place which not even the well-intentioned efforts of the Gothic restorers of forty years ago have been able to spoil—though their restoration was then glaring white—we seemed to have quite forgotten the unpleasant episode of the morning. The old lime tree with its great trunk gnarled with the passing of nearly nine centuries, the deep well cut through the heart of the rock by those captives of old, and the lovely view from the city wall whence we heard, spread over almost a full quarter of an hour, the multitudinous chimes of the city, had all helped to wipe out from our minds the incident of the slain kitten.

We were the only visitors who had entered the Torture Tower that morning—so at least said the old custodian—and as we had the place all to ourselves were able to make a minute and more satisfactory survey than would have otherwise been possible. The custodian, looking to us as the sole source of his gains for the day, was willing to meet our wishes in any way. The Torture Tower is truly a grim place, even now when many thousands of visitors have sent a stream of life, and the joy that follows life, into the place; but at the time I mention, it wore its grimmest and most gruesome aspect. The dust of ages seemed to have settled on it, and the darkness and the horror of its memories seem to have become sentient in a way that would have satisfied the Pantheistic souls of Philo or Spinoza. The lower chamber, where we entered, was seemingly, in its normal state, filled with incarnate darkness; even the hot sunlight streaming in through the door seemed to be lost in the vast thickness of the walls, and only showed the masonry rough as when the builder's scaffolding had come down, but coated with dust and marked here and there with patches of dark stain which, if walls could speak, could have given their own dread memories of fear and pain. We were glad to pass up the dusty wooden staircase, the custodian leaving the outer door open to light us somewhat on our way; for to our eyes the one long-wick'd, evil-smelling candle stuck in a sconce on the wall gave an inadequate light. When we came up through the open trap in the corner of the chamber overhead, Amelia held on to me so tightly that I could actually feel her heart beat. I must say for my own part that I was not surprised at her fear, for this room was even more gruesome than that below. Here there was certainly more light, but only just sufficient to realise the horrible surroundings of the place. The builders of the tower had evidently intended that only they who should gain the top should have any of the joys of light and prospect. There, as we had noticed from below, were ranges of windows, albeit of medieval smallness, but elsewhere in the tower were only a very few narrow slits such as were habitual in places of medieval defence. A few of these only lit the chamber, and these were so high up in the wall that from no part could the sky be seen through the thickness of the walls. In racks, and leaning in disorder against the walls, were a number of headsmen's swords, great double-handed weapons with broad blade and keen edge. Hard by were several blocks whereon the necks of the victims had lain, with here and there deep notches where the steel had bitten through the guard of flesh and shored into the wood. Round the chamber, placed in all sorts of irregular ways, were many implements of torture which made one's heart ache to see—chairs full of spikes which gave instant and excruciating pain; chairs and couches with dull knobs whose torture was seemingly less, but which, though slower, were equally efficacious; racks, belts, boots, gloves, collars, all made for compressing at will; steel baskets in which the head could be slowly crushed into a pulp if necessary; watchmen's hooks with long handle and knife that cut at resistance—this a specialty of the old Nurnberg police system; and many, many other devices for man's injury to man. Amelia grew quite pale with the horror of things, but fortunately did not faint, for being a little overcome she sat down on a torture chair, but jumped up again with a shriek, all tendency to faint gone. We both pretended that it was the injury done to her dress by the dust of the chair and the rusty spikes which had upset her, and Mr Hutcheson acquiesced in accepting the explanation with a kind-hearted laugh.

But the central object in the whole of this chamber of horrors was the engine known as the Iron Virgin, which stood near the centre of the room. It was a rudely-shaped figure of a woman, something of the bell order, or, to make a closer comparison, of the figure of Mrs Noah in the children's Ark, but without that slimness of waist and perfect *rondeur* of hip which marks the aesthetic type of the Noah family. One would hardly have recognised it as intended for a human figure at all had not the founder shaped on the forehead a rude semblance of a woman's face. This machine was coated with rust without, and covered with dust; a rope was fastened to a ring in the front of the figure, about where the waist should have been, and was drawn through a pulley, fastened on the wooden pillar which sustained the flooring above. The custodian pulling this rope showed that a section of the front was hinged like a door at one side; we then saw that the engine was of considerable thickness, leaving just room enough inside for a man to be placed. The door was of equal thickness and of great weight, for it took the custodian all his strength, aided though he was by the contrivance of the pulley, to open it. This weight was partly due to the fact that the door was of manifest purpose hung so as to throw its weight downwards, so that it might shut of its own accord when the strain was released. The inside was honeycombed with rust—nay more, the rust alone that comes through time would hardly have eaten so deep into the iron walls; the rust of the cruel stains was deep indeed! It was only, however, when we came to look at the inside of the door that the diabolical intention was manifest to the full. Here were several long spikes, square and massive, broad at the base and sharp at the points, placed in such a position that when the door should close, the upper ones would pierce the eyes of the victim and the lower ones his heart and vitals. The sight was too much for poor Amelia, and this time she fainted dead off, and I had to carry her down the stairs and place her on a bench outside till she recovered. That she felt it to the quick was afterwards shown by the fact that my eldest son bears to this day a rude birthmark on his breast, which has, by family consent, been accepted as representing the Nurnberg Virgin.

When we got back to the chamber, we found Hutcheson still opposite the Iron Virgin; he had been evidently philosophising, and now gave us the benefits of this thought in the shape of a sort of exordium.

'Wall, I guess I've been learnin' somethin' here while madam has been getting over her faint. 'Pears to me that we're a long way behind the times on our side of the big drink. We uster think out on the plains that the Injun could give us points in tryin' to make a man oncomfortable; but I guess your old medieval law-and-order party could raise him every time. Splinters was pretty good in his bluff on the squaw, but this here young miss held a straight flush all high on him. The points of them spikes air sharp enough still, though even the edges air eaten out by what uster be on them. It'd be a god thing for our Indian section to get some specimens of this here play-toy to send round to the Reservations jest to knock the stuffin' out of the bucks, and the squaws too, by showing them as how old civilisation lays over them at their best. Guess but I'll get in that box a minute jest to see how it feels!'

'Oh no! no!!' said Amelia. 'It is too terrible!'

'Guess, ma'am, nothin's too terrible to the explorin' mind. I've been in some queer places in my time. Spent a night inside a dead horse while a prairie fire swept over me in Montana Territory— an' another time slept inside a dead buffler when the Comanches was on the war path an' didn't keer to leave my kyard on them. I've been two days in a caved-in tunnel in the Billy Broncho gold mine in New Mexico an' was one of the four shut up for three parts of a day in the caisson what slid over on her side when we was settin' the foundations of the Buffalo Bridge. I've not funked an odd experience yet, an' I don't propose to begin now!'

We saw that he was set on the experiment, so I said: 'Well, hurry up, old man, and get through it quick!'

'All right, General,' said he, 'but I calculate we ain't quite ready yet. The gentlemen, my predecessors, what stood in that thar canister, didn't volunteer for the office—not much! And I guess there was some ornamental tyin' up before the big stroke was made. I want to go into this thing fair and square, so I must get fixed up proper first. I dare say this old galoot can rise some string and tie me up accordin' to sample?'

This was said interrogatively to the old custodian, but the latter, who understood the drift of his speech, though perhaps not appreciating to the full the niceties of dialect and imagery, shook his head. His protest was, however, only formal and made to be overcome. The American thrust a gold piece into his hand, saying, 'Take it, pard! it's your pot; and don't be skeer'd. This ain't no necktie party that you're asked to assist in!' He produced some thin frayed rope and proceeded to bind our companion with sufficient strictness for the purpose. When the upper part of his body was bound, Hutcheson said:

'Hold on a moment, Judge. Guess I'm too heavy for you to tote into the canister. You jest let me walk in, and then you can wash up regardin' my legs!'

Whilst speaking he had backed himself into the opening which was just enough to hold him. It was a close fit and no mistake. Amelia looked on with fear in her eyes, but she evidently did not like to say anything. Then the custodian completed his task by tying the American's feet together so that he was now absolutely helpless and fixed in his voluntary prison. He seemed to really enjoy it, and the incipient smile which was habitual to his face blossomed into actuality as he said:

'Guess this here Eve was made out of the rib of a dwarf! There ain't much room for a full-grown citizen of the United States to hustle. We uster make our coffins more roomier in Idaho territory. Now, Judge, you jest begin to let this door down, slow, on to me. I want to feel the same pleasure as the other jays had when those spikes began to move toward their eyes!'

'Oh no! no! no!' broke in Amelia hysterically. 'It is too terrible! I can't bear to see it!—I can't I can't!'

But the American was obdurate. 'Say, Colonel,' said he, 'why not take Madame for a little promenade? I wouldn't hurt her feelin's for the world; but now that I am here, havin' kem eight thousand miles, wouldn't it be too hard to give up the very experience I've been pinin' an' pantin' fur? A man can't get to feel like canned goods every time! Me and the Judge here'll fix up this thing in no time, an' then you'll come back, an' we'll all laugh together!'

Once more the resolution that is born of curiosity triumphed, and Amelia stayed holding tight to my arm and shivering whilst the custodian began to slacken slowly inch by inch the rope that held back the iron door. Hutcheson's face was positively radiant as his eyes followed the first movement of the spikes.

'Wall!' he said, 'I guess I've not had enjoyment like this since I left Noo York. Bar a scrap with a French sailor at Wapping—an' that warn't much of a picnic neither—I've not had a show fur real pleasure in this dod-rotted Continent, where there ain't no b'ars nor no Injuns, an' wheer nary man goes heeled. Slow there, Judge! Don't you rush this business! I want a show for my money this game—I du!'

The custodian must have had in him some of the blood of his predecessors in that ghastly tower, for he worked the engine with a deliberate and excruciating slowness which after five minutes, in which the outer edge of the door had not moved half as many inches, began to overcome Amelia. I saw her lips whiten, and felt her hold upon my arm relax. I looked around an instant for a place whereon to lay her, and when I looked at her again found that her eye had become fixed on the side of the Virgin. Following its direction I saw the black cat crouching out of sight. Her green eyes shone like danger lamps in the gloom of the place, and their colour was heightened by the blood which still smeared her coat and reddened her mouth. I cried out:

'The cat! look out for the cat!' for even then she sprang out before the engine. At this moment she looked like a triumphant demon. Her eyes blazed with ferocity, her hair bristled out till she seemed twice her normal size, and her tail lashed about as does a tiger's when the quarry is before it. Elias P. Hutcheson when he saw her was amused, and his eyes positively sparkled with fun as he said:

'Darned if the squaw hain't got on all her war paint! Jest give her a shove off if she comes any of her tricks on me, for I'm so fixed everlastingly by the boss, that durn my skin if I can keep my eyes from her if she wants them! Easy there, Judge! don't you slack that ar rope or I'm euchered!'

At this moment Amelia completed her faint, and I had to clutch hold of her round the waist or she would have fallen to the floor. Whilst attending to her I saw the black cat crouching for a spring, and jumped up to turn the creature out.

But at that instant, with a sort of hellish scream, she hurled herself, not as we expected at Hutcheson, but straight at the face of the custodian. Her claws seemed to be tearing wildly as one sees in the Chinese drawings of the dragon rampant, and as I looked I saw one of them light on the poor man's eye and actually tear through it and down his cheek, leaving a wide band of red where the blood seemed to spurt from every vein.

With a yell of sheer terror which came quicker than even his sense of pain, the man leaped back, dropping as he did so the rope which held back the iron door. I jumped for it, but was too late, for the cord ran like lightning through the pulley-block, and the heavy mass fell forward from its own weight.

As the door closed I caught a glimpse of our poor companion's face. He seemed frozen with terror. His eyes stared with a horrible anguish, as if dazed, and no sound came from his lips.

And then the spikes did their work. Happily the end was quick, for when I wrenched open the door they had pierced so deep that they had locked in the bones of the skull through which they had crushed, and actually tore him—it—out of his iron prison till, bound as he was, he fell at full length with a sickly thud upon the floor, the face turning upward as he fell.

THE SQUAW 17

I rushed to my wife, lifted her up and carried her out, for I feared for her very reason if she should wake from her faint to such a scene. I laid her on the bench outside and ran back. Leaning against the wooden column was the custodian moaning in pain whilst he held his reddening handkerchief to his eyes. And sitting on the head of the poor American was the cat, purring loudly as she licked the blood which trickled through the gashed socket of his eyes.

I think no one will call me cruel because I seized one of the old executioner's swords and shore her in two as she sat.

The Tiger

A.E. Coppard

*T*he tiger was coming at last; the almost fabulous beast, the subject of so much conjecture for so many months, was at the docks twenty miles away. Yak Pedersen had gone to fetch it, and Barnabe Woolf's Menagerie was about to complete its unrivalled collection by the addition of a full-grown Indian tiger of indescribable ferocity, newly trapped in the forest and now for the first time exhibited, and so on, and so on. All of which, as it happened, was true. On the previous day, Pedersen the Dane and some helpers had taken a brand new four-horse exhibition waggon, painted and carved with extremely legendary tigers lapped in blood—even the bars were gilded—to convey this unmatchable beast to its new masters. The show had had to wait a long time for a tiger, but it had got a beauty at last, a terror indeed by all accounts, though it is not to be imagined that everything recorded of it by Barnabe Woolf was truth and nothing but truth. Showmen do not work in that way.

Yak Pedersen was the tamer and menagerie manager, a tall, blonde, angular man about thirty-five, of dissolute and savage blood himself, with the very ample kind of moustache that bald men often develop; yes, bald, intemperate, lewd, and an interminable smoker of Cuban cigarettes, which seemed constantly to threaten a conflagration in that moustache. Marie the Cossack hated him, but Yak loved her with a fierce deep passion. Nobody knew why she was called Marie the Cossack. She came from Canning Town—everybody knew that, and her proper name was Fascota, Mrs Fascota, wife of Jimmy Fascota, who was the architect and carpenter and builder of the show. Jimmy was not much to look at, so little in fact that you couldn't help wondering what it was Marie had seen in him when she could have had the King of Poland, as you might say, almost for the asking. But still Jimmy was the boss ganger of the show, and even that young gentleman in frock coat and silk hat who paraded the platform entrance to the arena and rhodomontadoed you into it, often against your will, by the seductive recital of the seven ghastly wonders of the world, all certainly to be seen, to be seen inside, waiting to be seen, must be seen, roll up—even he was subject to the commands of Jimmy Fascota when the time came to dismantle and pack up the show, although the transfer of his activities involved him temporarily in a change, a horrid change, of attire and language. Marie was not a lady, but she was not for Pedersen anyway. She swore like a factory foreman, or a young soldier, and when she got tipsy she was full of freedoms. By the power of god she was beautiful, and by the same gracious power she was virtuous. Her husband knew it; he knew all about Master Pedersen's passion, too, and it did not interest him. Marie did feats in the lion cages, whipping poor decrepit beasts, desiccated by captivity, through a hoop or over a stick of wood and other kindergarten disportings; but there you are, people must live, and Marie lived that way. Pedersen was always wooing her. Sometimes he was gracious and kind, but at other times when his failure wearied him, he would be cruel and sardonic, with a suggestive tongue whose vice would have scourged her were it not that Marie was impervious, or too deeply inured to mind it. She always grinned at him or fobbed him off with pleasantries, whether he was amorous or acrid.

'God Almighty!' he would groan, 'she is not good for me, this Marie. What can I do for her? She is burning me alive and the Skaggerack could not quench me, not all of it. The devil! What can I do with this? Some day I shall smash her across the eyes, yes, across the eyes.'

So you see the man really loved her.

When Pedersen returned from the docks, the car with its captive was dragged to a vacant place in the arena, and the wooden front panel was let down from the bars. The marvellous tiger was revealed. It sprung into a crouching attitude as the light surprised the appalling beauty of its smooth fox-coloured coat, its ebony stripes, and snowy pads and belly. The Dane, who was slightly drunk, uttered a yell and struck the bars of the cage with his whip. The tiger did not blench, but all the malice and ferocity in the world seemed to congregate in its eyes and impress with a pride and ruthless grandeur the colossal brutality of its face. It did not move its body, but its tail gradually stiffened out behind it as stealthily as fire moves in the forest undergrowth, and the hair along the ridge of its back rose in fearful spikes. There was the slightest possible distension of the lips, and it fixed its marvellous baleful gaze upon Pedersen. The show people were hushed into silence, and even Pedersen was started. He showered a few howls and curses at the tiger, who never ceased to fix him with eyes that had something of a contempt in them and something of a horrible presage. Pedersen was thrusting a sharp spike through the bars when a figure stepped from the crowd. It was an old negro, a hunchback with a white beard, dressed in a red fez cap, long tunic of buff cotton, and blue trousers. He laid both his hands on the spike and shook his head deprecatingly, smiling all the while. He said nothing, but there was nothing he could say—he was dumb.

'Let him alone, Yak; let the tiger alone, Yak!' cried Barnabe Woolf. 'What is this feller?'

Pedersen, with some reluctance, turned from the cage and said: 'He is come with the animal.'

'So?' said Barnabe. 'Vell, he can go. Ve do not vant any black feller.'

'He cannot speak—no tongue—it is gone—it is gone,' Yak replied.

'No tongue! Vot, have they cut him out?'

'I should think it,' said the tamer. 'There was two of them, a white keeper, but that man fell off the ship one night and they do not see him any more. This chap he feed it and look after it. No information of him, dumb, you see, and a foreigner; don't understand. He have no letters, no money, no name, nowheres to go. Dumb, you see, he has nothing, nothing but a flote. The captain said to take him away with us. Give a job to him, he is a proposition.'

'Vot is he got you say?'

'Flote.' Pedersen imitated with his fingers and lips the actions of a flute-player.

'Oh ya, a vloot! Vell, ve don't want no vloots now; ve feeds our own tigers, don't ve, Yak?' And Mr Woolf, oily but hearty—and well he might be so for he was beautifully rotund, hair like satin, extravagantly clothed, and rich with jewellery—surveyed first with a contemplative grin, and then compassionately the figure of the old negro, who stood unsmiling with his hands crossed humbly before him. Mr Woolf was usually perspiring and usually being addressed by perspiring workmen, upon whom he bellowed orders and such anathemas as reduced each recipient to the importance of a potato, and gave him the aspect of a consumptive sheep. But today Mr Woolf was affable and calm. He took his cigar from his mouth and poured a flood of rich grey air from his lips. 'Oh ya, look after him a day, or a couple of days.' At that one of the boys began to lead the hunchback away as if he were a horse. 'Come on, Pompoon,' he cried, and thenceforward the unknown negro was called by that name.

Throughout the day the tiger was the sensation of the show, and the record of its ferocity attached to the cage received thrilling confirmation whenever Pedersen appeared before the bars. The sublime concentration of hatred was so intense that children screamed, women shuddered, and even men held their breath in awe. At the end of the day the beasts were fed. Great hacks of bloody flesh were forked into the bottoms of the cages, the hungry victims pouncing and snarling in ecstasy. But no sooner were they served than the front panel of each cage was swung up, and the inmate in the seclusion of his den slaked his appetite and slept. When the public had departed, the lights were put out and the doors of the arena closed. Outside in the darkness only its great rounded oblong shape could be discerned, built high of painted wood, roofed with striped canvas, and adorned with flags. Beyond this matchbox coliseum was a row of caravans, tents, naphtha flares, and buckets of fire on which suppers were cooking. Groups of the show people sat or lounged about, talking, cackling with laughter, and even singing. No one observed the figure of Pompoon as he passed silently on the grass. The outcast, doubly chained to his solitariness by the misfortune of dumbness and strange nationality, was hungry. He had not tasted food that day. He could not understand it any more than he could understand the speech of these people. In the end caravan, nearest the arena, he heard a woman quietly singing. He drew a shining metal flute from his breast, but stood silently until the singer ceased. Then he repeated the tune very accurately and sweetly on his flute. Marie the Cossack came to the door in her green silk tights and high black boots with gilded fringes; her black velvet doublet had plenty of gilded buttons upon it. She was a big, finely moulded woman, her dark and splendid features were burned healthily by the sun. In each of her ears two gold discs tinkled and gleamed as she moved. Pompoon opened his mouth very widely and supplicatingly; he put his hand upon his stomach and rolled his eyes so dreadfully that Mrs Fascota sent her little daughter Sophy down to him with a basin of soup and potatoes. Sophy was partly undressed, in bare feet and red petticoat. She stood gnawing the bone of a chicken, and grinning at the black man as he swallowed and dribbled as best he could without a spoon. She cried out: 'Here, he's going to eat the blood basin and all, mum!' Her mother cheerfully ordered her to 'give him those fraggiments, then!' The child did so, pausing now and again to laugh at the satisfied roll of the old man's eyes. Later on Jimmy Fascota found him a couple of sacks, and Pompoon slept upon them beneath their caravan. The last thing the old man saw was Pedersen, carrying a naphtha flare, unlocking a small door leading into the arena, and closing it with a slam after he had entered. Soon the light went out.

II

After a week the show shifted and Pompoon accompanied it. Mrs Kavanagh, who looked after the birds, was, a little fortunately for him, kicked in the stomach by a mule and had to be left at an infirmary. Pompoon, who seemed to understand birds, took charge of the parakeets, love birds, and other highly coloured fowl, including the quetzal with green mossy head, pink breast, and flowing tails, and the primrose-breasted toucans, with bills like a butcher's cleaver.

The show was always moving on and on. Putting it up and taking it down was a more entertaining affair than the exhibition itself. With Jimmy Fascota in charge, and the young man of the frock coat in an ecstasy of labour, half-clothed husky men swarmed up the rigged frameworks, dismantling poles, planks, floors, ropes, roofs, staging, tearing at bolts and bars, walking at dizzying altitudes on narrow boards, swearing at their mates, staggering under vast burdens, sweating till they looked like seals, packing and disposing incredibly of it all, furling the flags, rolling up the filthy awnings, then Right O! for a market town twenty miles away.

In the autumn the show would be due at a great gala town in the north, the supreme opportunity of the year, and by that time Mr Woolf expected to have a startling headline about a new tiger act and the intrepid tamer. But somehow Pedersen could make no progress at all with this. Week after week went by, and the longer he left that initial entry into the cage of the tiger, notwithstanding the comforting support of firearms, and hot irons, the more remote appeared the possibility of its capitulation. The tiger's hatred did not manifest itself in roars and gnashing of teeth, but by its rigid implacable pose and a slight flexion of its protruded claws. It seemed as if endowed with an imagination of blood-lust, Pedersen being the deepest conceivable excitation of this. Week after week went by and the show people became aware that Pedersen, their Pedersen, the unrivalled, the dauntless tamer, had met his match. They were proud of the beast. Some said it was Yak's bald crown that the tiger disliked, but Marie swore it was his moustache, a really remarkable piece of hirsute furniture, that he would not have parted with for a pound of gold—so he said. But whatever it was—crown, moustache, or the whole conglomerate Pedersen—the tiger remarkably loathed it and displayed his loathing, while the unfortunate tamer had no more success with it than he had ever had with Marie the Cossack, though there was at least a good humour in her treatment of him which was horribly absent from the attitude of the beast. For a long time Pedersen blamed the hunchback for it all. He tried to elicit from him, by gesticulations in front of the cage, the secret of the creature's enmity, but the barriers to their intercourse were too great to be overcome, and to all Pedersen's illustrative frenzies Pompoon would only shake his sad head and roll his great eyes until the Dane would cuff him away with a curse of disgust and turn to find the eyes of the tiger, the dusky, smooth-skinned tiger with bitter bars of ebony, fixed upon him with tenfold malignity. How he longed in his raging impotence to transfix the thing with a sharp spear through the cage's gilded bars, or to bore a hole into its vitals with a red-hot iron! All the traditional treatment in such cases, combined first with starvation and then with rich feeding, proved unavailing. Pedersen always had the front flap of the cage left down at night so that he might, as he thought, establish some kind of working arrangement between them by the force of propinquity. He tried to sleep on a bench just outside the cage, but the horror of the beast so penetrated him that he had to turn his back upon it. Even then the intense enmity pierced the back of his brain and forced him to seek a bench elsewhere out of range of the tiger's vision.

Meanwhile, the derision of Marie was not concealed—it was even blatant—and to the old contest of love between herself and the Dane was now added a new contest of personal courage, for it had come to be assumed, in some undeclarable fashion, that if Yak Pedersen could not tame that tiger, Marie the Cossack would. As this situation crystallised daily, the passion of Pedersen changed to jealousy and hatred. He began to regard the smiling Marie in much the same way as the tiger regarded him.

'The hell-devil! May some lightning scorch her like a toasted fish!'

But in a short while this mood was displaced by one of anxiety; he became even abject. Then, strangely enough, Marie's feelings underwent some modification. She was proud of the chance to subdue and defeat him, but it might be at a great price—too great a price for her. Addressing herself in turn to the dim understanding of Pompoon, she had come to perceive that he believed the tiger to be not merely quite untamable, but full of mysterious dangers. She could not triumph over the Dane unless she ran the risk he feared to run. The risk was colossal then, and with her realisation of this some pity for Yak began to exercise itself in her; after all, were they not in the same boat? But the more she sympathised the more she jeered. The thing had to be done somehow.

Meanwhile Barnabe Woolf wants that headline for the big autumn show, and a failure will mean a nasty interview with that gentleman. It may end by Barnabe kicking Yak Pedersen out of the wild beast show. Not that Mr Woolf is so gross as to suggest that. He senses the difficulty, although his manager in his pride will not confess to any. Mr Woolf declares that his tiger is a new tiger; Yak must watch out for him, be careful. He talks as if it were just a question of giving the cage a coat of whitewash. He never hints at contingencies; but still, there is his new untamed tiger, and there is Mr Yak Pedersen, his wild beast tamer—at present.

III

One day the menagerie did not open. It had finished an engagement, and Jimmy Fascota had gone off to another town to arrange the new pitch. The show folk made holiday about the camp, or flocked into the town for marketing or carousals. Mrs Fascota was alone in her caravan, clothed in her jauntiest attire. She was preparing to go into the town when Pedersen suddenly came silently in and sat down.

'Marie,' he said, after a few moments, 'I give up that tiger. To me he has given a spell. It is like a mesmerise.' He dropped his hands upon his knees in complete humiliation. Marie did not speak, so he asked: 'What you think?'

She shrugged her shoulders, and put her brown arms akimbo. She was a grand figure so, in a cloak of black satin and a huge hat trimmed with crimson feathers.

'If you can't trust him,' she said, 'who can?'

'It is myself I am not to trust. Shameful! But that tiger will do me, yes, so I will not conquer him. It's bad, very, very bad, is it not so? Shameful, but I will not do it!' he declared excitedly.

'What's Barnabe say?'

'I do not care. Mr Woolf can think what he can think! Damn Woolf! But for what I do think of my own self.... Ah!' He paused for a moment, dejected beyond speech. 'Yes, miserable it is, in my own heart very shameful, Marie. And what you think of me, yes, that too!'

There was a note in his voice that almost confounded her—why, the man was going to cry! In a moment she was all melting compassion and bravado.

'You leave the devil to me, Yak. What's come over you, man? God love us, I'll tiger him!'

But the Dane had gone as far as he could go. He could admit his defeat, but he could not welcome her all too ready amplification of it.

'Na, na, you are good for him, Marie, but you beware. He is not a tiger; he is beyond everything, foul—he has got a foul heart and a thousand demons in it. I would not bear to see you touch him; no, no, I would not bear it!'

'Wait till I come back this afternoon—you wait!' cried Marie, lifting her clenched fist. 'So help me I'll tiger him, you'll see!'

Pedersen suddenly awoke to her amazing attraction. He seized her in his arms. 'Na, na, Marie! God above! I will not have it.'

'Aw, shut up!' she commanded impatiently, and pushing him from her she sprang down the steps and proceeded to the town alone.

She did not return in the afternoon; she did not return in the evening. She was not there when the camp closed up for the night. Sophy, alone, was quite unconcerned. Pompoon sat outside the caravan, while the flame of the last lamp was perishing weakly above his head. He now wore a coat of shag-coloured velvet. He was old and looked very wise, often shaking his head, not wearily, but as if in doubt. The flute lay glittering upon his knees and he was wiping his lips with a green silk handkerchief when barefoot Sophy, in her red petticoat, crept behind him, unhooked the lamp, and left him in darkness. Then he departed to an old tent the Fascotas had found for him.

When the mother returned, the camp was asleep in its darkness and she was very drunk. Yak Pedersen had got her. He carried her into the arena, and bolted and barred the door.

IV

Marie Fascota awoke the next morning in broad daylight; through chinks and rents in the canvas roof of the arena the brightness was beautiful to behold. She could hear a few early risers bawling outside, while all around her the caged beasts and birds were squeaking, whistling, growling, and snarling. She was lying beside the Dane on a great bundle of straw. He was already awake when she became aware of him, watching her with amused eyes.

'Yak Pedersen! Was I drunk?' Marie asked dazedly in low, husky tones, sitting up. 'What's this Yak Pedersen? Was I drunk? Have I been here all night?'

He lay with his hands behind his head, smiling in the dissolute ugliness of his abrupt yellow skull so incongruously bald, his moustache so profuse, his nostrils and ears teeming with hairs.

'Can't you speak?' cried the wretched woman. 'What game do you call this? Where's my Sophy, and my Jimmy—is he back?'

Again he did not answer; he stretched out a hand to caress her. Unguarded as he was, Marie smashed down both her fists full upon his face. He lunged back blindly at her, and they both struggled to their feet, his fingers clawing in her thick strands of hair as she struck at him in frenzy. Down rolled the mass, and he seized it; it was her weakness, and she screamed. Marie was a rare woman—a match for most men—but the capture of her hair gave her utterly into his powerful hands. Uttering a torrent of filthy oaths, Pedersen pulled the yelling woman backwards to him and, grasping her neck with both hands, gave a murderous wrench and flung her to the ground. As she fell, Marie's hands clutched a small cage of fortune-telling birds. She hurled this at the man, but it missed him; the cage burst against a pillar and the birds scattered in the air.

'Marie! Marie!' shouted Yak, 'listen! listen!'

Remorsefully he flung himself before the raging woman, who swept at him with an axe, her hair streaming, her eyes blazing with the fire of a thousand angers.

'Drunk, was I!' she screamed at him. 'That's how ye got me, Yak Pedersen? Drunk, was I?'

He warded the blow with his arm, but the shock and pain of it was so great that his own rage burst out again, and leaping at the woman he struck her a horrible blow across the eyes. She sank of her knees and huddled there without a sound, holding her hands to her bleeding face, her loose hair covering it like a net. At the pitiful sight the Dane's grief conquered him again, and bending over her imploringly he said: 'Marie, my love, Marie! Listen! It is not true! Swear me to god, good woman, it is not true, it is not possible! Swear me to god!' he raged distractedly. 'Swear me to god!' Suddenly he stopped and gasped. They were in front of the tiger's cage, and Pedersen was as if transfixed by that fearful gaze. The beast stood with hatred concentrated in every bristling hair upon its hide, and in its eyes a malignity that was almost incandescent. Still as a stone, Marie observed this and began to creep away from the Dane, stealthily, stealthily. On a sudden, with incredible agility, she sprang up the steps of the tiger's cage, tore the pin from the catch, flung open the door, and, yelling in madness, leapt in. As she did so, the cage emptied. In one moment she saw Pedersen grovelling on his knees, stupid, and the next...

All the hidden beasts, stirred by instinctive knowledge of the tragedy, roared and raged. Marie's eyes and mind were opened to its horror. She plugged her fingers into her ears; screamed; but her voice was a mere wafer of sound in that pandemonium. She heard vast crashes of some one smashing in the small door of the arena, and then swooned upon the floor of the cage.

The bolts were torn from their sockets at last, the slip door swung back, and in the opening appeared Pompoon, alone, old

Pompoon with a flaming lamp and an iron spear. As he stepped forward into the gloom he saw the tiger, dragging something in its mouth, leap back into its cage.

The Doll's Ghost

F. Marion Crawford

It was a terrible accident, and for one moment the splendid machinery of Cranston House got out of gear and stood still. The butler emerged from the retirement in which he spent his elegant leisure, two grooms of the chambers appeared simultaneously from opposite directions, there were actually housemaids on the grand staircase, and those who remember the facts most exactly assert that Mrs Pringle herself positively stood upon the landing. Mrs Pringle was the housekeeper. As for the head nurse, the under nurse and the nursery-maid, their feelings cannot be described.

The Lady Gwendolen Lancaster-Douglas-Scroop, youngest daughter of the ninth Duke of Cranston, and aged six years and three months, picked herself up quite alone and sat down on the third step of the grand staircase in Cranston House.

'Oh!' ejaculated the butler, and he disappeared again.

'Ah!' responded the grooms of the chambers, as they also went away.

'It's only that doll,' Mrs Pringle was distinctly heard to say, in a tone of contempt.

The under nurse heard her say it. Then the three nurses gathered round Lady Gwendolen and patted her, and gave her unhealthy things out of their pockets and hurried her out of Cranston House as fast as they could, lest it should be found out upstairs that they had allowed the Lady Gwendolen Lancaster-Douglas-Scroop to tumble down the grand staircase with her doll in her arms. And as the doll was badly broken, the nursery-maid carried it, with the pieces wrapped up in Lady Gwendolen's little cloak. It was not far to Hyde Park, and when they had reached a quiet place they took means to find out that Lady Gwendolen had no bruises. For the carpet was very thick and soft, and there was thick stuff under it to make it softer.

Lady Gwendolen Lancaster-Douglas-Scroop sometimes yelled, but she never cried. It was because she had yelled that the nurse had allowed her to go downstairs alone with Nina, the doll, under one arm, while she steadied herself with her other hand on the balustrade, and trod upon the polished marble steps beyond the edge of the carpet. So she had fallen, and Nina had come to grief.

Mr Bernard Puckler and his little daughter lived in a little house in a little alley, which led out off a quiet little street not very far from Belgrave Square. He was the great doll doctor, and his extensive practice lay in the most aristocratic quarter. He mended dolls of all sizes and ages, boy dolls and girl dolls, baby dolls in long clothes, and grown-up dolls in fashionable gowns, talking dolls and dumb dolls, those that shut their eyes when they lay down, and those whose eyes had to be shut for them by means of a mysterious wire. His daughter Else was only just over twelve years old, but she was already very clever at mending dolls' clothes and at doing their hair, which is harder than you might think, though the dolls sit quite still while it is being done.

Mr Puckler had originally been a German, but he had dissolved his nationality in the ocean of London many years ago, like a great many foreigners. He still had one or two German friends, however, who came on Saturday evenings and smoked with him and played picquet or 'skat' with him for farthing points, and called him 'Herr Doktor', which seemed to please Mr Puckler very much.

He looked older than he was, for his beard was rather long and ragged, his hair was grizzled and thin, and he wore horn-rimmed spectacles.

As for Else, she was a thin, pale child, very quiet and neat, with dark eyes and brown hair that was plaited down her back and tied with a bit of black ribbon. She mended the dolls' clothes and took the dolls back to their homes when they were quite strong again.

The house was a little one, but too big for the two people who lived in it. There was a small sitting-room on the street, and the workshop was at the back, and there were three rooms upstairs. But the father and daughter lived most of their time in the workshop, because they were generally at work, even in the evenings.

Mr Puckler laid Nina on the table and looked at her a long time, till the tears began to fill his eyes behind the horn-rimmed spectacles. He was a very susceptible man, and he often fell in love with the dolls he mended and found it hard to part with them when they had smiled at him for a few days. They were real little people to him, with characters and thoughts and feelings of their own, and he was very tender with them all. But some attracted him especially from the first, and when they were brought to him maimed and injured, their state seemed so pitiful to him that the tears came easily. You must remember that he had lived among dolls during a great part of his life, and understood them.

'How do you know that they feel nothing?' he went on to say to Else. 'You must be gentle with them. It costs nothing to be kind to the little beings, and perhaps it makes a difference to them.'

And Else understood him, because she was a child, and she knew that she was more to him than all the dolls.

He fell in love with Nina at first sight, perhaps because her beautiful brown glass eyes were something like Else's own, and he loved Else first and best, with all his heart. And, besides, it was a very sorrowful case. Nina had evidently not been long in the world, for her complexion was perfect, her hair was smooth where it should be smooth, and curly where it should be curly, and her silk clothes were perfectly new. But across her face was that frightful gash, like a sabre-cut, deep and shadowy within, but clean and sharp at the edges. When he tenderly pressed her head to close the gaping wound, the edges made a fine, grating sound that was painful to hear, and the lids of the dark eyes quivered and trembled as though Nina were suffering dreadfully.

'Poor Nina!' he exclaimed sorrowfully. 'But I shall not hurt you much, though you will take a long time to get strong.'

He always asked the names of the broken dolls when they were brought to him, and sometimes the people knew what the children called them, and told him. He liked 'Nina' for a name. Altogether and in every way she pleased him more than any doll he had seen for many years, and he felt drawn to her and made up his mind to make her perfectly strong and sound, no matter how much labour it might cost him.

Mr Puckler worked patiently a little at a time, and Else watched him. She could do nothing for poor Nina, whose clothes needed no mending. The longer the doll doctor worked the more fond he became of the yellow hair and the beautiful brown glass eyes. He sometimes forgot all the other dolls that were waiting to be mended, lying side by side on a shelf, and sat for an hour gazing at Nina's face, while he racked his ingenuity for some new invention by which to hide even the smallest trace of the terrible accident.

She was wonderfully mended. Even he was obliged to admit that; but the scar was still visible to his keen eyes, a very fine line right across the face, downwards from right to left. Yet all the conditions had been most favourable for a cure, since the cement had set quite hard at the first attempt and the weather had been fine and dry, which makes a great difference in a dolls' hospital.

At last he knew that he could do no more, and the under nurse had already come twice to see whether the job was finished, as she coarsely expressed it.

'Nina is not quite strong yet,' Mr Puckler had answered each time, for he could not make up his mind to face the parting.

And now he sat before the square deal table at which he worked, and Nina lay before him for the last time with a big brown-paper box beside her. It stood there like her coffin, waiting for her, he thought. He must put her into it and lay tissue paper over her dear face, and then put on the lid, and at the thought of tying the string his sight was dim with tears again. He was never to look into the glassy depths of the beautiful brown eyes any more, nor to hear the little wooden voice say 'Pa-pa' and 'Ma-ma'. It was a very painful moment.

In the vain hope of gaining time before the separation, he took up the little sticky bottles of cement and glue and gum and colour, looking at each one in turn, and then at Nina's face. And all his small tools lay there, neatly arranged in a row, but he knew that he could not use them again for Nina. She was quite strong at last, and in a country where there should be no cruel children to hurt her she might live a hundred years, with only that almost imperceptible line across her face, to tell of the fearful thing that had befallen her on the marble steps of Cranston House.

Suddenly Mr Puckler's heart was quite full, and he rose abruptly from his seat and turned away.

'Else,' he said unsteadily, 'you must do it for me. I cannot bear to see her go into the box.'

So he went and stood at the window with his back turned, while Else did what he had not the heart to do.

'Is it done?' he asked, not turning round. 'Then take her away, my dear. Put on your hat, and take her to Cranston House quickly, and when you are gone I will turn round.'

Else was used to her father's queer ways with the dolls, and though she had never seen him so much moved by a parting, she was not much surprised.

'Come back quickly,' he said, when he heard her hand on the latch. 'It is growing late, and I should not send you at this hour. But I cannot bear to look forward to it any more.'

When Else was gone, he left the window and sat down in his place before the table again to wait for the child to come back. He touched the place where Nina had lain, very gently, and he recalled the softly-tinted pink face, and the glass eyes and the ringlets of yellow hair, till he could almost see them.

The evenings wore long, for it was late in the spring. But it began to grow dark soon, and Mr Puckler wondered why Else did not come back. She had been gone an hour and a half, and that was much longer than he had expected, for it was barely half a mile from Belgrave Square to Cranston House. He reflected that the child might have been kept waiting, but as the twilight deepened he grew anxious and walked up and down in the dim workshop, no longer thinking of Nina, but of Else, his own living child, whom he loved.

An indefinable, disquieting sensation came upon him by fine degrees, a chilliness and a faint stirring of his thin hair, joined with a wish to be in any company rather than to be alone much longer. It was the beginning of fear.

He told himself in strong German-English that he was a foolish old man, and he began to feel about for the matches in the dusk. He knew just where they should be, for he always kept them in the same place, close to the little tin box that held bits of sealing-wax of various colours, for some kinds of mending. But somehow he could not find the matches in the gloom.

Something had happened to Else, he was sure, and as his fear increased, he felt as though it might be allayed if he could get a light and see what time it was. Then he called himself a foolish old man again, and the sound of his own voice startled him in the dark. He could not find the matches.

The window was grey still; he might see what time it was if he went close to it, and he could go and get matches out of the cupboard afterwards. He stood back from the table, to get out of the way of the chair, and began to cross the board floor.

Something was following him in the dark. There was a small pattering, as of tiny feet upon the boards. He stopped and listened, and the roots of his hair tingled. It was nothing and he was a foolish old man. He made two steps more, and he was sure that he heard the little pattering again. He turned his back to the window, leaning against the sash so that the panes began to crack, and he faced the dark. Everything was quite still, and it smelt of paste and cement and wood-filings as usual.

'Is that you, Else?' he asked, and he was surprised by the fear in his voice.

There was no answer in the room, and he held up his watch and tried to make out what time it was by the grey dusk that was just not darkness. So far as he could see, it was within two or three minutes of ten o'clock. He had been a long time alone. He was shocked and frightened for Else, out in London, so late, and he almost ran across the room to the door. As he fumbled for the latch, he distinctly heard the running of the little feet after him.

'Mice!' he exclaimed feebly, just as he got the door open.

He shut it quickly behind him and felt as though some cold thing had settled on his back and was writhing upon him. The passage was quite dark, but he found his hat and was out in the alley in a moment, breathing more freely, and surprised to find how much light there still was in the open air. He could see the pavement clearly under his feet, and far off in the street to which the alley led he could hear the laughter and calls of children, playing some game out of doors. He wondered how he could have been so nervous, and for an instant he thought of going back into the house to wait quietly for Else. But instantly he felt that nervous fright of something stealing over him again. In any case it was better to walk up to Cranston House and ask the servants about the child. One of the women had perhaps taken a fancy to her, and was even now giving her tea and cake.

He walked quickly to Belgrave Square, and then up the broad streets, listening as he went, whenever there was no other sound, for the tiny footsteps. But he heard nothing, and was laughing at himself when he rang the servants' bell at the big house. Of course, the child must be there.

The person who opened the door was quite an inferior person—for it was a back door—but affected the manners of the front, and stared at Mr Puckler superciliously.

No little girl had been seen, and he knew 'nothing about no dolls'.

'She is my little girl,' said Mr Puckler tremulously, for all his anxiety was returning tenfold, 'and I am afraid something has happened.'

The inferior person said rudely that 'nothing could have happened to her in that house, because she had not been there, which was a jolly good reason why'; and Mr Puckler was obliged to admit that the man ought to know, as it was his business to keep the door and let people in. He wished to be allowed to speak to the under nurse, who knew him; but the man was ruder than ever, and finally shut the door in his face.

When the doll doctor was alone in the street, he steadied himself by the railing, for he felt as though he were breaking in two, just as some dolls break, in the middle of the backbone.

Presently he knew that he must be doing something to find Else, and that gave him strength. He began to walk as quickly as he could through the streets, following every highway and byway which his little girl might have taken on her errand. He also asked several policemen in vain if they had seen her, and most of them answered him kindly, for they saw that he was a sober man and in his right senses, and some of them had little girls of their own.

It was one o'clock in the morning when he went up to his own door again, worn out and hopeless and broken-hearted. As he turned the key in the lock, his heart stood still, for he knew that he was awake and not dreaming, and that he really heard those tiny footsteps pattering to meet him inside the house along the passage.

But he was too unhappy to be much frightened any more, and his heart went on again with a dull regular pain, that found its way all through him with every pulse. So he went in and hung up his hat in the dark, and found the matches in the cupboard and the candlestick in its place in the corner. Mr Puckler was so much overcome and so completely worn out that he sat down in his chair before the work-table and almost fainted, as his face dropped forward upon his folded hands. Beside him the solitary candle burned steadily with a low flame in the still warm air.

'Else! Else!' he moaned against his yellow knuckles. And that was all he could say, and it was no relief to him. On the contrary, the very sound of the name was a new and sharp pain that pierced his ears and his head and his very soul. For every time he repeated the name it meant that little Else was dead, somewhere out in the streets of London in the dark.

He was so terribly hurt that he did not even feel something pulling gently at the skirt of his old coat, so gently that it was like the nibbling of a tiny mouse. He might have thought that it was really a mouse if he had noticed it.

'Else! Else!' he groaned, right against his hands.

Then a cool breath stirred his thin hair, and the low flame of the one candle dropped down almost to a mere spark, not flickering, as though a draught were going to blow it out, but just dropping down as if it were tired out. Mr Puckler felt his hands stiffening with fright under his face; and there was a faint rustling sound, like some small silk thing blown in a gentle breeze. He sat up straight, stark and scared, and a small wooden voice spoke in the stillness.

'Pa-pa,' it said, with a break between the syllables.

Mr Puckler stood up in a single jump, and his chair fell over backwards with a smashing noise upon the wooden floor. The candle had almost gone out.

It was Nina's doll-voice that had spoken, and he should have known it among the voices of a hundred other dolls. And yet there was something more in it, a little human ring, with a pitiful cry and a call for help, and the wail of a hurt child. Mr Puckler stood up, stark and stiff, and tried to look round, but at first he could not, for he seemed to be frozen from head to foot.

Then he made a great effort and raised one hand to each of his temples, and pressed his own head round as he would have turned a doll's. The candle was burning so low that it might as well have been out altogether, for any light it gave, and the room seemed quite dark at first. Then he saw something. He would not have believed that he could be more frightened than he had been just before that. But he was, and his knees shook, for he saw the doll standing in the middle of the floor, shining with a faint and ghostly radiance, her beautiful glassy brown eyes fixed on his. And across her face the very thin line of the break he had mended shone as though it were drawn in light with a line point of white flame

Yet there was something more in the eyes, too; there was something human, like Else's own, but as if only the doll saw him through them, and not Else. And there was enough of Else to bring back all his pain and to make him forget his fear.

'Else! My little Else!' he cried aloud.

The small ghost moved, and its doll-arm slowly rose and fell with a stiff, mechanical motion.

'Pa-pa,' it said.

It seemed this time that there was even more of Else's tone echoing somewhere between the wooden notes that reached his ears so distinctly and yet so far away. Else was calling him, he was sure.

His face was perfectly white in the gloom, but his knees did not shake any more, and he felt that he was less frightened.

'Yes, child! But where? Where?' he asked. 'Where are you, Else?'

'Pa-pa!'

The syllables died away in the quiet room.

There was a low rustling of silk, the glassy brown eyes turned slowly away, and Mr Puckler heard the pitter-patter of the small feet in the bronze kid slippers as the figure ran straight to the door.

Then the candle burned high again, the room was full of light, and he was alone.

Mr Puckler passed his hand over his eyes and looked about him. He could see everything quite clearly, and he felt that he must have been dreaming, though he was standing instead of sitting down, as he should have been if he had just waked up. The candle burned brightly now. There were the dolls to be mended, lying in a row with their toes up. The third one had lost her right shoe, and Else was making one. He knew that, and he was certainly not dreaming now. He had not been dreaming when he had come in from his fruitless search and had heard the doll's footsteps running to the door. He had not fallen asleep in his chair. How could he possibly have fallen asleep when his heart was breaking? He had been awake all the time.

He steadied himself, set the fallen chair upon its legs, and said to himself again very emphatically that he was a foolish old man. He ought to be out in the streets looking for his child, asking questions, and enquiring at the police stations where all accidents were reported as soon as they were known, or at the hospitals.

'Pa-pa!'

The longing, wailing, pitiful little wooden cry rang from the passage, outside the door, and Mr Puckler stood for an instant with white face, transfixed and rooted to the spot. A moment later his hand was on the latch. Then he was in the passage, with the light streaming from the open door behind him.

Quite at the other end he saw the little phantom shining clearly in the shadow, and the right hand seemed to beckon to him as the arm rose and fell once more. He knew all at once that it had not come to frighten him but to lead him, and when it disappeared, and he walked boldly towards the door, he knew that it was in the street outside, waiting for him. He forgot that he was tired and had eaten no supper, and had walked many miles, for a sudden hope ran through and through him, like a golden stream of life.

And sure enough, at the corner of the alley, and at the corner of the street, and out in Belgrave Square, he saw the small ghost flitting before him. Sometimes it was only a shadow, where there was other light, but then the glare of the lamps made a pale green sheen on its little Mother Hubbard frock of silk; and sometimes, where the streets were dark and silent, the whole figure shone out brightly with its yellow curls and rosy neck. It seemed to trot along like a tiny child, and Mr Puckler could hear the pattering of the bronze kid slippers on the pavement as it ran. But it went very fast, and he could only just keep up with it, tearing along with his hat on the back of his head and his thin hair blown by the night breeze, and his horn-rimmed spectacles firmly set upon his broad nose.

On and on he went, and he had no idea where he was. He did not even care, for he knew certainly that he was going the right way.

Then at last, in a wide, quiet street, he was standing before a big, sober-looking door that had two lamps on each side of it, and a polished brass bell-handle, which he pulled.

And just inside, when the door was opened, in the bright light, there was the little shadow, and the pale green sheen of the little silk dress, and once more the small cry came to his ears, less pitiful, more longing.

'Pa-pa!'

The shadow turned suddenly bright, and out of the brightness the beautiful brown glass eyes were turned up happily to his, while the rosy mouth smiled so divinely that the phantom doll looked almost like a little angel just then.

'A little girl was brought in soon after ten o'clock,' said the quiet voice of the hospital doorkeeper. 'I think they thought she was only stunned. She was holding a big brown-paper box against her, and they could not get it out of her arms. She had a long plait of brown hair that hung down as they carried her.'

'She is my little girl,' said Mr Puckler, but he hardly heard his own voice.

He leaned over Else's face in the gentle light of the children's ward, and when he had stood there a minute, the beautiful brown eyes opened and looked up to his.

'Pa-pa!' cried Else softly, 'I knew you would come!'

Then Mr Puckler did not know what he did or said for a moment, and what he felt was worth all the fear and terror and despair that had almost killed him that night. But by and by Else was telling her story, and the nurse let her speak, for there were only two other children in the room, who were getting well and were sound asleep.

'They were big boys with bad faces,' said Else, 'and they tried to get Nina away from me, but I held on and fought as well as I could till one of them hit me with something, and I don't remember any more, for I tumbled down and I suppose the boys ran away, and somebody found me there. But I'm afraid Nina is all smashed.'

'Here is the box,' said the nurse. 'We could not take it out of her arms till she came to herself. Would you like to see if the doll is broken?'

And she undid the string cleverly, but Nina was all smashed to pieces. Only the gentle light of the children's ward made a pale green sheen in the folds of the little Mother Hubbard frock.

The Skeleton

Jerome K. Jerome

One evening Jephson asked me if I believe in spiritualism to its fullest extent.

'That is rather a large question,' I answered. 'What do you mean by "spiritualism to its fullest extent"?'

'Well, do you believe that the spirits of the dead have not only the power of revisiting this earth at their will, but that, when here, they have the power of action, or rather, of exciting to action? Let me put a definite case. A spiritualist friend of mine, a sensible and by no means imaginative man, once told me that a table, through the medium of which the spirit of a friend had been in the habit of communicating with him, came slowly across the room towards him, of its own accord, one night as he sat alone, and pinioned him against the wall. Now can any of you believe that, or can't you?'

'I could,' Brown took it upon himself to reply; 'but, before doing so, I should wish for an introduction to the friend who told you the story. Speaking generally,' he continued, 'it seems to me that the difference between what we call the natural and the supernatural is merely the difference between frequency and rarity of an occurrence. Having regard to the phenomena we are compelled to admit, I think it illogical to disbelieve anything we are unable to disprove.'

'For my part,' remarked MacShaughnassy, 'I can believe in the ability of our spirit friends to give the quaint entertainments credited to them much easier than I can in their desire to do so.'

'You mean,' added Jephson, 'that you cannot understand why a spirit, not compelled as we are by the exigencies of society, should care to spend its evenings on a laboured and childish conversation with a room full of abnormally uninteresting people.'

'That is precisely what I cannot understand,' MacShaughnassy agreed.

'Nor I, either,' said Jephson. 'But I was thinking of something very different altogether. Suppose a man died with the dearest wish of his heart unfulfilled, do you believe that his spirit might have power to return to earth and complete the interrupted work?'

'Well,' answered MacShaughnassy, 'if one admits the possibility of spirits retaining any interest in the affairs of this world at all, it is certainly more reasonable to imagine them engaged upon a task such as you suggest, than to believe that they occupy themselves with the performance of mere drawing-room tricks. But what are you leading up to?'

'Why, to this,' replied Jephson, seating himself straddle-legged across his chair, and leaning his arms upon the back. 'I was told a story this morning at the hospital by an old French doctor. The actual facts are few and simple; all that is known can be read in the Paris police records of sixty-two years ago.

'The most important part of the case, however, is the part that is not known, and that never will be known.

'The story begins with a great wrong done by one man unto another man. What the wrong was I do not know. I am inclined to think, however, it was connected with a woman. I think that, because he who had been wronged hated him who had wronged him with a hate such as does not often burn in a man's brain, unless it be fanned by the memory of a woman's breath.

'Still that is only conjecture, and the point is immaterial. The man who had done the wrong fled, and the other man followed him. It became a point-to-point race, the first man having the advantage of a day's start. The course was the whole world, and the stakes were the first man's life.

'Travellers were few and far between in those days, and this made the trail easy to follow. The first man, never knowing how far or how near the other was behind him, and hoping now and again that he might have baffled him, would rest for a while. The second man, knowing always just how far the first one was before him, never paused, and thus each day the man who was spurred by hate drew nearer to the man who was spurred by Fear.

'At this town the answer to the never-varied question would be:

'"At seven o'clock last evening, Monsieur."

'"Seven—ah; eighteen hours. Give me something to eat, quick, while the horses are being put to."

'At the next the calculation would be sixteen hours.

'Passing a lonely châlet, Monsieur puts his head out of the window:

'"How long since a carriage passed this way, with a tall, fair man inside?"

'"Such a one passed early this morning, Monsieur."

'"Thanks, drive on, a hundred francs apiece if you are through the pass before daybreak."

'"And what for dead horses, Monsieur?"

'"Twice their value when living."

'One day the man who was ridden by Fear looked up, and saw before him the open door of a cathedral, and passing in, knelt down and prayed. He prayed long and fervently, for men, when they are in sore straits, clutch eagerly at the straws of faith. He prayed that he might be forgiven his sin, and, more important still, that he might be pardoned the consequences of his sin, and be delivered from his adversary; and a few chairs from him, facing him, knelt his enemy, praying also.

'But the second man's prayer, being a thanksgiving merely, was short, so that when the first man raised his eyes, he saw the face of his enemy gazing at him across the chair-tops, with a mocking smile upon it.

'He made no attempt to rise, but remained kneeling, fascinated by the look of joy that shone out of the other man's eyes. And the other man moved the high-backed chairs one by one, and came towards him softly.

'Then, just as the man who had been wronged stood beside the man who had wronged him, full of gladness that his opportunity had come, there burst from the cathedral tower a sudden clash of bells, and the man, whose opportunity had come, broke his heart and fell back dead, with that mocking smile still playing round his mouth.

'And so he lay there.

'Then the man who had done the wrong rose up and passed out, praising god.

'What became of the body of the other man is not known. It was the body of a stranger who had died suddenly in the cathedral. There was none to identify it, none to claim it.

'Years passed away, and the survivor in the tragedy became a worthy and useful citizen, and a noted man of science.

'In his laboratory were many objects necessary to him in his researches, and prominent among them stood in a certain corner a human skeleton. It was a very old and much-mended skeleton, and one day the long-expected end arrived, and it tumbled to pieces.

'Thus it became necessary to purchase another.

'The man of science visited a dealer he well knew—a little parchment-faced old man who kept a dingy shop, where nothing was ever sold, within the shadow of the towers of Notre Dame.

'The little parchment-faced old man had just the very thing that Monsieur wanted—a singularly fine and well-proportioned "study". It should be sent round and set up in Monsieur's laboratory that very afternoon.

'The dealer was as good as his word. When Monsieur entered his laboratory that evening, the thing was in its place.

'Monsieur seated himself in his high-backed chair, and tried to collect his thoughts. But Monsieur's thoughts were unruly, and inclined to wander, and to wander always in one direction.

'Monsieur opened a large volume and commenced to read. He read of a man who had wronged another and fled from him, the other man following. Finding himself reading this, he closed the book angrily and went and stood by the window and looked out. He saw before him the sun-pierced nave of a great cathedral, and on the stones lay a dead man with a mocking smile upon his face.

'Cursing himself for a fool, he turned away with a laugh. But his laugh was short-lived, for it seemed to him that something else in the room was laughing also. Struck suddenly still, with his feet glued to the ground, he stood listening for a while: then sought with starting eyes the corner from where the sound had seemed to come. But the white thing standing there was only grinning.

'Monsieur wiped the damp sweat from his head and hands, and stole out.

'For a couple of days he did not enter the room again. On the third, telling himself that his fears were those of a hysterical girl, he opened the door and went in. To shame himself, he took his lamp in his hand, and crossing over to the far corner where the skeleton stood, examined it. A set of bones bought for three hundred francs. Was he a child, to be scared by such a bogey!

'He held his lamp up by the front of the thing's grinning head. The flame of the lamp flickered as though a faint breath had passed over it.

'The man explained this to himself by saying that the walls of the house were old and cracked, and that the wind might creep in anywhere. He repeated this explanation to himself as he re-crossed the room, walking backwards, with his eyes fixed on the thing. When he reached his desk, he sat down and gripped the arms of his chair till his fingers turned white.

'He tried to work, but the empty sockets in that grinning head seemed to be drawing him towards them. He rose and battled with his inclination to fly screaming from the room. Glancing fearfully about him, his eye fell upon a high screen, standing before the door. He dragged it forward, and placed it between himself and the thing, so that he could not see it—nor it see him. Then he sat down again to his work. For a while he forced himself to look at the book in front of him, but at last, unable to control himself any longer, he suffered his eyes to follow their own bent.

'It may have been a hallucination. He may have accidentally placed the screen so as to favour such an illusion. But what he saw was a bony hand coming round the corner of the screen, and, with a cry, he fell to the floor in a swoon.

'The people of the house came running in, and lifting him up, carried him out, and laid him upon his bed. As soon as he recovered, his first question was, where had they found the thing—where was it when they entered the room? When they told him they had seen it standing where it always stood, and had gone down into the room to look again, because of his frenzied entreaties, and returned trying to hide their smiles, he listened to their talk about overwork and the necessity for change and rest, and said they might do with him as they would.

'So for many months the laboratory door remained locked. Then there came a chill autumn evening when the man of science opened it again, and closed it behind him.

'He lighted his lamp and gathered his instruments and books around him, and sat down before them in his high-backed chair. And the old terror returned to him.

'But this time he meant to conquer himself. His nerves were stronger now, and his brain clearer; he would fight his unreasoning fear. He crossed to the door and locked himself in, and flung the key to the other end of the room, where it fell among jars and bottles with an echoing clatter.

'Later on, his old housekeeper, going her final round, tapped at his door and wished him good-night, as was her custom. She received no response, at first, and, growing nervous, tapped louder and called again; and at length an answering 'good-night' came back to her.

'She thought little about it at the time, but afterwards she remembered that the voice that had replied to her had been strangely grating and mechanical. Trying to describe it, she likened it to such a voice as she would imagine coming from a statue.

'Next morning his door remained still locked. It was no unusual thing for him to work all night and far into the next day, so no one was surprised. When, however, evening came, and yet he did not appear, his servants gathered outside the room and whispered, remembering what had happened once before.

'They listened, but could hear no sound. They shook the door and called to him, then beat with their fists upon the wooden panels. But still no sound came from the room.

'Becoming alarmed, they decided to burst open the door, and, after many blows, it gave way, and they crowded in.

'He sat bolt upright in his high-backed chair. They thought at first he had died in his sleep. But when they drew nearer and the light fell upon him, they saw the livid marks of bony fingers round his throat; and in his eyes there was a terror such as is not often seen in human eyes.'

The Staircase

Hugh Walpole

It doesn't matter in the least where this old house is. There were once many houses like it. Now there are very few.

It was born in 1540 (you can see the date of its birth over the lintel of the porch, cut into the stone). It is E-shaped, with a central porch and wings at each end. Its stone is now, in its present age, weathered to a beautiful colour of pearl-grey, purple-shadowed. This stone makes the house seem old, but it is not old; its heart and veins are strong and vigorous, only its clothes now are shabby.

It is a small house as Tudor manor-houses go, but its masonry is very solid, and it was created by a spirit who cared that it should have every grace of proportion and strength. The wings have angle buttresses, and the porch rises to twisted terminals; there are twisted terminals with cupola tops also upon the gables, and the chimneys too are twisted. The mullioned windows have arched heads, and the porch has a Tudor arch. The arch is an entrance to a little quadrangle, and there are rooms above and gables on either side. Here and there is rich carving very fancifully designed.

It is set upon a little hill, and the lawn runs down to a small formal garden with box-hedges mounted by animals fancifully cut, a sun-dial, a little stone temple. Fields spread on either side of it and are bordered completely by a green tangled wood. The trees climb skywards on every side, but they are not too close about the house. They are too friendly to it to hurt it in any way. Over the arched porch a very amiable gargoyle hangs his head. He has one eye closed and a protruding chin from which the rain drips on a wet day, and in the winter icicles hang from it.

All the country about the house is very English, and the villages have names like Croxton, Little Pudding, Big Pudding, Engleheart and Applewain. A stream runs at the end of the lower field, runs through the wood, under the road, by other fields, so far as Bonnet where it becomes a river and broadens under bridges at Peckwit, the country town.

The house is called Candil Place, and is very proud of its name. Its history for the last hundred years has been very private and personal. No one save myself and the house knows the real crises of its history, just as no one knows the real crisis of your history save yourself. You have doubtless been often surprised that neighbours think that such and such events have been the dramatic changing moments in your life—as when you lost your wife or your money or had scarlet fever—when in reality it was the blowing of a window curtain, the buying of a ship in silver, or the cry of a child on the stair.

So it has been with this house which has had its heart wrung by the breaking of a bough in the wind, a spark flying from the chimney, or a mouse scratching in the wainscot. From its birth it has had its own pride, its own reserve, its own consequence. Everything that has happened in it, every person who has come to it or gone from it, every song that has been sung in it, every oath sworn in it, every shout, every cry, every prayer, every yawn has found a place in its history.

Its heart has been always kind, hospitable, generous; it has had as many intentions as we have all had, towards noble ends and fine charities. But life is not so easy as that.

Its first days were full of light and colour. Of course it was always a small house; Sir Mortimer Candil, who helped to create it, loved it, and the house gave him its heart. The house knew that he did for it what he could with his means; the house suffered with him when his first wife died of the plague, rejoiced with him when he married again so beautiful a lady, suffered with him once more when the beautiful lady ran away to Spain with a rascal.

There is a little room, the Priest's Room, where Sir Mortimer shut himself in and cried, one long summer day, his heart away. When he came out of there he had no heart any more, and the house, the only witness of that scene, put its arms about him, loved him more dearly than it had ever done, and mourned him most bitterly when he died.

Sir Edmund had a sister Henrietta, who was the cause of all the later trouble. The house never from the beginning liked Henrietta.

The house was willing to grant that Henrietta loved her brother, but in a mean, grasping, greedy manner, and jealousy was her other name.

They were children of a late marriage and their parents died of the smallpox when Edmund was nineteen and Henrietta twenty-one. After that Henrietta ruled the house because Edmund was scarcely ever there, and the house disliked exceedingly her rule. This house was, as I have said, a loyal and faithful friend and servant of the Candil family. Some houses are always hostile to their owners, having a great unreasoning pride of their own and considering the persons who inhabit them altogether unworthy of their good fortune. But partly for the sake of Sir Mortimer, who had created and loved it, and partly because it was by nature kindly, and partly because it always hoped for the best, the house had always chosen only the finest traits in the Candil character and refused to look at any other.

But, if there is one thing that a house resents, it is to be shabbily and meanly treated. When a carpet is worn, a window rattling in the breeze, a pipe in rebellion, a chair on the wobble, the house does everything towards drawing the attention of its master. This house had been always wonderfully considerate of expense and the costliness of all repair. It knew that its masters were not men of great wealth and must go warily with their purposes, but, until Henrietta, the Candils had been generous within their powers. They had had a pride in the house which made them glad to be generous. Henrietta had no such pride. She persisted in what she called an 'adequate economy,' declaring that it was her duty to her brother who drove her, but as the house (who was never deceived about anything) very well knew, this so-called 'economy' became her god and to save money her sensual passion.

She grew into a long bony woman with a faint moustache on her upper lip and a strange, heavy, flat-footed way of walking. The Staircase, a little conceited perhaps because of its lovely banisters that were as delicate as lace, hated her tread and declared that she was so common that she could not be a Candil. Several times the Staircase tripped her up out of sheer maliciousness. The Storeroom hated her more than did any other part of the house. Every morning she was there, skimping and cheese-paring, making this last and doing without that, wondering whether this were not too expensive and that too 'outrageous'. Of course, her maidservants would not stay with her. She found it cheapest to engage little charity-girls, and when she had them she starved them. It is true that she also starved herself, but that was no virtue; the house would see the little charity-girls crying from sheer hunger in their beds, and its heart would ache for them.

This was of course to some degree different when Edmund came home from his travels, but not very different, because he was always considerably under his sister's influence. He was soft-hearted and she was hard, and, as the house very well knew, the hard ones always win.

Henrietta loved her brother, but she was also afraid of him. She was very proud of him but yet more proud of her domination over him. When he was thirty and she thirty-two, she was convinced that he would never marry. It had been once her terror that he should, and she would lie awake thinking one moment of the household accounts and the next of wicked girls who might entrap her brother. But it seemed that he was never in love; he returned from every travel as virgin as before.

She said to him one morning, smiling her rather grim smile: 'Well, brother, you are a bachelor for life, I think.'

It was then that he told her that he was shortly to marry Miss Dorothy Preston of Cathwick Hall.

He spoke very quietly, but, as the armchair in the Adam Room noticed, he was not quite at his ease. They were speaking in the Adam Room at the time, and this armchair had only recently been purchased by Edmund Candil. The room was not known then as the Adam Room (it had that title later) but it was the room of Edmund's heart. The fireplace was in the Adam style and so were the ceiling, and the furniture, the chairs, the table, the sofa, the commode Edmund had had made for him in London.

Very lovely they were, of satin-wood and mahogany, with their general effect of straight line but modified by lovely curves, delicate and shining. In the centre of the commode was a painted vase of flowers, on the ceiling a heavenly tracing of shell-like circles. Everywhere grace and strength and the harmony of perfect workmanship.

This room was for Edmund the heart of England, and he would stand in it, his dark eyes glowing, fingering his stock, slapping his tight thigh with his riding-whip, a glory at his heart. Many things he had brought with him from foreign countries. There was the Chinese room, and the little dining-room was decorated with Italian pictures. In his own room that he called the Library there was an ink-horn that had been (they said) Mirabeau's, a letter of Marie Antoinette's, a yellow lock cut from the hair of a mermaid and some of the feathers from the head-dress of an African chieftain. Many more treasures than these. But it was the Parlour with the fine furniture bought by him in London that was England, and it was of this room that he thought when he was tossing on the Bay of Biscay or studying pictures in Florence or watching the ablutions of natives in the Sacred River.

It was in this room that he told his sister that he intended marriage.

She made no protest. She knew well enough when her brother's mind was made up. But it was a sunny morning when he told her, and as the sun, having embraced merrily the box-hedge peacocks and griffins, looked in to wish good-morning to the sofa and the round shining satin-wood table that balanced itself so beautifully on its slim delicate legs, it could tell that the table and chairs were delighted about something.

'What is it?' said the sun, rubbing its chin on the window-sill.

'There's a new mistress coming,' said the table and chairs.

And, when she came, they all fell at once in love with her. Was there ever anyone so charming and delicate in her primrose-coloured gown, her pretty straw bonnet and the grey silk scarf about her shoulders? Was there ever anyone so charming?

Of course, Henrietta did not think so. This is an old story, this one of the family relations greeting so suspiciously the new young bride, but it is always actual enough in its tragedy and heartbreak, however often it may have happened before.

Is it sentimental to be sorry because the new Lady Candil was sad and lonely and cried softly for hours at night while her husband slept beside her? At that time at least the house did not think so. Possibly by now it has grown more cynical. It cannot, any more than the humans who inhabit it, altogether be unaware of the feeling and colour of its time.

In any case the house loved Dorothy Candil and was deeply grieved at her trouble. That trouble was, one must realise, partly of her own making.

Her husband loved her, nay, he adored her with all the tenderness and tenacity that were part of his character. He adored her and was bored by her: as everyone knows, this is a most aggravating state of feeling. He thought her beautiful, good, amiable and honest, but he had nothing at all to say to her. For many a man she would have been exactly fitting, for it was not so much that she was stupid as that she had no education and no experience. He gave her none of these things as he should have done. Nor did he realise that this life, in the depths of English country, removed from all the enterprise and movement of the town, removed also by the weather from any outside intercourse for weeks at a time, was for someone without any great resources in herself depressing and enervating.

And then she was frightened of him. How well the house understood this! It too was, at times, afraid of him, of his silences, his obstinacy and easy capacity of semi-liveliness, a sensitiveness that his reticence forbade him to express.

How often in the months that followed the marriage did the house long to advise her as to her treatment of him. The sofa in the parlour was especially wise in such cases. Long before it had been covered with its gay cherry-coloured silk, it had been famous among friends and neighbours for its delicacy in human tactics.

There came a morning when Lady Candil sat on a corner of it, her lovely little hand (she was delicate, slim, fragile, her body had the consistency of egg-shell china) clenching the shining wood of its strong arm for support, and a word from her would have put everything right. The sofa could feel the throbbing of her heart, and looking across to the thick, stiff, obstinate body of her husband, longed to throw her into his arms. But she could not say the word, and the mischanced moment became history for both of them. Had they not loved so truly it might have been easier for them; as it was, shyness and obstinacy built the barrier.

And of course Henrietta assisted. How grimly was she pleased as she sat in her ugly old russet gown, pretending to read Lord Clarendon's History (for she made a great pretence of improving her mind), but in reality listening to the unhappy silences between them and watching for the occasion when a word from her to her brother would skilfully widen the breach. For she hated poor Dorothy. She must in any case have done so out of jealousy and disappointment, but Dorothy was also precisely the example in woman whom she most despised. A weak, feckless, helpless thing whose pretty looks were an insult!

Then Dorothy felt her peril and rose to meet it. The house may have whispered in her ear!

Yes, she rose to meet it, but, as life only too emphatically teaches us, it is no good crying for the moon—and it is no good, however urgent we may be, begging for qualities that we have not got. She had a terrible habit of being affectionate at the wrong time. A kind of fate pursued her in this. He would return from his afternoon's ride, pleasantly weary, eager for his wife and happy in the thought of a little romantic dalliance, and she, fancying that he would not be disturbed, would leave him to snore beside the fire. Or, a neighbour squire would visit him and he be off with him for the afternoon and she feel neglected. Or, he would be absorbed in a newsletter with a lively account of French affairs and she choose that moment to sit on his knee and tug his hair.

Dorothy was in truth one of those unfortunate persons—and they are among the most unfortunate in the world—who are insensitive to the moods and atmospheres of others. These err not through egotism nor stupidity, but rather through a sort of colour-blindness so that they see their friend red when he is yellow and green when he is blue. Neither Dorothy nor Edmund had any gift of words.

So, a year and a half after his marriage, Edmund, with an ache in his heart, although he would own this to nobody, went once again to foreign parts. The house implored him not to go: he almost heard its protests.

On one of his last evenings there—a windy spring evening—he came in from a dark twilight walk, splashed with the mud of the country paths, the sense of the pale hedgerow primroses yet in his eye, the chatter of birds in his ear, and standing in the hall heard the William and Mary clock with the moon and stars, the banisters of the staircase, the curtains of the long hall window whisper to him:

'Don't' go! Don't go! Don't go!'

He stood there and thought: 'By Gemini, I'll not leave this!' Dorothy came down the stairs to greet him and, seeing him lost in thought, stole upstairs again. In any case he had taken his seat in the coach, and his place in the packet-boat was got for him by a friend in London.

'Don't go!' said the portrait of old Uncle Candil.

He strode upstairs and Dorothy was reading *Grandison* by the fire, and although her heart was beating with love for him, was too timid to say so.

So to foreign parts he went again and, loving her so dearly, wrote letters to her which he tore up without sending lest she should think him foolish—such being the British temperament.

How the house suffered then, that Dorothy should be left to the harsh economies of sister Henrietta. Henrietta was not a bad woman, but she was mean, selfish, proud and stupid. She was also jealous. Very quickly and with little show of rebellion Dorothy submitted to her ways. If true love is in question, absence does indeed make the heart grow fonder, and Dorothy thought of her husband night, morning, and night again.

She was snubbed, starved, and given a thorough sense of her insufficiencies. It is surprising how completely one human being can convince another of incompetence, ignorance and silly vanity if they be often alone together and one of them a woman. Women are more whole-hearted than men in what they do, whether for good or ill, and Henrietta was very whole-hearted indeed in this affair.

She convinced Dorothy before her husband's return that she was quite unworthy of his love, that he found her dull and unresponsive, that he was deeply disappointed in the issue of his marriage, and that she had deceived him most basely. You may say that she was a poor-spirited little thing, but she was very lonely, half-starved, and her love made her defenceless.

The appetite grows with what it feeds on, and Henrietta found that 'educating Dorothy,' as she called it, was a very worthy and soul-satisfying occupation. Dorothy began to be frightened, not only of herself and of Henrietta but of everything around her, the house, the gardens, the surrounding country.

The house did its utmost to reassure her. When she lay awake in her bed at night, the house would hush any noise that might disturb her—the furniture of her room, the hangings above her bed, the old chest of Cromwell's time, the Queen Anne wardrobe, the warming-pan, the fire-irons that had the heads of grinning dogs, the yellow rug from Turkey, the Italian lamp beside her bed, they all crowded about her to tell her that they loved her. After a while she was conscious of their affection. Her bedroom and the parlour were for her the happiest places in the house, the only places indeed where she was not afraid.

She did not know that they were saying anything to her—she had not that kind of perception—but she felt reassured by them, and she would lock herself into her bedroom and sit there for hours thinking of her husband and wondering where he might be.

She became so painfully aware of Henrietta that she saw her when she wasn't there. She saw her always just around a corner, behind a tree, on the other side of the rose-garden well, peering over the sun-dial, hiding behind the curtain. She became a slave to her, doing all that she was told, going where she was bid. The house considered it a disgusting business.

One evening she broke into a flash of rebellion.

'Edmund loves me!' she cried, her little breasts panting, her small hands clenched. 'And you hate me! Why do you hate me? I have never done you any harm.'

'Hate! Hate! I have other things to do—and if he loves you, why does he stay so long away?'

Ah! why indeed? The house echoed the question, the very floors trembling with agitation. The stupid fool! Could he not see the treasure that he had? Did he think that such glories were to be picked up anywhere, any day, for the asking? The fire spat a piece of coal on to the hearthrug in contempt of human blindness.

When the time arrived at last for Edmund's return, Dorothy was in a fitting condition of miserable humility. Edmund did not love her. He was bored with her too dreadfully. But indeed how could he love her? How could anybody love her, poor incompetent stupid thing that she was! And yet in her heart she knew that she was not so stupid. Did Edmund love her only a little she could jump all the barriers and be really rather brilliant—much more brilliant than Henrietta, who was certainly not brilliant at all. It was this terrible shyness that held her back, that and Henrietta's assurance that Edmund did not love her. And indeed he did not seem to. It was but too likely that Henrietta was right.

As the time approached for Edmund's return, Henrietta was in a fine bustle and the house was in one, too. The house smiled contemptuously at Henrietta's parsimonious attempts to freshen it up. As though the house could not do that a great deal better than Henrietta ever could! Bees-waxing the floors, rubbing the furniture, shining up the silver—what were these little superficialities compared with the inner spiritual shake that the house gave itself when it wanted to? A sort of glow stole over windows, stairs and hall; a silver shine, a richer colour crept into the amber curtains, the cherry-coloured sofa; the faces in the portraits smiled, the fire-irons glittered, the mahogany shone again. Edmund had been away too long; the house would not let him go so easily next time.

The night before his return, Dorothy did not sleep, but lay there, here eyes burning, her heart thickly beating, determining on the bold demonstrative person she would be. She would show Henrietta whether he loved her or not. But at the thought of Henrietta she shivered and drew the bed-clothes closely about her. She seemed to be standing beside the bed, illumined in the darkness by her own malignant fires, her yellow skin drawn tightly across the supercilious bones, her hands curving over some fresh mean economy, her ridiculous head-dress wagging like a mocking spirit above her small red-rimmed eyes. Yes, if only Henrietta were not there…

And the old chest murmured softly: 'If only Henrietta were not there…'

The post-chaise came up to the door darkly like a ghost, for it had been snowing all day and the house was wrapped in silence. The animals on the box-tree hedge stood out fantastically against the silver-grey of the evening sky, and the snow fell like the scattering feathers of a heavenly geese-flock.

Edmund stepped into the hall and had Dorothy in his arms. At that moment they knew how truly they loved one another. He wondered as he flung his mind back in an instant's retrospect over a phantasmagoria of Indian Moguls, Chinese rivers and the flaming sunsets of Arabia how it could be that he had not known that his life was here, here with his beloved house above him, his adored wife in his arms. His head up like a conqueror's, he mounted the stairs, almost running into his wonderful parlour, to see once again the vase of flowers on the commode, the slender beautiful legs of his chair, the charming circles of his delicate ceiling. 'How could I have stayed away?' he thought. 'I will never leave this again!'

And that night, clasped in one another's arms, they discovered one another again: shyness fled and heart was open to heart.

Nevertheless, there remained Henrietta. Would you believe that one yellow-faced old maid could direct and dominate two normal healthy creatures? You know that she can, and is doing it somewhere or the other at this very moment. And all for their good. No one ever did anything mean to anyone else yet save for their good, and so it will be until the end of this frail planet.

She told Edmund that she had been 'educating Dorothy'. He would find her greatly improved; she feared that her worst fault was Hardness of Heart. Hardness of Heart! A sad defect!

During those snowy days Henrietta tried to show her brother that no one in the world truly loved him but herself. She had shown him this before and found the task easy; now it was more difficult. Dorothy's shyness had been melted by this renewed contact; he could not doubt the evidence of his eyes and the many little unconscious things that spoke for her when she had no idea that they were speaking. Now they rode and walked together and he explained to her how *he* was, how that at a time his thoughts would be far, far away in Cairo or Ispahan and that she must not think that he did not care for her because he was dreaming, and she told him that when he had frightened her she had been stupid, but that now that he frightened her no longer she would soon be brilliant. ... So Henrietta's task was difficult.

And then in the spring, when the daffodils blew among the long grasses and the white violets were shining in the copse, a chance word of hers showed her the way. She hated Dorothy now because she suspected that Dorothy was planning to be rid of her.

The fear that she would be turned out of the house never left her, and so, as fear always does, it drove her to baser things than belonged truly to her nature. She hinted that in Edmund's absence Dorothy had found a neighbouring squire 'good company'. And there had been perhaps another or two ... men ... At that word every frustrated instinct in Henrietta's body turned in rebellion. She had not spoken before she believed it true. She had this imaginative gift, common to lonely persons. She was herself amazed at the effect of her words on Edmund. If she had ever doubted Edmund's love for his wife (and she had not really doubted it) she was certain of the truth at last. Dorothy ... Dorothy ... His stout body trembled; his eyes were wounded; he turned from his sister as though he were ashamed both of her and of himself. After that there was no peace.

It was now that the house wondered most deeply at these strange human beings. The little things that upset them, the odd things that, at a moment, they would believe! Here, for instance, was their Edmund, whom they so truly admired, loving his Dorothy and entirely trusting her. Now, at a moment's word from a sour-faced virgin, there is a fire of torment in his heart. He looks on every male with an eager restless suspicion. While attempting to appear natural he watches Dorothy at every corner and counters in his mind her lightest word.

'Why,' said the Italian lamp (which from its nationality knew everything about jealousy) to the Cromwellian chest, 'I have never known so foolish a suspicion,' to which the Cromwellian chest replied in its best Roundhead manner: 'Woman ... the devil's bait ... always has been ... always will be.'

He attacked his sister again and again. 'With whom has she been? Has she ever stayed from the house a night? What friends has she made?'

To which Henrietta would indignantly reply: 'Brother, brother. What are you about? This jealousy is most unbecoming. I have suggested no impropriety ... only a little foolishness born of idleness.'

But it did not need time for Dorothy to discover that something was once again terribly amiss.

This strange husband of hers, so unable to express himself—she had but just won him back to her and now he was away again! With the courage born of their new relationship she asked him what was the trouble. And he told her: 'Nothing. ... Nothing! Nothing at all! Why should there be trouble? You are for ever imagining...' And then looked at her so strangely that she blushed and turned away as though she were indeed guilty. Guilty of what? She had not the least idea. But what she did know was that it was dear sister Henrietta who was responsible, and now, as May came with a flourish of birds and blossom and star-lit nights, she began to hate Henrietta with an intensity quite new to her gentle nature.

So, with jealousy and hatred, alive and burning, the house grew very sad. It hated these evil passions and had said long ago that they ruined with their silly bitterness every good house in the world. The little Chinese cabinet with the purple dragons on its doors said that in China everything was much simpler—you did not drag a situation to infinity as these sluggish English do, but simply called Death in to make a settlement—a much simpler way. In any case the house began to watch and listen with the certainty that the moment was approaching when it must interfere.

Jealousy always heightens love, and so, if Edmund had loved Dorothy at the first, that cool, placid anticipation was nothing to the fevered passion which he now felt. When he was away from her he longed to have her in his arms, covering her with kisses and assuring her that he had never doubted her, and when he was with her he suspected her every look, her every word. And she, miserable now and angry and ill, could not tell what possessed him, her virtue being so secure that she could not conceive that anyone should suspect it. Only she was well aware that Henrietta was to blame.

These were also days of national anxiety and unrest; the days when Napoleon jumping from Elba alighted in France and for a moment promised to stay there. Warm, stuffy, breathless days, when everyone was waiting, the house with the rest.

On the staircase one summer evening Dorothy told Henrietta something of her mind. 'If I had my way,' she ended in a shaking rage, 'you would not be here plotting against us!'

So that was it! At last Henrietta's suspicions were confirmed. In a short while Dorothy would have her out of the house; and then where would she go? The thought of her desolation, loneliness, loss of power, gripped her heart like a cat's claws. The two little charity-girls had a time of it during those weeks and cried themselves to sleep in their attic that smelt of mice and apples, dreaming afterwards of strong lovers who beat their mistress into a pulp.

'Give me proof!' said Edmund, so bitterly tormented. 'If it is true, give me proof!'

And Henrietta answered, sulkily: 'I have never said anything,' and a window-sash fell on his fingers and bruised them just to teach him not to be so damnable a fool.

Nevertheless, Henrietta had her proof. She had been cherishing it for a year at least. This was a letter written by a young Naval Lieutenant, cousin of a neighbouring squire, after he had danced with Dorothy at a Christmas ball. It was only a happy careless boy's letter, he in love with Dorothy's freshness, and because he was never more than a moment in any one place, careless of consequences. He said in his letter that she was the most beautiful of god's creatures, that he would dream of her at sea, and the rest. Dorothy kept it. Henrietta stole it....

The day came when the coach brought the news of the Waterloo victory. On that summer evening rockets were breaking into the pale sky above the dark soft shelter of the wood; on Bendon Hill they were waiting for dark to light the bonfire. You could hear the shouting and singing from the high-road. The happiness at the victory and the sense that England was delivered blew some of the cobwebs from Edmund's brain; he took Dorothy into the garden and there, behind the sun-dial, put his arms around her and kissed her.

Henrietta, watching the rockets strike the sky from her window, saw them, and fear, malice, loneliness, greed, hurt pride and jealousy all rose in her together. She turned over the letter in her drawer and vowed that her brother should not go to bed that night before he had heard of it.

'Look out! Look out!' cried her room to the rest of the house. 'She will make mischief with the letter. We must prevent her...'

'She has done mischief enough,' chattered the clock from the hall. 'She must be prevented...' whistled the chimneys. Something must be done and at once. But how? By whom?

She is coming. She stands outside her door, glancing about the dim sunset passage. The picture of Ranelagh above her head wonders—shall it fall on her? The chairs along the passage watch her anxiously as she passes them. But what can they do? Each must obey his own laws.

Stop her! Stop her! Stop her! Edmund and Dorothy are coming in from the garden. The sun is sinking, the shadows lengthening across the lawn. One touch on his arm: 'Brother, may I have a word?' and all the harm is done—misery and distress, unhappiness in the house, separation and loneliness. Stop her! Stop her!

All the house is quivering with agitation. The curtains are blowing, the chimneys are twisting, the tables and chairs are creaking: Stop her! Stop her! Stop her!

The order has gone out. She is standing now at the head of the staircase leading to the hall. She waits, her head bent a little, listening. Something seems to warn her. Edmund and Dorothy are coming in from the garden. The fireworks are beginning beyond the wood, and their gold and crimson showers are rivalling the stars.

Henrietta, nodding her head as though in certainty, has taken her step, some roughness in the wood has caught her heel (was it there a moment ago?), she stumbles, she clutches at the balustrade, but it is slippery and refuses to aid her. She is falling; her feet are away in air, her head strikes the board; she screams, once and then again; a rush, a flash of huddled colour, and her head has struck the stone of the hall floor.

How odd a silence followed! Dorothy and Edmund were still a moment lingering by the door looking back to the shower of golden stars, hearing the happy voices singing in the road. Henrietta was dead and so made no sound.

But all through the house there was a strange humming as though everything from top to bottom were whispering.

Everything in the house is moving save the woman at the bottom of the stairs.

The Haunted Doll's House

M.R. James

'I suppose you get stuff of that kind through your hands pretty often?' said Mr Dillet, as he pointed with his stick to an object which shall be described when the time comes: and when he said it, he lied in his throat, and knew that he lied. Not once in twenty years—perhaps not once in a lifetime—could Mr Chittenden, skilled as he was in ferreting out the forgotten treasures of half-a-dozen counties, expect to handle such a specimen. It was collectors' palaver, and Mr Chittenden recognised it as such.

'Stuff of that kind, Mr Dillet! It's a museum piece, that is.'

'Well, I suppose there are museums that'll take anything.'

'I've seen one, not as good as that, years back,' said Mr Chittenden, thoughtfully. 'But that's not likely to come into the market: and I'm told they 'ave some fine ones of the period over the water. No: I'm only telling you the truth, Mr Dillet, when I say that if you was to place an unlimited order with me for the very best that could be got—and you know I 'ave facilities for getting to know of such things, and a reputation to maintain—well, all I can say is, I should lead you straight up to that one and say. "I can't do no better for you than that, Sir."'

'Hear, hear!' said Mr Dillet, applauding ironically with the end of his stick on the floor of the shop. 'How much are you sticking the innocent American buyer for it, eh?'

'Oh, I shan't be over hard on the buyer, American or otherwise. You see, it stands this way, Mr Dillet—if I knew just a bit more about the pedigree——'

'Or just a bit less,' Mr Dillet put in.

'Ha, ha! You will have your joke, Sir. No, but as I was saying, if I knew just a little more than what I do about the piece—though anyone can see for themselves it's a genuine thing, every last corner of it, and there's not been one of my men allowed to so much as touch it since it came into the shop—there'd be another figure in the price I'm asking.'

'And what's that: five and twenty?'

'Multiply that by three and you've got it, Sir. Seventy-five's my price.'

'And fifty's mine,' said Mr Dillet.

The point of agreement was, of course, somewhere between the two, it does not matter exactly where—I think sixty guineas. But half an hour later the object was being packed, and within an hour Mr Dillet had called for it in his car and driven away. Mr Chittenden, holding the cheque in his hand, saw him off from the door with smiles, and returned, still smiling, into the parlour where his wife was making tea. He stopped at the door.

'It's gone,' he said.

'Thank god for that!' said Mrs Chittenden, putting down the teapot. 'Mr Dillet, was it?'

'Yes, it was.'

'Well, I'd sooner it was him than another.'

'Oh, I don't know, he ain't a bad feller, my dear.'

'Maybe not, but in my opinion he'd be none the worse for a bit of a shake up.'

'Well, if that's your opinion, it's my opinion he's put himself into the way of getting one. Anyhow, we shan't have no more of it, and that's something to be thankful for.'

And so Mr and Mrs Chittenden sat down to tea.

And what of Mr Dillet and of his new acquisition? What it was, the title of this story will have told you. What it was like, I shall have to indicate as well as I can.

There was only just room enough for it in the car, and Mr Dillet had to sit with the driver: he had also to go slow, for though the rooms of the Doll's House had all been stuffed carefully with soft cotton-wool, jolting was to be avoided, in view of the immense number of small objects which thronged them; and the ten-mile drive was an anxious time for him, in spite of all the precautions he insisted upon. At last his front door was reached, and Collins, the butler, came out.

'Look here, Collins, you must help me with this thing—it's a delicate job. We must get it out upright, see? It's full of little things that mustn't be displaced more than we can help. Let's see, where shall we have it?' (After a pause for consideration.) 'Really, I think I shall have to put it in my own room, to begin with at any rate. On the big table—that's it.'

It was conveyed—with much talking—to Mr Dillet's spacious room on the first floor, looking out on the drive. The sheeting was unwound from it, and the front thrown open, and for the next hour or two Mr Dillet was fully occupied in extracting the padding and setting in order the contents of the rooms.

When this thoroughly congenial task was finished, I must say that it would have been difficult to find a more perfect and attractive specimen of a Doll's House in Strawberry Hill Gothic than that which now stood on Mr Dillet's large kneehole table, lighted up by the evening sun which came slanting through three tall sash-windows.

It was quite six feet long, including the chapel or oratory which flanked the front on the left as you faced it, and the stable on the right. The main block of the house was, as I have said, in the Gothic manner: that is to say, the windows had pointed arches and were surmounted by what are called ogival hoods, with crockets and finials such as we see on the canopies of tombs built into church walls. At the angles were absurd turrets covered with arched panels. The chapel had pinnacles and buttresses and a bell in the turret and coloured glass in the windows. When the front of the house was open you saw four large rooms, bedroom, dining-room, drawing-room and kitchen, each with its appropriate furniture in a very complete state.

The stable on the right was in two storeys, with its proper complement of horses, coaches and grooms, and with its clock and Gothic cupola for the clock bell.

Pages, of course, might be written on the outfit of the mansion—how many frying pans, how many gilt chairs, what pictures, carpets, chandeliers, four-posters, table linen, glass, crockery and plate it possessed; but all this must be left to the imagination. I will only say that the base or plinth on which the house stood (for it was fitted with one of some depth which allowed of a flight of steps to the front door and a terrace, partly balustraded) contained a shallow drawer or drawers in which were neatly stored sets of embroidered curtains, changes of raiment for the inmates, and, in short, all the materials for an infinite series of variations and refittings of the most absorbing and delightful kind.

'Quintessence of Horace Walpole, that's what it is: he must have had something to do with the making of it.' Such was Mr Dillet's murmured reflection as he knelt before it in a reverent ecstasy. 'Simply wonderful; this is my day and no mistake. Five hundred pound coming in this morning for that cabinet which I never cared about, and now this tumbling into my hands for a tenth, at the very most, of what it would fetch in town. Well, well! It almost makes one afraid something'll happen to counter it. Let's have a look at the population, anyhow.'

Accordingly, he set them before him in a row. Again, here is an opportunity, which some would snatch at, of making an inventory of costume: I am incapable of it.

There were a gentleman and lady, in blue satin and brocade respectively. There were two children, a boy and a girl. There was a cook, a nurse, a footman, and there were the stable servants, two postillions, a coachman, two grooms.

'Anyone else? Yes, possibly.'

The curtains of the four-poster in the bedroom were closely drawn round four sides of it, and he put his finger in between them

THE HAUNTED DOLL'S HOUSE 83

and felt in the bed. He drew the finger back hastily, for it almost seemed to him as if something had—not stirred, perhaps, but yielded—in an odd live way as he pressed it. Then he put back the curtains, which ran on rods in the proper manner, and extracted from the bed a white-haired old gentleman in a long linen nightdress and cap, and laid him down by the rest. The tale was complete.

Dinner time was now near, so Mr Dillet spent but five minutes in putting the lady and children into the drawing-room, the gentleman into the dining-room, the servants into the kitchen and stables, and the old man back into his bed. He retired into his dressing room next door, and we see and hear no more of him until something like eleven o'clock at night.

His whim was to sleep surrounded by some of the gems of his collection. The big room in which we have seen him contained his bed: bath, wardrobe, and all the appliances of dressing were in a commodious room adjoining: but his four-poster, which itself was a valued treasure, stood in the large room where he sometimes wrote, and often sat, and even received visitors. Tonight he repaired to it in a highly complacent frame of mind.

There was no striking clock within earshot—none on the staircase, none in the stable, none in the distant church tower. Yet, it is indubitable that Mr Dillet was startled out of a very pleasant slumber by a bell tolling one.

He was so much startled that he did not merely lie breathless with wide-open eyes, but actually sat up in his bed.

He never asked himself, till the morning hours, how it was that, though there was no light at all in the room, the Doll's House on the kneehole table stood out with complete clearness. But it was so. The effect was that of a bright harvest moon shining full on the front of a big white stone mansion—a quarter of a mile away it might be, and yet every detail was photographically sharp. There were trees about it, too—trees rising behind the chapel and the house. He seemed to be conscious of the scent of a cool still September night. He thought he could hear an occasional stamp and clink from the stables, as of horses stirring. And with another shock he realised that, above the house, he was looking, not at the wall of his room with its pictures, but into the profound blue of a night sky.

There were lights, more than one, in the windows, and he quickly saw that this was no four-roomed house with a movable front, but one of many rooms, and staircases—a real house, but seen as if through the wrong end of a telescope. 'You mean to show me something,' he muttered to himself, and he gazed earnestly on the lighted windows. They would in real life have been shuttered or curtained, no doubt, he thought; but, as it was, there was nothing to intercept his view of what was being transacted inside the rooms.

Two rooms were lighted—one on the ground floor to the right of the door, one upstairs, on the left—the first brightly enough, the other rather dimly. The lower room was the dining-room: a table was laid, but the meal was over, and only wine and glasses were left on the table. The man of the blue satin and the woman of the brocade were alone in the room, and they were talking very earnestly, seated close together at the table, their elbows on it: every now and again stopping to listen, as it seemed. Once *he* rose, came to the window and opened it and put his head out and his hand to his ear. There was a lighted taper in a silver candlestick on a sideboard.

When the man left the window, he seemed to leave the room also; and the lady, taper in hand, remained standing and listening. The expression on her face was that of one striving her utmost to keep down a fear that threatened to master her—and succeeding. It was a hateful face, too; broad, flat and sly. Now the man came back and she took some small thing from him and hurried out of the room. He, too, disappeared, but only for a moment or two. The front door slowly opened and he stepped out and stood on the top of the *perron*, looking this way and that; then turned towards the upper window that was lighted, and shook his fist.

It was time to look at that upper window. Through it was seen a four-post bed: a nurse or other servant in an arm-chair, evidently sound asleep; in the bed an old man lying: awake, and, one would say, anxious, from the way in which he shifted about and moved his fingers, beating tunes on the coverlet. Beyond the bed a door opened. Light was seen on the ceiling, and the lady came in: she set down her candle on a table, came to the fireside and roused the nurse. In her hand she had an old-fashioned wine bottle, ready uncorked. The nurse took it, poured some of the contents into a little silver sauce-pan, added some spice and sugar from casters on the table, and set it to warm on the fire. Meanwhile, the old man in the bed beckoned feebly to the lady, who came to him smiling, took his wrist as if to feel his pulse, and bit her lip as if in consternation. He looked at her anxiously, and then pointed to the window, and spoke. She nodded, and did as the man below had done; opened the casement and listened—perhaps rather ostentatiously: then drew in her head and shook it, looking at the old man, who seemed to sigh.

By this time the posset on the fire was steaming, and the nurse poured it into a small two-handled silver bowl and brought it to the bedside. The old man seemed disinclined for it and was waving it away, but the lady and the nurse together bent over him and evidently pressed it upon him. He must have yielded, for they supported him into a sitting position, and put it to his lips. He drank most of it, in several draughts, and they laid him down. The lady left the room, smiling good-night to him, and took the bowl, the bottle and the silver sauce-pan with her. The nurse returned to the chair, and there was an interval of complete quiet.

Suddenly the old man started up in his bed—and he must have uttered some cry, for the nurse started out of her chair and made but one step of it to the bedside. He was a sad and terrible sight—flushed in the face, almost to blackness, the eyes glaring whitely, both hands clutching at his heart, foam at his lips.

For a moment the nurse left him, ran to the door, flung it wide open, and, one supposes, screamed aloud for help, then darted back to the bed and seemed to try feverishly to soothe him—to lay him down—anything. But as the lady, her husband, and several servants, rushed into the room with horrified faces, the old man collapsed under the nurse's hands and lay back, and the features, contorted with agony and rage, relaxed slowly into calm.

A few moments later, lights showed out to the left of the house, and a coach with flambeaux drove up to the door. A white-wigged man in black got nimbly out and ran up the steps, carrying a small leather trunk-shaped box. He was met in the doorway by the man and his wife, she with her handkerchief clutched between her hands, he with a tragic face, but retaining his self-control. They led the newcomer into the dining-room, where he set his box of papers on the table, and, turning to them, listened with a face of consternation at what they had to tell. He nodded his head again and again, threw out his hands slightly, declined, it seemed, offers of refreshment and lodging for the night, and within a few minutes came slowly down the steps entering the coach and driving off the way he had come. As the man in blue watched him from the top of the steps, a smile not pleasant to see stole slowly over his fat white face. Darkness fell over the whole scene as the lights of the coach disappeared.

But Mr Dillet remained sitting up in the bed: he had rightly guessed that there would be a sequel. The house front glimmered out again before long. But now there was a difference. The lights were in other windows, one at the top of the house, the other illuminating the range of coloured windows of the chapel. How he saw through these is not quite obvious, but he did. The interior was as carefully furnished as the rest of the establishment, with its minute red cushions on the desks, its Gothic stall-canopies, and its western gallery and pinnacled organ with gold pipes. On the centre of the black and white pavement was a bier: four tall candles burned at the corners. On the bier was a coffin covered with a pall of black velvet.

As he looked the folds of the pall stirred. It seemed to rise at one end: it slid downwards: it fell away, exposing the black coffin with its silver handles and name-plate. One of the tall candlesticks swayed and toppled over. Ask no more, but turn, as Mr Dillet hastily did, and look in at the lighted window at the top of the house, where a boy and girl lay in two truckle-beds, and a four-poster for the nurse rose above them. The nurse was not visible for the moment; but the father and mother were there, dressed now in mourning, but with very little sign of mourning in their demeanour. Indeed, they were laughing and talking with a good deal of animation, sometimes to each other, and sometimes throwing a remark to one or other of the children, and again laughing at the answers. Then the father was seen to go on tiptoe out of the room, taking with him as he went a white garment that hung on a peg near the door. He shut the door after him. A minute or two later it was slowly opened again, and a muffled head poked round it. A bent form of sinister shape stepped across to the truckle-beds and suddenly stopped, threw up its arms and revealed, of course, the father, laughing. The children were in agonies of terror, the boy with the bed clothes over his head, the girl throwing herself out of bed into her mother's arms. Attempts at consolation followed— the parents took the children on their laps, patted them, picked up the white gown and showed there was no harm in it, and so forth; and at last putting the children back into bed, left the room with encouraging waves of the hand. As they left it, the nurse came in, and soon the light died down.

Still, Mr Dillet watched immovable.

A new sort of light—not of lamp or candle—a pale ugly light, began to dawn around the door-case at the back of the room. The door was opening again. The seer does not like to dwell upon what he saw entering the room: he says it might be described as a frog— the size of a man—but it had scanty white hair about its head. It was busy about the truckle-beds, but not for long. The sound of cries—faint, as if coming out of a vast distance—but, even so, infinitely appalling, reached the ear.

There were signs of a hideous commotion all over the house: lights passed along and up, and doors opened and shut, and running figures passed within the windows. The clock in the stable turret tolled one, and darkness fell again.

It was only dispelled once more to show the house front. At the bottom of the steps dark figures were drawn up in two lines, holding flaming torches. More dark figures came down the steps, bearing, first one, then another small coffin. And the lines of torch-bearers with the coffins between them moved silently onward to the left.

The hours of night passed on—never so slowly, Mr Dillet thought. Gradually he sank down from sitting to lying in his bed—but he did not close an eye: and early next morning he sent for the doctor.

The doctor found him in a disquieting state of nerves, and recommended sea-air. To a quiet place on the East Coast he accordingly repaired by easy stages in his car.

One of the first people he met on the sea front was Mr Chittenden, who, it appeared, had likewise been advised to take his wife away for a bit of a change.

Mr Chittenden looked somewhat askance upon him when they met: and not without cause.

'Well, I don't wonder at you being a bit upset, Mr Dillet. What? yes, well, I might say 'orrible upset, to be sure, seeing what me and my poor wife went through ourselves. But I put it to you, Mr Dillet, one of two things: was I going to scrap a lovely piece like that on the one 'and, or was I going to tell customers: "I'm selling you a regular picture-palace-dramar in reel life of the olden time, billed to perform regular at one o'clock a.m.?" Why, what would you 'ave said yourself? And next thing you know, two Justices of the Peace in the back parlour, and pore Mr and Mrs Chittenden off in a spring cart to the County Asylum and everyone in the street saying, "Ah, I thought it 'ud come to that. Look at the way the man drank!"—and me next door, or next door but one, to a total abstainer, as you know. Well, there was my position. What? Me 'ave it back in the shop? Well, what do *you* think? No, but I'll tell you what I will do. You shall have your money back, bar the ten pound I paid for it, and you make what you can.'

Later in the day, in what is offensively called the 'smoke-room' of the hotel, a murmured conversation between the two went on for some time.

'How much do you really know about that thing, and where it came from?'

'Honest, Mr Dillet, I don't know the 'ouse. Of course, it came out of the lumber room of a country 'ouse—that anyone could guess. But I'll go as far as say this, that I believe it's not a hundred miles from this place. Which direction and how far I've no notion. I'm only judging by guess-work. The man as I actually paid the cheque to ain't one of my regular men, and I've lost sight of him; but I 'ave the idea that this part of the country was hi-beat, and that's every word I can tell you. But now, Mr Dillets there's one thing that rather physicks me—that old chap—I suppose you saw him drive up to the door—I thought so: now, would he have been the medical man, do you take it? My wife would have it so, but I stuck to it that was the lawyer, because he had papers with him, and one he took out was folded up.'

'I agree,' said Mr Dillet. 'Thinking it over, I came to the conclusion that was the old man's will, ready to be signed.'

'Just what I thought,' said Mr Chittenden, 'and I took it that will would have cut out the young people, eh? Well, well! It's been a lesson to me, I know that. I shan't buy no more dolls' houses, nor waste no more money on the pictures—and as to this business of poisonin' grandpa, well, if I know myself, I never 'ad much of a turn for that. Live and let live: that's bin my motto throughout life, and I ain't found it a bad one.'

Filled with these elevated sentiments, Mr Chittenden retired to his lodgings. Mr Dillet next day repaired to the local institute, where he hoped to find some clue to the riddle that absorbed him. He gazed in despair at a long file of the Canterbury and York Society's publications of the Parish Registers of the district. No print resembling the house of his nightmare was among those that hung on the staircase and in the passages. Disconsolate, he found himself at last in a derelict room, staring at a dusty model of a church in a dusty glass case: *Model of St Stephen's Church, Coxham. Presented by J. Merewether, Esq., of Ilbridge House, 1877. The work of his ancestor James Merewether, d. 1786.* There was something in the fashion of it that reminded him dimly of his horror. He retraced his steps to a wall map he had noticed, and made out that Ilbridge House was in Coxham Parish. Coxham was, as it happened, one of the parishes of which he had retained the name when he glanced over the file of printed registers, and it was not long before he found in them the record of the burial of Roger Milford, aged seventy-six, on the 11th of September, 1757, and of Roger and Elizabeth Merewether, aged nine and seven, on the 19th of the same month. It seemed worthwhile to follow up this clue, frail as it was; and in the afternoon he drove out to Coxham. The east end of the north aisle of the church is a Milford chapel, and on its north wall are tablets to the same persons; Roger, the elder, it seems, was distinguished by all the qualities which adorn 'the Father, the Magistrate, and the Man': the memorial was erected by his attached daughter Elizabeth, 'who did not long survive the loss of a parent ever solicitous for her welfare, and of two amiable children'. The last sentence was plainly an addition to the original inscription.

A yet late slab told of James Merewether, husband of Elizabeth, 'who in the dawn of life practised, not without success, those arts which, had he continued their exercise, might in the opinion of the most competent judges have earned for him the name of the British Vitruvius: but who, overwhelmed by the visitation which deprived him of an affectionate partner and a blooming offspring, passed his Prime and Age in a secluded yet elegant Retirement: his grateful Nephew and Heir indulges a pious sorrow by this too brief a recital of his excellences'.

The children were more simply commemorated. Both died on the night of the 12th of September.

Mr Dillet felt sure that in Ilbridge House he had found the scene of his drama. In some old sketch-book, possibly in some old print, he may yet find convincing evidence that he is right. But the Ilbridge House of today is not that which he sought; it is an Elizabethan erection of the forties, in red brick with stone quoins and dressings. A quarter of a mile from it, in a low part of the park, backed by ancient, stag-horned, ivy-strangled trees and thick undergrowth, are marks of a terraced platform overgrown with rough grass. A few stone balusters lie here and there, and a heap or two, covered with nettles and ivy, of wrought stones with badly carved crockets. This, someone told Mr Dillet, was the site of an older house.

As he drove out of the village, the hall clock struck four, and Mr Dillet started up and clapped his hands to his ears. It was not the first time he had heard that bell.

Awaiting an offer from the other side of the Atlantic, the doll's house still reposes, carefully sheeted, in a loft over Mr Dillet's stables, whither Collins conveyed it on the day when Mr Dillet started for the sea-coast.

The Ghost

By Walter de la Mare

'Who knocks?' 'I, who was beautiful,
  Beyond all dreams to restore,
I, from the roots of the dark thorn am hither.
  And knock on the door.'

'Who speaks?' 'I—once was my speech
  Sweet as the bird's on the air,
When echo lurks by the waters to heed;
  'Tis I speak thee fair.'

'Dark is the hour!' 'Ay, and cold.'
  'Lone is my house.' 'Ah, but mine?'
'Sight, touch, lips, eyes yearned in vain.'
  'Long dead these to thine...'

Silence. Still faint on the porch
  Brake the flames of the stars.

In gloom groped a hope-wearied hand
    Over keys, bolts, and bars.

A face peered. All the grey night
    In chaos of vacancy shone;
Naught but vast sorrow was there—
    The sweet cheat gone.

Mrs Amworth

E.F. Benson

The village of Maxley, where last summer and autumn these strange events took place, lies on a heathen and pine-clad upland of Sussex. In all England you could not find a sweeter and saner situation. Should the wind blow from the south, it comes laden with the spices of the sea; to the east, high downs protect it from the inclemencies of March; and from the west and north the breezes which reach it travel over miles of aromatic forest and heather. The village itself is insignificant enough in point of population, but rich in amenities and beauty. Half-way down the single street, with its broad road and spacious areas of grass on each side, stands the little Norman Church and the antique graveyard long disused: for the rest there are a dozen small, sedate Georgian houses, red-bricked and long-windowed, each with a square of flower garden in front, and an ampler strip behind; a score of shops, and a couple of score of thatched cottages belonging to labourers on neighbouring estates, complete the entire cluster of its peaceful habitations. The general peace, however, is sadly broken on

Saturdays and Sundays, for we lie on one of the main roads between London and Brighton and our quiet street becomes a race-course for flying motor-cars and bicycles. A notice just outside the village begging them to go slowly only seems to encourage them to accelerate, for the road lies open and straight, and there is really no reason why they should do otherwise. By way of protest, therefore, the ladies of Maxley cover their noses and mouths with their handkerchiefs as they see a motor-car approaching, though, as the street is asphalted, they need not really take these precautions against dust. But late on Sunday night the horde of scorchers has passed, and we settle down again to five days of cheerful and leisurely seclusion. Railway strikes which agitate the country so much leave us undisturbed because most of the inhabitants of Maxley never leave it at all.

I am the fortunate possessor of one of these small Georgian houses, and consider myself no less fortunate in having so interesting and stimulating a neighbour as Francis Urcombe, who, the most confirmed of Maxleyites, has not slept away from his house, which stands just opposite to mine in the village street, for nearly two years, at which date, though still in middle life he resigned his Physiological Professorship at Cambridge University, and devoted himself to the study of those occult and curious phenomena which seem equally to concern the physical and psychical sides of human nature. Indeed his retirement was not unconnected with his passion for the strange uncharted places that lie on the confines and borders of science, the existence of which is so stoutly denied by the more materialistic minds, for he advocated that all medical students should be obliged to pass some sort of examination in mesmerism, and that one of the tripos papers should be designed to test their knowledge in such subjects as appearances at the time of death, haunted houses, vampirism, automatic writing, and possession.

'Of course they wouldn't listen to me,' ran his account of the matter, 'for there is nothing that these seats of learning are so frightened of as knowledge, and the road to knowledge lies in the study of things like these. The functions of the human frame are, broadly speaking, known. They are a country, anyhow, that has been charted and mapped out. But outside that lie huge tracts of undiscovered terrain, which certainly exist, and the real pioneers of knowledge are those who, at the cost of being derided as credulous and superstitious, want to push on into those misty and probably perilous places. I felt that I could be of more use by setting out without compass or knapsack into the mists than by sitting in a cage like a canary and chirping about what was known. Besides, teaching is very bad for a man who knows himself only to be a learner: you only need to be a self-conceited ass to teach.'

Here, then, in Francis Urcombe, was a delightful neighbour to one who, like myself, has an uneasy and burning curiosity about what he called the 'misty and perilous places', and this last spring we had a further and most welcome addition to our pleasant little community, in the person of Mrs Amworth, widow of an Indian civil servant. Her husband had been a judge in the North-West Provinces, and after his death at Peshawar she came back to England, and after a year in London found herself starving for the ampler air and sunshine of the country to take the place of the fog and griminess of town. She had, too, a special reason for settling in Maxley, since her ancestors up until a hundred years ago had long been native to the place, and in the old churchyard, now disused, are many gravestones bearing her maiden name of Chaston. Big and energetic, her vigorous and genial personality speedily woke Maxley up to a higher degree of sociality than it ever had known. Most of us were bachelors or spinsters or elderly folk not much inclined to exert ourselves in the expense and effort of hospitality, and hitherto the gaiety of a small tea party, with bridge afterwards and galoshes (when it was wet) to trip home in again for a solitary dinner, was about the climax of our festivities. But Mrs Amworth showed us a more gregarious way, and set an example of luncheon parties and little dinners, which we began to follow. On other nights when no such hospitality was on foot, a lone man like myself found it pleasant to know that a call on the telephone to Mrs Amworth's house, not a hundred yards off, and an inquiry as to whether I might come over after dinner for a game of piquet before bedtime would probably evoke a response of welcome. There she would be, with comrade-like eagerness for companionship, and there was a glass of port and a cup of coffee and a cigarette and a game of piquet. She played the piano too, in a free and exuberant manner, and had a charming voice and sang to her own accompaniment; and as the days grew long and the light lingered late, we played our game in her garden, which in the course of a few months she had turned from being a nursery for slugs and snails into a glowing patch of luxuriant blossomings. She was always cheery and jolly; she was interested in everything; and in music, in gardening, in games of all sorts was a competent performer. Everybody (with one exception) liked her, everybody found her bringing with her the tonic of a sunny day. That one exception was Francis Urcombe; he, though he confessed he did not like her, acknowledged that he was vastly interested in her. This always seemed strange to me, for pleasant and jovial as she was, I could see nothing in her that could call forth conjecture or intrigued surmise, so healthy and unmysterious a figure did she present. But of the genuineness of Urcombe's interest there could be no doubt; one could see him watching and scrutinising her. In the matter of age, she frankly volunteered the information that she was forty-five; but her briskness, her activity, her unravaged skin, her coal-black hair, made it difficult to believe that she was not adopting an unusual device and adding ten years on to her age instead of subtracting them.

Often, also, as our quite unsentimental friendship ripened, Mrs Amworth would ring me up and propose her advent. If I was busy writing, I was to give her, so we definitely bargained, a frank negative, and in answer I could hear her jolly laugh and her wishes for a successful evening of work. Sometimes, before her proposal arrived, Urcombe would already have stepped across from his house opposite for a smoke and a chat, and he, hearing who my intended visitor was, always urged me to beg her to come. She and I should play our piquet, said he, and he would look on, if we did not object and learn something of the game. But I doubt whether he paid much attention to it, for nothing could be clearer than that, under that penthouse of forehead and thick eyebrows, his attention was fixed not on the cards, but on one of the players. But he seemed to enjoy an hour spent thus, and often, until one particular evening in July, he would watch her with the air of a man who has some deep problem in front of him. She, enthusiastically keen about our game, seemed not to notice his scrutiny. Then came that evening when, as I see in the light of subsequent events, began the first twitching of the veil that hid the secret horror from my eyes. I did not know it then, though I noticed that thereafter if she rang up to propose coming round, she always asked not only if I was at leisure, but whether Mr Urcombe was with me. If so, she said, she would not spoil the chat of two old bachelors, and laughingly wished me goodnight. Urcombe, on this occasion, had been with me for some half-hour before Mrs Amworth's appearance, and had been talking to me about the medieval beliefs concerning vampirism, one of those border-land subjects which he declared had not been sufficiently studied before it had been consigned by the medical profession to the dustheap of exploded superstitions. There he sat, grim and eager, tracing with that pellucid clearness which had made him in his Cambridge days so admirable a lecturer, the history of those mysterious visitations. In them all there was the same general features; one of those ghoulish spirits took up its abode in a living man or woman, conferring supernatural powers of bat-like flight and glutting itself with nocturnal blood-feasts. When its host died, it continued to dwell in the corpse, which remained undecayed. By day it rested, by night it left the grave and went on its awful errands. No European country in the Middle Ages seemed to have escaped them; earlier yet, parallels were to be found in Roman and Greek and in Jewish history.

'It's a large order to set all that evidence aside as being moonshine,' he said. 'Hundreds of totally independent witnesses in many ages have testified to the occurrence of these phenomena, and there's no explanation known to me which covers all the facts. And if you feel inclined to say "Why, then, if these are facts, do we not come across them now?" there are two answers I can make you. One is that there were diseases known in the Middle Ages, such as the black death, which were certainly existent then and which have become extinct since, but for that reason we do not assert that such diseases never existed. Just as the black death visited England and decimated the population of Norfolk, so here in this very district, about three hundred years ago, there was certainly an outbreak of vampirism, and Maxley was the centre of it. My second answer is even more convincing, for I tell you that vampirism is by no means extinct now. An outbreak of it certainly occurred in India a year or two ago.'

At that moment I heard my knocker plied in the cheerful and peremptory manner in which Mrs Amworth is accustomed to announce her arrival, and I went to the door to open it.

'Come in at once,' I said, 'and save me from having my blood curdled. Mr Urcombe has been trying to alarm me.'

Instantly her vital, voluminous presence seemed to fill the room.

'Ah, but how lovely!' she said. 'I delight in having my blood curdled. Go on with your ghost story, Mr Urcombe. I adore ghost stories.'

I saw that, as his habit was, he was intently observing her.

'It wasn't a ghost story exactly,' said he. 'I was only telling our host how vampirism was not extinct yet. I was saying that there was an outbreak of it in India only a few years ago.'

There was a more than perceptible pause, and I saw that, if Urcombe was observing her, she on her side was observing him with fixed eye and parted mouth. Then her jolly laugh invaded that rather tense silence.

'Oh, what a shame!' she said. 'You're not going to curdle my blood at all. Where did you pick up such a tale, Mr Urcombe? I have lived for years in India and never heard a rumour of such a thing. Some storyteller in the bazaars must have invented it; they are famous at that.'

I could see that Urcombe was on the point of saying something further, but checked himself.

'Ah! Very likely that was it,' he said.

But something had disturbed our usual peaceful sociability that night, and something had dampened Mrs Amworth's usual high spirits. She had no gusto for her piquet, and left after a couple of games. Urcombe had been silent too, indeed he hardly spoke again until she departed.

'That was unfortunate,' he said, 'for the outbreak of a very mysterious disease, let us call it, took place at Peshawar where she and her husband were. And—'

'Well?' I asked.

'He was one of the victims of it' said he. 'Naturally I had quite forgotten that when I spoke.'

The summer was unreasonably hot and rainless, and Maxley suffered much from drought, and also from a plague of big black night-flying gnats, the bite of which was very irritating and virulent. They came sailing in on an evening, settling on one's skin so quietly that one perceived nothing until the sharp stab announced that one had been bitten. They did not bite the hands or face, but chose always the neck and throat for their feeding-ground, and most of us, as the poison spread, assumed a temporary goitre. Then about the middle of August appeared the first of those mysterious cases of illness which our local doctor attributed to the long-continued heat coupled with the bite of these venomous insects. The patient was a boy of sixteen or seventeen, the son of Mrs Amworth's gardener, and the symptoms were an anaemic pallor and a languid prostration, accompanied by great drowsiness and an abnormal appetite. He had, too, on his throat two small punctures where, so Dr Ross conjectured, one of these great gnats had bitten him. But the odd thing was that there was no swelling or inflammation round the place where he had been bitten. The heat at this time had begun to abate, but the cooler weather failed to restore him, and the boy, in spite of the quantity of food which he so ravenously swallowed, wasted away to a skinclad skeleton.

I met Dr Ross in the street one afternoon about this time, and in answer to my inquiries about his patient he said that he was afraid the boy was dying. The case, he confessed, completely puzzled him: some obscure form of pernicious anaemia was all he could suggest. But he wondered whether Mr Urcombe would consent to see the boy, on the chance of his being able to throw some new light on the case, and since Urcombe was dining with me that night, I proposed to Dr Ross to join us. He could not do this, but said he would look in later. When he came, Urcombe at once consented to put his skill at the other's disposal, and together they went off at once. Being thus shorn of my sociable evening, I telephoned Mrs Amworth to know if I might inflict myself on her for an hour. Her answer was a welcoming affirmative, and between piquet and music the hour lengthened itself into two. She spoke of the boy who was so desperately and mysteriously ill, and told me that she had often been to see him, taking him nourishing and delicate food. But today—and her kind eyes moistened as she spoke—she was afraid she had paid her last visit. Knowing the antipathy between her and Urcombe, I did not tell her that he had been called into consultation; and when I returned home she accompanied me to the door, for the sake of a breath of night air, and in order to borrow a magazine which contained an article on gardening which she wished to read.

'Ah, this delicious night air,' she said, luxuriously sniffing in the coolness. 'Night air and gardening are the great tonics. There is nothing so stimulating as bare contact with rich mother earth. You are never so fresh as when you have been grubbing in the soil—black hands, black nails, and boots covered with mud.' She gave her great jovial laugh.

'I'm a glutton for air and earth,' she said. 'Positively I look forward to death, for then I shall be buried and have the kind earth all round me. No leaden caskets for me—I have given explicit directions. But what shall I do about air? Well, I suppose one can't have everything. The magazine? A thousand thanks, I will faithfully return it. Good-night: garden and keep your windows open, and you won't have anaemia.'

'I always sleep with my windows open,' said I.

I went straight up to my bedroom, of which one of the windows looks out over the street, and as I undressed I thought I heard voices talking outside not far away. But I paid no particular attention, put out my lights, and falling asleep plunged into the depths of a most horrible dream, distortedly suggested, no doubt, by my last words with Mrs Amworth. I dreamed that I awoke, and found that both my bedroom windows were shut. Half-suffocating, I dreamed that

I sprang out of bed, and went across to open them. The blind over the first one was drawn down, and pulling it up I saw, with the indescribable horror of incipient nightmare, Mrs Amworth's face suspended close to the pane in the darkness outside, nodding and smiling at me. Pulling down the blind again to keep that terror out, I rushed to the second window on the other side of the room, and there again was Mrs Amworth's face. Then the panic came upon me in full blast; here was I suffocating in the airless room, and whichever window I opened Mrs Amworth's face would float in. The nightmare rose to screaming point, and with strangled yells I awoke to find my room cool and quiet with both windows open and blinds up and a half-moon high in its course, casting an oblong of tranquil light on the floor. But even when I was awake, the horror persisted, and I lay tossing and turning. I must have slept long before the nightmare seized me, for now it was nearly day, and soon in the east the drowsy eyelids of morning began to lift.

I was scarcely downstairs next morning—for after the dawn I slept late—when Urcombe rang up to know if he might see me immediately. He came in, grim and preoccupied, and I noticed that he was pulling on a pipe that was not even filled.

'I want your help,' he said, 'and so I must tell you first of all what happened last night. I went round with the little doctor to see his patient, and found him just alive, but scarcely more. I instantly diagnosed in my own mind what this anaemia, unaccountable by any other explanation, meant. The boy is the prey of a vampire.'

He put his empty pipe on the breakfast table, by which I had just sat down, and folded his arms, looking at me steadily from under his overhanging brows.

'Now about last night,' he said. 'I insisted that he should be moved from his father's cottage into my house. As we were carrying him on a stretcher, whom should we meet but Mrs Amworth! She expressed shocked surprise that we were moving him. Now why do you think she did that?'

With a start of horror, as I remembered my dream that night before, I felt an idea come into my mind so preposterous and unthinkable that I instantly turned it out again.

'I haven't the smallest idea,' I said.

'Then listen, while I tell you about what happened later. I put out all the lights in the room where the boy lay, and watched. One window was a little open, for I had forgotten to close it, and about midnight I heard something outside, trying apparently to push it farther open. I guessed who it was—yes, it was full twenty feet from the ground—and I peeped round the corner of the blind. Just outside was the face of Mrs Amworth and her hand was on the frame of the window. Very softly I crept close, and then banged the window down, and I think I just caught the tip of one of her fingers.'

'But it's impossible,' I cried. 'How could she be floating in the air like that? And what had she come for? Don't tell me such—'

Once more, with closer grip, the remembrance of my nightmare seized me.

'I am telling you what I saw,' said he. 'And all night long, until it was nearly day, she was fluttering outside like some terrible bat, trying to gain admittance. Now put together various things I have told you.'

He began checking them off on his fingers.

'Number one,' he said: 'there was an outbreak of disease similar to that which this boy is suffering from at Peshawar, and her husband died of it. Number two: Mrs Amworth protested against my moving the boy to my house. Number three: she or the demon that inhabits her body, a creature powerful and deadly, tries to gain admittance. And add this, too: in medieval times there was an epidemic of vampirism here at Maxley. The vampire, so the accounts run, was found to be Elizabeth Chaston.... I see you remember Mrs Amworth's maiden name. Finally, the boy is stronger this morning. He would certainly not have been alive if he had been visited again. And what do you make of it?'

There was a long silence, during which I found this incredible horror assuming the hues of reality.

'I have something to add,' I said, 'which may or may not bear on it. You say that the—spectre went away shortly before dawn?'

'Yes.'

I told him of my dream, and he smiled grimly.

'Yes, you did well to awake,' he said. 'That warning came from your subconscious self, which never wholly slumbers, and cried out to you of deadly danger. For two reasons, then you must help me: one to save others, the second to save yourself.'

'What do you want me to do?' I asked.

'I want you first of all to help me in watching this boy, and ensuring that she does not come near him. Eventually I want you to help me in tracking the thing down, in exposing and destroying it. It is not human: it is an incarnate fiend. What steps we shall have to take I don't know.'

It was now eleven of the forenoon, and presently I went across to his house for a twelve-hour vigil while he slept, to come on duty again that night, so that for the next twenty-four hours either Urcombe or myself was always in the room where the boy, now getting stronger every hour, was lying. The day following was Saturday and a morning of brilliant pellucid weather, and already when I went across to his house to resume my duty, the stream of motors down to Brighton had begun. Simultaneously I saw Urcombe with a cheerful face, which boded good news of his patient, coming out of his house, and Mrs Amworth, with a gesture of salutation to me, and a basket in her hand, walking up the broad strip of grass which bordered the road. There we all three met. I noticed (and saw that Urcombe noticed it too) that one finger on her left hand was bandaged.

'Good morning to you both,' said she. 'And I hear your patient is doing well, Mr Urcombe. I have come to bring him a bowl of jelly, and to sit with him for an hour. He and I are great friends. I am overjoyed at his recovery.'

Urcombe paused a moment, as if making up his mind, and then shot out a pointing finger at her.

'I forbid that,' he said. 'You shall not sit with him or see him. And you know the reason as well as I do.'

I have never seen so horrible a change pass over a human face as that which now blanched hers to the colour of grey mist. She put up her hand as if to shield herself from the pointing finger, which drew the sign of the cross in the air, and shrank back cowering on the road. There was a wild hoot from a horn, a grinding of brakes, a shout—too late—from a passing car, and one long scream suddenly cut short. Her body rebounded from the roadway after the first wheel had gone over it, and the second followed it. It lay there, quivering and twitching and was still.

She was buried three days afterwards in the cemetery outside Maxley, in accordance with the wishes she had told me that she had devised about her internment, and the shock which her sudden and awful death had caused to the little community began by degrees to pass off. To two people only, Urcombe and myself, the horror of it was mitigated from the first by the nature of the relief that her death brought; but, naturally enough, we kept our own counsel, and no hint of what greater horror had been thus averted was ever let slip. But, oddly enough, so it seemed to me, he was still not satisfied about something in connnection with her, and would give no answer to my questions on the subject. Then as the days of a tranquil mellow September and the October that followed began to drop away like the leaves of the yellowing trees, his uneasiness relaxed. But before the entry of November the seeming tranquillity broke into a hurricane.

I had been dining one night at the far end of the village, and about eleven o'clock was walking home again. The moon was of an unusual brilliance, rendering all that it shone on as distinct as in some etching. I had just come opposite the house which Mrs Amworth had occupied, where there was a board up saying that it was to let, when I heard the click of her front gate, and the next moment I saw, with a sudden chill and quaking of my very spirit, that she stood there. Her profile vividly illuminated, was turned to me, and I could not be mistaken in my identification of her. She appeared not to see me (indeed the shadow of the yew hedge in front of her garden enveloped me in its blackness), and she went swiftly across the road and entered the gate of the house directly opposite. There I lost sight of her completely.

My breath was coming in short pants as if I had been running—and now indeed I ran, with fearful backward glances, along the hundred yards that separated me from my house and Urcombe's. It was to his that my flying steps took me, and next minute I was within.

'What have you come to tell me?' he asked. 'Or shall I guess?'

'You can't guess.' said I.

'No; it's no guess. She has come back and you have seen her. Tell me about it.'

I gave my story.

'That's Major Pearsall's house,' he said. 'Come back with me there at once.'

'But what can we do?' I asked.

'I've no idea. That's what we have got to find out.'

A minute later, we were opposite the house. When I had passed it before, it was all dark; now lights gleamed from a couple of windows upstairs. Even as we faced it, the front door opened, and next moment Major Pearsall emerged from the gate. He saw us and stopped.

'I'm on my way to Dr Ross,' he said quickly. 'My wife has been taken suddenly ill. She had been in bed an hour when I came upstairs, and found her white as a ghost and utterly exhausted. She had been to sleep, it seemed—But you will excuse me.'

'One moment, Major,' said Urcombe. 'Was there any mark on her throat?'

'How did you guess that?' said he. 'There was; one of those beastly gnats must have bitten her twice there. She was streaming with blood.'

'And there's someone with her?' asked Urcombe.

'Yes, I roused her maid.'

He went off, and Urcombe turned to me. 'I know now what we have to do,' he said. 'Change your clothes, and I'll join you at your house.'

'What is it?' I asked.

'I'll tell you on our way. We're going to the cemetery.'

He carried a pick, a shovel, and a screwdriver when he rejoined me, and wore round his shoulders a long coil of rope. As we walked, he gave me the outlines of the ghastly hour that lay before us.

'What I have to tell you,' he said, 'will seem to you now too fantastic for credence, but before dawn we shall see whether it outstrips reality. By a most fortunate happening, you saw the spectre, the astral body, whatever you choose to call it, of Mrs Amworth going on its grisly business, and therefore, beyond doubt, the vampire spirit which abode in her during life animates her again in death. That is not exceptional—indeed, all these weeks since her death I have been expecting it. If I am right, we shall find her body undecayed and untouched by corruption.'

'But she has been dead nearly two months,' said I.

'If she had been dead two years it would still be so, if the vampire has possession of her. So remember: whatever you see done, it will be done not to her, who in the natural course would now be feeding the grasses above her grave, but to a spirit of untold evil and malignancy, which gives a phantom life to her body.'

'But what shall I see done?' said I.

'I will tell you. We know that now, at this moment, the vampire clad in her mortal semblance is out; dining out. But it must get back before dawn, and it will pass into the material form that lies in her grave. We must wait for that, and then with your help I shall dig up her body. If I am right, you will look on her as she was in life, with the full vigour of the dreadful nutriment she has received pulsing in her veins. And then, when dawn has come, and the vampire cannot leave the lair of her body, I shall strike her with this'—and he pointed to his pick—'through the heart, and she, who comes to life again only with the animation the fiend gives her, she and her hellish partner will be dead indeed. Then we must bury her again, delivered at last.'

We had come to the cemetery, and in the brightness of the moonshine there was no difficulty in identifying her grave. It lay some twenty yards from the small chapel, in the porch of which, obscured by shadow, we concealed ourselves. From there we had a clear and open sight of the grave, and now we must wait until its infernal visitor returned home. The night was warm and windless, yet even if a freezing wind had been raging I think I should have felt nothing of it, so intense was my preoccupation as to what the night and dawn would bring. There was a bell in the turret of the chapel that struck the quarters of the hour, and it amazed me to find how swiftly the chimes succeeded one another.

The moon had long set but a twilight of stars shone in a clear sky, when five o'clock of the morning sounded from the turret.

A few minutes more passed, and then I felt Urcombe's hand softly nudging me; and looking out in the direction of his pointing finger, I saw that the form of a woman, tall, and large in build, was approaching from the right. Noiselessly, with a motion more of gliding and floating than walking, she moved across the cemetery to the grave which was the centre of our observation. She moved round as if to be certain of its identity, and for a moment stood directly facing us. In the greyness, to which my eyes had now grown accustomed, I could easily see her face, and recognise its features.

She drew her hand across her mouth as if wiping it, and broke into a chuckle of such laughter as made my hair stir on my head. Then she leaped onto the grave, holding her hands high above her head, and inch by inch disappeared into the earth. Urcombe's hand was laid on my arm, in an injunction to keep still, but now he removed it.

'Come,' he said.

With pick and shovel and rope we went to the grave. The earth was light and sandy, and soon after six struck, we had delved down to the coffin lid. With his pick he loosened the earth around it, and, adjusting the rope through the handles by which it had been lowered, we tried to raise it. This was a long and laborious business, and the light had begun to herald day in the east before we had it out and lying by the side of the grave. With his screwdriver he loosened the fastenings of the lid, and slid it aside, and standing there we looked on the face of Mrs Amworth. The eyes, once closed in death, were open, the cheeks were flushed with colour, the red, full-lipped mouth seemed to smile.

'One blow and it is all over,' he said. 'You need not look.'

Even as he spoke he took up the pick again, and laying the point of it on her left breast, measured his distance. And though I knew what was coming I could not look away...

He grasped the pick in both hands, raised it an inch or two for the taking of his aim, and then with full force brought it down on her breast, A fountain of blood, though she had been dead so long, spouted high in the air, falling with the thud of a heavy splash over the shroud, and simultaneously from those red lips came one long, appalling cry, swelling up like some hooting siren, and dying away again, With that, instantaneous as a lightning flash, came the touch of corruption on her face, the colour of it faded to ash, the plump cheeks fell in, the mouth dropped.

'Thank God, that's over,' said he, and without pause slipped the coffin lid back into its place.

Day was coming fast now, and, working like men possessed, we lowered the coffin into its place again, and shovelled the earth over it... The birds were busy with their earliest pipings as we went back to Maxley.

The White Wolf of the Hartz Mountains

Frederick Marryat

Before noon Philip and Krantz had embarked, and made sail in the peroqua.

They had no difficulty in steering their course; the islands by day, and the clear stars by night, were their compass. It is true that they did not follow the more direct track, but they followed the more secure, working up the smooth waters, and gaining to the northward more than to the west. Many times they were chased by the Malay proas, which infested the islands, but the swiftness of their little peroqua was their security; indeed, the chase was, generally speaking, abandoned as soon as the smallness of the vessel was made out by the pirates, who expected that little or no booty was to be gained.

One morning, as they were sailing between the isles, with less wind than usual, Philip observed—

'Krantz, you said that there were events in your own life, or connected with it, which would corroborate the mysterious tale I confided to you. Will you now tell me to what you referred?'

'Certainly,' replied Krantz; 'I have often thought of doing so, but one circumstance or another has hitherto prevented me; this is, however, a fitting opportunity. Prepare therefore to listen to a strange story, quite as strange, perhaps, as your own.

'I take it for granted that you have heard people speak of the Hartz Mountains,' observed Krantz.

'I have never heard people speak of them, that I can recollect,' replied Philip; 'but I have read of them in some book, and of the strange things which have occurred there.'

'It is indeed a wild region,' rejoined Krantz, 'and many strange tales are told of it; but strange as they are, I have good reason for believing them to be true.

'My father was not born, or originally a resident, in the Hartz Mountains; he was a serf of a Hungarian nobleman, of great possessions, in Transylvania; but although a serf, he was not by any means a poor or illiterate man. In fact, he was rich and his intelligence and respectability were such that he had been raised by his lord to the stewardship; but whoever may happen to be born a serf, a serf must he remain, even though he become a wealthy man: such was the condition of my father. My father had been married for about five years; and by his marriage had three children—my eldest brother Caesar, myself (Hermann), and a sister named Marcella. You know, Philip, that Latin is still the language spoken in that country; and that will account for our high-sounding names. My mother was a very beautiful woman, unfortunately more beautiful than virtuous: she was seen and admired by the lord of the soil; my father was sent away upon some mission; and during his absence, my mother, flattered by the attentions, and won by the assiduities of this nobleman, yielded to his wishes. It so happened that my father returned very unexpectedly, and discovered the intrigue. The evidence of my mother's shame was positive: he surprised her in the company of her seducer! Carried away by the impetuosity of his feelings, he watched the opportunity of a meeting taking place between them, and murdered both his wife and her seducer. Conscious that, as a serf, not even the provocation which he had received would be allowed as a justification of his conduct, he hastily collected together what money he could lay his hands upon, and, as we were then in the depth of winter, he put his horses to the sleigh, and taking his children with him, he set off in the middle of the night, and was far away before the tragical circumstance had transpired. Aware that he would be pursued, and that he had no chance of escape if he remained in any portion of his native country (in which the authorities could lay hold of him), he continued his flight without intermission until he had buried himself in the intricacies and seclusions of the Hartz Mountains. Of course, all that I have now told you I learned afterwards. My oldest recollections are knit to a rude, yet comfortable, cottage in which I lived with my father, brother, and sister. It was on the confines of one of those vast forests which cover the northern part of Germany; around it were a few acres of ground, which, during the summer months, my father cultivated, and which, though they yielded a doubtful harvest, were sufficient for our support. In the winter we remained much indoors, for, as my father followed the chase, we were left alone, and the wolves during that season incessantly prowled about. My father had purchased the cottage, and land about it, off one of the rude foresters, who gain their livelihood partly by hunting and partly by burning charcoal, for the purpose of smelting the ore from the neighbouring mines; it was distant about two miles from any other habitation. I can call to mind the whole landscape now; the tall pines which rose up on the mountain above us, and the wide expanse of the forest beneath, on the topmost boughs and heads of whose trees we looked down from our cottage, as the mountain below us rapidly descended into the distant valley. In summer time the prospect was beautiful: but during the severe winter a more desolate scene could not well be imagined.

'I said that, in the winter, my father occupied himself with the chase; every day he left us, and often would he lock the door, that we might not leave the cottage. He had no one to assist him, or to take care of us—indeed, it was not easy to find a female servant who would live in such a solitude; but, could he have found one, my father would not have received her, for he had imbibed a horror of the sex, as the difference of his conduct towards us, his two boys, and my poor little sister Marcella, evidently proved. You may suppose we were sadly neglected; indeed, we suffered much, for my father, fearful that we might come to some harm, would not allow us fuel when he left the cottage; and we were obliged, therefore, to creep under the heaps of bears' skins, and there to keep ourselves as warm as we could until he returned in the evening, when a blazing fire was our delight. That my father chose this restless sort of life may appear strange, but the fact was that he could not remain quiet; whether from the remorse for having committed murder, or from the misery consequent on his change of situation, or from both combined, he was never happy unless he was in a state of activity. Children, however, when left so much to themselves, acquire a thoughtfulness not common to their age. So it was with us; and during the short cold days of winter, we would sit silent, longing for the happy hours when the snow would melt and the leaves burst out, and the birds begin their songs, and when we should again be set at liberty.

'Such was our peculiar and savage sort of life until my brother Caesar was nine, myself seven, and my sister five years old, when the circumstances occurred on which is based the extraordinary narrative which I am about to relate.

'One evening my father returned home rather later than usual; he had been unsuccessful, and as the weather was very severe, and many feet of snow were upon the ground, he was not only very cold, but in a very bad humour. He had brought in wood, and we were all three gladly assisting each other in blowing on the embers to create a blaze, when he caught poor little Marcella by the arm and threw her aside; the child fell, struck her mouth, and bled very much. My brother ran to raise her up. Accustomed to ill-usage, and afraid of my father, she did not dare cry, but looked up in his face very piteously. My father drew his stool nearer to the hearth, muttered something in abuse of women, and busied himself with the fire, which both my brother and I had deserted when our sister was so unkindly treated. A cheerful blaze was soon the result of his exertions; but we did not, as usual, crowd round it. Marcella, still bleeding, retired to a corner, and my brother and I took our seats beside her, while my father hung over the fire gloomily and alone. Such had been our position for about half an hour when the howl of a wolf, close under the window of the cottage, fell on our ears. My father started up, and seized his gun; the howl was repeated; he examined the priming, and then hastily left the cottage, shutting the door after him. We all waited (anxiously listening), for we thought that if he succeeded in shooting the wolf, he would return in a better humour; and, although he was harsh to all of us, and particularly so to our little sister, still we loved our father, and loved to see him cheerful and happy, for what else had we to look up to? And I may here observe that perhaps there never were three children who were fonder of each other; we did not, like other children, fight and dispute together; and if, by chance, any disagreement did arise, between my elder brother and me, little Marcella would run to us, and kissing us both, seal, through her entreaties, the peace between us. Marcella was a lovely, amiable child; I can recall her beautiful features even now. Alas! poor little Marcella.'

'She is dead, then?' observed Philip.

'Dead! yes, dead! but how did she die?—But I must not anticipate, Philip; let me tell my story.

'We waited for some time, but the report of the gun did not reach us, and my elder brother then said, "Our father has followed the wolf, and will not be back for some time. Marcella, let us wash the blood from your mouth, and then we will leave this corner and go to the fire to warm ourselves."

'We did so, and remained there until near midnight, every minute wondering, as it grew later, why our father did not return. We had no idea that he was in any danger, but we thought that he must have chased the wolf for a very long time. "I will look out and see if father is coming," said my brother Caesar, going to the door. "Take care." said Marcella, "the wolves must be about now, and we cannot kill them, brother." My brother opened the door very cautiously, and but a few inches; he peeped out. "I see nothing," said he, after a time, and once more he joined us at the fire. "We have had no supper," said I, for my father usually cooked the meat as soon as he came home; and during his absence we had nothing but the fragments of the preceding day.

'"And if our father comes home, after his hunt, Caesar," said Marcella, "he will be pleased to have some supper; let us cook it for him and for ourselves." Caesar climbed upon the stool, and reached down some meat—I forget now whether it was venison or bear's meat, but we cut off the usual quantity, and proceeded to dress it, as we used to do under our father's superintendence. We were all busy putting it into the platters before the fire, to await his coming, when we heard the sound of a horn. We listened—there was a noise outside, and a minute afterwards my father entered, ushered in a young female and a large dark man in a hunter's dress.

'Perhaps I had better now relate what was only known to me many years afterwards. When my father had left the cottage, he perceived a large white wolf about thirty yards from him; as soon as the animal saw my father, it retreated slowly, growling and snarling. My father followed; the animal did not run, but always kept at some distance; and my father did not like to fire until he was pretty certain that his ball would take effect; thus they went on for some time, the wolf now leaving my father far behind, and then stopping and snarling defiance at him, and then, again, on his approach, setting off at speed.

'Anxious to shoot the animal (for the white wolf is very rare), my father continued the pursuit for several hours, during which he continually ascended the mountain.

'You must know, Philip, that there are peculiar spots on those mountains which are supposed, and, as my story will prove, truly supposed, to be inhabited by the evil influences: they are well known to the huntsmen, who invariably avoid them. Now, one of these spots, an open space in the pine forest above us, had been pointed out to my father as dangerous on that account. But whether he disbelieved these wild stories, or whether, in his eager pursuit of the chase, he disregarded them, I know not; certain, however, it is, that he was decoyed by the white wolf to his open space, when the animal appeared to slacken her speed. My father approached, came close up to her, raised his gun to his shoulder and was about to fire, when the wolf suddenly disappeared. He thought that the snow on the ground must have dazzled his sight, and he let down his gun to look for the beast—but she was gone; how she could have escaped over the clearance, without his seeing her, was beyond his comprehension. Mortified at the ill-success of his chase, he was about to retrace his steps, when he heard the distant sound of a horn. Astonishment at such a sound—at such an hour—in such a wilderness made him forget for the moment his disappointment, and he remained riveted to the spot. In a minute the horn was blown a second time, and at no great distance; my father stood still, and listened; a third time it was blown. I forget the term used to express it, but it was the signal which, my father well knew, implied that the party was lost in the woods. In a few minutes more my father beheld a man on horseback, with a female seated on the crupper, enter the cleared space, and ride up to him. At first, my father called to mind the strange stories which he had heard of the supernatural beings who were said to frequent these mountains; but the nearer approach of the parties satisfied him that they were mortals like himself. As soon as they came up to him, the man who guided the horse accosted him "Friend hunter, you are out late, the better fortune for us; we have ridden far, and are in fear of our lives, which are eagerly sought after. These mountains have enabled us to elude our pursuers; but if we find not shelter and refreshment, that will avail us little, as we must perish from hunger and the inclemency of the night. My daughter, who rides behind me, is now more dead than alive—say, can you assist us in our difficulty?"

'"My cottage is some few miles distant," replied my father, "but I have little to offer you besides a shelter from the weather; to the little I have you are welcome. May I ask whence you come?"

'"Yes, friend, it is no secret now; we have escaped from Transylvania, where my daughter's honour and my life were equally in jeopardy!"

'This information was quite enough to raise an interest in my father's heart. He remembered his own escape: he remembered the loss of his wife's honour, and the tragedy by which it was wound up. He immediately, and warmly, offered all the assistance which he could afford them.

'"There is no time to be lost, then, good sir," observed the horseman; "my daughter is chilled with the frost, and cannot hold out much longer against the severity of the weather."

'"Follow me," replied my father, leading the way towards his home.

'"I was lured away in pursuit of a large white wolf," observed my father; "it came to the very window of my hut, or I should not have been out at this time of night."

'"The creature passed by us just as we came out of the wood," said the female, in a silvery tone.

'"I was nearly discharging my piece at it," observed the hunter; "but since it did us such good service, I am glad that I allowed it to escape."

'In about an hour and a half, during which my father walked at a rapid pace, the party arrived at the cottage, and, as I said before, came in.

'"We are in good time, apparently," observed the dark hunter, catching the smell of the roasted meat, as he walked to the fire and surveyed my brother and sister and myself. "You have young cooks here, Meinheer." "I am glad that we shall not have to wait," replied my father. "Come, mistress seat yourself by the fire; you require warmth after your cold ride." "And where can I put up my horse, Meinheer?" observed the huntsman. "I will take care of him," replied my father, going out of the cottage door.

'The female must, however, be particularly described. She was young, and apparently twenty years of age. She was dressed in a travelling dress, deeply bordered with white fur, and wore a cap of white ermine on her head. Her features were very beautiful, at least I thought so, and so my father has since declared. Her hair was flaxen, glossy, and shining, and bright as a mirror; and her mouth, although somewhat large when it was open, showed the most brilliant teeth I have ever beheld. But there was something about her eyes, bright as they were, which made us children afraid; they were so restless, so furtive; I could not at that time tell why, but I felt as if there was cruelty in her eye; and when she beckoned us to come to her, we approached her with fear and trembling. Still she was beautiful, very beautiful. She spoke kindly to my brother and myself, patted our heads and caressed us; but Marcella would not come near her; on the contrary, she slunk away, and hid herself in bed, and would not wait for the supper, which half an hour before she had been so anxious for.

'My father, having put the horse into a close shed, soon returned, and supper was placed on the table. When it was over, my father requested the young lady take possession of the bed, and he would remain at the fire, and sit up with her father. After some hesitation on her part, this arrangement was agreed to, and I and my brother crept into the other bed with Marcella, for we had as yet always slept together.

'But we could not sleep; there was something so unusual, not only in seeing strange people, but in having those people sleep at the cottage, that we were bewildered. As for poor little Marcella, she was quiet, but I perceived that she trembled during the whole night, and sometimes I thought that she was checking a sob. My father had brought out some spirits, which he rarely used, and he and the strange hunter remained drinking and talking before the fire. Our ears were ready to catch the slightest whisper—so much was our curiosity excited.

'"You said you came from Transylvania?" observed my father.

"'Even so, Meinheer,' replied the hunter. "I was a serf to the noble house of——; my master would insist upon my surrendering up my fair girl to his wishes; it ended in my giving him a few inches of my hunting-knife."

"'We are countrymen and brothers in misfortune,' replied my father, taking the huntsman's hand and pressing it warmly.

"'Indeed! Are you then from that country?'

"'Yes; and I too have fled for my life. But mine is a melancholy tale.'

"'Your name?' inquired the hunter.

"'Krantz.'

"'What! Krantz of——? I have heard your tale; you need not renew your grief by repeating it now. Welcome, most welcome, Meinheer, and, I may say, my worthy kinsman. I am your second cousin, Wilfred of Barnsdorf,' cried the hunter, raising up and embracing my father.

'They filled their horn-mugs to the brim, and drank to one another after the German fashion. The conversation was then carried on in a low tone; all that we could collect from it was that our new relative and his daughter were to take up their abode in our cottage, at least for the present. In about an hour they both fell back in their chairs and appeared to sleep.

"'Marcella, dear, did you hear?' said my brother, in a low tone.

"'Yes,' replied Marcella, in a whisper, 'I heard all. Oh! brother, I cannot bear to look upon that woman—I feel so frightened.'

'My brother made no reply, and shortly afterwards we were all three fast asleep.

'When we awoke the next morning, we found that the hunter's daughter had risen before us. I thought she looked more beautiful than ever. She came up to little Marcella and caressed her; the child burst into tears, and sobbed as if her heart would break.

'But not to detain you with too long a story, the huntsman and his daughter were accommodated in the cottage. My father and he went out hunting daily, leaving Christina with us. She performed all the household duties; was very kind to us children; and gradually the dislike even of little Marcela wore away. But a great change took place in my father; he appeared to have conquered his aversion to the sex, and was most attentive to Christina. Often, after her father and we were in bed, would he sit up with her, conversing in a low tone by the fire. I ought to have mentioned that my father and the huntsman Wilfred slept in another portion of the cottage, and that the bed which he formerly occupied, and which was in the same room as ours, had been given up to the use of Christina. These visitors had been about three weeks at the cottage, when, one night, after we children had been sent to bed, a consultation was held. My father had asked Christina in marriage, and had obtained both her own consent and that of Wilfred; after this, a conversation took place, which was, as nearly as I can recollect, as follows:—

"'You may take my child, Meinheer Krantz, and my blessing with her, and I shall then leave you and seek some other habitation— it matters little where."

"'Why not remain here, Wilfred?"

"'No, no, I am called elsewhere; let that suffice, and ask no more questions. You have my child."

"'I thank you for her, and will duly value her but there is one difficulty."

"'I know what you would say; there is no priest here in this wild country; true; neither is there any law to bind. Still must some ceremony pass between you, to satisfy a father. Will you consent to marry her after my fashion? If so, I will marry you directly."

"'I will,' replied my father.

"'Then take her by the hand. Now, Meinheer, swear.'

"'I swear,' repeated my father.

"'By all the spirits of the Hartz Mountains—'

"'Nay, why not by Heaven?' interrupted my father.

"'Because it is not my humour,' rejoined Wilfred. "If I prefer that oath, less binding, perhaps, than another, surely you will not thwart me.'

"'Well, be it so, then; have your humour. Will you make me swear by that in which I do not believe?'

"'Yet many do so, who in outward appearance are Christians,' rejoined Wilfred; "say, will you be married, or shall I take my daughter away with me?'

"'Proceed,' replied my father impatiently.

"'I swear by all the spirits of the Hartz Mountains, by all their power for good or for evil, that I take Christina for my wedded wife; that I will ever protect her, cherish her, and love her; that my hand shall never be raised against her to harm her.'

'My father repeated the words after Wilfred.

"'And if I fail in this my vow, may all the vengeance of the spirits fall upon me and upon my children; may they perish by the vulture, by the wolf, or other beasts of the forest; may their flesh be torn from their limbs, and their bones blanch in the wilderness: all this I swear.'

My father hesitated, as he repeated the last words; little Marcella could not restrain herself, and as my father repeated the last sentence, she burst into tears. This sudden interruption appeared to discompose the party, particularly my father; he spoke harshly to the child, who controlled her sobs, burying her face under the bedclothes.

'Such was the second marriage of my father. The next morning, the hunter Wilfred mounted his horse and rode away.

'My father resumed his bed, which was in the same room as ours; and things went on much as before the marriage, except that our new stepmother did not show any kindness towards us; indeed, during my father's absence, she would often beat us, particularly little Marcella, and her eyes would flash fire, as she looked eagerly upon the fair and lovely child.

'One night my sister awoke me and my brother.

'"What is the matter?" said Caesar.

'"She has gone out," whispered Marcella.

'"Gone out!"

'"Yes, gone out at the door, in her night-clothes," replied the child; "I saw her get out of bed, look at my father to see if he slept, and then she went out at the door."

'What could induce her to leave her bed, and all undressed to go out, in such bitter wintry weather, with the snow deep on the ground, was to us incomprehensible; we lay awake, and in about an hour we heard the growl of a wolf close under the window.

'"There is a wolf," said Caesar. "She will be torn to pieces."

'"Oh, no!" cried Marcella.

'In a few minutes our stepmother appeared; she was in her night-dress, as Marcella had stated. She let down the latch of the door, so as to make no noise, went to a pail of water, and washed her face and hands, and then slipped into the bed where my father lay.

'We all three trembled—we hardly knew why; but we resolved to watch the next night. We did so; and not only on the ensuing night, but on many others, and always at about the same hour would our stepmother rise from her bed and leave the cottage; and after she was gone we invariably heard the growl of a wolf under our window, and always saw her on her return wash herself before she retired to bed. We observed also that she seldom sat down to meals, and that when she did she appeared to eat with dislike; but when the meat was taken down to be prepared for dinner, she would often furtively put a raw piece into her mouth.

'My brother Caesar was a courageous boy; he did not like to speak to my father until he knew more. He resolved that he would follow her out, and ascertain what she did. Marcella and I endeavoured to dissuade him from the project; but he would not be controlled; and the very next night he lay down in his clothes, and as soon as our stepmother had left the cottage he jumped up, took down my father's gun, and followed her.

'You may imagine in what a state of suspense Marcella and I remained during his absence. After a few minutes we heard the report of a gun. It did not awaken my father; and we lay trembling with anxiety. In a minute afterwards we saw our stepmother enter the cottage—her dress was bloody. I put my hand to Marcella's mouth to prevent her crying out, although I was myself in great alarm. Our stepmother approached my father's bed, looked to see if he was asleep, and then went to the chimney and blew up the embers into a blaze.

'"Who is there?" said my father, waking up.

'"Lie still, dearest," replied my stepmother; "it is only me; I have lighted the fire to warm some water; I am not quite well."

'My father turned round, and was soon asleep; but we watched our stepmother. She changed her linen, and threw the garments she had worn into the fire; and we then perceived that her right leg was bleeding profusely, as if from a gun-shot wound. She bandaged it up, and then dressing herself remained before the fire until the break of day.

'Poor little Marcella, her heart beat quick as she pressed me to her side—so indeed did mine. Where was our brother Caesar? How did my stepmother receive the wound unless from his gun? At last my father rose, and then for the first time I spoke, saying, "Father, where is my brother Caesar?"

'"Your brother?" exclaimed he; "why, where can he be?"

'"Merciful Heaven! I thought as I lay very restless last night," observed our stepmother, "that I heard somebody open the latch of the door; and, dear me, husband, what has become of your gun?"

'My father cast his eyes up above the chimney, and perceived that his gun was missing for a moment he looked perplexed; then, seizing a broad axe, he went out of the cottage without saying another world.

'He did not remain away from us long; in a few minutes he returned, bearing in his arms the mangled body of my poor brother; he laid it down, and covered up his face.

'My stepmother rose up, and looked at the body, while Marcella and I threw ourselves by its side, wailing and sobbing bitterly.

'"Go to bed again, children," said she sharply. "Husband," continued she, "your boy must have taken the gun down to shoot a wolf, and the animal has been too powerful for him. Poor boy! He has paid dearly for his rashness."

'My father made no reply. I wished to speak—to tell all—but Marcella, who perceived my intention, held me by the arm, and looked at me so imploringly, that I desisted.

'My father, therefore, was left in his error; but Marcella and I, although we could not comprehend it, were conscious that our stepmother was in some way connected with my brother's death.

'That day my father went out and dug a grave; and when he laid the body in the earth he piled up stones over it, so that the wolved should not be able to dig it up. The shock of this catastrophe was to my poor father very severe; for several days he never went to the chase, although at times he would utter bitter anathemas and vengeance against the wolves.

'But during this time of mourning on his part, my stepmother's nocturnal wanderings continued with the same regularity as before.

'At last my father took down his gun to repair to the forest; but he soon returned, and appeared much annoyed.

'"Would you believe it, Christina, that the wolves—perdition to the whole race!—have actually contrived to dig up the body of my poor boy, and now there is nothing left of him but his bones."

'"Indeed!" replied my stepmother. Marcella looked at me, and I saw in her intelligent eye all she would have uttered.

'"A wolf growls under our window every night, father," said I.

'"Ay, indeed! Why did you not tell me, boy? Wake me the next time you hear it."

'I saw my stepmother turn away; her eyes flashed fire, and she gnashed her teeth.

'My father went out again, and covered up with a larger pile of stones the little remains of my poor brother which the wolves had spared. Such was the first act of the tragedy.

'The spring now came on; the snow disappeared, and we were permitted to leave the cottage; but never would I quit for one moment my dear little sister, to whom, since the death of my brother, I was more ardently attached than ever; indeed, I was afraid to leave her alone with my stepmother, who appeared to have a particular pleasure in ill-treating the child. My father was now employed upon his little farm, and I was able to render him some assistance.

'Marcella used to sit by us while we were at work, leaving my stepmother alone in the cottage. I ought to observe that, as the spring advanced, so did my stepmother decrease her nocturnal rambles, and that we never heard the growl of the wolf under the window after I had spoken of it to my father.

'One day, when my father and I were in the field, Marcella being with us, my stepmother came out, saying that she was going into the forest to collect some herbs that my father wanted, and that Marcella must go to the cottage and watch the dinner. Marcella went; and my stepmother soon disappeared in the forest, taking a direction quite contrary to that in which the cottage stood, and leaving my father and me, as it were, between her and Marcella.

'About an hour afterwards we were startled by shrieks from the cottage—evidently the shrieks of little Marcella. "Marcella has burnt herself, father," said I, throwing down my spade. My father threw down his, and we both hastened to the cottage. Before we could gain the door, out darted a large white wolf, which fled with the utmost celerity. My father had no weapon; he rushed into the cottage, and there saw poor little Marcella expiring. Her body was dreadfully mangled and the blood pouring from it had formed a large pool on the cottage floor. My father's first intention had been to seize his gun and pursue; but he was checked by this horrid spectacle; he knelt down by his dying child, and burst into tears. Marcella could just look kindly on us for a few seconds, and then her eyes were closed in death.

'My father and I were still hanging over my poor sister's body when my stepmother came in. At the dreadful sight she expressed much concern; but she did not appear to recoil from the sight of blood, as most people do.

'"Poor child!" said she, "it must have been that great white wolf which passed me just now, and frightened me so. She's quite dead, Krantz."

'"I know it!—I know it!" cried my father, in agony.

'I thought my father would never recover from the effects of this second tragedy; he mourned bitterly over the body of his sweet child, and for several days would not consign it to its grave, although frequently requested by my stepmother to do so. At last he yielded, and dug a grave for her close by that of my poor brother, and took every precaution that the wolves should not violate her remains.

'I was now really miserable as I lay alone in the bed which I had formerly shared with my brother and sister. I could not help thinking that my stepmother was implicated in both their deaths, although I could not account for the manner; but I no longer felt afraid of her; my little heart was full of hatred and revenge.

'The night after my sister had been buried, as I lay awake, I perceived my stepmother get up and go out of the cottage. I waited some time, then dressed myself, and looked out through the door, which I half opened. The moon shone bright, and I could see the spot where my brother and my sister had been buried; and what was my horror when I perceived my stepmother busily removing the stones from Marcella's grave!

'She was in her white night-dress, and the moon shone full upon her. She was digging with her hands, and throwing away the stones behind her with all the ferocity of a wild beast. It was some time before I could collect my senses and decide what I should do. At last I perceived that she had arrived at the body, and raised it up to the side of the grave. I could bear it no longer: I ran to my father and awoke him.

'"Father, father!" cried I, "dress yourself, and get your gun."

'"What!" cried my father, "the wolves are there, are they?"

'He jumped out of bed, threw on his clothes, and in his anxiety did not appear to perceive the absence of his wife. As soon as he was ready, I opened the door; he went out, and I followed him.

'Imagine his horror, when (unprepared as he was for such a sight) he beheld, as he advanced towards the grave, not a wolf, but his wife, in her night-dress, on her hands and knees, crouching by the body of my sister, and tearing off large pieces of flesh, and devouring them with all the avidity of a wolf. She was too busy to be aware of our approach. My father dropped his gun; his hair stood on end, so did mine; he breathed heavily, and then his breath for a time stopped. I picked up the gun and put it into his hand. Suddenly he appeared as if concentrated rage had restored him to double vigour; he levelled his piece, fired, and with a loud shriek down fell the wretch whom he had fostered in his bosom.

'"God of heaven!" cried my father, sinking down upon the earth in a swoon, as soon as he had discharged his gun.

'I remained some time by his side before he recovered. "Where am I?" said he, "what has happened? Oh!—yes, yes! I recollect now. Heaven forgive me!"

'He rose and we walked up to the grave; imagine our astonishment and horror to find that, instead of the dead body of my stepmother, as we expected, there was, lying over the remains of my poor sister, a large white she-wolf.

'"The white wolf," exclaimed my father, "the white wolf which decoyed me into the forest—I see it all now—I have dealt with the spirits of the Hartz Mountains."

'For some time my father remained in silence and deep thought. He then carefully lifted the body of my sister, replaced it in the grave, and covered it over as before, having struck the head of the dead animal with the heel of his boot, and raving like a madman. He walked back to the cottage, shut the door, and threw himself on the bed; I did the same, for I was in a stupor of amazement.

'Early in the morning we were both roused by a loud knocking at the door, and in rushed the hunter Wilfred.

'"My daughter—man—my daughter!—where is my daughter?" cried he in a rage.

"'Where the wretch, the fiend should be, I trust," replied my father, starting up, and displaying equal choler: "where she should be—in hell! Leave this cottage, or you may fare worse."

"'Ha—ha!" replied the hunter, "would you harm a potent spirit of the Hartz Mountains? Poor mortal, who must needs wed a werewolf."

"'Out, demon! I defy thee and thy power."

"'Yet shall you feel it; remember your oath—your solemn oath—never to raise your hand against her to harm her."

"'I made no compact with evil spirits."

"'You did, and if you failed in your vow, you were to meet the vengeance of the spirits. Your children were to perish by the vulture, the wolf——"

"'Out, out, demon!"

"'And their bones blanch in the wilderness. Ha—ha!"

'My father, frantic with rage, seized his axe and raised it over Wilfred's head to strike.

"'All this I swear," continued the huntsman mockingly.

'The axe descended; but it passed through the form of the hunter, and my father lost his balance, and fell heavily on the floor.

"'Mortal!" said the hunter, striding over my father's body, "we have power over those only who have committed murder. You have been guilty of a double murder: you shall pay the penalty attached to your marriage vow. Two of your children are gone, the third is yet to follow—and follow them he will, for your oath is registered. Go—it were kindness to kill thee—your punishment is, that you live!"

'With these words the spirit disappeared. My father rose from the floor, embraced me tenderly, and knelt down in prayer.

'The next morning he quitted the cottage for ever. He took me with him, and bent his steps to Holland, where we safely arrived. He had some little money with him; but he had not been many days in Amsterdam before he was seized with a brain fever, and died raving mad. I was put into the asylum, and afterwards was sent to sea before the mast. You now know all my history. The question is, whether I am to pay the penalty of my father's oath? I am myself perfectly convinced that, in some way or another, I shall.'

II

On the twenty-second day the high land of the south of Sumatra was in view: as there were no vessels in sight, they resolved to keep their course through the Straits, and run for Pulo Penang, which they expected, as their vessel lay so close to the wind, to reach in seven or eight days. By constant exposure Philip and Krantz were now so bronzed that with their long beards and Mussulman dresses, they might easily have passed off for natives. They had steered during the whole of the days exposed to a burning sun; they had lain down and slept in the dew of the night; but their health had not suffered. But for several days, since he had confided the history of his family to Philip, Krantz had become silent and melancholy; his usual flow of spirits had vanished, and Philip had often questioned him as to the cause. As they entered the Straits, Philip talked of what they should do upon their arrival at Goa; when Krantz gravely replied, 'For some days, Philip, I have had a presentiment that I shall never see that city.'

'You are out of health, Krantz,' replied Philip.

'No, I am in sound health, body and mind. I have endeavoured to shake off the presentiment, but in vain; there is a warning voice that continually tells me that I shall not be long with you Philip; will you oblige me by making me content on one point? I have gold about my person which may be useful to you; oblige me by taking it, and securing it on your own.'

'What nonsense, Krantz.'

'It is no nonsense, Philip. Have you not had your warnings? Why should I not have mine? You know that I have little fear in my composition, and that I care not about death; but I feel the presentiment which I speak of more strongly every hour....'

'These are the imaginings of a disturbed brain, Krantz; why you, young, in full health and vigour, should not pass your days in peace, and live to a good old age, there is no cause for believing. You will be better to-morrow.'

'Perhaps so,' replied Krantz; 'but you still must yield to my whim, and take the gold. If I am wrong, and we do arrive safe, you know, Philip, you can let me have it back,' observed Krantz, with a faint smile—'but you forget, our water is nearly out, and we must look out for a rill on the coast to obtain a fresh supply.'

'I was thinking of that when you commenced this unwelcome topic. We had better look out for the water before dark, and as soon as we have replenished our jars, we will make sail again.'

At the time that this conversation took place, they were on the eastern side of the Strait, about forty miles to the northward. The interior of the coast was rocky and mountainous, but it slowly descended to low lands of alternate forest and jungles, which continued to the beach; the country appeared to be uninhabited. Keeping close in to the shore, they discovered, after two hours' run, a fresh stream which burst in a cascade from the mountains, and swept its devious course through the jungle, until it poured its tribute into the waters of the Strait.

They ran close into the mouth of the stream, lowered the sails, and pulled the peroqua against the current until they had advanced far enough to assure them that the water was quite fresh. The jars were soon filled, and they were again thinking of pushing off, when enticed by the beauty of the spot, the coolness of the fresh water, and wearied with their long confinement on board of the peroqua, they proposed to bathe—a luxury hardly to be appreciated by those who have not been in a similar situation. They threw off their Mussulman dresses, and plunged into the stream, where they remained for some time. Krantz was the first to get out; he complained of feeling chilled, and he walked on to the banks where their clothes had been laid. Philip also approached nearer to the beach, intending to follow him.

'And now, Philip,' said Krantz, 'this will be a good opportunity for me to give you the money. I will open my sash and pour it out, and you can put it into your own before you put it on.'

Philip was standing in the water, which was about level with his waist.

'Well, Krantz,' said he, 'I suppose if it must be so, it must; but it appears to me an idea so ridiculous—however, you shall have your own way.'

Philip quitted the run, and sat down by Krantz, who was already busy in shaking the doubloons out of the folds of his sash; at last he said—

'I believe, Philip, you have got them all, now?—I feel satisfied.'

'What danger there can be to you, which I am not equally exposed to, I cannot conceive,' replied Philip: 'however——'

Hardly had he said these words, when there was a tremendous roar—a rush like a mighty wind through the air—a blow which threw him on his back—a loud cry—and a contention. Philip recovered himself, and perceived the naked form of Krantz carried off with the speed of an arrow by an enormous tiger through the jungle. He watched with distended eyeballs; in a few seconds the animal and Krantz had disappeared.

'God of heaven! Would that Thou hadst spared me this,' cried Philip, throwing himself down in agony on his face. 'O Krantz! my friend—my brother—too sure was your presentiment. Merciful God! Have pity—but Thy will be done.' And Philip burst into a flood of tears.

For more than an hour did he remain fixed upon the spot, careless and indifferent to the danger by which he was surrounded. At last, somewhat recovered, he rose, dressed himself, and then again sat down—his eyes fixed upon the clothes of Krantz, and the gold which still lay on the sand.

'He would give me that gold. He foretold his doom. Yes! Yes! It was his destiny, and it has been fulfilled. *His bones will bleach in the wilderness,* and the spirit-hunter and his wolfish daughter are avenged.'

Dracula's Guest

Bram Stoker

When we started for our drive, the sun was shining brightly on Munich and the air was full of the joyousness of early summer. Just as we were about to depart, Herr Delbruck (the *maître d'hôtel* of the Quatre Saisons, where I was staying) came down, bareheaded, to the carriage and, after wishing me a pleasant drive, said to the coachman, still holding his hand on the handle of the carriage door: 'Remember you are back by nightfall. The sky looks bright but there is a shiver in the north wind that says there may be a sudden storm. But I am sure you will not be late.' Here he smiled and added, 'for you know what night it is.'

Johann answered with an emphatic, *'Ja, mein Herr,'* and, touching his hat, drove off quickly. When we had cleared the town, I said, after signalling to him to stop: 'Tell me, Johann, what is tonight?'

He crossed himself as he answered laconically: 'Walpurgisnacht.' Then he took out his watch, a great, old-fashioned German silver thing as big as a turnip, and looked at it, with his eyebrows gathered together and a little impatient shrug of his shoulders. I realised that this was his way of respectfully protesting against the unnecessary delay and I sank back in the carriage, merely motioning him to proceed. He started off rapidly, as if to make up for lost time. Every now and then the horses seemed to throw up their heads and sniffed the air suspiciously. On such occasions I often looked round in alarm. The road was pretty bleak, for we were traversing a sort of high, wind-swept plateau. As we drove, I saw a road that looked but little used and which seemed to dip through a little, winding valley. It looked so inviting that, even at the risk of offending him, I called Johann to stop and when he had pulled up I told him I would like to drive down that road. He made all sorts of excuses and frequently crossed himself as he spoke. This somewhat piqued my curiosity so I asked him various questions. He answered fencingly and repeatedly looked at his watch in protest. Finally I said: 'Well, Johann, I want to go down this road. I shall not ask you to come unless you like; but tell me why you do not like to go, that is all I ask.' For an answer he seemed to throw himself off the box, so quickly did he reach the ground. Then he stretched out his hands appealingly to me and implored me not to go. There was just enough of English mixed with German for me to understand the drift of his talk. He seemed always just about to tell me something—the very idea of which evidently frightened him, but each time he pulled himself up, saying, as he crossed himself: 'Walpurgisnacht!'

I tried to argue with him, but it was difficult to argue with a man when I did not know his language. Then the horses became restless and sniffed the air. At this he grew very pale and, looking around in a frightened way, he suddenly jumped forward, took them by the bridles and led them on some twenty feet. I followed and asked why he had done this. For answer he crossed himself, pointed to the spot we had left and drew his carriage in the direction of the other road, indicating a cross, and said, first in German, then in English: 'Buried him—him what killed themselves.'

I remembered the old custom of burying suicides at cross-roads: 'Ah! I see, a suicide. How interesting!' But for the life of me I could not make out why the horses were frightened.

Whilst we were talking we heard a sort of sound between a yelp and a bark. It was far away, but the horses got very restless and it took Johann all his time to quiet them. He was pale and said, 'It sounds like a wolf—but yet there are no wolves here now.'

'No?' I said, questioning him; 'isn't it long since the wolves were so near the city?'

'Long, long,' he answered. 'in the spring and summer, but with the snow the wolves have been here not so long.'

Whilst he was petting the horses and trying to quiet them, dark clouds drifted rapidly across the sky. The sunshine passed away and a breath of cold wind seemed to drift past us. It was only a breath, however, and more in the nature of a warning than a fact, for the sun came out brightly again. Johann looked under his lifted hand at the horizon and said: 'The storm of snow, he comes before long time.' Then he looked at his watch again and, straightaway, holding his reins firmly—for the horses were still pawing the ground restlessly and shaking their heads—he climbed to his box as though the time had come for proceeding on our journey.

I felt a little obstinate and did not at once get into the carriage.

'Tell me,' I said, 'about this place where the road leads,' and I pointed down.

Again he crossed himself and mumbled a prayer before he answered, 'It is unholy.'

'What is unholy?' I enquired.

'The village.'

'Then there is a village?'

'No, no. No one lives there hundreds of years.' My curiosity was piqued, 'But you said there was a village.'

'There was.'

'Where is it now?'

Whereupon he burst out into a long story in German and English, so mixed up that I could not quite understand exactly what he said, but roughly I gathered that hundreds of years ago, men had died there and been buried in their graves; and sounds were heard under the clay and when the graves were opened, men and women were found rosy with life, and their mouths red with blood. And so, in haste to save their lives (aye, and their souls!—and here he crossed himself) those who were left fled away to other places, where the living lived and the dead were dead and not—not something. He was evidently afraid to speak the last words. As he proceeded with his narration, he grew more and more excited. It seemed as if his imagination had got hold of him and he ended in a perfect paroxysm of fear—white-faced, perspiring, trembling and looking round him, as if expecting that some dreadful presence would manifest itself there in the bright sunshine on the open plain. Finally, in an agony of desperation, he cried; 'Walpurgisnacht!' and pointed to the carriage for me to get in. All my blood rose at this and, standing back, I said: 'You are afraid, Johann—you are afraid. Go home, I shall return alone; the walk will do me good.' The carriage door was open. I took from the seat my oak walking-stick—which I always carry on my holiday excursions—and closed the door, pointing back to Munich, and said, 'Go home, Johann—Walpurgisnacht doesn't concern me.'

The horses were now more restive than ever and Johann was trying to hold them in, while excitedly imploring me not to do anything so foolish. It began to be a little tedious. After giving the direction, 'Home!' I turned to go down the crossroad into the valley.

With a despairing gesture, Johann turned his horses towards Munich. I leaned on my stick and looked after him. He went slowly along the road for a while: then there came over the crest of the hill a man tall and thin. I could only see so much in the distance. When he drew near the horses, they began to jump and kick about, then to scream with terror. Johann could not hold them in; they bolted down the road, running away madly. I watched them out of sight, then looked for the stranger, but I found that he, too, was gone.

With a light heart I turned down the side road through the deepening valley to which Johann had objected. There was not the slightest reason, that I could see, for his objection, and I daresay I tramped for a couple of hours without thinking of time or distance, and certainly without seeing a person or a house. So far as the place was concerned, it was desolation itself. But I did not notice this particularly until, on turning a bend in the road, I came upon a scattered fringe of wood; then I recognised that I had been impressed unconsciously by the desolation of the region through which I had passed.

I sat down to rest myself and began to look around. It struck me that it was considerably colder than it had been at the commencement of my walk—a sort of sighing sound seemed to be around me, with, now and then, high overhead, a sort of muffled roar. Looking upwards I noticed that great thick clouds were drifting rapidly across the sky from north to south at a great height. There were signs of a coming storm in some lofty stratum of the air. I was a little chilly and, thinking that it was the sitting still after the exercise of walking, I resumed my journey.

The ground I passed over was now much more picturesque. There were no striking objects that the eye might single out, but in all there was a charm of beauty. I took little heed of time and it was only when the deepening twilight forced itself upon me that I began to think of how I should find my way home. The brightness of the day had gone. The air was cold and the drifting of clouds high overhead was more marked. They were accompanied by a sort of far-away rushing sound, through which seemed to come at intervals, that mysterious cry which the driver had said came from a wolf. For a while I hesitated. I had said I would see the deserted village, so on I went and presently came on a wide stretch of open country, shut in by hills all around. Their sides were covered with trees which spread down to the plain, dotting, in clumps, the gentler slopes and hollows which showed here and there. I followed with my eye the winding of the road and saw that it cured close to one of the densest of these clumps and was lost behind it.

As I looked, there came a cold shiver in the air and the snow began to fall. I thought of the miles and miles of bleak country

I had passed and then hurried on to seek the shelter of the wood in front. Darker and darker grew the sky and faster and heavier fell the snow, until the earth before and around me was a glistening white carpet, the farther edge of which was lost in misty vagueness. The road was here but crude and when on the level, its boundaries were not so marked, as when it passed through the cuttings; and in a little while I found that I must have strayed from it, for I missed underfoot the hard surface and my feet sank deeper in the grass and moss. Then the wind grew strong and blew with ever increasing force, until I was fain to run before it. The air became icy cold and in spite of my exercise I began to suffer. The snow was now falling so thickly and whirling around me in such rapid eddies that I could hardly keep my eyes open. Every now and then the heavens were torn asunder by vivid lightning, and in the flashes I could see ahead of me a great mass of trees, chiefly yew and cypress, all heavily coated with snow.

I was soon amongst the shelter of the trees, and there, in comparative silence, I could hear the rush of the wind high overhead. Presently the blackness of the storm had become merged in the darkness of the night. By and by the storm seemed to be passing away: it now only came in fierce puffs or blasts. At such moments the weird sound of the wolf appeared to be echoed by many similar sounds around me.

Now and again, through the black mass of drifting cloud, came a straggling ray of moonlight, which lit up the expanse and showed me that I was at the edge of a dense mass of cypress and yew trees. As the snow had ceased to fall, I walked out from the shelter and began to investigate more closely. It appeared to me that, amongst so many old foundations as I had passed, there might be still standing a house in which, though in ruins, I could find some sort of shelter for a while. As I skirted the edge of the copse I found that a low wall encircled it, and following this I presently found an opening. Here the cypresses formed an alley leading up to a square mass of some kind of a building. Just as I caught sight of this, however, the drifting clouds obscured the moon and I passed up the path in darkness. The wind must have grown colder, for I felt myself shiver as I walked; but there was hope of shelter and I groped my way blindly on.

I stopped, for there was a sudden stillness. The storm had passed and, perhaps in sympathy with nature's silence, my heart seemed to cease to beat. But this was only momentarily, for suddenly the moonlight broke through the clouds, showing me that I was in a graveyard and that the square object before me was a great massive tomb of marble, as white as the snow that lay on and all around it. With the moonlight there came a fierce sigh of the storm, which appeared to resume its course with a long, low howl, as of many dogs or wolves. I was awed and shocked and felt the cold perceptibly grow upon me until it seemed to grip me by the heart. Then, while the flood of moonlight still fell on the marble tomb, the storm gave further evidence of renewing, as though it was returning on its track. Impelled by some sort of fascination I approached the sepulchre to see what it was and why such a thing stood alone in such a place. I walked around it and read, over the Doric door, in German:

Countess Dolingen of Gratz in Styria
Sought and Found Death
1801

On the top of the tomb, seemingly driven through the solid marble—for the structure was composed of a few vast blocks of stone—was a great iron spike or stake. On going to the back I saw, graven in great Russian letters:

The Dead Travel Fast

There was something so weird and uncanny about the whole thing that it gave me a turn and made me feel quite faint. I began to wish, for the first time, that I had taken Johann's advice. Here a thought struck me, which came under almost mysterious circumstances and with a terrible shock. This was Walpurgis Night!

Walpurgis Night, when, according to the belief of millions of people, the devil was abroad—when the graves were opened and the dead came forth and walked. When evil things of earth and air and water held revel. This very place the driver had especially shunned. This was the depopulated village of centuries ago. This was where the suicides lay; and this was the place where I was alone—unmanned, shivering with cold in a shroud of snow with a wild storm gathering again upon me! It took all my philosophy, all the religion I had been taught, all my courage, not to collapse in a paroxysm of fright.

And now a perfect tornado burst upon me. The ground shook as though thousands of horses thundered across it, and this time the storm bore on its icy wings, not snow, but great hailstones which drove with such violence that they might have come from the thongs of Balearic slingers—hailstones that beat down leaf and branch and made the shelter of the cypresses of no more avail than though their stems were standing corn. At the first I had rushed to the nearest tree, but I was soon fain to leave it and seek the only spot that seemed to afford refuge, the deep Doric doorway of the marble tomb. There, crouching against the massive bronze door, I gained a certain amount of protection from the beating of the hailstones, for now they only drove against me as they ricocheted from the ground and the side of the marble.

As I leaned against the door it moved slightly and opened inwards. The shelter of even a tomb was welcome in that pitiless tempest and I was about to enter it when there came a flash of forked lightning that lit up the whole expanse of the heavens. In the instant, as I am a living man, I saw, as my eyes were turned into the darkness of the tomb, a beautiful woman with rounded cheeks and red lips, seemingly sleeping on a bier. As the thunder broke overhead I was grasped as by the hand of a giant and hurled out into the storm. The whole thing was so sudden that, before I could realise the shock, moral as well as physical, I found the hailstones beating me down. At the same time I had a strange, dominating feeling that I was not alone. I looked towards the tomb. Just then there came another blinding flash, which seemed to strike the iron stake that surmounted the tomb and to pour through to the earth, blasting and crumbling the marble, as in a burst of flame. The dead woman rose for a moment of agony, while she was lapped in the flame, and her bitter scream of pain was drowned in the thundercrash. The last thing I heard was this mingling of dreadful sound, as again I was seized in the giant-grasp and dragged away, while the hailstones beat on me, and the air around seemed reverberant with the howling of wolves. The last sight that I remembered was a vague, white, moving mass, as if all the graves around me had sent out the phantoms of their sheeted dead, and that they were closing in on me through the white cloudiness of the driving hail.

Gradually there came a sort of vague beginning of consciousness, then a sense of weariness that was dreadful. For a time I remembered nothing, but slowly my senses returned. My feet seemed positively racked with pain, yet I could not move them. They seemed to be numbed. There was an icy feeling at the back of my neck and all down my spine, and my ears, like my feet, were dead, yet in torment; but there was in my breast a sense of warmth which was, by comparison, delicious. It was as a nightmare—a physical nightmare, if one may use such an expression—for some heavy weight on my chest made it difficult for me to breathe.

This period of semi-lethargy seemed to remain a long time, and as it faded away I must have slept or swooned. Then came a sort of loathing, like the first stage of sea-sickness, and a wild desire to be free from something—I knew not what. A vast stillness enveloped me, as though all the world were asleep or dead—only broken by the low panting as of some animal close to me. I felt a warm rasping at my throat, then came a consciousness of the awful truth, which chilled me to the heart and sent the blood surging up through my brain. Some great animal was lying on me and now licking my throat. I feared to stir, for some instinct of prudence bade me lie still, but the brute seemed to realise that there was now some change in me, for it raised its head. Through my eyelashes I saw above me the two great flaming eyes of a gigantic wolf. Its sharp white teeth gleamed in the gaping red mouth and I could feel its hot breath, fierce and acrid, upon me.

For another spell of time I remembered no more. Then I became conscious of a low growl, followed by a yelp, renewed again and again. Then, seemingly very far away, I heard a 'Holloa! holloa!' as of many voices calling in unison. Cautiously I raised my head and looked in the direction whence the sound came, but the cemetery blocked my view. The wolf still continued to yelp in a strange way and a red glare began to move round the grove of cypresses, as though following the sound. As the voices drew closer, the wolf yelped faster and louder. I feared to make either sound or motion. Nearer came the red glow, over the white pall which stretched into the darkness around me. Then all at once from beyond the trees there came at a trot, a troop of horsemen bearing torches. The wolf rose from my breast and made for the cemetery. I saw one of the horsemen (soldiers, by their caps and their long military cloaks) raise his carbine and take aim. A companion knocked up his arm, and I heard the ball whizz over my head. He had evidently taken my body for that of the wolf. Another sighted the animal as it slunk away and a shot followed. Then, at a gallop, the troop rode forward—some towards me, others following the wolf as it disappeared amongst the snow-clad cypresses.

As they drew nearer I tried to move, but was powerless, although I could see and hear all that went on around me. Two or three of the soldiers jumped from their horses and knelt beside me. One of them raised my head and placed his hand over my heart.

'Good news, comrades!' he cried. 'His heart still beats!'

Then some brandy was poured down my throat; it put vigour into me and I was able to open my eyes fully and look around. Lights and shadows were moving among the trees and I heard men call one another. They drew together, uttering frightened exclamations, and the lights flashed as the others came pouring out of the cemetery pell-mell, like men possessed. When the farther ones came close to us, those who were around me asked them eagerly: 'Well, have you found him?'

The reply rang out hurriedly: 'No! no! Come away quick—quick! This is no place to stay, and on this of all nights!'

'What was it?' was the question, asked in all manner of keys. The answer came variously and all indefinitely as though the men were moved by some common impulse to speak, yet were restrained by some common fear from giving their thoughts.

'It—it—indeed!' gibbered one, whose wits had plainly given out for the moment.

'A wolf—and yet not a wolf!' another put in shudderingly.

'No use trying for him without the sacred bullet,' a third remarked in a more ordinary manner.

'Serve us right for coming out on this night! Truly we have earned our thousand marks!' were the ejaculations of a fourth.

'There was blood on the broken marble,' another said after a pause—'the lightning never brought that there. And as for him—is he safe? Look at his throat! See, comrades, the wolf had been lying on him and keeping his blood warm.'

The officer looked at my throat and replied: 'He is all right, the skin is not pierced. What does it all mean? We should never have found him but for the yelping of the wolf.'

'What became of it?' asked the man who was holding up my head and who seemed the least panic-stricken of the party, for his hands were steady and without tremor. On his sleeve was the chevron of a petty officer.

'It went to its home,' answered the man, whose long face was pallid and who actually shook with terror as he glanced around him fearfully. 'There are graves enough there in which it may lie. Come, comrades come quickly! Let us leave this cursed spot.'

The officer raised me to a sitting posture, as he uttered a word of command, then several men placed me upon a horse. He sprang to the saddle behind me, took me in his arms, gave the word to advance and, turning our faces away from the cypresses, we rode away in swift, military order.

As yet my tongue refused its office and I was perforce silent. I must have fallen asleep, for the next thing I remembered was finding myself standing up, supported by a soldier on each side of me. It was almost broad daylight, and to the north a red streak of sunlight was reflected, like a path of blood, over the waste of snow. The officer was telling the men to say nothing of what they had seen, except that they found an English stranger, guarded by a large dog.

'Dog! That was no dog,' cut in the man who had exhibited such fear. 'I think I know a wolf when I see one.'

The young officer answered calmly: 'I said a dog.' 'Dog!' reiterated the other ironically. It was evident that his courage was rising with the sun and, pointing to me, he said, 'Look at his throat. Is that the work of a dog, master?'

Instinctively I raised my hand to my throat, and as I touched it I cried out in pain. The men crowded round to look, some stooping down from their saddles, and again there came the calm voice of the young officer: 'A dog, as I said. If aught else were said we should only be laughed at.'

I was then mounted behind a trooper and we rode on into the suburbs of Munich. Here we came across a stray carriage, into which I was lifted, and it was driven off to the Quatre Saisons— the young officer accompanying me, whilst a trooper followed with his horse and the others rode off to their barracks.

When we arrived, Herr Delbrück rushed so quickly down the steps to meet me that it was apparent he had been watching within. Taking me by both hands he solicitously led me in. The officer saluted me and was turning to withdraw when I recognised his purpose, and insisted that he should come to my rooms. Over a glass of wine I warmly thanked him and his brave comrades for saving me. He replied simply that he was more than glad and that Herr Delbrück had at the first taken steps to make all the searching party pleased; at which ambiguous utterance the *maître d'hôtel* smiled, while the officer pleaded duty and withdrew.

'But Herr Delbrück,' I enquired, 'how and why was it that the soldiers searched for me?'

He shrugged his shoulders, as if in depreciation of his own deed, as he replied: 'I was so fortunate as to obtain leave from the commander of the regiment in which I served, to ask for volunteers.'

'But how did you know I was lost?' I asked.

'The driver came hither with the remains of his carriage, which had been upset when the horses ran away.'

'But surely you would not send a search-party of soldiers merely on his account?'

'Oh, no!' he answered, 'but even before the coachman arrived I had this telegram from the Boyar whose guest you are,' and he took from his pocket a telegram which he handed to me, and I read:

Bistritz. Be careful of my guest—his safety is most precious to me. Should aught happen to him, or if he be missed, spare nothing to find him and ensure his safety. He is English and therefore adventurous. There are often dangers from snow and wolves and night. Lose not a moment if you suspect harm to him. I answer your zeal with my fortune—*Dracula*.

As I held the telegram in my hand, the room seemed to whirl around me, and if the attentive *maître d 'hôtel* had not caught me I think I should have fallen. There was something so strange in all this, something so weird and impossible to imagine, that there grew on me a sense of my being in some way the sport of opposite forces—the mere vague idea of which seemed in a way to paralyse me. I was certainly under some form of mysterious protection. From a distant country had come, in the very nick of time, a message that took me out of the danger of the snow-sleep and the jaws of the wolf.

Carnival on the Downs

GERALD KERSH

We are a queer people: I do not know what to make of us. Whatever anyone says for us is right; whatever anyone says against us is right. A conservative people, we would turn out our pockets for a rebel; and prim as we are, we love an eccentric.

We are an eccentric people. For example: we make a cult of cold baths—and of our lack of plumbing—and a boast of such characters as Dirty Dick of Bishopsgate, and Mr Lagg who is landlord of The White Swan at Wettendene.

Dirty Dick of Bishopsgate had a public house, and was a dandy, once upon a time. But it seems that on the eve of his marriage to a girl with whom he was in love he was jilted, with the wedding breakfast on the table. Thereafter, everything had, by his order, to be left exactly as it was on that fatal morning. The great cake crumbled, the linen mouldered, the silver turned black. The bar became filthy. Spiders spun their webs, which grew heavy and grey with insects and dirt. Dick never changed his wedding suit, nor his linen, either. His house became a byword for dirt and neglect... whereupon, he did good business there, and died rich.

Mr Lagg, who had a public house in Wettendene, which is in Sussex, seeing The Green Man redecorated and furnished with chromium chairs, capturing carriage trade, was at first discouraged. His house, The White Swan, attracted the local men who drank nothing but beer—on the profit of which, at that time, a publication could scarcely live.

Lagg grew depressed; neglected the house. Spiders spun their webs in the cellar, above and around the empty, mouldering barrels, hogsheads, kilderkins, nipperkins, casks and pins. He set up a bar in this odorous place—and so made his fortune. As the dirtiest place in Sussex, it became a meeting place for people who bathed every day. An American from New Orleans started the practice of pinning visiting cards to the beams. Soon, everybody who had a card pinned it up, so that Lagg's cellar was covered with them.

When he went to town, Lagg always came back with artificial spiders and beetles on springy wires, to hang from the low ceiling; also, old leather jacks, stuffed crocodiles and spiky rays from the Caribbean gulfs, and even a dried human head from the Amazon. Meanwhile, the cards accumulated, and so did the bills advertising local attractions—cattle shows, flower shows, theatricals, and what not.

And the despisers of what they called the 'great Unwashed' congregated there—the flickers-away of specks of dust—the ladies and gentlemen who could see a thumb print on a plate. Why? Homesickness for the gutter, perhaps—it is an occupational disease of people who like strong perfumes.

I visited The White Swan, in passing, on holiday. The people in Wettendene called it—not without affection—The Mucky Duck. There was the usual vociferous gathering of long-toothed women in tight-cut tweeds, and ruddy men with two slits to their jackets, howling confidences, while old Lagg, looking like a half-peeled beetroot, brooded under the cobwebs.

He took notice of me when I offered him something to drink, and said: 'Stopping in Wettendene, sir?'

'Overnight,' I said. 'Anything doing?'

He did not care. 'There's the flower show,' he said, flapping about with a loose hand. 'There's the Christian Boys' Sports. All pinned up. Have a dekko. See for yourself.'

So I looked about me.

That gentleman from New Orleans, who had pinned up the first card on the lowest bean, had started a kind of chain reaction. On the beams, the ceiling, and the very barrels, card jostled card, and advertisement jostled advertisement. I saw the card of the Duke of Chelsea overlapped by the large, red-pinned trade card of one George Grape, Rat-Catcher; a potato-crisp salesman's card half overlaid by that of the Hon. Iris Greene. The belly of a stuffed trout was covered with cards as an autumn valley with leaves.

But the great hogshead, it seemed, was set aside for the bills advertising local attractions. Many of these were out of date—for example, an advertisement of a Baby Show in 1932, another of a Cricket Match in 1934, and yet another for 'Sports' in 1923. As Mr Lagg had informed me, there were the printed announcements of the Christian Boys' affair and the Flower Show.

Under the Flower Show, which was scheduled for 14 August, was pinned a wretched little bill advertising, for the same fate, a 'Grand Carnival' in Wagnall's Barn on Long Meadow, Wettendene. Everything was covered with dust.

It is a wonderful place for dust. It is necessary, in The Mucky Duck cellar, to take your drink fast or clasp your hand over the top of the glass before it accumulates a grey scum or even a dead spider: the nobility and gentry like it that way. The gnarled old four-ale drinkers go to The Green Man: they have no taste for quaintness.

I knew nobody in Wettendene, and am shy of making new acquaintances. The 'Grand Carnival' was to begin at seven o'clock; entrance fee sixpence, children half price. It could not be much of a show, I reflected, at that price and in that place: a showman must be hard up, indeed, to hire a barn for his show in such a place. But I like carnivals and am interested in the people that follow them; so I set off at five o'clock.

Long Meadow is not hard to find: you go to the end of Wettendene High Street, turn sharp right at Scott's Corner where the village ends, and take the winding lane, Wettendene Way. This will lead you, through a green tunnel, to Long Meadow, where the big Wagnall's Barn is.

Long Meadow was rich grazing land in better times, but now it is good for nothing but a pitiful handful of sheep that nibble the coarse grass. There has been no use for the barn these last two generations. It was built to last hundreds of years; but the land died first. This had something to do with water—either a lack or an excess of it. Long Meadow is good for nothing much, at present, but the Barn stands firm and four-square to the capricious rains and insidious fogs of Wettendene Marsh. (If it were not for the engineers who dammed the river, the whole area would, by now, be under water.) However, the place is dry in dry weather.

Still, Long Meadow has the peculiarly dreary atmosphere of a swamp and Wagnall's Barn is incongruously sturdy in that wasteland. It is a long time since any produce was stocked in Wagnall's Barn. Mr Etheridge, who owns it, rents it for dances, amateur theatrical shows and what not.

That playbill aroused my curiosity. It was boldly printed in red, as follows:

!!! JOLLY JUMBO'S CARNIVAL !!!
!! THE ONE AND ONLY !!
COME AND SEE
!! GORGON, The Man Who Eats Bricks & Swallows Glass !!
!! THE HUMAN SKELETON !!
!! THE INDIA RUBBER BEAUTY –
She Can Put Her Legs Around Her Neck & Walk On Her Hands !!
!! A LIVE MERMAID !!
!! ALPHA, BETA, AND DOT.
The World–Famous Tumblers
With The Educated Dog !!
! JOLLY JUMBO !
!! JOLLY JUMBO !!

I left early, because I like to look behind the scenes, and have a chat with a wandering freak or two. I remembered a good friend of mine who had been a Human Skeleton—six foot six and weighed a hundred pounds—ate five meals a day, and was as strong as a bull. He told good stories in that coffee-bar that is set up where the Ringling Brothers and Barnum and Bailey Combined Circuses rest in Florida for the winter. I 'tasted sawdust', as the saying goes, and had a yearning to sit on the ground and hear strange stories. Not that I expected much of Wettendene. All the same the strangest people turn up at the unlikeliest places...

Then the rain came down, as it does in an English summer. The sky sagged, rumbled a borborygmic threat of thunderstorms, which seemed to tear open clouds like bags of water.

Knowing our English summer, I had come prepared with a mackintosh, which I put on as I ran for the shelter of the barn.

I was surprised to find it empty. The thunder was loud, now, and there were zigzags of lightning in the east; the pelting rain sounded on the meadow like a maraca. I took off my raincoat and lit a cigarette—and then, in the light of the match flame, I caught a glimpse of two red-and-green eyes watching me, in a far corner, about a foot away from the floor.

It was not yet night, but I felt in that moment such a pang of horror as comes only in the dark; but I am so constituted that, when frightened, I run forward. There was something unholy about Wagnall's Barn, but I should have been ashamed not to face it, whatever it might be. So I advanced, with my walking-stick; but then there came a most melancholy whimper, and I knew that the eyes belonged to a dog.

I made a caressing noise and said: 'Good dog, good doggie! Come on, doggie!'—feeling grateful for his company. By the light of another match, I saw a grey poodle, neatly clipped in the French style. When he saw me, he stood up on his hindlegs and danced.

In the light of that same match I saw, also, a man squatting on his haunches with his head in his hands. He was dressed only in trousers and a tattered shirt. Beside him lay a girl. He had made a bed for her out of his clothes and, the rain falling softer, I could hear her breathing, harsh and laborious. The clouds lifted. A little light came into the barn. The dog danced, barking, and the crouching man awoke, raising a haggard face.

'Thank God you've come,' he said. 'She can't breathe. She's got an awful pain in her chest, and a cough. She can't catch her breath, and she's burning. Help her, Doctor—Jolly Jumbo has left us high and dry.'

'What?' I said. 'Went on and left you here, all alone?'

'Quite right, Doctor.'

I said: 'I'm not a doctor.'

'Jumbo promised to send a doctor from the village,' the man said, with a laugh more unhappy than tears. 'Jolly Jumbo promised! I might have known. I did know. Jolly Jumbo never kept his word. Jumbo lives for hisself. But he didn't ought to leave us here in the rain, and Dolores in a bad fever. No, nobody's got the right. No!'

I said: 'You might have run down to Wettendene yourself, and got the doctor.'

' "Might" is a long word, mister. I've broke my ankle and my left wrist. Look at the mud on me, and see if I haven't tried… Third time, working my way on my elbows—and I am an agile man— I fainted with the pain, and half drowned in the mud…But Jumbo swore his Bible oath to send a physician for Dolores. Oh, dear me!'

At this the woman between short, agonised coughs, gasped: '*Alma de mi corazon*—heart of my soul—not leave? So cold, so hot, so cold. Please, not go?'

'I'll see myself damned first,' the man said, 'and so will Dot. Eh, Dot?'

At this the poodle barked and stood on its hindlegs, dancing.

The man said, drearily: 'She's a woman, do you see, sir. But one of the faithful kind. She come out of Mexico. That *alma de mi corazon*—she means it. Actually, it means 'soul of my heart'. There's nothing much more you can say to somebody you love, if you mean it... So you're not a doctor? More's the pity! I'd hoped you was. But oh, sir, for the sake of Christian charity, perhaps you'll give us a hand.

'She and me, we're not one of that rabble of layabouts, and gyppos, and what not. Believe me, sir, we're artists of our kind. I know that a gentleman like you doesn't regard us, because we live rough. But it would be an act of kindness for you to get a doctor up from Wettendene, because my wife is burning and coughing, and I'm helpless.

'I'll tell you something, guv'nor—poor little Dot, who understands more than the so-called Christians in these parts, she knew, *she* knew! She ran away. I called her: "Dot—Dot—Dot!"—but she run on. I'll swear she went for a doctor, or something.

'And in the meantime Jolly Jumbo has gone and left us high and dry. Low and wet is the better word, sir, and we haven't eaten this last two days.'

The girl, gripping his wrist, sighed: 'Please, not to go, not to leave?'

'Set your hear at ease, sweetheart,' the man said. 'Me and Dot, we are with you. And here's a gentleman who'll get us a physician. Because, to deal plainly with you, my one and only, I've got a bad leg now and a bad arm, and I can't make it through the mud to Wettendene. The dog tried and she come back with a bloody mouth where somebody kicked her...'

I said: 'Come on, my friends, don't lose heart. I'll run down to Wettendene and get an ambulance, or at least a doctor. Meanwhile,' I said, taking off my jacket, 'peel off some of those damp clothes. Put this on her. At least it's dry. Then I'll run down and get you some help.'

He said: 'All alone? It's a dretful thing, to be all alone. Dot'll go with you, if you will, God love you! But it's no use, I'm afraid.'

He said this in a whisper, but the girl heard him, and said, quite clearly: 'No use. Let him not go. Kind voice. Talk'—this between rattling gasps.

He said: 'All right, my sweet, he'll go in a minute.'

The girl said: 'Only a minute. Cold. Lonely—'

'What, Dolores, lonely with me and Dot?'

'Lonely, lonely, lonely.'

So the man forced himself to talk. God grant that no circumstances may compel any of you who read this to talk in such a voice. He was trying to speak evenly; but from time to time, when some word touched his heart, his voice broke like a boy's, and he tried to cover the break with a laugh that went inward, a sobbing laugh.

Holding the girl's hand and talking for her comfort, interrupted from time to time by the whimpering of the poodle Dot, he went on:

'They call me Alpha, you see, because my girl's name is Beta. That is her real name—short for Beatrice Dolores. But my real name is Alfred, and I come from Hampshire.

'They call us "tumblers", sir, but Dolores is an artist. I can do the forward rolls and the triple back-somersaults; but Dolores is the genius. Dolores, and that dog, Dot, do you see?

'It's a hard life, sir, and it's a rough life. I used to be a Joey— a kind of a clown—until I met Dolores in Southampton, where she'd been abandoned by a dago that run a puppet show, with sideshows, as went broke and left Dolores high and dry. All our lives, from Durham to Land's End, Carlisle to Brighton, north, south, east, west, I've been left high and dry when the rain came down and the money run out. Not an easy life, sir. A hard life, as a matter of fact. You earn your bit of bread, in this game.

'Ever since Dolores and me joined Jolly Jumnbo's Carnival, there was a run of bad luck. At Immersham, there was a cloudburst; Jumbo had took Grote's Meadow—we was two foot under water. The weather cleared at Athelboro' and they all came to see Pollux, the Strong Man, because, do you see, the blacksmith, at Athelboro' could lift an anvil over his head, and there was a fi'–pun prize for anybody who could out-lift Pollux (his name was really Michaels).

'Well, as luck would have it, at Athelboro' Pollux sprained his wrist. The blacksmith out-lifted him, and Jolly Jumbo told him to come back next morning for his fiver. We pulled out about midnight: Jumbo will never go to Athelboro' again. Then, in Pettydene, something happened to Gorgon, the man that eats bricks and swallows glass. His act was to bite lumps out of a brick, chew them up, wash them down with a glass of water, and crunch up and swallow the glass. We took the Drill Hall at Pettydene, and had a good house. And what happens, but Gorgon breaks a tooth!

'I tell you, sir, we had no luck. After that, at Firestone, something went wrong with the Mermaid. She was my property, you know—an animal they call a manatee—I bought her for a round sum from a man who caught her in South America. A kind of seal, but with breasts like a woman, and almost a human voice. She got a cough, and passed away.

'There was never such a round. Worst of all, just here, Dolores caught a cold.

'I dare say you've heard of my act, Alpha, Beta and Dot?... Oh, a stranger here; are you sir? I wish you could have seen it. Dolores is the genius—her and Dot. I'm only the under-stander. I would come rolling and somersaulting in, and stand. Then Dolores'd come dancing in and take what looked like a standing jump—I gave her a hand-up—on to my shoulders, so we stood balanced. Then, in comes poor little Dot, and jumps; first on to my shoulder, then on to Dolores' shoulder from mine, and so on to Dolores' head where Dot stands on her hind legs and dances...

'The rain comes down, sir. Dolores has got a cold in the chest. I beg her: "Don't go on, Dolores—don't do it!" But nothing will satisfy her, bless her heart: the show must go on. And when we come on, she was burning like a fire. Couldn't do the jump. I twist sidewise to take the weight, but her weight is kind of a deadweight, poor girl! My ankle snaps, and we tumbles.

'Tried to make it part of my act—making funny business, carrying the girl in my arms, hopping on one foot, with good old Dot dancing after us.

'That was the end of us in Wettendene. Jolly Jumbo says to us: "Never was such luck. The brick-eater's bust a tooth. The mermaid's good and dead. The strong-man has strained hisself ... and I'm not sure but that blacksmith won't be on my trail, with a few pals, for that fi'pun note. I've got to leave you to it, Alph, old feller, I'm off to Portsmouth."

'I said: "And what about my girl? I've only got one hand and one foot, and she's got a fever."

'He said: "Wait a bit, Alph, just wait a bit. My word of honour, and my Bible oath, I'll send a sawbones up from Wettendene."

' "And what about our pay?" I ask.

'Jolly Jumbo says: "I swear on my mother's grave, Alph, I haven't got it. But I'll have it in Portsmouth, on my Bible oath. You know me. Sacred word of honour! I'll be at The Hope and Anchor for a matter of weeks, and you'll be paid in full. And I'll send you a doctor, by my father's life I will. Honour bright! In the meantime, Alph, I'll look after Dot for you."

'And so he picked up the dog—I hadn't the strength to prevent him—and went out, and I heard the whips cracking and the vans squelching in the mud.

'But little Dot got away and came back...

'I've been talking too much, sir. I thought you was the doctor. Get one for the girl, if you've a heart in you—and a bit of meat for the dog. I've got a few shillings on me.'

I said: 'Keep still. I'll be right back.' And I ran in the rain, closely followed by the dog Dot, down through that dripping green tunnel into Wettendene, and rang long and loud at a black door to which was affixed the brass plate, well worn, of one Dr MacVitie, M.R.C.S., L.R.C.P.

The old doctor came out, brushing crumbs from his waistcoat. There was an air of decrepitude about him. He led me into his surgery. I saw a dusty old volume of Gray's Anatomy, two fishing rods, four volumes of the Badminton Library—all unused these past twenty years. There were also some glass-stoppered bottles that seemed to contain nothing but sediment; a spirit lamp without spirit; some cracked test-tubes; and an ancient case-book into the cover of which was stuck a rusty scalpel.

He was one of the cantankerous old Scotch school of doctors that seem incapable of graciousness, and grudging even of a civil word. He growled; 'I'm in luck this evening. It's six months since I sat down to my bit of dinner without the bell going before I had the first spoonful of soup half-way to my mouth. Well, you've let me finish my evening meal. Thank ye.'

He was ponderously ironic, this side of offensiveness. 'Well, out with it. What ails ye? Nothing, I'll wager. Nothing ever ails 'em hereabouts that a dose of castor oil or an aspirin tablet will not cure—excepting always rheumatism. Speak up, man!'

I said: 'There's nothing wrong with me at all. I've come to fetch you to treat two other people up at Wagnall's Barn. There's a man with a broken ankle and a girl with a congestion of the lungs. So get your bag and come along.'

He snapped at me like a turtle, and said: 'And since when, may I ask, were you a diagnostician? And who are you to be giving a name to symptoms? In any case, young fellow, I'm not practising. I'm retired. My son runs the practice, and he's out on a child-bed case... Damn that dog—he's barking again!'

The poodle, Dot, was indeed barking hysterically and scratching at the front door.

I said: 'Doctor, these poor people are in desperate straits.'

'Aye, poor people always are. And who's to pay the bill?'

'I'll pay,' I said, taking out my wallet.

'Put it up, man, put it up! Put your hand in your pocket for all the riff-raff that lie about in barns and ye'll end in the workhouse.'

He got up laboriously, sighing: 'Alex is over Iddlesworth way with the car. God give us strength to bear it. I swore my oath and so I'm bound to come, Lord preserve us!'

'If——' I said, 'if you happen to have a bit of meat in the house for the dog, I'd be glad to pay for it——'

'——And what do you take this surgery for? A butcher's shop?' Then he paused. 'What sort of a dog, as a matter of curiosity, would ye say it was?'

'A little grey French poodle.'

'Oh, aye? Very odd. Ah well, there's a bit of meat on the chop bones, so I'll put 'em in my pocket for the dog, if you like... Wagnall's Barn, did ye say? A man and a girl, is that it? They'll be some kind of vagrant romanies, or gyppos, no doubt?'

I said: 'I believe they are some kind of travelling performers. They are desperately in need of help. Please hurry, Doctor.'

His face was sour and his voice harsh, but his eyes were bewildered, as he said: 'Aye, no doubt. I dare say, very likely. A congestion of the lungs, ye said? And a fractured ankle, is that it? Very well.' He was throwing drugs and bandages into his disreputable-looking black bag. I helped him into his immense black mackintosh.

He said: 'As for hurrying, young man, I'm seventy-seven years old, my arteries are hard, and I could not hurry myself for the crack of doom. Here, carry the bag. Hand me my hat and my stick, and we'll walk up to Wagnall's Barnon, this fool's errand of yours. Because a fool's errand it is, I fancy. Come on.'

The little dog, Dot, looking like a bit of the mud made animate, only half distinguishable in the half dark, barked with joy, running a little way backwards and a long way forwards, leading us back to the Barn through that darkened green tunnel.

The doctor had a flash-lamp. We made our way to the barn, he grumbling and panting and cursing the weather. We went in. He swung the beam of his lamp from corner to corner, until it came to rest on my jacket. It lay as I had wrapped it over poor Dolores, but it was empty.

I shouted: 'Alpha, Beta! Here's the doctor!'

The echo answered: *'Octor!'*

I could only pick up my jacket and say: 'They must have gone away.'

Dr MacVitie said, drily: 'Very likely, if they were here at all.'

'Here's my jacket, damp on the inside and dry on the outside,' I said. 'And I have the evidence of my own eyes——'

'No doubt. Very likely. In a lifetime of practice I have learned, sir, to discredit the evidence of my eyes, and my other four senses, besides. Let's away. Come!'

'But where have they gone?'

'Ah, I wonder!'

'And the dog, where's the dog?' I cried.

He said, in his dour way: 'For that, I recommend you consult Mr Lindsay, the vet.'

So we walked down again, without exchanging a word until we reached Dr MacVitie's door. Then he said: 'Where did you spend your evening?'

I said: 'I came straight to the Barn from The White Swan.'

'Well, then,' he said, 'I recommend ye go back, and take a whisky and water, warm; and get ye to bed in a dry night-shirt. And this time take a little more water with it. Goodnight to ye—,' and slammed the door in my face.

I walked the half mile to The White Swan, which was still open. The landlord, Mr Lagg, looked me up and down, taking notice of my soaking wet clothes and muddy boots. 'Been out?' he asked.

In Sussex they have a way of asking unnecessary, seemingly innocent questions of this nature which lead to an exchange of witticisms—for which, that night, I was not in the mood.

I said: 'I went up to Wagnall's Barn for Jolly Jumbo's Carnival but he pulled out, it seems, and left a man, a woman, and a dog—'

'You hear that, George?' said Mr Lagg to a very old farmer whose knobbed ash walking-stick seemed to have grown out of the knobbed root of his earthy, arthritic hand, and who was smoking a pipe mended in three places with insulating tape.

'I heerd,' said old George, with a chuckle. 'Dat gen'lemen'll been a liddle bit late for dat carnival, like.'

At this they both laughed. But then Mr Lagg said, soothingly, as to a cash customer: 'Didn't you look at the notice on the bill, sir? Jolly Jumbo was here all right, and flitted in a hurry too. And he did leave a man and a girl (not lawfully married, I heerd) and one o' them liddle shaved French dogs.

'I say, you'm a liddle late for Jolly Jumbo's Carnival, sir, 'cause if you look again at Jolly Jumbo's bill, you'll see—I think the programme for the Cricket Match covers up the corner—you'll see the date on it is August the fourteenth, 1904. I was a boy at the time; wasn't I, George?'

'Thirteen-year-old,' old George said, 'making you sixty-three to my seventy-two. Dat were a sad business, but as ye sow, so shall ye reap, they says. Live a vagabond, die a vagabond. Live in sin, die in sin—'

'All right, George,' said Mr Lagg, 'you're not in chapel now...I don't know how you got at it, sir, but Jolly Jumbo (as he called hisself) lef' two people and a dog behind. Hauled out his vans, eleven o'clock at night, and left word with Dr MacVitie (the old one, that was) to go up to Wagnall's Barn.

'But he was in the middle o' dinner, and wouldn't go. Then he was called out to the Squire's place, and didn't get home until twelve o'clock next night. And there was a liddle dog that kep' barking and barking, and trying to pull him up the path by the trousis-leg. But Dr MacVitie—'

'Dat were a mean man, dat one, sure enough!'

'You be quiet, George. Dr MacVitie kicked the liddle dog into the ditch, and unhooked the bell, and tied up the knocker, and went to bed. Couple o' days later, Wagnall, going over his land, has a look at that barn, and he sees a young girl stone dead, a young fellow dying, and a poor liddle dog crying fit to break your heart. Oh, he got old Dr MacVitie up to the barn then all right, but t'was too late. The fellow, he died in the Cottage Hospital.

'They tried to catch the dog, but nobody could. It stood off and on, like, until that pair was buried by the parish. Then it run off into the woods, and nobody saw it again——'

'Oh, but didn't they, though?' said old George.

Mr Lagg said: 'It's an old wives' tale, sir. They *do* say that this here liddle grey French dog comes back every year on August the fourteenth to scrat and bark at the doctor's door, and lead him to Wagnall's Barn. And be he in the middle of his supper or be he full, be he weary or rested, wet or dry, sick or well, go he must... *He* died in 1924, so you see it's nothing but an old wives' tale—'

'Dey did used to git light-headed, like, here on the marshes,' said old George, 'but dey do say old Dr MacVitie mustn't rest. He mus' pay dat call to dat empty barn, every year, because of his hard heart. Tomorrow, by daylight, look and see if doctor's door be'nt all scratted up, like.'

'George, you're an old woman in your old age,' said Mr Lagg. 'We take no stock of such things in these parts, sir. Would you like to come up to the lounge and look at the television until closing time?'

The House of Strange Stories

ANDREW LANG

The House of Strange Stories, as I prefer to call it (though it is not known by that name in the country), seems the very place for a ghost. Yet, though so many people have dwelt upon its site and in its chambers, though the ancient Elizabethan oak, and all the queer tables and chairs that a dozen generations have bequeathed, might well be tenanted by ancestral spirits, and disturbed by rappings, it is a curious fact that there is *not* a ghost in the House of Strange Stories. On my earliest visit to this mansion, I was disturbed, I own, by a not unpleasing expectancy. There *must*, one argued, be a shadowy lady in green in the bedroom, or, just as one was falling asleep, the spectre of a Jesuit would creep out of the priest's hole, where he was starved to death in the 'spacious times of great Elizabeth,' and would search for a morsel of bread.

'Does the priest of your "priest-hole" walk?' I asked the squire one winter evening in the House of Strange Stories.

Darkness had come to the rescue of the pheasants at about four in the afternoon, and all of us, men and women, were sitting at afternoon tea in the firelit study, drowsily watching the flicker of the flames on the black panelling. The characters will introduce themselves, as they take part in the conversation.

'No,' said the squire, 'even the priest does not walk. Somehow very few of the Jesuits have left ghosts in country houses. They are just the customers you would expect to "walk", but they don't....'

'The only ghost *I* ever came across, or, rather, came within measurable distance of, never appeared at all so far as one knew,' remarked the Girton girl.

'Miss Lebas has a story,' said the squire, 'Won't she tell us her story?'

The ladies murmured, 'Do, please.'

'It really cannot be called a ghost-story,' remarked Miss Lebas, 'it was only an uncomfortable kind of coincidence, and I never think of it without a shudder. But I know there is not any reason at all why it should make any of *you* shudder; so don't be disappointed.

'It was the long vacation before last, and I went on a reading party to Bantry Bay. Term-time was drawing near, and Bantry Bay was getting pretty cold, when I received an invitation from Lady Garryowen to stay with them at Dundellan on my way south. They were two very dear, old, hospitable Irish ladies, the last of their race, Lady Garryowen and her sister, Miss Patty. They were *so* hospitable that, though I did not know it, Dundellan was quite full when I reached it, overflowing with young people. The house has nothing very remarkable about it: a grey, plain building, with remains of the château about it, and a high park wall. In the garden wall there is a small round tower, just like those in the precinct wall at St Andrews. The ground floor is not used. On the first floor there is a furnished chamber with a deep round niche, almost a separate room, like that in Queen Mary's apartments in Holy Rood. The first floor has long been fitted up as a bedroom and dressing-room, but it had not been occupied, and a curious old spinning-wheel in the corner (which has nothing to do with my story, if you can call it a story), must have been unused since 1798, at least. I reached Dublin late; our train should have arrived at half-past six—it was ten before we toiled into the station. The Dundellan carriage was waiting for me, and, after an hour's drive, I reached the house. The dear old ladies had sat up for me, and I went to bed as soon as possible in a very comfortable room. I fell asleep at once, and did not waken until broad daylight, between seven and eight, when, as my eyes wandered about, I saw, by the pictures on the wall, and the names on the books beside my bed, that Miss Patty must have given up her own room to me. I was quite sorry and, as I dressed, determined to get her to let me change into any den rather than accept this sacrifice. I went downstairs, and found breakfast ready, but neither Lady Garryowen nor Miss Patty. Looking out of the window into the garden, I heard, for the only time in my life, the wild Irish *keen* over the dead, and saw the old nurse wailing and wringing her hands and hurrying to the house. As soon as she entered she told me, with a burst of grief, and in a language I shall not try to imitate, that Miss Patty was dead.

'When I arrived the house was so full that there was literally no room for me. But "Dundellan was never beaten yet", the old ladies had said. There was still the room in the tower. But this room had such an evil reputation for being "haunted" that the servants could hardly be got to go near it, at least after dark, and the dear old ladies never dreamed of sending any of their guests to pass a bad night in a place with a bad name. Miss Patty, who had the courage of a Bayard, did not think twice. She went herself to sleep in the haunted tower, and left her room to me. And when the old nurse went to call her in the morning, she could not waken Miss Patty. She was dead. Heart-disease, they called it. Of course,' added the Girton girl, 'as I said, it was only a coincidence. But the Irish servants could not be persuaded that Miss Patty had not seen whatever the thing was that they believed to be in the garden tower. I don't know what it was. You see the context was dreadfully vague, a mere fragment.

There was a little silence after the Girton girl's story.

'I never heard before in my life,' said the maiden aunt, at last, 'of any host or hostess who took the haunted room themselves, when the house happened to be full. They always send the stranger within their gates to it, and then pretend to be vastly surprised when he does not have a good night. I had several bad nights myself once. In Ireland too.'

'Tell us all about it, Judy,' said her brother, the squire.

'No,' murmured the maiden aunt. 'You would only laugh at me. There was no ghost. I didn't hear anything. I didn't see anything. I didn't even *smell* anything, as they do in that horrid book, *The Haunted Hotel*.'

'Then why had you such bad nights?'

'Oh, I *felt*,' said the maiden aunt, with a little shudder.

'What did you *feel*, Aunt Judy?'

'I *know* you will laugh,' said the maiden aunt, abruptly entering on her nervous narrative. 'I felt all the time *as if somebody was looking through the window*. Now, you know, there *couldn't* be anybody. It was in an Irish country house where I had just arrived, and my room was on the second floor. The window was old-fashioned and narrow, with a deep recess. As soon as I went to bed, my dears, I *felt* that someone was looking through the window, and meant to come in. I got up, and bolted the window, though I knew it was impossible for anybody to climb up there, and I drew the curtains, but I could not fall asleep. If ever I began to doze, I would waken with a start, and turn and look in the direction of the window. I did not sleep all night, and the next night, though I was dreadfully tired, it was just the same thing. So I had to take my hostess into my confidence, though it was extremely disagreeable, my dears, to seem so foolish. I only told her that I thought the air, or something, must disagree with me, for I could not sleep. Then, as someone was leaving the house that day, she implored me to try another room, where I slept beautifully, and afterwards had a very pleasant visit. But, the day I went away, my hostess asked me if I had been kept awake by anything in particular, for instance, by a feeling that someone was trying to come in at the window. Well, I admitted that I *had* a nervous feeling of that sort, and she said that she was very sorry, and that everyone who lay in the room had exactly the same sensation. She supposed they must all have heard the history of the room, in childhood, and forgotten that they had heard it, and then been unconsciously reminded of it by reflex action. It seems, my dears, that that is the new scientific way of explaining all these things, presentiments and dreams and wraiths, and all that sort of thing. We have seen them before, and remember them without being aware of it. So I said I'd never heard the history of the room; but she said I *must* have, and so must all the people who felt as if someone was coming in by the window. And I said that it was rather a curious thing they should *all* forget they knew it, and *all* be reminded of it without being aware of it, and that, if she did not mind, I'd like to be reminded of it again. So she said that these objections had all been replied to (just as clergymen always say in sermons), and then she told me the history of the room. It only came to this that three generations before, the family butler (whom everyone had always thought a most steady, respectable man), dressed himself up like a ghost, or like his notion of a ghost, and got a ladder, and came in by the window to steal the diamonds of the lady of the house, and he frightened her to death, poor woman! That was all. But, ever since, people who sleep in the room don't sleep, so to speak, and keep thinking that someone is coming in by the casement. That's all; and I told you it was not an interesting story, but perhaps you will find more interest in the scientific explanation of all these things.'

The story of the maiden aunt, so far as it recounted her own experience, did not contain anything to which the judicial faculties of the mind refused assent. Probably the Bachelor of Arts felt that something a good deal more unusual was wanted, for he instantly started, without being asked, on the following narrative:

'I also was staying,' said the Bachelor of Arts, 'at the home of my friends, the aristocracy in Scotland. The name of the house, and the precise rank in the peerage of my illustrious host, it is not necessary for me to give. All those, however, who know of feudal and baronial halls are aware that the front of the castle looks forth on a somewhat narrow drive, bordered by black and funereal pines. On the night of my arrival at the castle, although I went late to bed, I did not feel at all sleepy. Something, perhaps, in the mountain air, or in the vicissitudes of *baccarat*, may have banished slumber. I had been in luck, and a pile of sovereigns and notes lay, in agreeable confusion, on my dressing table. My feverish blood declined to be tranquillised, and at last I drew up the blind, threw open the latticed window, and looked out on the drive and the pinewood. The faint and silvery blue of dawn was just wakening in the sky, and a setting moon hung, with a peculiarly ominous and wasted appearance, above the crests of the forest. But conceive my astonishment when I beheld, on the drive, and right under my window, a large and well-appointed hearse, with two white horses, with plumes complete and attended by mutes, whose black staffs were tipped with silver that glittered pallid in the dawn.

'I exhausted my ingenuity in conjectures as to the presence of this remarkable vehicle with the white horses, so unusual, though, when one thinks of it, so appropriate to the chariot of Death. Could some belated visitor have arrived in a hearse, like the lady in Miss Ferrier's novel? Could one of the domestics have expired, and was it the intention of my host to have the body thus honourably removed without casting a gloom over his guests?

'Wild as these hypotheses appeared, I could think of nothing better, and was just about to leave the window, and retire to bed, when the driver of the strange carriage, who had hitherto sat motionless, turned, and looked me full in the face. Never shall I forget the appearance of this man, whose sallow countenance, close-shaven dark skin, and a small, black moustache, combined with I know not what of martial in his air, struck into me a certain indefinable alarm. No sooner had he caught my eye than he gathered up his reins, raised his whip, and started the mortuary vehicle at a walk down the road. I followed it with my eyes until a bend in the avenue hid it from my sight. So wrapt up was my spirit in the exercise of the single sense of vision that it was not until the hearse became lost to view that I noticed the entire absence of sound which accompanied its departure. Neither had the bridles and trappings of the white horses jingled as the animals shook their heads, nor had the wheels of the hearse crashed upon the gravel of the avenue. I was compelled by all these circumstances to believe that what I had looked upon was not of this world, and, with a beating heart, I sought refuge in sleep.

'Next morning, feeling far from refreshed, I arrived among the latest at a breakfast which was a desultory and movable feast. Almost all the men had gone forth to hill, forest, or river, in pursuit of the furred, finned, or feathered denizens of the wilds——'

'You speak,' interrupted the schoolboy, 'like a printed book! I like to hear you speak like that. Drive on, old man! Drive on your hearse!'

The Bachelor of Arts 'drove on', without noticing this interruption. 'I tried to "lead up" to the hearse,' he said, 'in conversation with the young ladies of the castle. I endeavoured to assume the languid and preoccupied air of the guest who, in ghost-stories, has had a bad night with the family spectre. I drew the conversation to the topic of apparitions, and even warnings of death. I knew that every family worthy of the name has its omen: the Oxenhams a white bird, another house a brass band, whose airy music in poured forth by invisible performers, and so on. Of course I expected someone to cry, "Oh, *we've* got a hearse with white horses", for that is the kind of heirloom an ancient house regards with complacent pride. But nobody offered any remarks on the local omen, and even when I drew near the topic of *hearses*, one of the girls, my cousin, merely quoted, "Speak not like a death's-head, good Doll" (my name is Adolphus), and asked me to play lawn-tennis.'

'In the evening, in the smoking-room, it was no better, nobody had ever heard of an omen in this particular castle. Nay, when I told my story, for it came to that at last, they only laughed at me, and said I must have dreamed it. Of course I expected to be wakened in the night by some awful apparition, but nothing disturbed me. I never slept better, and hearses were the last things I thought of during the remainder of my visit. Months passed, and I had almost forgotten the vision, or dream, for I began to feel apprehensive that, after all, it *was* a dream. So costly and elaborate an apparition as a hearse, with white horses and plumes complete, could never have been got up, regardless of expense, for one occasion only, and to frighten one undergraduate, yet it was certain that the hearse was not 'the old family coach'. My entertainers had undeniably never heard of it in their lives before. Even tradition at the castle said nothing of a spectral hearse, though the house was credited with a white lady deprived of her hands, and a luminous boy.'

Here the Bachelor of Arts paused, and a shower of chaff began.

'Is that really all?' asked the Girton girl. 'Why, this is the third ghost-story tonight without any ghost in it!'

'I don't remember saying that it *was* a ghost-story,' replied the Bachelor of Arts; 'but I thought a little anecdote of a mere "warning" might not be unwelcome.'

'But where does the warning come in?' asked the schoolboy.

'That's just what I was arriving at,' replied the narrator, 'when I was interrupted with as little ceremony as if I had been Mr Gladstone in the middle of a most important speech. I was going to say that, in the Easter Vacation after my visit to the castle, I went over to Paris with a friend, a fellow of my college. We drove to the *Hôtel d' Alsace* (I believe there is no hotel of that name; if there is, I beg the spirited proprietor's pardon, and assure him that nothing personal is intended). We marched upstairs with our bag and baggage, and jolly high stairs they were. When we had removed the soil of travel from our persons, my friend called out to me, "I say, Jones, why shouldn't we go down by the lift?" "All right," said I, and my friend walked to the door of the mechanical apparatus, opened it, and got in. I followed him, when the porter whose business it is to "personally conduct" the inmates of the hotel, entered also, and was closing the door.

'His eyes met mine, and I knew him in a moment. I had seen him once before. His sallow face, black, closely shaven chin, furtive glance, and military bearing, were the face and the glance and bearing of the driver of that awful hearse!

'In a moment—more swiftly than I can tell you—I pushed past the man, threw open the door, and just managed, by a violent effort, to drag my friend on to the landing. Then the lift rose with a sudden impulse, fell again, and rushed, with frightful velocity, to the basement of the hotel, whence we heard an appalling crash, followed by groans. We rushed downstairs, and the horrible spectacle of destruction that met our eyes I shall never forget. The unhappy porter was expiring in agony; but the warning had saved my life and my friend's.'

'*I was that friend*, said I—the collector of these anecdotes; 'and so far I can testify to the truth of Jones's story.'

At this moment, however, the gong for dressing sounded, and we went to our several apartments, after this emotional specimen of 'Evenings at Home'.

The Overcoat

Ruskin Bond

It was clear frosty weather, and as the moon came up over the Himalayan peaks, I could see that patches of snow still lay on the roads of the hill-station. I would have been quite happy in bed, with a book and a hot-water bottle at my side, but I'd promised the Kapadias that I'd go to their party, and I felt it would be churlish of me to stay away. I put on two sweaters, an old football scarf, and an overcoat, and set off down the moonlit road.

It was a walk of just over a mile to the Kapadias' house, and I had covered about half the distance when I saw a girl standing in the middle of the road.

She must have been sixteen or seventeen. She looked rather old-fashioned—long hair, hanging to her waist, and a flummoxy sequined dress, pink and lavender, that reminded me of the photos in my Grandmother's family album. When I went closer, I noticed that she had lovely eyes and a winning smile.

'Good evening,' I said. 'It's a cold night to be out.' 'Are you going to the party?' she asked.

'That's right. And I can see from your lovely dress that you're going, too. Come along, we're nearly there.'

She fell into step beside me and we soon saw lights from the Kapadias' house shining brightly through the deodars. The girl told me her name was Julie. I hadn't seen her before but, then, I'd only been in the hill-station a few months.

There was quite a crowd at the party, and no one seemed to know Julie. Everyone thought she was a friend of mine. I did not deny it. Obviously she was someone who was feeling lonely and wanted to be friendly with people. And she was certainly enjoying herself. I did not see her do much eating or drinking, but she flitted about from one group to another, talking, listening, laughing; and when the music began, she was dancing almost continuously, alone or with partners, it didn't matter which, she was completely wrapped up in the music.

It was almost midnight when I got up to go. I had drunk a fair amount of punch, and was ready for bed. As I was saying goodnight to my hosts and wishing everyone a merry Christmas, Julie slipped her arm into mine and said she'd be going home, too.

When we were outside I said, 'Where do you live, Julie?'

'At Wolfsburn,' she said. 'At the top of the hill.'

'There's a cold wind,' I said. 'And although your dress is beautiful, it doesn't look very warm. Here, you'd better wear my overcoat. I've plenty of protection.'

She did not protest, and allowed me to slip my overcoat over her shoulders. Then we started out on the walk home. But I did not have to escort her all the way. At about the spot where we had met, she said, 'There's a short cut from here. I'll just scramble up the hillside.'

'Do you know it well?' I asked. 'It's a very narrow path.'

'Oh, I know every stone on the path. I use it all the time. And besides, it's a really bright night.'

'Well, keep the coat on,' I said. 'I can collect it tomorrow.'

She hesitated for a moment, then smiled and nodded to me. She then disappeared up the hill, and I went home alone.

The next day I walked up to Wolfsburn. I crossed a little brook, from which the house had probably got its name, and entered an open iron gate. But of the house itself little remained. Just a roofless ruin, a pile of stones, a shattered chimney, a few Doric pillars where a verandah had once stood.

Had Julie played a joke on me? Or had I found the wrong house?

I walked around the hill, to the mission house where the Taylors lived and asked old Mrs Taylor if she knew a girl called Julie.

'No, I don't think so,' she said. 'Where does she live?' 'At Wolfsburn, I was told. But the house is just a ruin.'

'Nobody has lived at Wolfsburn for over forty years. The Mackinnons lived there. One of the old families who settled here. But when their girl died....' She stopped and gave me a queer look. 'I think her name was Julie...Anyway, when she died, they sold the house and went away. No one ever lived in it again, and it fell into decay. But it couldn't be the same Julie you're looking for. She died of consumption—there wasn't much you could do about it in those days. Her grave is in the cemetery, just down the road.'

I thanked Mrs Taylor and walked slowly down the road to the cemetery: not really wanting to know any more, but propelled forward almost against my will.

It was a small cemetery under the deodars. You could see the eternal snows of the Himalayas standing out against the pristine blue of the sky. Here lay the bones of forgotten Empire-builders—soldiers, merchants, adventurers, their wives and children. It did not take me long to find Julie's grave. It had a simple headstone with her name clearly outlined on it:

> Julie Mackinnon
> 1923-39
> 'With us one moment,
> Taken the next
> Gone to her Maker,
> Gone to her rest.'

Although many monsoons had swept across the cemetery wearing down the stones, they had not touched this little tombstone.

I was turning to leave when I caught a glimpse of something familiar behind the headstone. I walked round to where it lay.

Neatly folded on the grass was my overcoat.

The Mirror

Reeta Dutta Gupta

Outside, in the fresh green lawn at 7 Chowrangee Street, Ruby was playing a game of her own. And along the edges of the green grass, white lilies and tuberoses bloomed. So did sweet-smelling jasmines on the trailing creeper. The monsoon had arrived. Among the white flowers, creamish, powder-puff butterflies flitted about when the rains took a rest.

Sitting on the windowsill, inhaling the perfumed air, Anjoli watched her little sister. She was always playing games. Little brat! How Mom indulged in her whims and fancies! And what a wild imagination she had! 'I can see ghosts,' she often said with a straight face. Liar! It sometimes worried Mom and Dad. But, they laughed it off. The other day, when Ruby and Anjoli stood out after dinner in their garden in the silver moonlight, to have a moonlight bath—which Ruby said was better than sunbathing in the hot humid climate of Calcutta—she suddenly looked up into the dark terrace streaked with faint moonbeams.

'There's aunty up there on the terrace, standing all alone in the moonlight,' Ruby had said. 'She is looking at us.'

Aunty was Dad's only sister. Only a year ago she had died of cancer.

How frightened Anjoli was that night! Mom and Dad were away at a party to which children were not invited. Why not? Wondered Anjoli. She was fifteen, going on sixteen and she loved to go to parties. Dress up. Put on her light blue chiffon dress embroidered with little white pearls and sequins. Mom had given her that beautiful dress on her fifteenth birthday, only a month ago. And the ornate dresser with a beautiful mirror, which had inlay work with mother-of-pearl along the edges, was a gift from Dad.

'Aunty is calling us,' Ruby had persisted as she stared into the empty space with her eyes and followed the movement of someone walking about.

'What utter nonsense,' Anjoli had snapped back, putting up a brave face. She didn't want to let her sister discover how afraid she was when she spoke like that. For instance, on her birthday, when she was most happy, Ruby had told her just before going to bed, 'He'll come!'

'Who'll come?... What on earth are you talking about?' Anjoli had asked, pinching her sister's chubby cheek so firmly that it left a red patch on her smooth fair skin. That serves her right for making me worry, she thought.

But Ruby had screamed into her ears, her eyes round like two white-and-black marbles, 'Of course, he will! Don't you believe me?'

The next morning, when Anjoli told her mother about the strange things Ruby had been telling her, her mother kept her cool.

At least, she pretended to look all right. And she even sided with the baby of the house.

'She is seven years younger to you, Ann. Why do you take everything she says so seriously? Children of her age play games like that. They live in a world of their own.'

Anjoli said nothing but felt a little hurt and angry inside. Her mother was always taking her sister's side. Spoilt child! Wasn't she glad that evening when Dad had chided Ruby as he was helping Anjoli solve a mathematical problem and Ruby came yelling into the room. 'He'll come! He'll come!'

Dad had sharply said, 'That's enough, Ruby! Mom has been telling me about all the naughty things you say! Have you not heard the story "Cry Wolf"? If you go on pretending, no one will believe you. Now, don't make a noise here, your Didi is studying.'

Days and weeks had passed since that evening. Almost a month was over. Ruby was away at her Grandma's house for the weekend and Anjoli was glad for that. She could now have her Mom all to herself for two days, thought Anjoli. Not that she didn't like going to Grandma's, but monthly tests were round the corner. So, she sat at her desk studying, when the doorbell rang. A short buzz, followed by a long, impatient ring. It had been drizzling outside, which turned into a shower. Anjoli could hear the pitter-patter of rain.

Anjoli's mother was busy at her computer. She worked for an Internet company and was always very busy. Her Dad, too, was busy with his clients discussing legal matters. So, Anjoli got up to answer the doorbell. Opening the door she saw a man, a little away from the entrance. The gentleman wore a white shirt and a pair of neatly pressed white trousers. His hair was completely silver like moonlight. He was thin and frail. Anjoli thought he looked like a stick of tuberose plucked from the garden outside. But how did he come in through the rain? He didn't have an umbrella. The man half-smiled.

'Yes?' Anjoli asked.

At first the man didn't say a word but continued to stare at Anjoli for sometime. Anjoli blinked and stared back. He didn't look happy. He seemed to have a sad countenance.

'Have you come to see Dad?' Anjoli asked looking away from the man as if trying hard to break away from the hold of his stare.

'It's the mirror,' the man said at length, almost in a whisper. I've come for it. Could I please have it back? The mirror you had bought a month ago from The Roy's Auction Mart at Freeschool Street? You see, it belonged to me. I'd no intention of putting it up for the sale. There was some mistake about it.'

Anjoli was horrified. She had grown much too fond of her mirror to part with it. She quickly looked back over her shoulders. Thank god, her parents were unaware they had a visitor. Thank god, Ruby was away. She would never come to know about this man and tattle about it to her mother. Anjoli had no intention of parting with the mirror. She was just discovering the world of teenage cosmetics and junk jewellery. She loved to look pretty for she had a feeling deep inside her—which no one knew—that she was not as good looking as her little sister. So when she was not studying, she spent time before the mirror doing her make up, combing her hair this way and that way and generally fussing over her looks.

In a hushed voice, she quickly replied, 'Ah, well! But I think it was sold to us. We'd bought it. You see, it was my birthday present.'

The man shook his head resolutely.

Anjoli shrugged up her shoulders. 'I'm sorry,' she said and before the man could say another word, she shut the door.

A week passed. Anjoli kept the visit of the man a closely guarded secret. She almost forgot about it. Then, one evening, when Ruby and she sat on the windowsill listening to the wind making strange noises among the palm fronds just outside their garden—for it had begun to drizzle and they couldn't go out for a stroll—Ruby suddenly stood up, closed her eyes and in a low whisper said, 'He's on his way. That man in white.'

Anjoli's heart missed a beat. Suddenly, she remembered the man who had come asking for her mirror. Of course, Ruby had told her, 'He'll come.' And now she was saying, 'That man in white.' How did Ruby know so much? Perhaps, her sister was not playing any game after all. There was something real about what she said. There was something uncanny about her that made her afraid. Was she what people called a clairvoyant? Was that the word, which meant a person who knew things in advance? Anjoli had read about it in a storybook.

For the first time giving her sister a measure of importance, Anjoli asked, testing her sister, 'How do you know he's on his way?'

'I know. I can see. He'll be back,' Ruby said.

'He'll be back—what do you mean?' Anjoli asked.

Ruby shrugged her shoulders and looked nonchalant.

Anjoli's heart began to pound. 'Tell me, why should he come?' she demanded. Ruby burst out laughing. 'Of course, you know! Don't pretend to be an angel.'

Anjoli held her breath, trying hard not to look too anxious as she continued with her interrogation, 'Tell me what else do you see?'

'I see him coming. I see him coming,' Ruby said closing her eyes and sniffing the air like a police dog.

'What makes you sniff the air, stupid?' Anjoli said.

'I can smell something like dad's eau-de-cologne. Now it is right in this room,' Ruby said, opening her eyes. 'Why, there he is!' she exclaimed.

Anjoli stared at her sister, totally bewildered. 'Where is he?' she whispered.

'He is in your mirror,' she said. 'He is not looking at me. He is looking at you.'

Anjoli was terrified. But, nonetheless, she managed to say, 'Nonsense. What utter nonsense!' giving a quick sidelong glance at the mirror. But there was nothing that she saw. She was sure, Ruby was playing—just playing a game. But how did she know about the man in white? Was it all a coincidence?

Thank god! The children's mother walked into the room just then. 'Ann and Ruby, dinner time!' She announced.

Anjoli wanted to run to her and hold her hand. But before she could get up—her legs were shaking—Ruby followed her mother out. Then, just as Anjoli was about to leave the room, a wind rose and a blast came in through the window. With a howl it banged the door shut. And just then, there was a flash of lightning in the sky. And a faint smell of men's cologne filled the room. Anjoli's heart began to race. She nervously glanced at the mirror and her heart missed a beat. Goodness gracious! There he was! That man in white. Staring hard at Anjoli. He looked displeased. Rather annoyed. Anjoli stumbled and fell and somehow managed to catch hold of the doorknob—it felt slippery and very cold; the room temperature too seemed to take a sudden dip—and opening the door, ran out and fell straight onto her Dad's lap.

'What's the matter, Ann? Why, you're perspiring?' the doting father asked, stroking his daughter's hair. Turning to Ruby, he chided her, 'Have you been frightening your sister, Ruby? Lying again?'

Now, for the first time Anjoli came to the rescue of her little sister. 'Ruby's not lying Dad. He is there—in the mirror! I saw him! There's a man in the mirror!'

Mr and Mrs Bannerji were speechless. They exchanged a long worried look. What was wrong with their girls? Were they reading too many nonsense tales? Too many ghost stories?

Mrs Bannerji, who sat frozen on her chair, was truly perturbed. 'This has been going on for sometime. First, Ruby said she saw him. And now Anjoli. Look at their faces!'

'And look at your face, ma'am,' Mr Bannerji smiled, addressing his wife. To lighten the situation he jokingly added. 'Are you going to say, too, that there's a man in Anjoli's mirror?'

Mr Bannerji laughed.

Mrs Bannerji laughed too. But her face was as pale as her girls were for she could sense the terror in Ann's heart. And that look of certainty on Ruby's face gave her the shivers. At once, she sent her husband to the children's room to check it out himself. This act, she was sure, would pacify her eldest daughter.

'Why, I see nothing. Nobody's in here, silly girls!' called back Mr Bannerji. He shut the door and came over shaking his head. 'How absurd can you all get?'

'Well girls, that settles it! There's no one there,' Mrs Bannerji said with visible relief.

But Anjoli insisted, 'I'm going to sleep with you, Mom! He's there in my mirror!'

'Tonight, you may sleep with us. Both of you. But tomorrow, I don't want anymore stories,' Mrs Bannerji reproved.

'But tomorrow, he isn't going to go away,' Ruby said with a straight face.

Anjoli gasped.

Mr Bannerji pretended to ignore the children and began to eat. Mrs Bannerji looked nervous.

That night, when the children fell asleep, Mr Bannerji said, 'We must consul Dr P. K. Majumdar. He's the best child psychologist in the city. I'm beginning to get really worried.'

'My daughters are not mad,' Mrs Bannerji protested. 'You never know with antique stuff!' his wife stated. 'I think you'd better sell if off. I don't want it in my house. A mirror like that, anyone will want to buy.'

Mr Bannerji sighed.

The next day, Anjoli avoided going to her room. Ruby fetched her sister's clothes and schoolbooks from her desk and Anjoli did her homework sitting in the dining room. It was Sunday, and after weeks the sky didn't pour. In the afternoon, Anjoli and Ruby went for a walk in the park. And guess whom they met? Mr Roy, the man who auctioned old furniture.

He called out. 'There you are Anjoli! Your father was there to see me this morning. He told me he was looking for a buyer for the mirror. Why, did you not like it? I've an antique three-legged table made of the finest teak. It came this evening. Would your father be interested?' he asked.

Anjoli was sad to hear that the mirror would now be sold off. However, she asked with growing curiosity, 'Where did you get that mirror from?'

'A lovely piece, isn't it? Exquisite, I'd say! Won't find another anywhere in India,' Mr Roy said.

Was the man deaf? Anjoli raised her voice, 'But where did you get it from, uncle?'

'It must be a hundred years old,' Mr Roy beamed.

'A hundred years old?' Anjoli exclaimed.

'Yes, a hundred years old. It belonged to Mr John's mother. She gave it to her daughter-in-law, Betty John, the beautiful lady of Park Circus. I'd always had an eye on it. John had been selling their old articles to me for many years. But he wouldn't agree to parting with the mirror, even after Mrs John died a couple of years ago. John said, "My mother was fond of it. My wife was fond of it. Betty spent hours at it doing up her lovely hair and make-up." But last year, when John died, a distant relation of theirs sold off all their possessions and their house. That's how I got the mirror. You've got it now, but your father doesn't want it suddenly. Why?' Mr Roy asked grinning at Anjoli. He was an aged man and had endearing ways.

'We know him! It's Mr John who is in our mirror!' Ruby suddenly blabbered.

'What, what?' Mr Roy asked looking curiously at the girl. 'Is she your sister?' he asked, and pointing his thin bony finger to his head he indicated that all was not right with her head.

Anjoli quickly turned her back and walked back home clutching Ruby's hand. 'Goodbye, uncle,' she called out.

That very evening the Bannerjis had visitors. A young man and his wife rang the doorbell and were ushered in straight to the children's bedroom.

'This is the mirror and the dressing-table for sale,' Mr Bannerji said.

'How beautiful!' the woman exclaimed.

Anjoli wanted to cry. She loved the mirror but was afraid of it. Standing at the door, she cast a quick sideways glance at it. Why, there was no one in it. Was it then her wild imagination? It was raining cats and dogs that awful night when she thought she saw him in it. The sky was drumming with thunder. The wind was tearing at the tops of the tress. In a situation like that one was bound to imagine things. Or, was it because of Ruby's influence? After all, if someone kept telling you stories and acted and behaved in the strange way she did, you were bound to be affected by it, thought Anjoli. Naughty girl! Because of Ruby, she was going to lose her mirror. An awful feeling of loss and sadness came over Anjoli. Then, she suddenly recalled the man in white who had actually come asking for the mirror. Anjoli had to admit that there was some mystery in it, after all.

With a sigh, Anjoli gave one last glance at the mirror as it was carted away. How beautiful it was! Suddenly, to her horror, Mr

John's face appeared in it. His hair shining like moonlight. His eyes blazing. His skin as white as the lilies. Only Anjoli could see him. And Ruby, who came in just then, stopped dead. The children screamed, 'There is Mr John!'

Mr Bannerji smiled with embarrassment at the man and the woman who looked puzzled. Then, suddenly, a loud smash, like glass breaking, came from the mirror. An awful sound it was! As if someone had got into a fit of rage and was pounding glass. And then, to everyone's horror, the mirror cracked.

The mirror, the lovely mirror, would never be of use to anyone, anymore. It could never be anyone's mirror, except Mrs John's. Mr John had made sure of that.

The Werewolf

C.A. KINCAID

It was a terribly hot afternoon in July, some fifty years ago, in Upper Sind. In the Deccan, cooling showers had turned the hard earth, baked by the summer winds, into a perfect paradise. The soil there was bright with long green grass. The hills rose emerald to the sky, although their summits were often veiled by the monsoon mists; and delightful breezes swept over the glad earth to the great joy of foreign sojourners in the Indian plateau. Even in the Punjab and the Gangetic valley, heavy rain had fallen, and if the air seemed stuffy to the traveller from southern India, his eyes rejoiced in the rich foliage and endless maize fields, while his ears listened joyfully to the murmuring sound of new-born streams, as they tinkled and splashed on their way to join the brimming rivers.

In Upper Sind, the landscape was quite different. Rain hardly ever falls there except in the cold weather, and while more favoured parts of India revel in the monsoon, none of it reaches that strange land. Irrigated by canals from the Indus, the fields are in winter gay with young wheat, and he who visits Upper Sind in January may well think that he has reached some heavenly spot. But let him go there in July or August and he will soon change his opinion. All day long the hot wind roars, driving the mercury up to 120° in the shade; nor is there much relief at night. The hot wind drops, but the thermometer still marks over a hundred; the sandflies and mosquitoes buzz all night, and moonbeams like the rays of a powerful electric headlight pour down on the would-be sleeper's face, making slumbering exceedingly difficult.

In the middle of this sunsplashed region is Sehwan, formerly an important town, but now greatly sunk in importance. One thing it still claims with justice is that it is one of the hottest places on earth. A Persian poet once in the bitterness of his heart asked the Almighty why, after making Sehwan and Sibi, he thought it worthwhile to make Hell. The afternoon on which this story opens was well worthy of Sehwan's ancient reputation. The train steamed slowly into Sehwan station from Sukkur. The railway on the left bank of the Indus had not then been built, so the railtrack passed through Sehwan on its way to Karachi and the seacoast. The last carriage on the train was the saloon of the Traffic Superintendent. It was far roomier than the ordinary first class carriages, as befitted the quarters of a senior railway official; but nothing could keep out the heat or make the interior cool. The shutters were closed. A railway coolie pulled a diminutive punka fixed on the roof, but he merely stirred into motion the heavy, hot air. There were two occupants of the saloon; one was the Traffic Superintendent, Frank Bollinger; the other was a Major Sinclair, whom he had known for some years. He had invited his friend to share the saloon instead of sweltering in the first class compartment and sharing it with two missionaries, their wives and babies.

'I shall be devoutly thankful,' said Bollinger, 'when we get out of this Hell into the monsoon area.'

'When will that be?'

'Once we pass the Lakhi gorge it will be better. They say the monsoon dies there and so they call the gorge the gate of Hell. It is true that once past that frightful mass of heated limestone, one does begin to feel a breath of cooler air. It gradually grows in strength; so we ought to get a good night on our way to Karachi.'

'I am very glad to hear that. I could not sleep a wink in this part of the world, could you?'

'Oh! I have had such a long experience of hot nights that I might; but thank God! there will be no need to make the experiment.'

Just then, the train drew up in Sehwan station. The station master, Isarmal, who had known Bollinger in earlier days, came running up to pay his respects. His face beamed all over with the pleasure that an Indian almost always feels at meeting a former English friend. Bollinger remembered well the little station master and was also very glad to see him and have a chat over old times.

To let the two old acquaintances have their talk out, Major Sinclair got out of the carriage and strolled about on the platform. After Bollinger and Isarmal had been gossiping together for about a quarter of an hour, the former said suddenly:

'I say, Mr Isarmal, why are we staying here so long? I never remember waiting more than five minutes at Sehwan before.'

'I am afraid, Sir—I am very sorry, Sir—the river has breached the line some four miles down and the train cannot go on until tomorrow morning.'

'Do you mean to say that we shall have to stay all night in this inferno? I am afraid, the Major Sahib will not like that at all. He was grumbling at the heat when the train was moving; what he'll say when he hears that we will have to pass the night in a stationary train, I can't think. He will swear horribly.'

'Yes indeed, Sir,' said Mr Isarmal, anxious to agree to everything his English friend said, 'the Major Sahib will swear horribly.'

Just then all doubts were settled by the arrival of Sinclair in a frightful temper. After so varied an outburst of blasphemy that it filled Bollinger with respectful awe, he shouted:

'Damn it all, Bollinger, have you heard that we have to spend the night in this hellhole?'

'Yes; I'm awfully sorry, old chap; but it cannot be helped. The Indus is in flood and it is just as capricious as a spoilt harlot. Still, it will only be for one night and you'll be able to wipe out your arrears of sleep, when we near Karachi.'

'My dear chap, I'm not going to sleep in your saloon. I have just been talking to the khansama of the rest-house. He says it is up on the top of a hill and all night one gets a cool breeze from the river. He'll give us dinner and he'll call us at six a.m. so that we shan't miss the train. He'll put our beds out in the open and he swears that we'll be able to sleep like tops.'

Just then the khansama himself came up. He was a powerfully built Panjabi Musulman with a long black beard and very strange yellow eyes. His face in repose had a villainous expression. He had a smile that rarely came off, but it was a very unpleasant one; it was rather like the smile of a savage Alsatian fawning on its master. He could speak a little broken English, which in the case of poor linguists like Major Sinclair was a great attraction. On reaching the saloon he stood at the door and addressing Bollinger very deferentially, said:

'The Major Sahib, he coming to resthouse. Sahib, please come, too, and have good night in cool breeze. I give good dinner and you get good sleep and I wake you six a.m. Madras time. Down here too dammed hot, you get no sleep at all, Sahib.'

Bollinger could not help thinking of the old nursery rhyme 'Won't you walk into my parlour said the spider to the fly' and anyway he had no wish to leave his comfortable saloon and a dinner served by his own servants for a hard bed and a doubtful meal at a rest-house half a mile away. He politely thanked the khansama.

'No, Khansama; I shall be quite all right here. It may be hot, but I doubt whether it will be any cooler on the top of your Himalayan peak. After all, I have been there and it is only about thirty feet high and my dinner will be better than any you can give me.'

The khansama's yellow eyes flashed disagreeably, but he continued as before to smile in his canine way and to repeat mechanically:

'Sahib, I give you very good dinner. A cool breeze will blow all night. You get good sleep and to-morrow I call you at six a.m. Madras time.'

At last, Bollinger said impatiently: 'It's no use going on jabbering like that. I'm just not going to your rest-house. I'm going to stay here and there's an end of it.'

Suddenly, Sinclair broke in: 'Well, I'm not. I'm damned if I'm going to spend the night in your sardine box.' Turning to his butler, he said: 'Here, boy, get my luggage out of the saloon and put it in a tonga and tell the man to drive to the rest-house. You can come with the khansama in another.'

Bollinger, taken aback, replied with stiff courtesy: 'My dear Sinclair, you must, of course, please yourself. I shall stay in the old sardine box and you'll have a good dinner and a capital night. Goodnight!'

The Major, without troubling to answer, walked off with the khansama and Bollinger resumed his talk with Mr Isarmal, the station master.

When the khansama and Sinclair had passed out of sight, Isarmal suddenly said in a low earnest voice: 'Thank God, you did not go, Sahib, with that terrible man. If you had you would be as good as dead already. The Major Sahib will not be alive tomorrow.'

'What on earth are you talking about, Isarmal?'

'It is that khansama, sir. He is not really a man, but a—a—a—I have forgotten the English word; we call it in Sindi a *lakhibaghar*.'

'A hyena, you mean,' said Bollinger, who knew some Sindi.

'Yes, Sahib, he turns himself every night into a hyena and eats anyone whom he finds sleeping alone on a cot in the open. We say that he is the reincarnation of a horrible man called Anu Kasai.'

'Oh, you mean that fellow who ate up Bodlo Bahar?'

'Yes, I see the Sahib knows the story. Bodlo Bahar was the disciple of our great Sehwan saint Lal Shabaz. One day he disappeared. The following morning one of the saint's disciples saw that the bits of mutton that he was cooking for his dinner were jumping about strangely in his pot. Other disciples had the same tale to tell. So, Lal Shahbaz said: "It must be our Bodlo Bahar," and went to the Governor of Sehwan. He asked from whom they had bought the mutton. They all said, "From the butcher Anu Kasai." Now, this wicked man had once been very prosperous, but he had fallen on evil days; and having no money to buy sheep, he used to murder strangers and sell their flesh as mutton. The Governor arrested Anu Kasai and searched his shop and house. They were full of human bones. He had for months escaped punishment, but he was caught when he killed a saint like Bodlo Bahar.'

'How did the Governor punish him?'

'He walled him up in the battlements of Sehwan fort, that is the hill on which the rest-house now stands. As you pass it you can see a sort of hollow in the side of it. That is where they walled up Anu the butcher.'

'But what is this talk of the khansama being his reincarnation?'

'Well, Sahib, he has only been here three or four months and yet several people in the town have disappeared. Whenever they have done so, a large hyena has been seen galloping through Sehwan. Not only that, but two Chota Sahibs (subordinate Europeans) who went to the rest-house have also disappeared. The khansama said the same in both cases. They dined and slept outside the rest-house, but when he brought the tea next morning they had vanished. We say the khansama turns himself into a hyena and eats them during the night. You will never see the Major Sahib again,

I am afraid; but thank God you are here! Still, at night close the doors and windows of your saloon, otherwise that khansama may attack you even here. We always shut ourselves in at night, although it is so hot.'

Bollinger was far too wise to laugh at the station master's story. He did not believe that the khansama and the hyena were the same: but remembering his villainous expression he did think it possible that he was a murderer; and after Isarmal had left, he began to wonder what he should do.

At last, he determined to go to the rest-house and share the danger, if any, with Sinclair. He had no gun, but he had a long heavy hunting knife that, had it been a bit sharper, would have been a very efficient weapon. He did not bother to take his servant as he did not wish to have him on his hands, too. In the glare of the setting sun he walked alone along the dusty limestone road and then up the steep side of the old fort, now the rest-house. He noticed, as he walked, a depression in the fort wall and said to himself that that must be the place where they walled up Anu Kasai. At last, he reached the top of the old fort. It formed a plateau and in the centre was the rest-house. He arrived just as Sinclair was sitting down to dinner outside the building. It certainly was far cooler than in the station siding, for a cool breeze blew from the river.

'Come along, Bollinger, I am so glad you have come,' said Sinclair cordially. 'You must dine with me. We can get a good night here in the breeze. I say, I'm awfully sorry for having been so grumpy just now. I cannot make out what came over me.'

'Oh, that's all right!' said Bollinger cheerily, wondering secretly what Sinclair would think of Isarmal's tale. The khansama also welcomed Bollinger and made ready a place for him. He then served an excellent dinner and after dinner began to put the two officers' cots outside.

'Oh, don't do that, we shall sleep inside.'

'It will be damned hot, almost as hot as in your saloon below.'

'Oh no, we shall leave the windows open and so get a through draught. The station master tells me that the place is alive with scorpions and that one may well get stung if one sleeps outside.'

Sinclair looked towards the khansama, but he made no objection, so Sinclair said, 'Very well; but it will be so hot that we shall not get a wink of sleep.'

'Oh well, no matter, we'll play picquet until midnight. After that it will cool down sufficiently for us to sleep indoors."

'Right-o!' said Sinclair gloomily, wishing Bollinger in the infernal regions.

From nine on, the two men played cards and Bollinger deliberately played badly so that Sinclair might win and remain interested in the game. The simple device succeeded and Sinclair was so pleased that at 11 p.m. he was still absorbed in the picquet. Just then, someone tried the door, but Bollinger had bolted it. A few seconds later, the khansama appeared at the window in front of which had been fixed wire netting to keep the numerous pigeons from soiling the rooms.

'I have brought iced lemonade for the Sahibs,' said the khansama with an obsequious grin. Bollinger thought that he had never seen any man with such an odious expression, and his yellow eyes were twinkling, as if with some horrible anticipation.

'All right,' said Sinclair. 'I'll open the door.' He rose, and before Bollinger could stop him he had drawn the bolt. Bollinger pushed him aside and flung his weight against the door. It was too late. A huge paw and the muzzle of a monstrous hyena forced their way through the opening. Bollinger brought his knife down with all his strength on the paw. It was too blunt to cut deeply through the hair, but the blow was a heavy one and numbed the brute's limb. A bloodcurdling growl followed and the paw and snout were withdrawn. Bollinger slammed the door and shot the bolt.

'Thank God, we got the better of that brute. I fancy we're rid of it for the night!'

Hearing a noise he looked round and cried 'By God! we're not!' Through a gap in the netting of one of the windows the hyena had forced its head and in a few seconds would have been in the room. This time, Bollinger decided to use the point and not the edge of his knife. He made a thrust at the brute's throat. It swung its head aside in time to avoid a fatal stab; nevertheless, the knife scored a deep cut in its neck. It gave another bloodcurdling growl, dragged out its head and, with blood streaming from its wound, it raced off laughing in the diabolical way that hyenas do when hurt.

'By Jove! What an escape!' said Sinclair thankfully; 'but I suppose you fight that sort of brute everyday.'

'No, thank Heaven, I don't,' and then Bollinger told Sinclair the station master's story and how, on hearing it, he had come to the rest-house to see if his help was needed.

Sinclair went up to Bollinger and shook him cordially by the hand: 'Then, my dear chap, I owe you my life. I cannot say how grateful I feel. I shall never forget your help.'

The other smiled and said: 'Oh, nonsense! You'd have done the same for me. But, I say, didn't you bring your boy with you?'

'Yes, I did. I wonder where he is. I hope to goodness the khansama has not killed him.'

'Well, we had better go and look but we must be very wary, for if the hyena killed your boy, he'll come back.'

'All right, come along. You've got a knife, haven't you? I'am afraid I've got nothing.'

The two men went to the back of the rest-house and there they found below a slight slope the dead body of Sinclair's Goanese servant. His throat was completely torn open. The hyena must have crept up noiselessly to the servant's bed and torn out his throat, killing him instantly. Then, it must have again become the khansama and tried to enter the rest-house with the iced lemonade.

Sinclair stood sorrowfully by the dead man, who had been many years in his service and to whom he was greatly attached.

'I say, we can't do anything for the poor chap,' said Bollinger, 'so we had better go straight back to the rest-house. I have a horrid feeling that the brute is somewhere near, coming back to its kill. By God! there it is!'

He pointed to where a huge striped form was galloping straight for them. The two men ran for the rest-house as fast as they could; they only reached it in time through Bollinger throwing his coat at the brute's head and thus gaining a moment's respite.

'I wonder what it will do now,' said Sinclair, but it did nothing. It went slowly back to the body of the Goanese and began to crunch it up, every now and then breaking into screams of diabolical laughter when its neck hurt it.

'I wish to God I had a gun', said Bollinger, 'but as we haven't, let's try to get some sleep. One will sit up and watch while the other lies down. I'll sit up first.'

'All right,' said Sinclair, and lying down on one of the cots fell dead asleep in spite of the heat and his servant's death.

Bollinger sat in a chair and tried as best he could to keep awake. Still, he must have dropped off for a minute or so, for waking up with a start he saw in the bright moonlight the baleful glare of the hyena's eyes as it stared at him through the wire netting. He drew his knife and ran with a shout towards the netting, but the hyena with a growl of fury jumped back and galloped off.

Sinclair woke and hearing what had happened said: 'We must both sit up, otherwise the brute will return and get us.'

The two friends sat and smoked and talked through the weary hours until about 5:30 a.m. when their troubles came to an end. A crowd of Sindis, led by Isarmal, came to the rest-house to see what had happened to the two Englishmen.

'God be praised!' exclaimed Isarmal earnestly. 'Nothing has happened and you are both safe!'

'We are safe, but look at this,' and Bollinger led the crowd of Sindis to the half-eaten remains of the unfortunate Goanese: 'The khansama killed him!'

Isarmal's face grew grim, and turning to the rest of the crowd he cried: 'Brothers, we are Sindis. The khansama is a Panjabi and therefore of a race that we hate. He is clearly the reincarnation of Anu Kasai. When the train has gone we must deal with him.'

The two Englishmen walked back with Isarmal to the station, where the train was standing; as they walked, Bollinger related the events of the night. Afterwards, Isarmal repeated the story in Sindi to the men following him. On reaching the saloon nothing more was said. The two weary travellers got in and Isarmal, as he waved on the train, turned to the Sindis, who were mostly Musulmans, and cried: 'The Sahibs are safe, *Alhamdalilla* (God be praised)!'

After a hot, slow journey, the Englishmen reached Karachi. On the way Bollinger said: 'I fancy the khansama has had a bad quarter of an hour. He is a Panjabi and, as Isarmal said, of a race hated by the Sindis.'

'But why do the Sindis hate the Panjabis? I like them.'

'I really do not quite know. Perhaps, like French and Germans, Sindis and Panjabis live too near together. The Panjabis, too, are bigger men as a rule than the Sindis and they throw their weight about. The Sindis seem very much afraid of them. Indeed I remember hearing a Sindi proverb that says: "If one Panjabi comes, sit still and say nothing. If two come, then pack up your kit at once, abandon your house and clear out." Anyway, Panjabis are not liked in these parts.'

'They don't seem to be!'

Two mornings after their arrival, Davidson, the District Superintendent of Police, burst unceremoniously into Bollinger's bungalow and onto the verandah, where he was having his *chota hazri* or morning tea.

'I'm sorry, Bollinger, but I must see you. I have just received an official report from the Chief Constable of Sehwan to the effect that the villagers, led by the station master, broke into the khansama's house, dragged him out, although he was very ill, and walled him into the battlements of the old fort. He hints that you know something about it. In the meantime, he has arrested the station master, Isarmal I think he calls him.'

'Half a mo', Davidson! I fancy I have a letter from the station master in my morning post. I'll open it.' Tearing open the envelope, Bollinger read aloud the following note, very short and quaintly expressed:

> Honoured Sir,
> The Chief Constable of Sehwan, who is a Panjabi, is troubling us because of the death of that Anu Kasai, the khansama. After Your Honour's departure we went to his house and found him very ill from a severe wound in the throat. We found in his house the property of the two missing Chota Sahibs; seeing this he became very obstinate and refused to answer our questions. Very soon he died. When dead, we put him where Anu Kasai was walled up. The Sahib knows the facts and will kindly do the needful.

'Well, Bollinger, he says you know the facts, for goodness sake let me have them.'

Bollinger told the full story of the adventure and Sinclair supported him in every detail. Still, as told in an Englishman's house in Karachi, it did not sound very convincing.

'Hang it all, Bollinger!' You can't expect me to believe this tale of a werewolf.'

'Well, Isarmal says that they found in the khansama's house the property of those two missing subordinates. That raises a presumption that he is a murderer, anyway.'

'The Chief Constable says nothing about that.'

'He is a brother Panjabi and can scarcely be expected to. Look here, instead of arguing, let's go off and call on the Commissioner. He is the Inspector-General of Police, as well as of everything else and we'll abide by his orders.'

'Right-o!' said the District Superintendent and at 11 a.m. all three men met to call on Government House.

The Commissioner was a big genial man, who combined with a very cordial manner a vast amount of commonsense. He greeted all three men pleasantly. Then, he turned to the D.S.P. who was in uniform:

'Well, Davidson, what's the trouble?'

'I think, Sir, Bollinger had better tell you his yarn first and then I'll supplement it with my information.'

'Capital! Go ahead, Bollinger.'

The railwayman repeated his story and Sinclair confirmed it. Then, Davidson shewed the Commissioner his Chief Constable's report and Bollinger produced Isarmal's letter.

The Commissioner's keen intellect grasped immediately all the facts and came at once to a decision.

'Look here, Bollinger, you can't expect me to accept as gospel your story of the werewolf or werehyena; but the khansama seems to have been a murderer all right. The discovery in his house of the property of the two subordinates points to that. I have often been worried as to what became of them. Again, I do not see why we should not believe Isarmal's statement that they did not wall in the khansama until he was dead. Anyway, it will be impossible to disprove it; for all the eye-witnesses will support Isarmal. In any case, if you go into the witness box, Bollinger, and tell your adventure with the khansama-cum-hyena, my administration will be the laughing stock of all India. Think how the young lions of the *Pioneer* will sharpen their wit at our expense. No! No, we must stop the prosecution at all costs. Look here, Davidson, you wire to the Chief Constable to drop the case and release Isarmal and any others he may have arrested. I shall myself transfer to some other district the Chief Constable; for he seems to have been very slack over the disappearance of the two subordinates. Well, good morning.'

Isarmal was duly released and resumed his duties as station master. But Bollinger did not forget him. Using his influence with the railway chiefs, he got Isarmal first promoted to be station master of Radhan and then of Sukkur, a very important post. This Isarmal retained until his retirement. He lived for many years on an ample pension and nothing gave him greater pleasure than to tell the story of the Panjabi who could turn himself into a hyena and how he nearly ate up the two Sahibs. He gave ample credit to Bollinger Sahib for his courage and resource; but the person for whom he reserved the fullest commendation was none other than Mr Isarmal, late station master of Sukkur.

At The Pit's Mouth

RUDYARD KIPLING

Once upon a time there was a Man and his Wife and a Tertium Quid. All three were unwise, but the Wife was the unwisest. The Man should have looked after his Wife, who should have avoided the Tertium Quid, who, again, should have married a wife of his own, after clean and open flirtations, to which nobody can possibly object, round Jakko or Observatory Hill. When you see a young man with his pony in a white lather, and his hat on the back of his head flying downhill at fifteen miles an hour to meet a girl who will be properly surprised to meet him, you naturally approve of that young man, and wish him Staff appointments, and take an interest in his welfare, and, as the proper time comes, give them sugar-tongs or side-saddles according to your means and generosity.

The Tertium Quid flew downhill on horseback, but it was to meet the Man's Wife; and when he flew uphill it was for the same end. The Man was in the Plains, earning money for the Wife to spend on dresses and four-hundred-rupee bracelets, and inexpensive luxuries of that kind. He worked very hard, and sent her a letter or a post-card daily. She also wrote to him daily, and said that she was longing for him to come up to Simla. The Tertium Quid used to lean over her shoulder and laugh as she wrote the notes. Then the two would ride to the Post-office together.

Now, Simla is a strange place and its customs are peculiar; nor is any man who has not spent at least ten seasons there qualified to pass judgment on circumstantial evidence, which is the most untrustworthy in the Courts. For these reasons, and for others which need not appear, I decline to state positively whether there was anything irretrievably wrong in the relations between the Man's Wife and the Tertium Quid. If there was, and hereon you must form your own opinion, it was the Man's Wife's fault. She was kittenish in her manners, wearing generally an air of soft and fluffy innocence. But she was deadlily learned and evil-instructed; and, now and again, when the mask dropped, men saw this, shuddered and—almost drew back. Men are occasionally particular, and the least particular men are always the most exacting.

Simla is eccentric in its fashion of treating friendships. Certain attachments which have set and crystallised through half a dozen seasons acquire almost the sanctity of the marriage bond, and are revered as such. Again, certain attachments equally old, and, to all appearance, equally venerable, never seem to win any recognised official status; while a chance-sprung acquaintance, not two months born, steps into the place which by right belongs to the senior. There is no law reducible to print which regulates these affairs.

Some people have a gift which secures them infinite toleration, and others have not. The Man's Wife had not. If she looked over the garden wall, for instance, women taxed her with stealing their husbands. She complained pathetically that she was not allowed to choose her own friends. When she put up her big white muff to her lips, and gazed over it and under her eyebrows at you as she said this thing, you felt that she had been infamously misjudged, and that all the other women's instincts were all wrong; which was absurd. She was not allowed to own the Tertium Quid in peace; and was so strangely constructed that she would not have enjoyed peace had she been so permitted. She preferred some semblance of intrigue to cloak even her most commonplace actions.

After two months of riding, first round Jakko, then Elysium, then Summer Hill, then Observatory Hill, then under Jutogh, and lastly up and down the Cart Road as far as the Tara Devi gap in the dusk, she said to the Tertium Quid, 'Frank, people say we are too much together, and people are so horrid.'

The Tertium Quid pulled his moustache, and replied that horrid people were unworthy of the consideration of nice people.

'But they have done more than talk—they have written—written to my hubby—I'm sure of it,' said the Man's Wife, and she pulled a letter from her husband out of her saddle-pocket and gave it to the Tertium Quid.

It was an honest letter, written by an honest man, then stewing in the Plains on two hundred rupees a month (for he allowed his wife eight hundred and fifty), and in a silk banian and cotton trousers. It is said that, perhaps, she had not thought of the unwisdom of allowing her name to be so generally coupled with the Tertium

Quid's; that she was too much of a child to understand the dangers of that sort of thing; that he, her husband, was the last man in the world to interfere jealously with her little amusements and interests, but that it would be better were she to drop the Tertium Quid quietly and for her husband's sake. The letter was sweetened with many pretty little pet names, and it amused the Tertium Quid considerably. He and She laughed over it, so that you, fifty yards away, could see their shoulders shaking while the horses slouched along side by side.

Their conversation was not worth reporting. The upshot of it was that, next day, no one saw the Man's Wife and the Tertium Quid together. They had both gone down to the Cemetery, which, as a rule, is only visited officially by the inhabitants of Simla.

A Simla funeral with the clergyman riding, the mourners riding, and the coffin creaking as it swings between the bearers, is one of the most depressing things on this earth, particularly when the procession passes under the wet, dank dip beneath the Rockcliffe Hotel, where the sun is shut out, and all the hill streams are wailing and weeping together as they go down the valleys.

Occasionally, folk tend the graves, but we in India shift and are transferred so often that, at the end of the second year, the Dead have no friends—only acquaintances who are far too busy amusing themselves up the hill to attend to old partners. The idea of using a Cemetery as a rendezvous is distinctly a feminine one. A man would have said simply, 'Let people talk. We'll go down the Mall.' A woman is made differently, especially if she be such a woman as the Man's Wife. She and the Tertium Quid enjoyed each other's society among the graves of men and women whom they had known and danced with aforetime.

They used to take a big horse-blanket and sit on the grass a little to the left of the lower end, where there is a dip in the ground, and where the occupied graves stop short and the ready-made ones are not ready. Each well-regulated Indian Cemetery keeps half a dozen graves permanently open for contingencies and incidental wear and tear. In the Hills these are more usually baby's size, because children who come up weakened and sick from the Plains often succumb to the effects of the Rains in the Hills or get pneumonia from their *ayahs* taking them through damp pine-woods after the sun has set. In Cantonments, of course, the man's size is more in request; these arrangements varying with the climate and population.

One day when the Man's Wife and the Tertium Quid had just arrived in the Cemetery, they saw some coolies breaking ground. They had marked out a full-size grave, and the Tertium Quid asked them whether any Sahib was sick. They said that they did not know; but it was an order that they should dig a Sahib's grave.

'Work away,' said the Tertium Quid, 'and let's see how it's done.'

The coolies worked away, and the Man's Wife and the Tertium Quid watched and talked for a couple of hours while the grave was being deepened. Then a coolie, taking the earth in baskets as it was thrown up, jumped over the grave.

'That's queer,' said the Tertium Quid. 'Where's my ulster?'

'What's queer?' said the Man's Wife.

'I have got a chill down my back—just as if a goose had walked over my grave.'

'Why do you look at the thing, then?' said the Man's Wife. 'Let us go.'

The Tertium Quid stood at the head of the grave, and stared without answering for a space. Then he said, dropping a pebble down, 'It is nasty—and cold: horribly cold. I don't think I shall come to the Cemetery any more. I don't think grave-digging is cheerful.'

The two talked and agreed that the Cemetery was depressing. They also arranged for a ride next day out from the Cemetery through the Mashobra Tunnel up to Fagoo and back, because all the world was going to a garden-party at Viceregal Lodge, and all the people of Mashobra would go too.

Coming up the Cemetery road, the Tertium Quid's horse tried to bolt uphill, being tired with standing so long, and managed to strain a back sinew.

'I shall have to take the mare tomorrow,' said the Tertium Quid, 'and she will stand nothing heavier than a snaffle.'

They made their arrangements to meet in the Cemetery, after allowing all the Mashobra people time to pass into Simla. That night it rained heavily, and, next day, when the Tertium Quid came to the trysting-place, he saw that the new grave had a foot of water in it, the ground being a tough and sour clay.

'Jove! That looks beastly,' said the Tertium Quid. 'Fancy being boarded up and dropped into that well!'

They then started off to Fagoo, the mare playing with the snaffle and picking her way as though she were shod with satin, and the sun shining divinely. The road below Mashobra to Fagoo is officially styled the Himalayan-Thibet Road; but in spite of its name it is not much more than six feet wide in most places, and the drop into the valley below may be anything between one and two thousand feet.

'Now we're going to Thibet,' said the Man's Wife merrily, as the horses drew near to Fagoo. She was riding on the cliff-side.

'Into Thibet,' said the Tertium Quid, 'ever so far from people who say horrid things, and hubbies who write stupid letters. With you—to the end of the world!'

A coolie carrying a log of wood came round a corner, and the mare went wide to avoid him—forefeet in and haunches out, as a sensible mare should go.

'To the world's end,' said the Man's Wife, and looked unspeakable things over her near shoulder at the Tertium Quid.

He was smiling, but, while she looked, the smile froze stiff as it were on his face, and changed to a nervous grin—the sort of grin men wear when they are not quite easy in their saddles. The mare seemed to be sinking by the stern, and her nostrils cracked while she was trying to realise what was happening. The rain of the night before had rotted the drop-side of the Himalayan-Thibet Road, and it was giving way under her. 'What are you doing?' said the man's Wife. The Tertium Quid gave no answer. He grinned nervously and set his spurs into the mare, who rapped with her forefeet on the road, and the struggle began. The Man's Wife screamed, 'Oh, Frank, get off!'

But the Tertium Quid was glued to the saddle—his face blue and white—and he looked into the Man's Wife's eyes. Then the Man's Wife clutched at the mare's head and caught her by the nose instead of the bridle. The brute threw up her head and went down with a scream, the Tertium Quid upon her, and the nervous grin still set on his face. The Man's Wife heard the tinkle-tinkle of little stones and loose earth falling off the roadway, and the sliding roar of the man and horse going down. Then everything was quiet, and she called on Frank to leave his mare and walk up. But Frank did not answer. He was underneath the mare, nine hundred feet below, spoiling a patch of Indian corn.

As the revellers came back from Viceregal Lodge in the mists of the evening, they met a temporarily insane woman, on a temporarily mad horse, swinging round the corners, with her eyes and her mouth open, and her head like the head of a Medusa. She was stopped by a man at the risk of his life, and taken out of the saddle, a limp heap, and put on the bank to explain herself. This wasted twenty minutes, and then she was sent home in a lady's rickshaw, still with her mouth open and her hands picking at her riding-gloves.

She was in bed through the following three days, which were rainy; so she missed attending the funeral of the Tertium Quid, who was lowered into eighteen inches of water, instead of the twelve to which he had first objected.

Boomerang

Oscar Cook

Warwick threw himself into a chair beside me, hitched up his trousers, and, leaning across, tapped me on the knee. 'You remember the story about Mendingham which you told me?' he asked.

I nodded. I was not likely to forget that affair. 'Well,' he went on, 'I've got as good a one to tell you. Had it straight from the filly's mouth, so to speak—and it's red-hot.'

I edged away in my chair, for there was something positively ghoulish in his delight, in the coarse way by which he referred to a woman, and one who, if my inference were correct, must have known tragedy. But there is no stopping Warwick: he knows or admits no finer feelings or shame when his thirst for 'copy' is aroused. Like the little boy in the well-known picture, 'he won't be happy till he's "quenched" it'.

I ordered drinks, and when they had been served and we were alone, bade him get on with his sordid story.

'It's a wild tale,' he began, 'of two planter fellows in the interior of Borneo—and, as usual, there's a woman.'

'*The* woman?' I could not refrain from asking, thinking of his earlier remark.

'The same,' he replied. 'A veritable golden-haired filly, only her mane is streaked with grey and there's a great livid scar or weal right round her neck. She's the wife of Leopold Thring. The other end of the triangle is Clifford Macy'

'And where do you come in?' I inquired.

Warwick closed one eye and pursed his lips.

'As a spinner of yarns,' he answered sententiously. Then, with a return to his usual cynicism, 'The filly is down and out, but for some silly religious scruples feels she must live. I bought the story, therefore, after verifying the facts. Shall I go on?'

I nodded, for I must admit I was genuinely interested. The eternal triangle always intrigues: set in the wilds of Borneo it promised a variation of incident unusually refreshing in these sophisticated days. Besides, that scar was eloquent.

Warwick chuckled.

'The two men were partners,' he went on, 'on a small experimental estate far up in the interior. They had been at it for six years and were just about to reap the fruits of their labours very handsomely. Incidentally, Macy had been out in the Colony the full six years—and the strain was beginning to tell. Thring had been home eighteen months before, and on coming back had brought his bride, Rhona.

'That was the beginning of the trouble. It split up the partnership: brought in a new element: meant the building of a new bungalow.'

'For Macy?' I asked.

'Yes. And he didn't take kindly to it. He had got set. And then there was the loneliness of night after night alone, while the others—you understand?'

I nodded.

'Well,' Warwick continued, 'the expected happened. Macy flirted, philandered, and then fell violently in love. He was one of those fellows who never do things by halves. If he drank, he'd get fighting drunk: if he loved, he went all out on it: if he hated—well, hell was let loose.'

'And—Mrs Thring?' I queried, for it seemed to me that she might have a point of view.

'Fell between two stools—as so many women of a certain type do. She began by being just friendly and kind—you know the sort of thing—cheering the lonely man up, drifted into woman's eternal game of flirting, and then began to grow a little afraid of the fire she'd kindled. Too late she realised that she couldn't put the fire out—either hers or Macy's—and all the while she clung to some hereditary religious scruples.

'Thring was in many ways easygoing, but at the same time possessed of a curiously intense strain of jealous possessiveness. He was generous, too. If asked, he would share or give away his last shirt or crust. But let him think or feel that his rights or dues were being curtailed or taken and—well, he was a tough customer of rather primitive ideas.

'Rhona—that's the easiest way to think of the filly—soon found she was playing a game beyond her powers. Hers was no poker face, and Thring began to sense that something was wrong. She couldn't dissemble, and Macy made no attempt to hide his feelings. He didn't make it easy for her, and I guess from what the girl told me, life about this time was for her a sort of glorified hell—a suspicious husband on one hand, and an impetuous, devil-may-care lover on the other. She was living on a volcano.'

'Which might explode any minute.' I quietly said.

Warwick nodded.

'Exactly; or whenever Thring chose to spring the mine. He held the key to the situation, or, should I say, the time-fuse? The old story, but set in a primitive land full of possibilities. You've got me?'

For answer I offered Warwick a cigarette, and, taking one myself, lighted both.

'So far,' I said, 'with all your journalistic skill you've not got off the beaten track. Can't you improve?'

He chuckled, blew a cloud of smoke, and once again tapped my knee in his irritating manner.

'Your cynicism,' he countered, 'is but a poor cloak for your curiosity. In reality you're jumping mad to know the end, eh?'

I made no reply, and he went on.

'Well, matters went on from day to day till Rhona became worn to the proverbial shadow. Thring wanted to send her home, but she wouldn't go. She owed a duty to her husband: she couldn't bear to be parted from her lover, and she didn't dare leave the two men alone. She was terribly, horribly afraid.

'Macy grew more and more openly amorous and less restrained. Thring watched whenever possible with the cunning of an iguana. Then came a rainy, damp spell that tried the nerves to the uttermost and the inevitable stupid little disagreements between Rhona and

Thring—mere trifles, but enough to let the lid off. He challenged her——'

'And she?' I could not help asking, for Warwick has, I must admit, the knack of keeping one on edge.

'Like a blithering but sublime little idiot admitted that it was all true.'

For nearly a minute I was speechless. Somehow, although underneath I had expected Rhona to behave so, it seemed such a senseless, unbelievable thing to do. Then at last I found my voice.

'And Thring?' I said simply.

Warwick emptied his glass at a gulp.

'That's the most curious thing in the whole yarn,' he answered slowly 'Thring took it as quietly as a lamb.'

'Stunned?' I suggested.

'That's what Rhona thought: what Macy believed when Rhona told him what had happened. In reality he must have been burning mad, a mass of white-hot revenge controlled by a devilish, cunning brain: he waited. A scene or a fight—and Macy was a big man—would have done no good. He would get his own back in his own time and in his own way. Meanwhile, there was the lull before the storm.

'Then, as so often happens, Fate played a hand. Macy went sick with malaria—really ill—and even Thring had to admit the necessity for Rhona to nurse him practically night and day. Macy owned his eventual recovery to her care, but even so his convalescence was a long job. In the end Rhona, too, crocked up through overwork, and Thring had them both on his hands. This was an opportunity better than he could have planned—it separated the lovers and gave him complete control.

'Obviously the time was ripe, ripe for Thring to score his revenge. The rains were over, the jungle had ceased wintering, and spring was in the air. The young grass and vegetation were shooting into new life: concurrently all the creepy, crawly insect life of the jungle and estate was young and vigorous and hungry, too. These facts gave Thring the germ of an idea which he was not slow to perfect—an idea as devilish as man could devise.'

Warwick paused to press out the stub of his cigarette, and noticing that even he seemed affected by his recital, I prepared myself as best I could for a really gruesome horror. All I said, however, was, 'Go on.'

'It seems,' he continued, 'that in Borneo there is a kind of mammoth earwig—a thing almost as fine and gossamer as a spider's web, as long as a good-sized caterpillar, that lives on waxy secretions. These are integral parts of some flowers and trees, and lie buried deep in their recesses. It is one of the terrors of these particular tropics, for it moves and rests so lightly on a human being that one is practically unconscious of it, while, like its English relation, it has a decided liking for the human ear: on account of man's carnivorous diet the wax in this has a strong and very succulent taste.'

As Warwick gave me those details, he sat upright on the edge of his easy-chair. He spoke slowly, emphasising each point by hitting the palm of his left hand with the clenched first of his right. It was impossible not to see the drift and inference of his remarks.

'You mean?' I began.

'Exactly,' he broke in quickly, blowing a cloud of smoke from a fresh cigarette which he had nervously lighted. 'Exactly. It was a devilish idea. To put the giant earwig on Macy's hair just above the ear.'

'And then...?' I knew the fatuousness of the question, but speech relieved the growing sense of ticklish horror that was creeping over me.

'Do nothing. But rely on the filthy insect running true to type. Once in Macy's ear, it was a thousand-to-one chance against it ever coming out the same way: it would not be able to turn: to back out would be almost an impossibility, and so, feeding as it went, it would crawl right across inside his head, with the result that——'

'The picture Warwick was drawing was more than I could bear: even my imagination, dulled by years of legal dry-as-dust affairs, saw and sickened at the possibilities. I put out a hand and gripped Warwick's arm.

'Stop, man!' I cried hoarsely 'For god's sake, don't say any more. I understand. My god, but the man Thring must be a fiend!'

Warwick looked at me, and I saw that even his face had paled.

'Was' he said meaningly. 'Perhaps you're right, perhaps he *was* a fiend. Yet, remember, Macy stole his wife.'

'But a torture like that! The deliberate creation of a living torment that would grow into madness. Warwick, you can't condone that!'

He looked at me for a moment and then slowly spread out his hands.

'Perhaps you're right,' he admitted. 'It was a bit thick, I know. But there's more to come.'

I closed my eyes and wondered if I could think of an excuse for leaving Warwick; but in spite of my real horror, my curiosity won the day.

'Get on with it,' I muttered, and leant back, eyes still shut, hands clenched. With teeth gritted together as if I myself were actually suffering the pain of that earwig slowly, daily creeping farther into and eating my brain, I waited.

Warwick was not slow to obey.

'I have told you,' he said, 'that Rhona had to nurse Macy, and even when he was better, though still weak, Thring insisted on her looking after him, though now he himself came more often.

'One afternoon Rhona was in Macy's bungalow alone with him: the house-boy was out. Rhona was on the veranda; Macy was asleep in the bedroom. Dusk was just falling; bats were flying about: the flying-foxes, heavy with fruit, were returning home; the inevitable house rats were scurrying about the floors; the lamps had not been lit. An eerie, devastating hour. Rhona dropped some needlework and fought back tears. Then from the bedroom came a shriek. 'My head! My ear! Oh, god! My ear! Oh, god! The pain!'

'That was the beginning. The earwig had got well inside. Rhona rushed in and did all she could. Of course, there was nothing to see. Then for a little while Macy would be quiet because the earwig was quiet, sleeping or gorged. Then the vile tiling would move or feed again, and Macy once more would shriek with the pain.

'And so it went on, day by day. Alternate quiet and alternate pain, each day for Macy, for Rhona a hell of nerve-rending expectancy. Waiting, always waiting for the pain that crept and crawled and twisted and writhed and moved slowly, ever slowly, through and across Macy's brain.'

Warwick paused so long that I was compelled to open my eyes. His face was ghastly. Fortunately I could not see my own.

'And Thring?' I asked.

'Came often each day. Pretended sorrow and served out spurious dope—Rhona found the coloured water afterwards. He cleverly urged that Macy should be carried down to the coast for medical treatment, knowing full well that he was too ill and worn to bear the smallest strain. Then when Macy was an utter wreck, broken completely in mind and body, with hollow, hunted eyes, with ever-twitching fingers, with a body no part of which he could properly control or keep still, the earwig came out—at the other ear.

'As it happened, both Thring and Rhona were present. Macy must have suffered an excruciating pain, followed as usual by a period of quiescence: then, feeling a slight ticklish sensation on his cheek, put up his hand to rub or scratch. His fingers came in contact with the earwig and its fine gossamer hairs. Instinct did the rest. You follow?'

My tongue was still too dry to enable me to speak. Instead I nodded, and Warwick went on.

'He naturally was curious and looked to see what he was holding. In an instant he realised. Even Rhona could not be in doubt. The hairs were faintly but unmistakably covered here and there with blood, with wax and with grey matter.

'For a moment there was absolute silence between the three. At last Macy spoke.

' "My god!" he just whispered. "Oh, my god! What an escape!"

'Rhona burst into tears. Only Thring kept silent, and that was his mistake. The silence worried Macy, weak though he was. He looked from Rhona to Thring, and at the critical moment Thring could not meet his gaze. The truth was out. With an oath Macy *threw* the insect, now dead from the pressure of his fingers, straight into Thring's face. Then he crumpled up in his chair and sobbed and sobbed till even the chair shook.'

Again Warwick paused till I thought he would never go on. I had heard enough, I'll admit, and yet it seemed to me that at least there should be an epilogue.

'Is that all?' I tentatively asked.

Warwick shook his head.

'Nearly, but not quite,' he said. 'Rhona had ceased weeping and kept her eyes fixed on Thring—she dared not go and comfort Macy now. She saw him examine the dead earwig, having picked it up from the floor to which it had fallen, turn it this way and that, then produce from a pocket a magnifying-glass which he used daily for the inspection and detection of leaf disease on certain of the plants. As she watched, she saw the fear and disappointment leave his face, to be replaced by a look of cunning and evil satisfaction. Then for the first time he spoke.

'"Macy!" he called, in a sharp, loud voice.

'Macy looked up.

'Thring held up the earwig. "This is dead now," he said, "dead. As dead as my friendship for you, you swine of a thief, as dead as my love for that whore who was my wife. It's dead, I tell you, dead, but it's a female. D'you get me? A female, and a female lays eggs, and before it died it——"

'He never finished. His baiting at last roused Macy, endowing him with the strength of madness and despair. With one spring he was at Thring's throat, bearing him down to the ground. Over and over they rolled on the floor, struggling for the possession of the great hunting-knife stuck in Thring's belt. One moment Macy was on top, the next, Thring. Their breath and oaths came in great trembling gasps. They kicked and bit and scratched. And all the while Rhona watched, fascinated and terrified. Then Thring got definitely on top. He had one hand on Macy's throat, both knees on his chest, and with his free hand he was feeling for the knife. In that instant Rhona's religious scruples went by the board. She realised she only loved Macy, that her husband didn't count. She rushed to Macy's help. Thring saw her coming and let drive a blow at her head which almost stunned her. She fell on top of him just as he was whipping out the knife. Its edge caught her neck. The sudden spurt of blood shot into Thring's eyes, and blinded him. It was Macy's last chance. He knew it, and he took it.

'When Rhona came back to consciousness, Thring was dead. Macy was standing beside the body, which was gradually swelling to huge proportions as he worked, weakly but steadily, at the white ant exterminator pump, the nozzle of which was pushed down the dead man's throat.'

Warwick ceased. This last had been a long, unbroken recital, and mechanically he picked up his empty glass as if to drain it. The action brought me back to nearly normal. I rang for the waiter—the knob of the electric bell luckily being just over my head. While waiting, I had time to speak.

'I've heard enough,' I said hurriedly, 'to last me a lifetime. You've made me feel positively sick. But there's just one point. What happened to Macy? Did he live?'

Warwick nodded.

'That's another strange fact. He still lives. He was tried for the murder of Thring, but there was no real evidence. On the other hand, his story was too tall to be believed, with the result—well, you can guess.'

'A lunatic asylum—for life?' I asked.

Warwick nodded again. Then I followed his glance. A waiter was standing by my chair.

'Two double whisky-and-sodas,' I ordered tersely, and then, with shaking fingers, lighted a cigarette.

The Hollow Man

Thomas Burke

He came up one of the narrow streets which lead from the docks, and turned into a road whose farther end was gay with the light of London. At the end of this road he went deep into the lights of London, and sometimes into its shadows, farther and farther away from the river; and did not pause until he had reached a poor quarter near the centre.

He was a tall, spare figure, wearing a black mackintosh. Below this could be seen brown dungaree trousers. A peaked cap hid most of his face; the little that was exposed was white and sharp. In the autumn mist that filled the lighted streets, as well as the dark, he seemed a wraith; and some of those who passed him looked again, not sure whether they had indeed seen a living man. One or two of them moved their shoulders, as though shrinking from something.

His legs were long, but he walked with the short, deliberate steps of a blind man, though he was not blind. His eyes were open, and he stared straight ahead; but he seemed to see nothing and hear nothing.

Neither the mournful hooting of sirens across the black water of the river nor the genial windows of the shops in the big streets near the centre drew his head to the right or left. He walked as though he had no destination in mind, yet constantly, at this corner or that, he turned. It seemed that an unseen hand was guiding him to a given point, of whose location he was himself ignorant.

He was searching for a friend of fifteen years ago, and the unseen hand, or some dog-instinct, had led him from Africa to London, and was now leading him, along the last mile of his search, to a certain little eating-house. He did not know that he was going to the eating-house of his friend Nameless, but he did know, from the time he left Africa, that he was journeying towards Nameless, and he now knew that he was very near to Nameless.

Nameless didn't know that his old friend was anywhere near him, though, had he observed the conditions that evening, he might have wondered why he was sitting up an hour later than usual. He was seated in one of the pews of his prosperous little workmen's dining-rooms—a little gold-mine his wife's relations called it—and he was smoking and looking at nothing.

He had added up the till and written the copies of the bill of fare for next day, and there was nothing to keep him out of bed after his fifteen hours' attention to business. Had he been asked why he was sitting up later than usual, he would first have answered that he didn't know that he was, and would then have explained, in default of any other explanation, that it was for the purpose of having a last pipe. He was quite unaware that he was sitting up and keeping the door unlatched because a long-parted friend from Africa was seeking him and slowly approaching him, and needed his services.

He was quite unaware that he had left the door unlatched at that late hour—half-past eleven—to admit pain and woe.

But even as many bells sent dolefully across the night from their steeples their disagreement as to the point of half-past eleven, pain and woe were but two streets away from him. The mackintosh and dungarees and the sharp white face were coming nearer every moment.

There was silence in the house and in the streets; a heavy silence, broken, or sometimes stressed, by the occasional night-noises—motor horns, back-firing of lorries, shunting at a distant terminus. That silence seemed to envelop the house, but he did not notice it. He did not notice the bells, and he did not even notice the lagging step that approached his shop, and passed—and returned—and passed again—and halted. He was aware of nothing save that he was smoking a last pipe, and he was sitting in that state of hazy reverie which he called thinking, deaf and blind to anything not in his immediate neighbourhood.

But when a hand was laid on the latch, and the latch was lifted, he did hear that, and he looked up. And he saw the door open, and got up and went to it. And there, just within the door, he came face to face with the thin figure of pain and woe.

To kill a fellow-creature is a frightful thing. At the time the act is committed, the murderer may have sound and convincing reasons (to him) for his act. But time and reflection may bring regret; even remorse; and this may live with him for many years. Examined in wakeful hours of the night or early morning, the reasons for the act may shed their cold logic, and may cease to be reasons and become mere excuses.

And these naked excuses may strip the murderer and show him to himself as he is. They may begin to hunt his soul, and to run into every little corner of his mind and every little nerve, in search of it. And if to kill a fellow-creature and to suffer the recurrent regret for an act of heated blood is a frightful thing, it is still more frightful to kill a fellow-creature and bury his body deep in an African jungle, and then, fifteen years later, at about midnight, to see the latch of your door lifted by the hand you had stilled and to see the man, looking much as he did fifteen years ago, walk into your home and claim your hospitality.

When the man in mackintosh and dungarees walked into the dining-rooms, Nameless stood still; stared; staggered against a table; supported himself by a hand, and said 'Oh!'

The other man said 'Nameless!'

Then they looked at each other; Nameless with head thrust forward, mouth dropped; eyes wide; the visitor with a dull, glazed expression. If Nameless had not been the man he was—thick, bovine and costive—he would have flung up his arms and screamed. At that moment he felt the need of some such outlet, but did not know how to find it. The only dramatic expression he gave to the situation was to whisper instead of speak.

Twenty emotions came to life in his head and spine, and wrestled there. But they showed themselves only in his staring eyes and his whisper. His first thought, or rather, spasm, was Ghosts-

Indigestion-Nervous-Breakdown. His second, when he saw that the figure was substantial and real, was Impersonation. But a slight movement on the part of the visitor dismissed that.

It was a little habitual movement which belonged only to that man; an unconscious twitching of the third finger of the left hand. He knew then that it was Gopak. Gopak, a little changed, but still, miraculously, thirty-two. Gopak, alive, breathing and real. No ghost. No phantom of the stomach. He was as certain of that as he was that fifteen years ago he had killed Gopak stone-dead and buried him.

The blackness of the moment was lightened by Gopak. In thin, flat tones he asked, 'May I sit down? I'm tired.' He sat down, and said: 'So tired. So tired.'

Nameless still held the table. He whispered: 'Gopak...Gopak... But I—I *killed* you. I killed you in the jungle. You were dead. I know you were.'

Gopak passed his hand across his face. He seemed about to cry. 'I know you did. I know. That's all I can remember—about this earth. You killed me.' The voice became thinner and flatter. 'And I was so comfortable. So comfortable. It was—such a rest. Such a rest as you don't know. And then they came and—disturbed me. They woke me up. And brought me back.' He sat with shoulders sagged, arms drooping, hands hanging between knees. After the first recognition he did not look at Nameless; he looked at the floor.

'Came and disturbed you?' Nameless leaned forward and whispered the words. 'Woke you up? Who?'

'The Leopard Men.'

'The what?'

'The Leopard Men.' The watery voice said it as casually as if it were saying 'the night watchman'.

'The Leopard Men?' Nameless stared, and his fat face crinkled in an effort to take in the situation of a midnight visitation from a dead man, and the dead man talking nonsense. He felt his blood moving out of its course. He looked at his own hand to see if it was his own hand. He looked at the table to see if it was his table. The hand and the table were facts, and if the dead man was a fact—and he was—his story might be a fact. It seemed anyway as sensible as the dead man's presence. He gave a heavy sigh from the stomach.

'A-ah… The Leopard Men… Yes, I heard about them out there. Tales!'

Gopak slowly wagged his head. 'Not tales. They're real. If they weren't real—I wouldn't be here. Would I? I'd be at rest.'

Nameless had to admit this. He had heard many tales 'out there' about the Leopard Men, and had dismissed them as jungle yarns. But now, it seemed, jungle yarns had become commonplace fact in a little London shop.

The watery voice went on. 'They do it. I saw them. I came back in the middle of a circle of them. They killed a nigger to put his life into me. They wanted a white man—for their farm. So they brought me back. You may not believe it. You wouldn't *want* to believe it. You wouldn't want to—see or know anything like them. And I wouldn't want any man to. But it's true. That's how I'm here.'

'But I left you absolutely dead. I made every test. It was three days before I buried you. And I buried you deep.'

'I know. But that wouldn't make any difference to them. It was a long time after when they came and brought me back. And I'm still dead, you know. It's only my body they brought back.' The voice trailed into a thread. 'And I'm so tired. So tired. I want to go back—to rest.'

Sitting in his prosperous eating-house, Nameless was in the presence of an achieved miracle, but the everyday, solid appointments of the eating-house wouldn't let him fully comprehend it. Foolishly, as he realised when he had spoken, he asked Gopak to explain what had happened. Asked a man who couldn't really be alive to explain how he came to be alive. It was like asking Nothing to explain Everything.

Constantly, as he talked, he felt his grasp on his own mind slipping. The surprise of a sudden visitor at a late hour; the shock of the arrival of a long-dead man; and the realisation that this long-dead man was not a wraith, were too much for him.

During the next half-hour he found himself talking to Gopak as to the Gopak he had known seventeen years ago when they were partners. Then he would be halted by the freezing knowledge that he was talking to a dead man, and that a dead man was faintly answering him. He felt that the thing couldn't really have happened, but in the interchange of talk he kept forgetting the improbable side of it, and accepting it. With each recollection of the truth, his mind would clear and settle in one thought—'I've got to get rid of him. How am I going to get rid of him?'

'But how did you get here?'

'I escaped.' The words came slowly and thinly, and out of the body rather than the mouth.

'How.'

'I don't—know. I don't remember anything—except our quarrel. And being at rest.'

'But why come all the way here? Why didn't you stay on the coast?'

'I don't—know. But you're the only man I know. The only man I can remember.'

'But how did you find me?'

'I don't know. But I had to—find you. You're the only man—who can help me.'

'But how can I help you?'

The head turned weakly from side to side. 'I don't—know. But nobody else—can.'

Nameless stared through the window, looking on to the lamplit street and seeing nothing of it. The everyday being which had been his half an hour ago had been annihilated; the everyday beliefs and disbeliefs shattered and mixed together. But some shred of his old sense and his old standard remained. He must handle this situation. 'Well— what you want to do? What you going to do? I don't see how I can help you. And you can't stay here, obviously.' A demon of perversity sent a facetious notion into his head—introducing Gopak to his wife— 'This is my dead friend.'

But on his last spoken remark Gopak made the effort of raising his head and staring with the glazed eyes at Nameless. 'But I *must* stay here. There's nowhere else I can stay. I must stay here. That's why I came. You got to help me.'

'But you can't stay here. I got no room. All occupied. Nowhere for you to sleep.'

The wan voice said: 'That doesn't matter. I *don't* sleep.'

'Eh?'

'I *don't* sleep. I haven't slept since they brought me back. I can sit here—till you can think of some way of helping me.'

'But how *can* I?'

He again forgot the background of the situation, and began to get angry at the vision of a dead man sitting about the place waiting for him to think of something. 'How *can* I if you don't tell me how?'

'I don't—know. But you got to. You killed me. And I was dead—and comfortable. As it all came from you—killing me—you're responsible for me being—like this. So, you got to—help me. That's why I—came to you.'

'But what do you want me to do?'

'I don't—know. I can't—think. But nobody but you can help me. I had to come to you. Something brought me—straight to you. That means that you're the one—that can help me. Now I'm with you, something will—happen to help me. I feel it will. In time you'll—think of something.'

Nameless found his legs suddenly weak. He sat down and stared with a sick scowl at the hideous and the incomprehensible. Here was a dead man in his house—a man he had murdered in a moment of black temper—and he knew in his heart that he couldn't turn the man out. For one thing, he would have been afraid to touch him; he couldn't see himself touching him. For another, faced with the miracle of the presence of a fifteen-years-dead man, he doubted whether physical force or any material agency would be effectual in moving the man.

His soul shivered, as all men's souls shiver at the demonstration of forces outside their mental or spiritual horizon. He had murdered this man, and often, in fifteen years, he had repented the act. If the man's appalling story were true, then he had some sort of right to turn to Nameless. Nameless recognised that, and knew that whatever happened he couldn't turn him out. His hot-tempered sin had literally come home to him.

The wan voice broke into his nightmare. 'You go to rest, Nameless. I'll sit here. You go to rest.' He put his face down to his hands and uttered a little moan. 'Oh, why can't I rest? Why can't I go back to my beautiful rest?'

Nameless came down early next morning with a half-hope that Gopak would not be there. But he was there, seated where Nameless had left him last night. Nameless made some tea, and showed him where he might wash. He washed listlessly, and crawled back to his seat, and listlessly drank the tea which Nameless brought to him.

To his wife and the kitchen helpers Nameless mentioned him as an old friend who had had a bit of a shock. 'Shipwrecked and knocked on the head. But quite harmless, and he won't be staying long. He's waiting for admission to a home. A good pal to me in the past, and it's the least I can do to let him stay here a few days. Suffers from sleeplessness and prefers to sit up at night. Quite harmless.'

But Gopak stayed more than a few days. He outstayed everybody. Even when the customers had gone, Gopak was still there.

On the first morning of his visit when the regular customers came in at mid-day, they looked at the odd, white figure sitting vacantly in the first pew, then stared, then moved away.

All avoided the pew in which he sat. Nameless explained him to them, but his explanation did not seem to relieve the slight tension which settled on the dining-room. The atmosphere was not so brisk and chatty as usual. Even those who had their backs to the stranger seemed to be affected by his presence.

At the end of the first day Nameless, noticing this, told him that he had arranged a nice corner of the front room upstairs, where he could sit by the window, and took his arm to take him upstairs. But Gopak feebly shook the hand away, and sat where he was. 'No. I don't want to go. I'll stay here. I'll stay here. I don't want to move.'

And he wouldn't move. After a few more pleadings Nameless realised with dismay that his refusal was definite; that it would be futile to press him or force him; that he was going to sit in that dining-room for ever. He was as weak as a child and as firm as a rock.

He continued to sit in that first pew, and the customers continued to avoid it, and to give queer glances at it. It seemed that they half-recognised that he was something more than a fellow who had had a shock.

During the second week of his stay, three of the regular customers were missing, and more than one of those that remained made acidly facetious suggestions to Nameless that he park his lively friend somewhere else. He made things too exciting for them; all that whoopee took them off their work, and interfered with digestion. Nameless told them he would be staying only a day or so longer, but they found that this was untrue, and at the end of the second week eight of the regulars had found another place.

Each day, when the dinner-hour came, Nameless tried to get him to take a little walk, but he always refused.

He would go out only at night, and then never more than two hundred yards from the shop. For the rest, he sat in his pew, sometimes dozing in the afternoon, at other times staring at the floor. He took his food abstractedly, and never knew whether he had had food or not. He spoke only when questioned, and the burden of his talk was 'I'm so tired. So tired.'

One thing only seemed to arouse any light of interest in him; one thing only drew his eyes from the floor. That was the seventeen-year-old daughter of his host, who was known as Bubbles, and who helped with the waiting. And Bubbles seemed to be the only member of the shop and its customers, who did not shrink from him.

She knew nothing of the truth about him, but she seemed to understand him, and the only response he ever gave to anything was to her childish sympathy. She sat and chatted foolish chatter to him—'bringing him out of himself' she called it—and sometimes he would be brought out to the extent of a watery smile. He came to recognise her step, and would look up before she entered the room. Once or twice in the evening, when the shop was empty, and Nameless was sitting miserably with him, he would ask, without lifting his eyes. 'Where's Bubbles?' and would be told that Bubbles had gone to the pictures or was out at a dance, and would relapse into deeper vacancy. Nameless didn't like this. He was already visited by a curse which, in four weeks, had destroyed most of his business. Regular customers had dropped off two by two, and no new customers came to take their place. Strangers who dropped in once for a meal did not come again; they could not keep their eyes or their minds off the forbidding, white-faced figure sitting motionless in the first pew. At mid-day, when the place had been crowded and late-comers had to wait for a seat, it was now two-thirds empty; only a few of the most thick-skinned remained faithful.

And on top of this there was the interest of the dead man in his daughter, an interest which seemed to be having an unpleasant effect. Nameless hadn't noticed it, but his wife had. 'Bubbles don't seem as bright and lively as she was. You noticed it lately? She's getting quiet— and a bit slack. Sits about a lot. Paler than she used to be.'

'Her age, perhaps.'

'No, She's not one of these thin dark sort. No—it's something else. Jus the last week or two I've noticed it. Off her food. Sits about doing nothing. No interest. May be nothing; just out of sorts, perhaps ... How much longer's that horrible friend of yours going to stay?'

The horrible friend stayed some weeks longer—ten weeks in all—while Nameless watched his business drop to nothing and his daughter get pale and peevish. He knew the cause of it. There was no home in all England like his: no home that had a dead man sitting in it for ten weeks. A dead man brought, after a long time, from the grave, to sit and disturb his customers and take the vitality from his daughter. He couldn't tell this to anybody. Nobody would believe such nonsense.

But he *knew* that he was entertaining a dead man, and, knowing that a long-dead man was walking the earth, he could believe in any result of that fact. He could believe almost anything that he would have derided ten weeks ago. His customers had abandoned his shop, not because of the presence of a silent, white-faced man, but because of the presence of a dead-living man.

Their minds might not know it, but their blood knew it. And, as his business had been destroyed, so, he believed, would his daughter be destroyed. Her blood was not warming her; her blood told her only that this was a long-ago friend of her father's, and she was drawn to him.

It was at *this* point that Nameless, having no work to do, began to drink. And it was well that he did so. For out of the drink came an idea, and with drat idea he freed himself from the curse upon him and his house.

The shop now served scarcely half a dozen customers at midday. It had become ill-kempt and dusty, and the service and the food were bad. Nameless took no trouble to be civil to his few customers. Often, when he was notably under drink, he went to the trouble of being very rude to them. They talked about this. They talked about the decline of his business and the dustiness of the shop and the bad food. They talked about his drinking, and, of course, exaggerated it.

And they talked about the queer fellow who sat there day after day and gave everybody the creeps. A few outsiders, hearing the gossip, came to the dining-rooms to see the queer fellow and the always-tight proprietor; but they did not come again, and there were not enough of the curious to keep the place busy. It went down until it served scarcely two customers a day. And Nameless went down with it into drink.

Then, one evening, out of the drink he fished an inspiration.

He took it downstairs to Gopak, who was sitting in his usual seat, hands hanging, eyes on the floor. 'Gopak—listen. You came here because I was the only man who could help you in your trouble. You listening?'

A faint 'Yes' was his answer.

'Well, now. You told me I'd got to think of something. I've thought of something... Listen. You say I'm responsible for your condition and got to get you out of it, because I killed you. I did. We had a row. You made me wild. You dared me. And what with that sun and the jungle and the insects, I wasn't meself. I killed you. The moment it was done I could a-cut me right hand off. Because you and me were pals. I could a-cut me right hand off.'

'I know. I felt that directly it was over. I knew you were suffering.' 'Ah!... I have suffered. And I'm suffering now. Well, this is what I've thought. All your present trouble comes from me killing you in that jungle and burying you. An idea came to me. Do you think it would help you—do you think it would put you back to rest if I— if I—if I—killed you again?'

For some seconds Gopak continued to stare at the floor. Then his shoulders moved. Then, while Nameless watched every little response to his idea, the watery voice began. 'Yes. Yes. That's it. That's what I was waiting for. That's why I came here. I can see now. That's why I had to get here. Nobody else could kill me. Only you. I've got to be lolled again. Yes, I see. But nobody else—would be able—to kill me. Only the man who first killed me.... Yes, you've found—what we're both—waiting for. Anybody else could shoot me—stab me—hang me—but they couldn't kill me. Only you. That's why I managed to get here and find you.'

The watery voice rose to a thin strength. 'That's it. And you must do it. Do it now. You don't want to, I know. But you must. You *must*.'

His head dropped and he stared at the floor. Nameless, too, stared at the floor. He was seeing things. He had murdered a man and had escaped all punishment save that of his own mind, which had been terrible enough. But now he was going to murder him again—not in a jungle but in a city; and he saw the slow points of the result.

He saw the arrest. He saw the first hearing. He saw the trial. He saw the cell. He saw the rope. He shuddered.

Then he saw the alternative—the breakdown of his life—a ruined business, poverty, the poorhouse, a daughter robbed of her health and perhaps dying, and always the curse of the dead-living man, who might follow him to the poorhouse. Better to end it all, he thought. Rid himself of the curse which Gopak had brought upon him and his family, and then rid his family of himself with a revolver. Better to follow up his idea.

He got stiffly to his feet. The hour was late evening—half-past ten—and the streets were quiet. He had pulled down the shop-blinds and locked the door. The room was lit by one light at the further end.

He moved about uncertainly and looked at Gopak. 'Er—how would you—how shall I—'

'Gopak said, 'You did it with a knife. Just under the heart. You must do it that way again.'

Nameless stood and looked at him for some seconds. Then, with an air of resolve, he shook himself. He walked quickly to the kitchen.

Three minutes later his wife and daughter heard a crash, as though a table had been overturned. They called but got no answer, When they came down they found him sitting in one of the pews, wiping sweat from his forehead. He was white and shaking, and appeared to be recovering from a faint.

'Whatever's the matter? You all right?'

He waved them away. 'Yes, I'm all right. Touch of giddiness. Smoking too much, I think.'

'Mmmm. Or drinking.... Where's your friend? Out for a walk?'

'No. He's gone off. Said he wouldn't impose any longer, and'd go and find an infirmary.' He spoke weakly and found trouble in picking words. 'Didn't you hear that bang—when he shut the door?'

'I thought that was you fell down.'

'No. It was him when he went. I couldn't stop him.'

'Mmmm. Just as well, I think.' She looked about her. 'Things seem to a-gone wrong since he's been here.'

There was a general air of dustiness about the place. The tablecloths were dirty, not from use but from disuse. The windows were dim. A long knife, very dusty, was lying on the table under the window. In a corner by the door leading to the kitchen, unseen by her, lay a dusty mackintosh and dungaree, which appeared to have been tossed there. But it was over by the main door, near the first pew, that the dust was thickest—a long trail of it—greyish-white dust.

'Reely this place gets more and more slapdash. Why can't you attend to business? You didn't use to be like this. No wonder it's gone down, letting the place get into this state. Why don't you pull yourself together. Just *look* at that dust by the door. Looks as though somebody's been spilling ashes all over the place.'

Nameless looked at it, and his hands shook a little. But he answered, more firmly than before: 'Yes, I know. I'll have a proper clean-up tomorrow. I'll put it all to rights to-morrow. I been getting a bit slack.'

For the first time in ten weeks he smiled at them; a thin, haggard smile, but a smile.

The Beast with Five Fingers

W.F. Harvey

The story, I suppose, begins with Adrian Borlsover, whom I met when I was a little boy and he an old man. My father had called to appeal for a subscription, and before he left, Mr Borlsover laid his right hand in blessing on my head. I shall never forget the awe in which I gazed up at his face and realised for the first time that eyes might be dark and beautiful and shining, and yet not able to see.

For Adrian Borlsover was blind.

He was an extraordinary man, who came of an eccentric stock. Borlsover sons for some reason always seemed to marry very ordinary women, which perhaps accounted for the fact that no Borlsover had been a genius, and only one Borlsover had been mad. But they were great champions of little causes, generous patrons of odd sciences, founders of querulous sects, trustworthy guides to the bypath meadows of erudition.

Adrian was an authority on the fertilisation of orchids. He had held at one time the family living at Borlsover Conyers, until a congenital weakness of the lungs obliged him to seek a less rigorous climate in the sunny south-coast watering-place where I had seen him. Occasionally he would relieve one or other of the local clergy. My father described him as a fine preacher, who gave long and inspiring sermons from what many men would have considered unprofitable texts. 'An excellent proof,' he would add, 'of the truth of the doctrine of direct verbal inspiration.'

Adrian Borlsover was exceedingly clever with his hands. His penmanship was exquisite. He illustrated all his scientific papers, made his own woodcuts, and carved the reredos that is at present the chief feature of interest in the church at Borlsover Conyers. He had an exceedingly clever knack in cutting silhouettes for young ladies and paper pigs and cows for little children, and made more than one complicated wind instrument of his own devising.

When he was fifty years old, Adrian Borlsover lost his sight. In a wonderfully short time he adapted himself to the new conditions of life. He quickly learnt to read Braille. So marvellous indeed was his sense of touch, that he was still able to maintain his interest in botany. The mere passing of his long supple fingers over a flower was sufficient means for its identification, though occasionally he would use his lips. I have found several letters of his among my father's correspondence; in no case was there anything to show that he was afflicted with blindness, and this in spite of the fact that he exercised undue economy in the spacing of lines. Towards the close of his life, Adrian Borlsover was credited with the powers of touch that seemed almost uncanny. It has been said that he could tell at once the colour of a ribbon placed between his fingers. My father would neither confirm nor deny the story.

Adrian Borlsover was a bachelor. His elder brother, Charles, had married late in life, leaving one son, Eustace, who lived in the gloomy Georgian mansion at Borlsover Conyers, where he could work undisturbed in collecting material for his great book on heredity.

Like his uncle, he was a remarkable man. The Borlsovers had always been born naturalists, but Eustace possessed in a special degree the power of systematising his knowledge. He had received his university education in Germany; and then, after post-graduate work in Vienna and Naples, had travelled for four years in South America and the East, getting together a huge store of material for a new study into the processes of variation.

He lived alone at Borlsover Conyers with Saunders, his secretary, a man who bore a somewhat dubious reputation in the district, but whose powers as a mathematician, combined with his business abilities, were invaluable to Eustace.

Uncle and nephew saw little of each other. The visits of Eustace were confined to a week in the summer or autumn—tedious weeks, that dragged almost as slowly as the bath-chair in which the old man was drawn along the sunny sea-front. In their way the two men were fond of each other, though their intimacy would, doubtless, have been greater, had they shared the same religious views. Adrian held to the old-fashioned evangelical dogmas of his early manhood; his nephew for many years had been thinking of embracing Buddhism. Both men possessed, too, the reticence the Borlsovers had always shown, and which their enemies sometimes called hypocrisy. With Adrian it was a reticence as to the things he had left undone; but with Eustace it seemed that the curtain which he was so careful to leave undrawn hid something more than a half-empty chamber.

Two years before his death, Adrian Borlsover developed, unknown to himself, the not uncommon power of automatic writing. Eustace made the discovery by accident. Adrian was sitting reading in bed, the forefinger of his left hand tracing the Braille characters, when his nephew noticed that a pencil the old man held in his right hand was moving slowly along the opposite page. He left his seat in the window and sat down beside the bed. The right hand continued to move, and now he could see plainly that they were letters and words which it was forming.

'Adrian Borlsover,' wrote the hand, 'Eustace Borlsover, Charles Borlsover, Francis Borlsover, Sigismund Borlsover, Adrian Borlsover, Eustace Borlsover, Saville Borlsover. B for Borlsover. Honesty is the Best Policy. Beautiful Belinda Borlsover.'

'What curious nonsense!' said Eustace to himself.

'King George ascended the throne in 1760,' wrote the hand. 'Crowd, a noun of multitude; a collection of individuals. Adrian Borlsover, Eustace Borlsover.'

'It seems to me,' said his uncle, closing the book, 'that you had much better make the most of the afternoon sunshine and take your walk now.'

'I think perhaps I will,' Eustace answered as he picked up the volume. 'I won't go far, and when I come back, I can read to you those articles in *Nature* about which we were speaking.'

He went along the promenade, but stopped at the first shelter, and, seating himself in the corner best protected from the wind, he examined the book at leisure. Nearly every page was scored with a meaningless jumble of pencil-marks; rows of capital letters, short words, long words, complete sentences, copy-book tags. The whole thing, in fact had the appearance of a copy-book, and, on a more careful scrutiny, Eustace thought that there was ample evidence to show that the handwriting at the beginning of the book, good though it was, was not nearly so good as the handwriting at the end.

He left his uncle at the end of October with a promise to return early in December. It seemed to him quite clear that the old man's power of automatic writing was developing rapidly, and for the first time he looked forward to a visit that would combine duty with interest.

But on his return he was at first disappointed. His uncle, he thought, looked older. He was listless, too, preferring others to read to him and dictating nearly all his letters. Not until the day before he left had Eustace an opportunity of observing Adrian Borlsover's new-found faculty.

The old man, propped up in bed with pillows, had sunk into a light sleep. His two hands lay on the coverlet, his left hand tightly clasping his right. Eustace took an empty manuscript-book and placed a pencil within reach of the fingers of the right hand. They snatched at it eagerly, then dropped the pencil to loose the left hand from its restraining grasp.

'Perhaps to prevent interference I had better hold that hand,' said Eustace to himself, as he watched the pencil. Almost immediately it began to write.

'Blundering Borlsovers, unnecessarily unnatural, extraordinarily eccentric, culpably curious.'

'Who are you?' asked Eustace in a low voice.

'Never you mind,' wrote the hand of Adrian.

'Is it my uncle who is writing?'

'O my prophetic soul, mine uncle!'

'Is it anyone I know?'

'Silly Eustace, you'll see me very soon.'

'When shall I see you?'

'When poor old Adrian's dead.'

'Where shall I see you?'

'Where shall you not?'

Instead of speaking his next question, Eustace wrote it. 'What is the time?'

The fingers dropped the pencil and moved three or four times across the paper. Then, picking up the pencil, they wrote: 'Ten minutes before four. Put your book away, Eustace. Adrian mustn't find us working at this sort of thing. He doesn't know what to make of it, and I won't have poor old Adrian disturbed. Au revoir!'

Adrian Borlsover awoke with a start.

'I've been dreaming again,' he said; 'such queer dreams of leaguered cities and forgotten towns. You were mixed up in this one, Eustace, though I can't remember how. Eustace, I want to warn you. Don't walk in doubtful paths. Choose your friends well. Your poor grandfather...'

A fit of coughing put an end to what he was saying, but Eustace saw that the hand was still writing. He managed unnoticed to draw the book away. 'I'll light the gas,' he said, 'and ring for tea.' On the other side of the bed-curtain he saw the last sentences that had been written.

'It's too late, Adrian,' he read. 'We're friends already, aren't we, Eustace Borlsover?'

On the following day Eustace left. He thought his uncle looked ill when he said good-bye, and the old man spoke despondently of the failure his life had been.

'Nonsense, uncle,' said his nephew. 'You have got over your difficulties in a way not one in a hundred thousand would have done. Everyone marvels at your splendid perseverance in teaching your hand to take the place of your lost sight. To me it's been a revelation of the possibilities of education.'

'Education,' said his uncle dreamily, as if the word had started a new train of thought. 'Education is good so long as you know to whom and for what purpose you give it. But with the lower orders of men, the base and more sordid spirits, I have grave doubts as to its results. Well, good-bye, Eustace; I may not see you again. You are a true Borlsover, with all the Borlsover faults. Marry, Eustace. Marry some good, sensible girl. And if by any chance I don't see you again, my will is at my solicitor's. I've not left you any legacy, because I know you're well provided for; but I thought you might like to have my books. Oh, and there's just one other thing. You know, before the end people often lose control over themselves and make absurd requests. Don't pay any attention to them, Eustace. Good-bye!' and he held out his hand. Eustace took it. It remained in his a fraction of a second longer than he had expected and gripped him with a virility that was surprising. There was, too, in its touch a subtle sense of intimacy.

'Why, uncle,' he said, 'I shall see you alive and well for many long years to come.'

Two months later Adrian Borlsover died.

Eustace Borlsover was in Naples at the time. He read the obituary notice in the *Morning Post* on the day announced for the funeral.

'Poor old fellow!' he said. 'I wonder whether I shall find room for all his books.'

The question occurred to him again with greater force when, three days later, he found himself standing in the library at Borlsover Conyers, a huge room built for use and not for beauty in the year of Waterloo by a Borlsover who was an ardent admirer of the great Napoleon. It was arranged on the plan of many college libraries, with tall projecting bookcases forming deep recesses of dusty silence, fit graves for the old hates of forgotten controversy, the dead passions of forgotten lives. At the end of the room, behind the bust of some unknown eighteenth-century divine, an ugly iron corkscrew stair led to a shelf-lined gallery. Nearly every shelf was full.

'I must talk to Saunders about it,' said Eustace. 'I suppose that we shall have to have the billiard-room fitted up with bookcases.'

The two men met for the first time after many weeks in the dining-room that evening.

'Hallo!' said Eustace, standing before the fire with his hands in his pockets. 'How goes the world, Saunders? Why these dress togs?' He himself was wearing an old shooting-jacket. He did not believe in mourning, as he had told his uncle on his last visit; and, though he usually went in for quiet-coloured ties, he wore this evening one of an ugly red, in order to shock Morton, the butler, and to make them thrash out the whole question of mourning for themselves in the servants' hall. Eustace was a true Borlsover. 'The world,' said Saunders, 'goes the same as usual, confoundedly slow. The dress togs are accounted for by an invitation from Captain Lockwood to bridge.'

'How are you getting there?'

'There's something the matter with the car, so I've told Jackson to drive me round in the dogcart. Any objection?'

'O dear me, no! We've had all things in common for far too many years for me to raise objections at this hour of the day.'

'You'll find your correspondence in the library,' went on Saunders. 'Most of it I've seen to. There are a few private letters I haven't opened. There's also a box with a rat or something inside it that came by the evening post. Very likely it's the six-toed beast Terry was sending us to cross with the four-toed albino. I didn't look because I didn't want to mess up my things; but I should gather from the way it's jumping about that it's pretty hungry.'

'Oh, I'll see to it,' said Eustace, 'while you and the captain earn an honest penny.'

Dinner over and Saunders gone, Eustace went into the library. Though the fire had been lit, the room was by no means cheerful.

'We'll have all the lights on, at any rate,' he said, as he turned the switches. 'And, Morton,' he added, when the butler brought the coffee, 'get me a screwdriver or something to undo this box. Whatever the animal is, he's kicking up the deuce of a row. What is it? Why are you dawdling?'

'If you please, sir, when the postman brought it, he told me that they'd bored the holes in the lid at the post office. There were no breathing holes in the lid, sir, and they didn't want the animal to die. That is all, sir.'

'It's culpably careless of the man, whoever he was,' said Eustace, as he removed the screws, 'packing an animal like this in a wooden box with no means of getting air. Confound it all! I meant to ask Morton to bring me a cage to put it in. Now I suppose I shall have to get one myself.'

He placed a heavy book on the lid from which the screws had been removed, and went into the billiard-room. As he came back into the library with an empty cage in his hand, he heard the sound of something falling, and then of something scuttling along the floor.

'Bother it! The beast's got out. How in the world am I to find it again in this library?'

To search for it did indeed seem hopeless. He tried to follow the sound of the scuttling in one of the recesses, where the animal seemed to be running behind the books on the shelves; but it was impossible to locate it. Eustace resolved to go on quietly reading. Very likely the animal might gain confidence and show itself. Saunders seemed to have dealt in his usual methodical manner with most of the correspondence. There were still the private letters.

What was that? Two sharp clicks and the lights in the hideous candelabra that hung from the ceiling suddenly went out.

'I wonder if something has gone wrong with the fuse,' said Eustace, as he went to the switches by the door. Then he stopped. There was a noise at the other end of the room, as if something was crawling up the iron corkscrew stair. 'If it's gone into the gallery,' he said, 'well and good.' He hastily turned on the lights, crossed the room, and climbed up the stair. But he could see nothing. His grandfather had placed a little gate at the top of the stair, so that children could run and romp in the gallery without fear of accident. This Eustace closed, and, having considerably narrowed the circle of his search, returned to his desk by the fire.

How gloomy the library was! There was no sense of intimacy about the room. The few busts that an eighteenth-century Borlsover had brought back from the grand tour might have been in keeping in the old library. Here they seemed out of place. They made the room feel cold in spite of the heavy red damask curtains and great gilt cornices.

With a crash two heavy books fell from the gallery to the floor; then, as Borlsover looked, another, and yet another.

'Very well. You'll starve for this, my beauty!' he said. 'We'll do some little experiments on the metabolism of rats deprived of water. Go on! Chuck them down! I think I've got the upper hand.' He turned once more to his correspondence. The letter was from the family solicitor. It spoke of his uncle's death, and of the valuable collection of books that had been left to him in the will.

'There was one request [he read] which certainly came as a surprise to me. As you know, Mr Adrian Borlsover had left instructions that his body was to be buried in as simple a manner as possible at Eastbourne. He expressed a desire that there should be neither wreaths nor flowers of any kind, and hoped that his friends and relatives would not consider it necessary to wear mourning. The day before his death we received a letter cancelling these instructions. He wished the body to be embalmed (he gave us the address of the man we were to employ—Pennifer, Ludgate Hill), with orders that his right hand should be sent to you stating that it was at your special request. The other arrangements about the funeral remained unaltered.'

'Good Lord,' said Eustace, 'what in the world was the old boy driving at? And what in the name of all that's holy is that?'

Someone was in the gallery. Someone had pulled the cord attached to one of the blinds, and it had rolled up with a snap. Someone must be in the gallery, for a second blind did the same. Someone must be walking round the gallery, for one after the other the blinds sprang up, letting in the moonlight.

'I haven't got to the bottom of this yet,' said Eustace, 'but I will do, before the night is very much older'; and he hurried up the corkscrew stair. He had just got to the top when the lights went out a second time, and he heard again the scuttling along the floor. Quickly he stole on tiptoe in the dim moonshine in the direction of the noise, feeling, as he went, for one of the switches. His fingers touched the metal knob at last. He turned on the electric light.

About ten yards in front of him, crawling along the floor, was a man's hand. Eustace stared at it in utter amazement. It was moving quickly in the manner of a geometer caterpillar, the fingers humped up one moment, flattened out the next; the thumb appeared to give a crablike motion to the while. While he was looking, too surprised to stir, the hand disappeared round the corner. Eustace ran forward. He no longer saw it, but he could hear it, as it squeezed its way behind the books on one of the shelves. A heavy volume had been displaced. There was a gap in the row of books, where it had got in. In his fear lest it should escape him again, he seized the first book that came to his hand and plugged it into the hole. Then, emptying two shelves of their contents, he took the wooden boards and propped them up in front to make his barrier doubly sure.

'I wish Saunders was back,' he said; 'one can't tackle this sort of thing alone.' It was after eleven, and there seemed little likelihood of Saunders returning before twelve. He did not dare to leave the shelf unwatched, even to run downstairs to ring the bell. Morton, the butler, often used to come round about eleven to see that the windows were fastened, but he might not come. Eustace was thoroughly unstrung. At last he heard steps down below.

'Morton!' he shouted. 'Morton!'

'Sir?'

'Has Mr Saunders got back yet?'

'Not yet, sir.'

'Well, bring me some brandy, and hurry up about it. I'm up in the gallery, you duffer.'

'Thanks,' said Eustace, as he emptied the glass. 'Don't go to bed yet, Morton. There are a lot of books that have fallen down by accident. Bring them up and put them back on their shelves.'

Morton had never seen Borlsover in so talkative a mood as on that night. 'Here,' said Eustace, when the books had been put back and dusted, 'you might hold up these boards for me, Morton. That beast in the box got out, and I've been chasing it all over the place.'

'I think I can hear it chewing at the books, sir. They're not valuable, I hope? I think that's the carriage, sir; I'll go and call Mr Saunders.'

It seemed to Eustace that he was away for five minutes, but it could hardly have been more than one, when he returned with Saunders. 'All right, Morton, you can go now. I'm up here, Saunders.'

'What's all the row?' asked Saunders, as he lounged forward with his hands in his pockets. The luck had been with him all the evening. He was completely satisfied, both with himself and with Captain Lockwood's taste in wines. 'What's the matter? You look to me to be in an absolutely blue funk.'

'That old devil of an uncle of mine,' began Eustace—'Oh, I can't explain it all. It's his hand that's been playing Old Harry all the evening. But I've got it cornered behind these books. You've got to help me to catch it.'

'What's up with you, Eustace? What's the game?'

'It's no game, you silly idiot! If you don't believe me, take out one of those books and put your hand in and feel.'

'All right,' said Saunders; 'but wait till I've rolled up my sleeve. The accumulated dust of centuries, eh?' He took off his coat, knelt down, and thrust his arm along the shelf.

'There's something there right enough,' he said. 'It's got a funny, stumpy end to it, whatever it is, and nips like a crab. Ah! no, you don't!' He pulled his hand out in a flash. 'Shove in a book quickly. Now it can't get out.'

'What was it?' asked Eustace.

'Something that wanted very much to get hold of me. I felt what seemed like a thumb and forefinger. Give me some brandy.'

'How are we to get it out of there?'

'What about a landing-net?'

'No good. It would be too smart for us. I tell you, Saunders, it can cover the ground far faster than I can walk. But I think I see how we can manage it. The two books at the end of the shelf are big ones, that go right back against the wall. The others are very thin. I'll take out one at a time, and you slide the rest along, until we have it squashed between the end two.'

It certainly seemed to be the best plan. One by one as they took out the books, the space behind grew smaller and smaller. There was something in it that was certainly very much alive. Once they caught sight of fingers feeling for a way of escape. At last they had it pressed between the two big books.

'There's muscle there, if there isn't warm flesh and blood,' said Saunders, as he held them together. 'It seems to be a hand right enough, too. I suppose this is a sort of infectious hallucination. I've read about such cases before.'

'Infectious fiddlesticks!' said Eustace, his face white with anger; 'bring the thing downstairs. We'll get it back into the box.'

It was not altogether easy, but they were successful at last. 'Drive in the screws,' said Eustace; 'we won't run any risks. Put the box in this old desk of mine. There's nothing in it that I want. Here's the key. Thank goodness there's nothing wrong with the lock.'

'Quite a lively evening,' said Saunders. 'Now let's hear more about your uncle.'

They sat up together until early morning. Saunders had no desire for sleep. Eustace was trying to explain and to forget; to conceal from himself a fear that he had never felt before—the fear of walking alone down the long corridor to his bedroom.

'Whatever it was,' said Eustace to Saunders on the following morning, 'I propose that we drop the subject. There's nothing to keep us here for the next ten days. We'll motor up to the Lakes and get some climbing.'

'And see nobody all day, and sit bored to death with each other every night. Not for me, thanks. Why not run up to town? Run's the exact word in this case, isn't it? We're both in such a blessed funk. Pull yourself together, Eustace, and let's have another look at the hand.'

'As you like,' said Eustace; 'there's the key.'

They went into the library and opened the desk. The box was as they had left it on the previous night.

'What are you waiting for?' asked Eustace.

'I am waiting for you to volunteer to open the lid. However, since you seem to funk it, allow me. There doesn't seem to be the likelihood of any rumpus this morning at all events.' He opened the lid and picked out the hand.

'Cold?' asked Eustace.

'Tepid. A bit below blood heat by the feel. Soft and supple too. If it's the embalming, it's a sort of embalming I've never seen before. Is it your uncle's hand?'

'Oh yes, it's his all right,' said Eustace. 'I should know those long thin fingers anywhere. Put it back in the box, Saunders. Never mind about the screws. I'll lock the desk, so that there'll be no chance of its getting out. We'll compromise by motoring up to town for a week. If we can get off soon after lunch, we ought to be at Grantham or Stamford by night.'

'Right,' said Saunders, 'and tomorrow—oh, well, by tomorrow we shall have forgotten all about this beastly thing.'

If, when the morrow came, they had not forgotten, it was certainly true that at the end of the week they were able to tell a very vivid ghost-story at the little supper Eustace gave on Hallow E'en.

'You don't want us to believe that it's true, Mr Borlsover? How perfectly awful!'

'I'll take my oath on it, and so would Saunders here; wouldn't you, old chap?'

'Any number of oaths,' said Saunders. 'It was a long thin hand, you know, and it gripped me just like that.'

'Don't, Mr Saunders! Don't! How perfectly horrid! Now tell us another one, do! Only a really creepy one, please.'

'Here's a pretty mess!' said Eustace on the following day, as he threw a letter across the table to Saunders. 'It's your affair, though. Mrs Merrit, if I understand it, gives a month's notice.'

'Oh, that's quite absurd on Mrs Merrit's part,' replied Saunders. 'She doesn't know what she's talking about. Let's see what she says.'

'Dear Sir [he read]. This is to let you know that I must give you a month's notice as from Tuesday, the 13th. For a long time I've felt the place too big for me; but when Jane Parfit and Emma Laidlaw go off with scarcely as much as an "If you please", after frightening the wits out of the other girls, so that they can't turn out a room by themselves or walk alone down the stairs for fear of treading on half-frozen toads or hearing it run along the passages at night, all I can say is that it's no place for me. So I must ask you, Mr Borlsover, sir, to find a new housekeeper, that has no objection to large and lonely houses, which some people do say, not that I believe them for a minute, my poor mother always having been a Wesleyan, are haunted.

'Yours faithfully,

'Elizabeth Merrit.

'P.S.—I should be obliged if you would give my respects to Mr Saunders. I hope that he won't run any risks with his cold.'

'Saunders,' said Eustace, 'you've always had a wonderful way with you in dealing with servants. You mustn't let poor old Merrit go.'

'Of course she shan't go,' said Saunders. 'She's probably only angling for a rise in salary. I'll write to her this morning.'

'No. There's nothing like a personal interview. We've had enough of town. We'll go back tomorrow, and you must work your cold for all it's worth. Don't forget that it's got on to the chest, and will require weeks of feeding up and nursing.'

'All right; I think I can manage Mrs Merrit.'

But Mrs Merrit was more obstinate than he had thought. She was very sorry to hear of Mr Saunders's cold, and how he lay awake all night in London coughing; very sorry indeed. She'd change his room for him, gladly, and get the south room aired, and wouldn't he have a hot basin of bread and milk last thing at night? But she was afraid that she would have to leave at the end of the month.

'Try her with an increase of salary,' was the advice of Eustace.

It was no use. Mrs Merrit was obdurate, though she knew of a Mrs Goddard, who had been housekeeper to Lord Gargrave, who might be glad to come at the salary mentioned.

'What's the matter with the servants, Morton?' asked Eustace that evening, when he brought the coffee into the library. 'What's all this about Mrs Merrit wanting to leave?'

'If you please, sir, I was going to mention it myself. I have a confession to make, sir. When I found your note, asking me to open that desk and take out the box with the rat, I broke the lock, as you told me, and was glad to do it, because I could hear the animal in the box making a great noise, and I thought it wanted food. So

I took out the box, sir, and got a cage, and was going to transfer it, when the animal got away.'

'What in the world are you talking about? I never wrote any such note.'

'Excuse me, sir; it was the note I picked up here on the floor on the day you and Mr Saunders left. I have it in my pocket now.'

It certainly seemed to be in Eustace's handwriting. It was written in pencil, and began somewhat abruptly.

'Get a hammer, Morton,' he read, 'or some other tool and break open the lock in the old desk in the library. Take out the box that is inside. You need not do anything else. The lid is already open. Eustace Borlsover.'

'And you opened the desk?'

'Yes, sir; and, as I was getting the cage ready, the animal hopped out.'

'What animal?'

'The animal inside the box, sir.'

'What did it look like?'

'Well, sir, I couldn't tell you,' said Morton nervously. 'My back was turned, and it was half way down the room when I looked up.'

'What was its colour?' asked Saunders. 'Black?'

'Oh no, sir; a greyish white. It crept along in a very funny way, sir. I don't think it had a tail.'

'What did you do then?'

'I tried to catch it; but it was no use. So I set the rat-traps and kept the library shut. Then that girl, Emma Laidlaw, left the door open when she was cleaning, and I think it must have escaped.'

'And you think it is the animal that's been frightening the maids?'

'Well, no sir, not quite. They said it was—you'll excuse me, sir—a hand that they saw. Emma trod on it once at the bottom of the stairs. She thought then it was a half-frozen toad, only white. And then Parfit was washing up the dishes in the scullery. She wasn't thinking about anything in particular. It was close on dusk. She took her hands out of the water and was drying them absent-minded like on the roller towel, when she found she was drying someone else's hand as well, only colder than hers.'

'What nonsense!' exclaimed Saunders.

'Exactly sir; that's what I told her; but we couldn't get her to stop.'

'You don't believe all this?' said Eustace, turning suddenly towards the butler.

'Me, sir? Oh no, sir! I've not seen anything.'

'Nor heard anything?'

'Well, sir, if you must know, the bells do ring at odd times, and there's nobody there when we go; and when we go round to draw the blinds of a night, as often as not somebody's been there before us. But, as I says to Mrs Merrit, a young monkey might do wonderful things, and we all know that Mr Borlsover has had some strange animals about the place.'

'Very well, Morton, that will do.'

'What do you make of it?' asked Saunders, when they were alone. 'I mean of the letter he said you wrote.'

'Oh, that's simple enough,' said Eustace. 'See the paper it's written on? I stopped using that paper years ago, but there were a few odd sheets and envelopes left in the old desk. We never fastened up the lid of the box before locking it in. The hand got out, found a pencil, wrote this note, and shoved it through the crack on to the floor, where Morton found it. That's plain as daylight.'

'But the hand couldn't write!'

'Couldn't it? You've not seen it do the things I've seen.'

And he told Saunders more of what had happened at Eastbourne.

'Well,' said Saunders, 'in that case we have at least an explanation of the legacy. It was the hand which wrote, unknown to your uncle, that letter to your solicitor bequeathing itself to you. Your uncle had no more to do with that request than I. In fact, it would seem that he had some idea of this automatic writing and feared it.'

'Then if it's not my uncle, what is it?'

'I suppose some people might say that a disembodied spirit had got your uncle to educate and prepare a little body for it. Now it's got into that little body and is off on its own.'

'Well, what are we to do?'

'We'll keep our eyes open,' said Saunders, 'and try to catch it. If we can't do that, we shall have to wait till the bally clockwork runs down. After all, if it's flesh and blood, it can't live for ever.'

For two days nothing happened. Then Saunders saw it sliding down the banister in the hall. He was taken unawares and lost a full second before he started in pursuit, only to find that the thing had escaped him. Three days later Eustace, writing alone in the library at night, saw it sitting on an open book at the other end of the room. The fingers crept over the page, as if it were reading; but before he had time to get up from his seat, it had taken the alarm, and was pulling itself up the curtains. Eustace watched it grimly, as it hung on to the cornice with three fingers and flicked thumb and forefinger at him in an expression of scornful derision.

'I know what I'll do,' he said. 'If I only get it into the open, I'll set the dogs on to it.'

He spoke to Saunders of the suggestion.

'It's a jolly good idea,' he said; 'only we won't wait till we find it out of doors. We'll get the dogs. There are the two terriers and the under-keeper's Irish mongrel, that's on to rats like a flash. Your spaniel has not got spirit enough for this sort of game.'

They brought the dogs into the house, and the keeper's Irish mongrel chewed up the slippers, and the terriers tripped up Morton, as he waited at table; but all three were welcome. Even false security is better than no security at all.

For a fortnight nothing happened. Then the hand was caught, not by the dogs, but by Mrs Merrit's grey parrot. The bird was in the habit of periodically removing the pins that kept its seed-and water-tin in place, and of escaping through the holes in the side of the cage. When once at liberty, Peter would show no inclination to return, and would often be about the house for days. Now, after six consecutive weeks of captivity, Peter had again discovered a new way of unloosing his bolts and was, at large, exploring the tapestried forests of the curtains and singing songs in praise of liberty from cornice and picture rail.

'It's no use your trying to catch him,' said Eustace to Mrs Merrit, as she came into the study one afternoon towards dusk with a stepladder. 'You'd much better leave Peter alone. Starve him into surrender, Mrs Merrit; and don't leave bananas and seed about for him to peck at when he fancies he's hungry. You're far too softhearted.'

'Well, sir, I see he's right out of reach now on that picture-rail; so, if you wouldn't mind closing the door, sir, when you leave the room, I'll bring his cage in tonight and put some meat inside it. He's that fond of meat, though it does make him pull out his feathers to suck the quills. They *do* say that if you cook——'

'Never mind, Mrs Merrit,' said Eustace, who was busy writing; 'that will do; I'll keep an eye on the bird.'

For a short time there was silence in the room.

'Scratch poor Peter,' said the bird. 'Scratch poor old Peter!'

'Be quiet, you beastly bird!'

'Poor old Peter! Scratch poor Peter; do!'

'I'm more likely to wring your neck, if I get hold of you.' He looked up at the picture-rail, and there was the hand, holding on to a hook with three fingers, and slowly scratching the head of the parrot with the fourth. Eustace ran to the bell and pressed it hard; then across to the window, which he closed with a bang. Frightened by the noise, the parrot shook its wings preparatory to flight, and, as it did so, the fingers of the hand got hold of it by the throat. There was a shrill scream from Peter, as he fluttered across the room, wheeling round in circles that ever descended, borne down under the weight that clung to him. The bird dropped at last quite suddenly, and Eustace saw fingers and feathers rolled into an inextricable mass on the floor. The struggle abruptly ceased, as finger and thumb squeezed the neck; the bird's eyes rolled up to show the white, and there was a faint, half-choked gurgle. But, before the fingers had time to loose their hold, Eustace had them in his own.

'Send Mr Saunders here at once,' he said to the maid who came in answer to the bell. 'Tell him I want him immediately.'

Then he went with the hand to the fire. There was a ragged gash across the back, where the bird's beak had torn it, but no blood oozed from the wound. He noted with disgust that the nails had grown long and discoloured.

'I'll burn the beastly thing,' he said. But he could not burn it. He tried to throw it into the flames, but his own hands, as if impelled by some old primitive feeling, would not let him. And so Saunders found him, pale and irresolute, with the hand still clasped tightly in his fingers.

'I've got it at last,' he said, in a tone of triumph.

'Good, let's have a look at it.'

'Not when it's loose. Get me some nails and a hammer and a board of some sort.'

'Can you hold it all right?'

'Yes, the thing's quite limp; tired out with throttling poor old Peter, I should say.'

'And now,' said Saunders, when he returned with the things, 'what are we going to do?'

'Drive a nail through it first, so that it can't get away. Then we can take our time over examining it.'

'Do it yourself,' said Saunders. 'I don't mind helping you with guinea-pigs occasionally, when there's something to be learned, partly because I don't fear a guinea-pig's revenge. This thing's different.'

'Oh, my aunt!' he giggled hysterically, 'look at it now.' For the hand was writhing in agonised contortions, squirming and wriggling upon the nail like a worm upon the hook.

'Well,' said Saunders, 'you've done it now. I'll leave you to examine it.'

'Don't go, in heaven's name! Cover it up, man; cover it up! Shove a cloth over it! Here!' and he pulled off the antimacassar from the back of a chair and wrapped the board in it. 'Now get the keys from my pocket and open the safe. Chuck the other things out. Oh, Lord, it's getting itself into frightful knots! Open it quick!' He threw the thing in and banged the door.

'We'll keep it there till it dies,' he said. 'May I burn in hell, if I ever open the door of that safe again.'

Mrs Merrit departed at the end of the month. Her successor, Mrs Handyside, certainly was more successful in the management of the servants. Early in her rule she declared that she would stand no nonsense, and gossip soon withered and died.

'I shouldn't be surprised if Eustace married one of these days,' said Saunders. 'Well, I'm in no hurry for such an event. I know him far too well for the future Mrs Borlsover to like me. It will be the same old story again; a long friendship slowly made—marriage—and a long friendship quickly forgotten.'

But Eustace did not follow the advice of his uncle and marry. Old habits crept over and covered his new experience. He was, if anything, less morose, and showed a great inclination to take his natural part in country society.

Then came the burglary. The man, it was said, broke into the house by way of the conservatory. It was really little more than an attempt, for they only succeeded in carrying away a few pieces of plate from the pantry. The safe in the study was certainly found open and empty, but, as Mr Borlsover informed the police inspector, he had kept nothing of value in it during the last six months.

'Then you're lucky in getting off so easily, sir,' the man replied. 'By the way they have gone about their business I should say they were experienced cracksmen. They must have caught the alarm when they were just beginning their evening's work.'

'Yes,' said Eustace, 'I suppose I am lucky.'

'I've no doubt,' said the inspector, 'that we shall be able to trace the men. I've said that they must have been old hands at the game. The way they got in and opened the safe shows that. But there's one little thing that puzzles me. One of them was careless enough not to wear gloves, and I'm bothered if I know what he was trying to do. I've traced his finger-marks on the new varnish on the window-sashes in every one of the downstairs rooms. They are very distinctive ones too.'

'Right hand or left or both?' asked Eustace.

'Oh, right every time. That's the funny thing. He must have been a foolhardy fellow, and I rather think it was him that wrote that.' He took out a slip of paper from his pocket. 'That's what he wrote, sir: "I've got out, Eustace Borlsover, but I'll be back before long." Some jailbird just escaped, I suppose. It will make it all the easier for us to trace him. Do you know the writing, sir?'

'No,' said Eustace. 'It's not the writing of anyone I know.'

'I'm not going to stay here any longer,' said Eustace to Saunders at luncheon. 'I've got on far better during the last six months than I expected, but I'm not going to run the risk of seeing that thing again. I shall go up to town this afternoon. Get Morton to put my things together, and join me with the car at Brighton on the day after tomorrow. And bring the proofs of those two papers with you. We'll run over them together.'

'How long are you going to be away?'

'I can't say for certain, but be prepared to stay for some time. We've stuck to work pretty closely through the summer, and I for one need a holiday. I'll engage the rooms at Brighton. You'll find it best to break the journey at Hitchin. I'll wire to you there at the "Crown" to tell you the Brighton address.'

The house he chose at Brighton was in a terrace. He had been there before. It was kept by his old college gyp, a man of discreet silence, who was admirably partnered by an excellent cook. The rooms were on the first floor. The two bedrooms were at the back, and opened out of each other. 'Mr Saunders can have the smaller one, though it is the only one with a fire-place,' he said. 'I'll stick to the larger of the two, since it's got a bathroom adjoining. I wonder what time he'll arrive with the car.'

Saunders came about seven, cold and cross and dirty. 'We'll light the fire in the dining-room,' said Eustace, 'and get Prince to unpack some of the things while we are at dinner. What were the roads like?'

'Rotten. Swimming with mud, and a beastly cold wind against us all day. And this is July. Dear Old England!'

'Yes,' said Eustace, 'I think we might do worse than leave Old England for a few months.'

They turned in soon after twelve.

'You oughtn't to feel cold, Saunders,' said Eustace, 'when you can afford to sport a great fur-lined coat like this. You do yourself very well, all things considered. Look at those gloves, for instance. Who could possibly feel cold when wearing them?'

'They are far too clumsy, though, for driving. Try them on and see'; and he tossed them through the door on to Eustace's bed and went on with his unpacking. A minute later he heard a shrill cry of terror. 'Oh, Lord,' he heard, 'it's in the glove! Quick, Saunders, quick!' Then came a smacking thud. Eustace had thrown it from him. 'I've chucked it into the bathroom,' he gasped; 'it's hit the wall and fallen into the bath. Come now, if you want to help.' Saunders, with a lighted candle in his hand, looked over the edge of the bath. There it was, old and maimed, dumb and blind, with a ragged hole in the middle, crawling, staggering, trying to creep up the slippery sides, only to fall back helpless.

'Stay there,' said Saunders. 'I'll empty a collar-box or something, and we'll jam it in. It can't get out while I'm away.'

'Yes, it can,' shouted Eustace. 'It's getting out now; it's climbing up the plug-chain.—No, you brute, you filthy brute, you don't!—Come back, Saunders; it's getting away from me. I can't hold it; it's all slippery. Curse its claws! Shut the window, you idiot! It's got out!' There was the sound of something dropping on to the hard flag-stones below, and Eustace fell back fainting.

For a fortnight he was ill.

'I don't know what to make of it,' the doctor said to Saunders. 'I can only suppose that Mr Borlsover has suffered some great emotional shock. You had better let me send someone to help you nurse him. And by all means indulge that whim of his never to be left alone in the dark. I would keep a light burning all night, if I were you. But he *must* have more fresh air. It's perfectly absurd, this hatred of open windows.'

Eustace would have no one with him but Saunders. 'I don't want the other man,' he said. 'They'd smuggle it in somehow. I know they would.'

'Don't worry about it, old chap. This sort of thing can't go on indefinitely. You know I saw it this time as well as you. It wasn't half so active. It won't go on living much longer, especially after that fall. I heard it hit the flags myself. As soon as you're a bit stronger, we'll leave this place, not bag and baggage, but with only the clothes on our backs, so that it won't be able to hide anywhere. We'll escape it that way. We won't give any address, and we won't have any parcels sent after us. Cheer up, Eustace! You'll be well enough to leave in a day or two. The doctor says I can take you out in a chair tomorrow.'

'What have I done?' asked Eustace. 'Why does it come after me? I'm no worse than other men. I'm no worse than you, Saunders; you know I'm not. It was you who was at the bottom of that dirty business in San Diego, and that was fifteen years ago.'

'It's not that, of course,' said Saunders. 'We are in the twentieth century, and even the parsons have dropped the idea of your old sins finding you out. Before you caught the hand in the library, it was filled with pure malevolence—to you and all mankind. After you spiked it through with that nail, it naturally forgot about other people and concentrated its attention on you. It was shut up in that safe, you know, for nearly six months. That gives plenty of time for thinking of revenge.'

Eustace Borlsover would not leave his room, but he thought there might be something in Saunders's suggestion of a sudden departure from Brighton. He began rapidly to regain his strength.

'We'll go on the first of September,' he said.

The evening of the thirty-first of August was oppressively warm. Though at midday the windows had been wide open, they had been shut an hour or so before dusk. Mrs Prince had long since ceased to wonder at the strange habits of the gentlemen on the first floor. Soon after their arrival she had been told to take down the heavy window curtains in the two bedrooms, and day by day the rooms had seemed to grow more bare. Nothing was left lying about.

'Mr Borlsover doesn't like to have any place where dirt can collect,' Saunders had said as an excuse. 'He likes to see into all the corners of the room.'

'Couldn't I open the window just a little?' he said to Eustace that evening. 'We're simply roasting in here, you know.'

'No, leave well alone. We're not a couple of boarding-school misses fresh from a course of hygiene lectures. Get the chess-board out.'

They sat down and played. At ten o'clock Mrs Prince came to the door with a note. 'I am sorry I didn't bring it before,' she said, 'but it was left in the letter-box.'

'Open it, Saunders, and see if it wants answering.'

It was very brief. There was neither address nor signature.

'Will eleven o'clock tonight be suitable for our last appointment?'

'Who is it from?' asked Borlsover.

'It was meant for me,' said Saunders. 'There's no answer, Mrs Prince,' and he put the paper into his pocket.

'A dunning letter from a tailor; I suppose he must have got wind of our leaving.'

It was a clever lie, and Eustace asked no more questions. They went on with their game.

On the landing outside Saunders could hear the grandfather's clock whispering the seconds, blurting out the quarter-hours.

'Check,' said Eustace. The clock struck eleven. At the same time there was a gentle knocking on the door; it seemed to come from the bottom panel.

'Who's there?' asked Eustace.

There was no answer.

'Mrs Prince, is that you?'

'She is up above,' said Saunders; 'I can hear her walking about the room.'

'Then lock the door; bolt it too. Your move, Saunders.'

While Saunders sat with his eyes on the chess-board, Eustace walked over to the window and examined the fastenings. He did the same in Saunders's room, and the bathroom. There were no doors between the three rooms, or he would have shut and locked them too.

'Now, Saunders,' he said, 'don't stay all night over your move. I've had time to smoke one cigarette already. It's bad to keep an invalid waiting. There's only one possible thing for you to do. What was that?'

'The ivy blowing against the window. There, it's your move now, Eustace.'

'It wasn't the ivy, you idiot! It was someone tapping at the window'; and he pulled up the blind. On the outer side of the window, clinging to the sash, was the hand.

'What is it that it's holding?'

'It's a pocket-knife. It's going to try to open the window by pushing back the fastener with the blade.'

'Well, let it try,' said Eustace. 'Those fasteners screw down; they can't be opened that way. Anyhow, we'll close the shutters. It's your move, Saunders; I've played.'

But Saunders found it impossible to fix his attention on the game. He could not understand Eustace, who seemed all at once to have lost his fear. 'What do you say to some wine?' he asked. 'You seem to be taking things coolly, but I don't mind confessing that I'm in a blessed funk.'

'You've no need to be. There's nothing supernatural about that hand, Saunders. I mean it seems to be governed by the laws of time and space. It's not the sort of thing that vanishes into thin air or slides through oaken doors. And since that's so, I defy it to get in here. We'll leave the place in the morning. I for one have bottomed the depths of fear. Fill your glass, man! The windows are all shuttered; the door is locked and bolted. Pledge me my Uncle Adrian! Drink, man! What are you waiting for?'

Saunders was standing with his glass half raised. 'It can get in,' he said hoarsely; 'it can get in. We've forgotten. There's the fireplace in my bed-room. It will come down the chimney.'

'Quick!' said Eustace, as he rushed into the other room; 'we haven't a minute to lose. What can we do? Light the fire, Saunders. Give me a match, quick!'

'They must be all in the other room. I'll get them.'

'Hurry, man, for goodness' sake! Look in the bookcase! Look in the bathroom! Here, come and stand here; I'll look.'

'Be quick!' shouted Saunders. 'I can hear something!'

'Then plug a sheet from your bed up the chimney. No, here's a match!' He had found one at last that had slipped into a crack in the floor.

'Is the fire laid? Good, but it may not burn. I know—the oil from that old reading-lamp and this cotton-wool. Now the match, quick! Pull the sheet away, you fool! We don't want it now.'

There was a great roar from the grate, as the flames shot up. Saunders had been a fraction of a second too late with the sheet. The oil had fallen on to it. It, too, was burning.

'The whole place will be on fire!' cried Eustace, as he tried to beat out the flames with a blanket. 'It's no good! I can't manage it. You must open the door, Saunders, and get help.'

Saunders ran to the door and fumbled with the bolts. The key was stiff in the lock. 'Hurry,' shouted Eustace, 'or the heat will be too much for me.' The key turned in the lock at last. For half a second Saunders stopped to look back. Afterwards he could never be quite sure as to what he had seen, but at the time he thought that something black and charred was creeping slowly, very slowly, from the mass of flames towards Eustace Borlsover. For a moment he thought of returning to his friend; but the noise and the smell of the burning sent him running down the passage, crying: 'Fire! Fire!' He rushed to the telephone to summon help, and then back to the bathroom—he should have thought of that before—for water. As he burst into the bedroom there came a scream of terror which ended suddenly, and then the sound of a heavy fall.

This is the story which I heard on successive Saturday evenings from the senior mathematical master at a second-rate suburban school. For Saunders has had to earn a living in a way which other men might reckon less congenial than his old manner of life. I had mentioned by chance the name of Adrian Borlsover, and wondered at the time why he changed the conversation with such unusual abruptness. A week later Saunders began to tell me something of his own history; sordid enough, though shielded with a reserve I could well understand, for it had to cover not only his failings, but those of a dead friend. Of the final tragedy he was at first especially loath to speak; and it was only gradually that I was able to piece together the narrative of the preceding pages. Saunders was reluctant to draw any conclusions. At one time he thought that the fingered beast had been animated by the spirit of Sigismund Borlsover, a sinister eighteenth-century ancestor, who, according to legend, built and worshipped in the ugly pagan temple that overlooked the lake. At another time Saunders believed the spirit to belong to a man whom Eustace had once employed as a laboratory assistant, 'a black-haired, spiteful little brute,' he said, 'who died cursing his doctor, because the fellow couldn't help him to live to settle some paltry score with Borlsover.'

From the point of view of direct contemporary evidence, Saunders's story is practically uncorroborated. All the letters mentioned in the narrative were destroyed, with the exception of the last note which Eustace received, or rather which he would have received, had not Saunders intercepted it. That I have seen myself. The handwriting was thin and shaky, the handwriting of an old man. I remember the Greek 'e' was used in 'appointment'. A little thing that amused me at the time was that Saunders seemed to keep the note pressed between the pages of his Bible.

I had seen Adrian Borlsover once. Saunders I learnt to know well. It was by chance, however, and not by design, that I met a third person of the story, Morton, the butler. Saunders and I were walking in the Zoological Gardens one Sunday afternoon, when he called my attention to an old man who was standing before the door of the Reptile House.

'Why, Morton,' he said, clapping him on the back, 'how is the world treating you?'

'Poorly, Mr Saunders,' said the old fellow, though his face lighted up at the greeting. 'The winters drag terribly nowadays. There don't seem no summers or springs.'

'You haven't found what you were looking for, I suppose?'

'No, sir, not yet; but I shall some day. I always told them that Mr Borlsover kept some queer animals.'

'And what is he looking for?' I asked, when we had parted from him.

'A beast with five fingers,' said Saunders. 'This afternoon, since he has been in the Reptile House, I suppose it will be a reptile with a hand. Next week it will be a monkey with practically no body. The poor old chap is a born materialist.'

The Lodger

Marie Belloc Lowndes

'There he is at last, and I'm glad of it, Ellen. 'tain't a night you would wish a dog to be out in.'

Mr Bunting's voice was full of unmistakable relief. He was close to the fire, sitting back in a deep leather armchair—a clean-shaven, dapper man, still in outward appearance what he had been so long, and now no longer was—a self-respecting butler.

'You needn't feel so nervous about him; Mr Sleuth can look out for himself, all right.' Mrs Bunting spoke in a dry, rather tart tone. She was less emotional, better balanced, than was her husband. On her the marks of past servitude were less apparent, but they were there all the same—especially in her neat black stuff dress and scrupulously clean, plain collar and cuffs. Mrs Bunting, as a single woman, had been for long years what is known as a useful maid.

'I can't think why he wants to go out in such weather. He did it in last week's fog, too,' Bunting went on complaining.

'Well, it's none of your business—now, is it?'

'No; that's true enough. Still, 'twould be a very bad thing for us if anything happened to him. This lodger's the first bit of luck we've had for a very long time.'

Mrs Bunting made no answer to this remark. It was too obviously true to be worth answering. Also she was listening—following in imagination her lodger's quick, singularly quiet—'stealthy', she called it to herself—progress through the dark, fog-filled hall and up the staircase.

'It isn't safe for decent folk to be out in such weather—not unless they have something to do that won't wait till tomorrow.' Bunting had at last turned round. He was now looking straight into his wife's narrow, colourless face; he was an obstinate man, and liked to prove himself right. 'I read you out the accidents in *Lloyd's* yesterday—shocking, they were, and all brought about by the fog! And then, that 'orrid monster at his work again—'

'Monster?' repeated Mrs Bunting absently. She was trying to hear the lodger's footsteps overhead; but her husband went on as if there had been no interruption:

'It wouldn't be very pleasant to run up against such a party as that in the fog, eh?'

'What stuff you do talk!' she said sharply; and then she got up suddenly. Her husband's remark had disturbed her. She hated to think of such things as the terrible series of murders that were just then horrifying and exciting the netherworld of London. Though she enjoyed pathos and sentiment—Mrs Bunting would listen with mild amusement to the details of a breach-of-promise action—she shrank from stories of either immorality or physical violence.

Mrs Bunting got up from the straight-backed chair on which she had been sitting. It would soon be time for supper.

She moved about the sitting-room, flecking off an imperceptible touch of dust here, straightening a piece of furniture there.

Bunting looked around once or twice. He would have liked to ask Ellen to leave off fidgeting, but he was mild and fond of peace, so he refrained. However, she soon gave over what irritated him of her own accord.

But even then Mrs Bunting did not at once go down to the cold kitchen, where everything was in readiness for her simple cooking. Instead, she opened the door leading into the bedroom behind, and there, closing the door quietly, stepped back into the darkness and stood motionless, listening.

At first she heard nothing, but gradually there came the sound of someone moving about in the room just overhead; try as she might, however, it was impossible for her to guess what her lodger was doing. At last she heard him open the door leading out on the landing. That meant that he would spend the rest of the evening in the rather cheerless room above the drawing-room floor—oddly enough, he liked sitting there best, though the only warmth obtainable was from a gas-stove fed by a shilling-in-the-slot arrangement.

It was indeed true that Mr Sleuth had brought the Buntings luck, for at the time he had taken their rooms, it had been touch and go with them.

After having each separately led the sheltered, impersonal, and, above all, the financially easy existence that is the compensation life offers to those men and women who deliberately take upon themselves the yoke of domestic service, these two, butler and useful maid, had suddenly, in middle age, determined to join their fortunes and savings.

Bunting was a widower; he had one pretty daughter, a girl of seventeen, who now lived, as had been the case ever since the death of her mother, with a prosperous aunt. His second wife had been reared in the Foundling Hospital, but she had gradually worked her way up into the higher ranks of the servant class and as useful maid she had saved quite a tidy sum of money.

Unluckily, misfortune had dogged Mr and Mrs Bunting from the very first. The seaside place where they had begun by taking a lodging-house became the scene of an epidemic. Then had followed a business experiment which had proved disastrous. But before going back into service, either together or separately, they had made up their minds to make one last effort, and, with the little money that remained to them, they had taken over the lease of a small house in the Marylebone Road.

Bunting, whose appearance was very good, had retained a connection with old employers and their friends, so he occasionally got a good job as waiter. During this last month, his jobs had perceptibly increased in number and in profit; Mrs Bunting was not superstitious, but it seemed that in this matter, as in everything else, Mr Sleuth, their new lodger, had brought them luck.

As she stood there, still listening intently in the darkness of the bedroom, she told herself, not for the first time, what Mr Sleuth's departure would mean to her and Bunting. It would almost certainly mean ruin.

Luckily, the lodger seemed entirely pleased both with the rooms and with his landlady. There was really no reason why he should ever leave such nice lodgings. Mrs Bunting shook off her vague sense of apprehension and unease. She turned round, took a step forward, and, feeling for the handle of the door giving into the passage, she opened it, and went down with light, firm steps into the kitchen.

She lit the gas and put a frying-pan on the stove, and then once more her mind reverted, as if in spite of herself, to her lodger, and there came back to Mrs Bunting, very vividly, the memory of all that had happened the day Mr Sleuth had taken her rooms.

The date of this excellent lodger's coming had been the twenty-ninth of December, and the time late afternoon. She and Bunting had been sitting, gloomily enough over their small banked-up fire. They had dined in the middle of the day—he on a couple of sausages, she on a little cold ham. They were utterly out of heart, each trying to pluck up courage to tell the other that it was no use trying any more. The two had also had a little tiff on that dreary afternoon. A newspaper-seller had come yelling down the Marylebone Road, shouting out, "'orrible murder in Whitechapel!' and just because Bunting had an old uncle living in the East End, he had gone and bought a paper, and at a time, too, when every penny, nay, every half-penny, had its full value! Mrs Bunting remembered the circumstances because that murder in Whitechapel had been the first of these terrible crimes—there had been four since—which she would never allow Bunting to discuss in her presence, and yet which had of late begun to interest curiously, uncomfortably, ever her refined mind.

But, to return to the lodger. It was then, on that dreary afternoon, that suddenly there had come to the front door a tremulous, uncertain double knock.

Bunting ought to have got up, but he had gone on reading the paper and so Mrs Bunting, with the woman's greater courage, had gone out into the passage, turned up the gas, and opened the door to see who it could be. She remembered, as if it were yesterday instead of nigh on a month ago, Mr Sleuth's peculiar appearance. Tall, dark, lanky, an old-fashioned top hat concealing his high bald forehead, he had stood there, an odd figure of a man, blinking at her.

'I believe—is it not a fact that you let lodgings?' he had asked in a hesitating, whistling voice, a voice that she had known in a moment to be that of an educated man—of a gentleman. As he had stepped into the hall, she had noticed that in his right hand he held a narrow bag—quite a new bag of strong brown leather.

Everything had been settled in less than a quarter of an hour. Mr Sleuth had at once 'taken' to the drawing-room floor, and then, as Mrs Bunting eagerly lit the gas in the front room above, he had looked around him and said, rubbing his hands with a nervous movement, 'Capital—capital! This is just what I've been looking for!'

The sink had specially pleased him—the sink and the gas-stove. 'This is quite first-rate!' he had exclaimed, 'for I make all sorts of experiments. I am, you must understand, Mrs—er—Bunting, a man of science.' Then he had sat down—suddenly. 'I'm very tired,' he had said in a low tone, 'very tired indeed! I have been walking about all day.'

From the very first the lodger's manner had been odd, sometimes distant and abrupt, and then, for no reason at all that she could see, confidential and plaintively confiding. But Mrs Bunting was aware that eccentricity has always been a perquisite, as it were the special luxury, of the well born and well educated. Scholars and such-like are never quite like other people.

And then, this particular gentleman had proved himself so eminently satisfactory as to the one thing that really matters to those who let lodgings. 'My name is Sleuth,' he said, 'S-l-e-u-t-h. Think of a hound, Mrs Bunting, and you'll never forget my name. I could give you references,' he had added, giving her, as she now remembered, a funny sidewise look, 'but I prefer to dispense with them. How much did you say? Twenty-three shillings a week, with attendance? Yes, that will suit me perfectly; and I'll begin by paying my first month's rent in advance. Now, four times twenty-three shillings is'—he looked at Mrs Bunting, and for the first time he smiled, a queer, wry smile—'ninety-two shillings.'

He had taken a handful of sovereigns out of his pocket and put them down on the table. 'Look here,' he had said, 'there's five pounds; and you can keep the change, for I shall want you to do a little shopping for me tomorrow.'

After he had been in the house about an hour, the bell had rung, and the new lodger had asked Mrs Bunting if she could oblige him with the loan of a Bible. She brought up to him her best Bible, the one that had been given to her as a wedding present by a lady with whose mother she had lived for several years. This Bible and one other book, of which the odd name was Cruden's Concordance, formed Mr Sleuth's only reading: he spent hours each day poring over the Old Testament and over the volume which Mrs Bunting had at last decided to be a queer kind of index to the Book.

However, to return to the lodger's first arrival. He had had no luggage with him, barring the small brown bag, but very soon parcels had begun to arrive addressed to Mr Sleuth, and it was then that Mrs Bunting first became curious. These parcels were full of clothes; but it was quite clear to the landlady's feminine eye that none of these clothes had been made for Mr Sleuth. They were, in fact, second-hand clothes, bought at good second-hand places, each marked, when marked at all, with a different name. And the really extraordinary thing was that occasionally a complete suit disappeared—became, as it were, obliterated from the lodger's wardrobe.

As for the bag he had brought with him, Mrs Bunting had never caught sight of it again. And this also was certainly very strange.

Mrs Bunting thought a great deal about that bag. She often wondered what had been in it; not a nightshirt and comb and brush, as she had at first supposed, for Mr Sleuth had asked her to go out and buy him a brush and comb and tooth-brush the morning after his arrival. That fact was specially impressed on her memory, for at the little shop, a barber's, where she had purchased the brush and comb, the foreigner who had served her had insisted on telling her some of the horrible details of the murder that had taken place the day before in Whitechapel, and it had upset her very much.

As to where the bag was now, it was probably locked up in the lower part of a chiffonnier in the front sitting-room. Mr Sleuth evidently always carried the key of the little cupboard on his person, for Mrs Bunting, though she looked well for it, had never been able to find it.

And yet, never was there a more confiding or trusting gentleman. The first four days that he had been with them he had allowed his money—the considerable sum of one hundred and eighty-four pounds in gold—to lie about wrapped up in pieces of paper on his dressing-table. This was a very foolish, indeed a wrong thing to do, as she had allowed herself respectfully to point out to him; but as only answer he had laughed, a loud, discordant shout of laughter.

Mr Sleuth had many other odd ways; but Mrs Bunting, a true woman in spite of her prim manner and love of order, had an infinite patience with masculine vagaries.

On the first morning of Mr Sleuth's stay in the Buntings' house, while Mrs Bunting was out buying things for him, the new lodger had turned most of the pictures and photographs hanging in his sitting-room with their faces to the wall! But this queer action on Mr Sleuth's part had not surprised Mrs Bunting as much as it might have done; it recalled an incident of her long-past youth—something that had happened a matter of twenty years ago, at a time when Mrs Bunting, then the still youthful Ellen Cottrell, had been maid to an old lady. The old lady had a favourite nephew, a bright, jolly young gentleman who had been learning to paint animals in Paris; and it was he who had had the impudence, early one summer morning, to turn to the wall six beautiful engravings of paintings done by the famous Mr Landseer! The old lady thought the world of those pictures, but her nephew, as only excuse for the extraordinary thing he had done, had observed that 'they put his eye out'.

Mr Sleuth's excuse had been much the same; for, when Mrs Bunting had come into his sitting-room and found all her pictures, or at any rate all those of her pictures that happened to be portraits of ladies, with their faces to the wall, he had offered as only explanation, 'Those women's eyes follow me about'.

Mrs Bunting had gradually become aware that Mr Sleuth had a fear and dislike of women. When she was 'doing' the staircase and landing, she often heard him reading bits of the Bible aloud to himself, and in the majority of instances the texts he chose contained uncomplimentary reference to her own sex. Only today she had stopped and listened while he uttered threateningly the awful words, 'A strange woman is a narrow pit. She also lieth in wait as for a prey, and increaseth the transgressors among men'. There had been a pause, and then had come, in a high singsong, 'Her house is the way to hell, going down to the chambers of death'. It had made Mrs Bunting feel quite queer.

The lodger's daily habits were also peculiar. He stayed in bed all morning, and sometimes part of the afternoon, and he never went out before the street lamps were alight. Then, there was his dislike of an open fire; he generally sat in the top front room, and while there he always used the large gas-stove, not only for his experiments, which he carried on at night, but also in the daytime, for warmth.

But there! Where was the use of worrying about the lodger's funny ways? Of course, Mr Sleuth was eccentric; if he hadn't been 'just a leetle "touched" upstairs'—as Bunting had once described it—he wouldn't be their lodger now; he would be living in a quite different sort of way with some of his relations, or with a friend of his own class.

Mrs Bunting, while these thoughts galloped disconnectedly through her brain, went on with her cooking, doing everything with a certain delicate and cleanly precision.

While in the middle of making the toast on which was to be poured some melted cheese, she suddenly heard a noise, or rather a series of noises. Shuffling, hesitating steps were creaking down the house above. She looked up and listened. Surely Mr Sleuth was not going out again into the cold, foggy night? But no; for the sounds did not continue down the passage leading to the front door.

The heavy steps were coming slowly down the kitchen stairs. Nearer and nearer came the thudding sounds, and Mrs Bunting's heart began to beat as if in response. She put out the gas-stove, unheedful of the fact that the cheese would stiffen and spoil in the cold air; and then she turned and faced the door. There was a fumbling at the handle, and a moment later the door opened and revealed, as she had known it would, her lodger.

Mr Sleuth was clad in a plaid dressing-gown, and in his hand was a candle. When he saw the lit-up kitchen, and the woman standing in it, he looked inexplicably taken aback, almost aghast.

'Yes, sir? What can I do for you, sir? I hope you didn't ring, sir?' Mrs Bunting did not come forward to meet her lodger; instead, she held her ground in front of the stove. Mr Sleuth had no business to come down like this into her kitchen.

'No, I—I didn't ring,' he stammered; 'I didn't know you were down here, Mrs Bunting. Please excuse my costume. The truth is, my gas-stove has gone wrong, or, rather, that shilling-in-the-slot arrangement has done so. I came down to see if *you* had a gas-stove. I am going to ask leave to use it tonight for an experiment I want to make.'

Mrs Bunting felt troubled—oddly, unnaturally troubled. Why couldn't the lodger's experiment wait till tomorrow? 'Oh, certainly, sir; but you will find it very cold down here.' She looked round her dubiously.

'It seems most pleasantly warm,' he observed, 'warm and cozy after my cold room upstairs.'

'Won't you let me make you a fire?' Mrs Bunting's housewifely instincts were roused. 'Do let me make you a fire in your bedroom, sir; I'm sure you ought to have one there these cold nights.'

'By no means—I mean, I would prefer not. I do not like an open fire, Mrs Bunting.' He frowned, and still stood, a strange-looking figure, just inside the kitchen door.

'Do you want to use this stove now, sir? Is there anything I can do to help you?'

'No, not now—thank you all the same, Mrs Bunting. I shall come down later, altogether later—probably after you and your husband have gone to bed. But I should be much obliged if you would see that the gas people come tomorrow and put my stove in order.'

'Perhaps Bunting could put it right for you, sir. I'll ask him to go up.'

'No, no—I don't want anything of that sort done tonight. Besides, he couldn't put it right. The cause of the trouble is quite simple. The machine is choked up with shillings: a foolish plan, so I have always felt it to be.'

Mr Sleuth spoke very pettishly, with far more heat than he was wont to speak; but Mrs Bunting sympathised with him. She had always suspected those slot-machines to be as dishonest as if they were human. It was dreadful, the way they swallowed up the shillings!

As if he were divining her thoughts, Mr Sleuth, walking forward, stared up at the kitchen slot-machine. 'Is it nearly full?' he asked abruptly. 'I expect my experiment will take some time, Mrs Bunting.'

'Oh, no, sir; there's plenty of room for shillings there still. We don't use our stove as much as you do yours, sir. I'm never in the kitchen a minute longer than I can help this cold weather.'

And then, with him preceding her, Mrs Bunting and her lodger made a slow progress to the ground floor. There Mr Sleuth courteously bade his landlady good night, and proceeded upstairs to his own apartments.

Mrs Bunting again went down into her kitchen, again she lit the stove, and again she cooked the toasted cheese. But she felt unnerved, afraid of she knew not what. The place seemed to her alive with alien presences, and once she caught herself listening, which was absurd, for of course she could not hope to hear what her lodger was doing two, if not three, flights upstairs. She had never been able to discover what Mr Sleuth's experiments really were; all she knew was that they required a very high degree of heat.

The Buntings went to bed early that night. But Mrs Bunting intended to stay awake. She wanted to know at what hour of the night her lodger would come down into the kitchen, and, above all, she was anxious as to how long he would stay there. But she had had a long day, and presently she fell asleep.

The church clock hard by struck two in the morning, and suddenly Mrs Bunting awoke. She felt sharply annoyed with herself.

How could she have dropped off like that? Mr Sleuth must have been down and up again hours ago.

Then, gradually, she became aware of a faint acrid odour; elusive, almost intangible, it yet seemed to encompass her and the snoring man by her side almost as a vapour might have done.

Mrs Bunting sat up in bed and sniffed; and then, in spite of the cold, she quietly crept out of the nice, warm bedclothes and crawled along to the bottom of the bed. There Mr Sleuth's landlady did a very curious thing; she leaned over the brass rail and put her face close to the hinge of the door. Yes, it was from there that this strange, horrible odour was coming; the smell must be very strong in the passage. Mrs Bunting thought she knew now what became of those suits of clothes of Mr Sleuth's that disappeared.

As she crept back, shivering, under the bedclothes, she longed to give her sleeping husband a good shake, and in fancy she heard herself saying: 'Bunting, get up! There is something strange going on downstairs that we ought to know about.'

But Mr Sleuth's landlady, as she lay by her husband's side, listening with painful intentness, knew very well that she would do nothing of the sort. The lodger had a right to destroy his clothes by burning if the fancy took him. What if he did make a certain amount of mess, a certain amount of smell, in her nice kitchen? Was he not—was he not such a good lodger! If they did anything to upset him, where could they ever hope to get another like him?

Three o'clock struck before Mrs Bunting heard slow, heavy steps creaking up her kitchen stairs. But Mr Sleuth did not go straight up to his own quarters, as she expected him to do. Instead, he went to the front door, and, opening it, put it on the chain. At the end of ten minutes or so he closed the front door, and by that time Mrs Bunting had divined why the lodger had behaved in this strange fashion—it must have been to get the strong acrid smell of burning wool out of the passage. But Mrs Bunting felt as if she herself would never get rid of the horrible odour. She felt herself to be all smell.

At last the unhappy woman fell into a deep, troubled sleep; and then she dreamed a most terrible and unnatural dream; hoarse voices seemed to be shouting in her ear, "'orrible murder off the Edgeware Road!' Then three words, indistinctly uttered, followed by '—at his work again! Awful details!'

Even in her dream Mrs Bunting felt angered and impatient; she knew so well why she was being disturbed by this horrid nightmare. It was because of Bunting—Bunting, who insisted on talking to her of those frightful murders, in which only morbid, vulgar-minded people took any interest. Why, even now, in her dream, she could hear her husband speaking to her about it.

'Ellen,'—so she heard Bunting say in her ear,—'Ellen, my dear, I am just going to get up to get a paper. It's after seven o'clock.'

Mrs Bunting sat up in bed. The shouting, nay, worse, the sound of tramping, hurrying feet smote on her ears. It had been no nightmare, then, but something infinitely worse—reality. Why couldn't Bunting have lain quietly in bed a while longer, and let his poor wife go on dreaming? The most awful dream would have been easier to bear than this awakening.

She heard her husband go to the front door, and, as he bought the paper, exchange a few excited words with the newspaper boy. Then he came back and began silently moving about the room.

'Well!' she cried. 'Why don't you tell me about it?'

'I thought you'd rather not hear.'

'Of course I like to know what happens close to our own front door!' she snapped out.

And then he read out a piece of the newspaper—only a few lines, after all—telling in brief, unemotional language that the body of a woman, apparently done to death in a peculiarly atrocious fashion some hours before, had been found in a passage leading to a disused warehouse off the Marylebone Road.

'It serves that sort of hussy right!' was Mrs Bunting's only comment.

When Mrs Bunting went down into the kitchen, everything there looked just as she had left it, and there was no trace of the acrid smell she had expected to find there. Instead, the cavernous whitewashed room was full of fog, and she noticed that, though the shutters were bolted and barred as she had left them, the windows behind them had been widely opened to the air. She, of course, had left them shut.

She stooped and flung open the oven door of her gas-stove. Yes, it was as she had expected; a fierce heat had been generated there since she had last used the oven, and a mass of black, gluey soot had fallen through to the stone floor below.

Mrs Bunting took the ham and eggs that she had bought the previous day for her own and Bunting's breakfast, and broiled them over the gas-ring in their sitting-room. Her husband watched her in surprised silence. She had never done such a thing before.

'I couldn't stay down there,' she said, 'it was so cold and foggy. I thought I'd make breakfast up here, just for today.'

'Yes,' he said kindly; 'that's quite right, Ellen. I think you've done quite right, my dear.'

But, when it came to the point, his wife could not eat any of the nice breakfast she had got ready; she only had another cup of tea.

'Are you ill?' Bunting asked solicitously.

'No,' she said shortly; 'of course I'm not ill. Don't be silly! The thought of that horrible thing happening so close by has upset me. Just hark to them, now!'

Through their closed windows penetrated the sound of scurrying feet and loud, ribald laughter. A crowd, nay, a mob, hastened to and from the scene of the murder.

Mrs Bunting made her husband lock the front gate. 'I don't want any of those ghouls in here!' she exclaimed angrily. And then, 'What a lot of idle people there must be in the world,' she said.

The coming and going went on all day. Mrs Bunting stayed indoors; Bunting went out. After all, the ex-butler was human— it was natural that he should feel thrilled and excited. All their neighbours were the same. His wife wasn't reasonable about such things. She quarrelled with him when he didn't tell her anything, and yet he was sure she would have been angry with him if he had said very much about it.

The lodger's bell rang about two o'clock, and Mrs Bunting prepared the simple luncheon that was also his breakfast. As she rested the tray a minute on the drawing-room floor landing, she heard Mr Sleuth's high, quavering voice reading aloud the words:

'She saith to him, Stolen waters are sweet, and bread eaten in secret is pleasant. But he knoweth not that the dead are there; and that her guests are in the depths of hell.'

The landlady turned the handle of the door and walked in with the tray. Mr Sleuth was sitting close by the window, and Mrs Bunting's Bible lay open before him. As she came in he hastily closed the Bible and looked down at the crowd walking along the Marylebone Road.

'There seem a great many people out today,' he observed, without looking round.

'Yes, sir, there do.' Mrs Bunting said nothing more, and offered no other explanation; and the lodger, as he at last turned to his landlady, smiled pleasantly. He had acquired a great liking and respect for this well-behaved, taciturn woman; she was the first person for whom he had felt any such feeling for many years past.

He took a half sovereign out of his waistcoat pocket; Mrs Bunting noticed that it was not the same waistcoat Mr Sleuth had been wearing the day before. 'Will you please accept this half sovereign for the use of your kitchen last night?' he said. 'I made as little mess as I could, but I was carrying on a rather elaborate experiment.'

She held out her hand, hesitated, and then took the coin. As she walked down the stairs, the winter sun, a yellow ball hanging in the smoky sky, glinted in on Mrs Bunting, and lent blood-red gleams, or so it seemed to her, to the piece of gold she was holding in her hand.

It was a very cold night—so cold, so windy, so snow-laden the atmosphere, that every one who could do so stayed indoors. Bunting, however, was on his way home from what had proved a very pleasant job; he had been acting as waiter at a young lady's birthday party, and a remarkable piece of luck had come his way. The young lady had come into a fortune that day, and she had had the gracious, surprising thought of presenting each of the hired waiters with a sovereign.

This birthday treat had put him in mind of another birthday. His daughter Daisy would be eighteen the following Saturday. Why shouldn't he send her a postal order for half a sovereign, so that she might come up and spend her birthday in London?

Having Daisy for three or four days would cheer up Ellen. Mr Bunting, slackening his footsteps, began to think with puzzled concern of how queer his wife had seemed lately. She had become so nervous, so 'jumpy,' that he didn't know what to make of her sometimes. She had never been a really good-tempered woman— your capable, self-respecting woman seldom is—but she had never been like what she was now. Of late she sometimes got quite hysterical; he had let fall a sharp word to her the other day, and she had sat down on a chair, thrown her black apron over her face, and burst out sobbing violently.

During the last ten days Ellen had taken to talking in her sleep. 'No, no, no!' she had cried out, only the night before. 'It isn't true! I won't have it said! It's a lie!' And there had been a wail of horrible fear and revolt in her unusually quiet, mincing voice. Yes, it would certainly be a good thing for her to have Daisy's company for a bit. Whew! It *was* cold; and Bunting had stupidly forgotten his gloves. He put his hands in his pockets to keep them warm.

Suddenly he became aware that Mr Sleuth, the lodger who seemed to have 'turned their luck', as it were, was walking along on the opposite side of the solitary street.

Mr Sleuth's tall, thin figure was rather bowed, his head bent toward the ground. His right arm was thrust into his long Inverness cape; the other occasionally sawed the air, doubtless in order to help him keep warm. He was walking rather quickly. It was clear that he had not yet become aware of the proximity of his landlord.

Bunting felt pleased to see his lodger; it increased his feeling of general satisfaction. Strange, was it not, that that odd, peculiar-looking figure should have made all the difference to his (Bunting's) and Mrs Bunting's happiness and comfort in life?

Naturally, Bunting saw far less of the lodger than did Mrs Bunting. Their gentleman had made it very clear that he did not like either the husband or wife to come up to his rooms without being definitely asked to do so, and Bunting had been up there only once since Mr Sleuth's arrival five weeks before. This seemed to be a good opportunity for a little genial conversation.

Bunting, still an active man for his years, crossed the road, and, stepping briskly forward, tried to overtake Mr Sleuth; but the more he hurried, the more the other hastened, and that without even turning to see whose steps he heard echoing behind him on the now freezing pavement.

Mr Sleuth's own footsteps were quite inaudible— an odd circumstance, when you came to think of it, as Bunting did think of it later, lying awake by Ellen's side in the pitch-darkness. What it meant was, of course, that the lodger had rubber soles on his shoes.

The two men, the pursued and the pursuer, at last turned into the Marylebone Road. They were now within a hundred yards of home; and so, plucking up courage, Bunting called out, his voice echoing freshly on the still air:

'Mr Sleuth, sir! Mr Sleuth!'

The lodger stopped and turned round. He had been walking so quickly, and he was in so poor a physical condition, that the sweat was pouring down his face.

'Ah! So it's you, Mr Bunting? I heard footsteps behind me, and I hurried on. I wish I'd known that it was only you; there are so many queer characters about at night in London.'

'Not on a night like this, sir. Only honest folk who have business out of doors would be out such a night as this. It *is* cold, sir!' And then into Bunting's slow and honest mind there suddenly crept the query as to what Mr Sleuth's own business out could be on this cold, bitter night.

'Cold?' the lodger repeated. 'I can't say that I find it cold, Mr Bunting. When the snow falls the air always becomes milder.'

'Yes, sir; but tonight there's such a sharp east wind. Why, it freezes the very marrow in one's bones!'

Bunting noticed that Mr Sleuth kept his distance in a rather strange way: he walked at the edge of the pavement, leaving the rest of it, on the wall side, to his landlord.

'I lost my way,' he said abruptly. 'I've been over Primrose Hill to see a friend of mine, and then, coming back, I lost my way.'

Bunting could well believe that, for when he had first noticed Mr Sleuth he was coming from the east, and not, as he should have done if walking home from Primrose Hill, from the north.

They had now reached the little gate that gave on to the shabby, paved court in front of the house. Mr Sleuth was walking up the flagged path, when, with a 'By your leave, sir', the ex-butler, stepping aside, slipped in front of his lodger, in order to open the front door for him.

As he passed by Mr Sleuth, the back of Bunting's bare left hand brushed lightly against the long Inverness cape the other man was wearing, and, to his surprise, the stretch of cloth against which his hand lay for a moment was not only damp, damp from the flakes of snow that had settled upon it, but wet—wet and gluey. Bunting thrust his left hand into his pocket; it was with the other that he placed the key in the lock of the door.

The two men passed into the hall together. The house seemed blackly dark in comparison with the lighted up road outside; and then, quite suddenly, there came over Bunting a feeling of mortal terror, an instinctive knowledge that some terrible and immediate danger was near him. A voice—the voice of his first wife, the long-dead girl to whom his mind so seldom reverted nowadays—uttered in his ear the words, 'Take care!'

'I'm afraid, Mr Bunting, that you must have felt something dirty, foul, on my coat? It's too long a story to tell you now, but I brushed up against a dead animal—a dead rabbit lying across a bench on Primrose Hill.'

Mr Sleuth spoke in a very quiet voice, almost in a whisper.

'No, sir; no, I didn't notice nothing. I scarcely touched you, sir,' It seemed as if a power outside himself compelled Bunting to utter these lying words. 'And now, sir, I'll be saying good night to you,' he added.

He waited until the lodger had gone upstairs, and then he turned into his own sitting-room. There he sat down, for he felt very queer. He did not draw his left hand out of his pocket till he heard the other man moving about in the room above. Then he lit the gas and held up his left hand; he put it close to his face. It was flecked, streaked with blood.

He took off his boots, and then, very quietly, he went into the room where his wife lay asleep. Stealthily he walked across to the toilet-table, and dipped his hand into the water-jug.

The next morning Mr Sleuth's landlord awoke with a start; he felt curiously heavy about the limbs and tired about the eyes.

Drawing his watch from under his pillow, he saw that it was nearly nine o'clock. He and Ellen had overslept. Without waking her, he got out of bed and pulled up the blind. It was snowing heavily, and, as is the way when it snows, even in London, it was strangely, curiously still.

After he had dressed he went out into the passage. A newspaper and a letter were lying on the mat. Fancy having slept through the postman's knock! He picked them both up and went into the sitting-room; then he carefully shut the door behind him, and, tossing the letter aside, spread the newspaper wide open on the table and bent over it.

As Bunting at last looked up and straightened himself, a look of inexpressible relief shone upon his stolid face. The item of news he had felt certain would be there, printed in big type on the middle sheet, was not there.

He folded the paper and laid it on a chair, and then eagerly took up his letter.

Dear Father [it ran]: I hope this finds you as well as it leaves me. Mrs Puddle's youngest child has got scarlet fever, and aunt thinks I had better come away at once, just to stay with you for a few days. Please tell Ellen I won't give her no trouble.

Your loving daughter,
Daisy.

Bunting felt amazingly light-hearted; and, as he walked into the next room, he smiled broadly.

'Ellen,' he cried out, 'here's news! Daisy's coming today. There's scarlet fever in their house, and Martha thinks she had better come away for a few days. She'll be here for her birthday!'

Mrs Bunting listened in silence; she did not even open her eyes. 'I can't have the girl here just now,' she said shortly; 'I've got just as much as I can manage to do.'

But Bunting felt pugnacious, and so cheerful as to be almost light-headed. Deep down in his heart he looked back to last night with a feeling of shame and self-rebuke. Whatever had made such horrible thoughts and suspicions come into his head?

'Of course Daisy will come here,' he said shortly. 'If it comes to that, she'll be able to help you with the work, and she'll brisk us both up a bit.'

Rather to his surprise, Mrs Bunting said nothing in answer to this, and he changed the subject abruptly. 'The lodger and me came in together last night,' he observed. 'He's certainly a funny kind of gentleman. It wasn't the sort of night one would choose to go for a walk over Primrose Hill, and yet that was what he had been doing—so he said.'

It stopped snowing about ten o'clock, and the morning wore itself away.

Just as twelve was striking, a four-wheeler drew up to the gate. It was Daisy—pink-cheeked, excited, laughing-eyed Daisy, a sight to gladden any father's heart. 'Aunt said I was to have a cab if the weather was bad,' she said.

There was a bit of a wrangle over the fare. King's Cross, as all the world knows, is nothing like two miles from the Marylebone

Road, but the man clamoured for one-and-six-pence, and hinted darkly that he had done the young lady a favour in bringing her at all.

While he and Bunting were having words, Daisy, leaving them to it, walked up the path to the door where her stepmother was awaiting her.

Suddenly there fell loud shouts on the still air. They sounded strangely eerie, breaking sharply across the muffled, snowy air.

'What's that?' said Bunting, with a look of startled fear. 'Why, whatever's that?'

The cabman lowered his voice: 'Them are crying out that 'orrible affair at King's Cross. He's done for two of 'em this time! That's what I meant when I said I might have got a better fare; I wouldn't say anything before Missy there, but folk 'ave been coming from all over London—like a fire; plenty of toffs, too. But there—there's nothing to see now!'

'What! Another woman murdered last night?' Bunting felt and looked convulsed with horror.

The cabman stared at him, surprised. 'Two of 'em, I tell yer— within a few yards of one another. He 'ave got a nerve—'

'Have they caught him?' asked Bunting perfunctorily.

'Lord, no! They'll never catch 'im! It must 'ave happened hours and hours ago—they was both stone-cold. One each end of an archway. That's why they didn't see 'em before.'

The hoarse cries were coming nearer and nearer—two news-venders trying to outshout each other.

' 'orrible discovery near King's Cross!' they yelled exultantly. And as Bunting, with his daughter's bag in his hand, hurried up the path and passed through his front door, the words pursued him like a dreadful threat.

Angrily he shut out the hoarse, insistent cries. No, he had no wish to buy a paper. That kind of crime wasn't fit reading for a young girl, such a girl as was his Daisy, brought up as carefully as if she had been a young lady by her strict Methody aunt.

As he stood in his little hall, trying to feel 'all right' again, he could hear Daisy's voice—high, voluble, excited—giving her stepmother a long account of the scarlet-fever case to which she owed her presence in London. But, as Bunting pushed open the door of the sitting-room there came a note of sharp alarm in his daughter's voice, and he heard her say: 'Why, Ellen! Whatever is the matter? You do look bad!' and his wife's muffled answer: 'Open the window—do.'

Rushing across the room, Bunting pushed up the sash. The newspaper-sellers were now just outside the house. 'Horrible discovery near King's Cross—a clue to the murderer!' they yelled. And then, helplessly, Mrs Bunting began to laugh. She laughed and laughed and laughed, rocking herself to and fro as if in an ecstasy of mirth.

'Why, father, whatever's the matter with her?' Daisy looked quite scared.

'She's in 'sterics—that's what it is,' he said shortly. 'I'll just get the water-jug. Wait a minute.'

Bunting felt very put out, and yet glad, too, for this queer seizure of Ellen's almost made him forget the sick terror with which he had been possessed a moment before. That he and his wife should be obsessed by the same fear, the same terror, never crossed his simple, slow-working mind.

The lodger's bell rang. That, or the threat of the water-jug, had a magical effect on Mrs Bunting. She rose to her feet, still trembling, but composed.

As Mrs Bunting went upstairs she felt her legs trembling under her, and put out a shaking hand to clutch at the bannister for support. She waited a few minutes on the landing, and then knocked at the door of her lodger's parlour.

But Mr Sleuth's voice answered her from the bedroom. 'I'm, not well,' he called out querulously; 'I think I caught a chill going out to see a friend last night. I'd be obliged if you'll bring me up a cup of tea and put it outside my door, Mrs Bunting.'

'Very well, sir.'

Mrs Bunting went downstairs and made her lodger a cup of tea over the gas-ring, Bunting watching her the while in heavy silence.

During their midday dinner the husband and wife had a little discussion as to where Daisy should sleep. It had already been settled that a bed should be made up for her in the sitting-room, but Bunting saw reason to change this plan. As the two women were clearing away the dishes, he looked up and said shortly: 'I think 'twould be better if Daisy were to sleep with you, Ellen, and I were to sleep in the sitting room.'

Ellen acquiesced quietly.

Daisy was a good-natured girl; she liked London, and wanted to make herself useful to her stepmother. 'I'll wash up; don't you bother to come downstairs,' she said.

Bunting began to walk up and down the room. His wife gave him a furtive glance; she wondered what he was thinking about.

'Didn't you get the paper?' she said at last.

'There's the paper,' he said crossly, 'the paper we always do take in, the *Telegraph*.' His look challenged her to a further question.

'I thought they was shouting something in the street—I mean just before I was took bad.'

But he made no answer; instead, he went to the top of the staircase and called out sharply: 'Daisy! Daisy, child, are you there?'

'Yes, father,' she answered from below.

'Better come upstairs out of that cold kitchen.'

He came back into the sitting-room again.

'Ellen, is the lodger in? I haven't heard him moving about. I don't want Daisy to be mixed up with him.'

'Mr Sleuth is not well today,' his wife answered; 'he is remaining in bed a bit. Daisy needn't have anything to do with him. She'll have her work cut out looking after things down here. That's where I want her to help me.'

'Agreed,' he said.

When it grew dark, Bunting went out and bought an evening paper. He read it out of doors in the biting cold, standing beneath a street lamp. He wanted to see what was the clue to the murderer.

The clue proved to be a very slender one—merely the imprint in the snowy slush of a half-worn rubber sole; and it was, of course, by no means certain that the sole belonged to the boot or shoe of the murderer of the two doomed women who had met so swift and awful a death in the arch near King's Cross station. The paper's special investigator pointed out that there were thousands of such soles being worn in London. Bunting found comfort in that obvious fact. He felt grateful to the special investigator for having stated it so clearly.

As he approached his house, he heard curious sounds coming from the inner side of the low wall that shut off the courtyard from the pavement. Under ordinary circumstances Bunting would have gone at once to drive whoever was there out into the roadway. Now he stayed outside, sick with suspense and anxiety. Was it possible that their place was being watched—already?

But it was only Mr Sleuth. To Bunting's astonishment, the lodger suddenly stepped forward from behind the wall on to the flagged path. He was carrying a brown-paper parcel, and, as he walked along, the new boots he was wearing creaked and the tap-tap of wooden heels rang out on the stones.

Bunting, still hidden outside the gate, suddenly understood what his lodger had been doing the other side of the wall. Mr Sleuth had been out to buy himself a pair of boots, and had gone inside the gate to put them on, placing his old footgear in the paper in which the new boots had been wrapped.

Bunting waited until Mr Sleuth had let himself into the house; then he also walked up the flagged pathway, and put his latch-key in the door.

In the next three days each of Bunting's waking hours held its meed of aching fear and suspense. From his point of view, almost any alternative would be preferable to that which to most people would have seemed the only one open to him. He told himself that it would be ruin for him and for his Ellen to be mixed up publicly in such a terrible affair. It would track them to their dying day.

Bunting was also always debating within himself as to whether he should tell Ellen of his frightful suspicion. He could not believe that what had become so plain to himself could long be concealed from all the world, and yet he did not credit his wife with the same intelligence. He did not even notice that, although she waited on Mr Sleuth as assiduously as ever, Mrs Bunting never mentioned the lodger.

Mr Sleuth, meanwhile, kept upstairs; he had given up going out altogether. He still felt, so he assured his landlady, far from well.

Daisy was another complication, the more so that the girl, whom her father longed to send away and whom he would hardly let out of his sight, showed herself inconveniently inquisitive concerning the lodger.

'Whatever does he do with himself all day?' she asked her stepmother.

'Well, just now he's reading the Bible,' Mrs Bunting had answered, very shortly and dryly.

'Well, I never! That's a funny thing for a gentleman to do!' Such had been Daisy's pert remark, and her stepmother had snubbed her well for it.

Daisy's eighteenth birthday dawned uneventfully. Her father gave her what he had always promised she should have on her eighteenth birthday—a watch. It was a pretty little silver watch, which Bunting had bought second-hand on the last day he had been happy; it seemed a long time ago now.

Mrs Bunting thought a silver watch a very extravagant present, but she had always had the good sense not to interfere between her husband and his child. Besides, her mind was now full of other things. She was beginning to fear that Bunting suspected something, and she was filled with watchful anxiety and unease. What if he were to do anything silly—mix them up with the police, for instance? It certainly would be ruination to them both. But there—one never knew, with men! Her husband, however, kept his own counsel absolutely.

Daisy's birthday was a Saturday. In the middle of the morning Ellen and Daisy went down into the kitchen. Bunting didn't like the feeling that there was only one flight of stairs between Mr Sleuth and himself, so he quietly slipped out of the house and went to buy himself an ounce of tobacco.

In the last four days Bunting had avoided his usual haunts. But today the unfortunate man had a curious longing for human companionship—companionship, that is, other than that of Ellen and Daisy. This feeling led him into a small, populous thoroughfare hard by the Edgeware Road. There were more people there than usual, for the housewives of the neighbourhood were doing their marketing for Sunday.

Bunting passed the time of day with the tobacconist, and the two fell into desultory talk. To the ex-butler's surprise, the man said nothing at all to him on the subject of which all the neighbourhood must still be talking.

And then, quite suddenly, while still standing by the counter, and before he had paid for the packet of tobacco he held in his hand, Bunting, through the open door, saw, with horrified surprise, that his wife was standing outside a green-grocer's shop just opposite. Muttering a word of apology, he rushed out of the shop and across the road.

'Ellen!' he gasped hoarsely. 'You've never gone and left my little girl alone in the house?'

Mrs Bunting's face went chalky white. 'I thought you were indoors,' she said. 'You *were* indoors. Whatever made you come out for, without first making sure I was there?'

Bunting made no answer; but, as they stared at each other in exasperated silence, *each knew that the other knew.*

They turned and scurried down the street.

'Don't run,' he said suddenly; 'we shall get there just as quickly if we walk fast. People are noticing you, Ellen. Don't run.'

He spoke breathlessly, but it was breathlessness induced by fear and excitement, not by the quick pace at which they were walking.

At last they reached their own gate. Bunting pushed past in front of his wife. After all, Daisy was his child—Ellen couldn't know how he was feeling. He made the path almost in one leap, and fumbled for a moment with his latch-key. The door opened.

'Daisy!' he called out in a wailing voice. 'Daisy, my dear, where are you?'

'Here I am, father; what is it?'

'She's all right!' Bunting turned his gray face to his wife. 'She's all right, Ellen!' Then he waited a moment, leaning against the wall of the passage. 'It did give me a turn,' he said; and then, warningly, 'Don't frighten the girl, Ellen.'

Daisy was standing before the fire in the sitting-room, admiring herself in the glass. 'Oh, father,' she said, without turning round, 'I've seen the lodger! He's quite a nice gentleman—though, to be sure, he does look a cure! He came down to ask Ellen for something, and we had quite a nice little chat. I told him it was my birthday, and he asked me to go to Madame Tussaud's with him this afternoon.' She laughed a little self-consciously. 'Of course I could see he was 'centric, and then at first he spoke so funnily. "And who be you?" he says, threatening-like. And I says to him, "I'm Mr Bunting's daughter, sir." "Then you're a very fortunate girl"—that's what he said, Ellen—"to 'ave such a nice stepmother as you've got. That's why," he says, "you look such a good, innocent girl." And then he quoted a bit of the prayer-book at me. "Keep innocency," he says, wagging his head at me. Lor'! It made me feel as if I was with aunt again.'

'I won't have you going out with the lodger—that's flat.' He was wiping his forehead with one hand, while with the other he mechanically squeezed the little packet of tobacco, for which, as he now remembered, he had forgotten to pay.

Daisy pouted. 'Oh, father, I think you might let me have a treat on my birthday! I told him Saturday wasn't a very good day—at least, so I'd heard—for Madame Tussaud's. Then he said we could go early, while the fine folk are still having their dinners. He wants you to come, too.' She turned to her stepmother, then giggled happily. 'The lodger has a wonderful fancy for you, Ellen; if I was father, I'd feel quite jealous!'

Her last words were cut across by a loud knock on the door. Bunting and his wife looked at each other apprehensively.

Both felt a curious thrill of relief when they saw that it was only Mr Sleuth—Mr Sleuth dressed to go out: the tall hat he had worn when he first came to them was in his hand, and he was wearing a heavy overcoat.

'I saw you had come in,'—he addressed Mrs Bunting in his high, whistling, hesitating voice,—'and so I've come down to ask if you and Miss Bunting will come to Madame Tussaud's now. I have never seen these famous waxworks, though I've heard of the place all my life.'

As Bunting forced himself to look fixedly at his lodger, a sudden doubt, bringing with it a sense of immeasurable relief, came to him. Surely it was inconceivable that this gentle, mild-mannered gentleman could be the monster of cruelty and cunning that Bunting had but a moment ago believed him to be!

'You're very kind, sir, I'm sure.' He tried to catch his wife's eye, but Mrs Bunting was looking away, staring into vacancy. She still, of course, wore the bonnet and cloak in which she had just been out to do her marketing. Daisy was already putting on her hat and coat.

Madame Tussaud's had hitherto held pleasant memories for Mrs Bunting. In the days when she and Bunting were courting they often spent part of their 'afternoon out' there. The butler had an acquaintance, a man named Hopkins, who was one of the waxworks' staff, and this man had sometimes given him passes for 'self and lady'. But this was the first time Mrs Bunting had been inside the place since she had come to live almost next door, as it were, to the big building.

The ill-sorted trio walked up the great staircase and into the first gallery; and there Mr Sleuth suddenly stopped short. The presence of those curious, still figures, suggesting death in life, seemed to surprise and affright him.

Daisy took quick advantage of the lodger's hesitation and unease.

'Oh, Ellen,' she cried, 'do let us begin by going into the Chamber of Horrors! I've never been in there. Aunt made father promise he wouldn't take me, the only time I've ever been here. But now that I'm eighteen I can do just as I like; besides, aunt will never know!'

Mr Sleuth looked down at her.

'Yes,' he said, 'let us go into the Chamber of Horrors; that's a good idea, Miss Bunting.'

They turned into the great room in which the Napoleonic relics are kept, and which leads into the curious, vaultlike chamber where waxen effigies of dead criminals stand grouped in wooden docks. Mrs Bunting was at once disturbed and relieved to see her husband's old acquaintance, Mr Hopkins, in charge of the turnstile admitting the public to the Chamber of Horrors.

'Well, you *are* a stranger,' the man observed genially. 'I do believe this is the very first time I've seen you in here, Mrs Bunting, since you married!'

'Yes,' she said; 'that is so. And this is my husband's daughter, Daisy; I expect you've heard of her, Mr Hopkins. And this'—she hesitated a moment—'is our lodger, Mr Sleuth.'

But Mr Sleuth frowned and shuffled away. Daisy, leaving her stepmother's side, joined him.

Mrs Bunting put down three sixpences.

'Wait a minute,' said Hopkins; 'you can't go into the Chamber of Horrors just yet. But you won't have to wait more than four or five minutes, Mrs Bunting. It's this way, you see; our boss is in there, showing a party round.' He lowered his voice. 'It's Sir John Burney—I suppose you know who Sir John Burney is?'

'No,' she answered indifferently; 'I don't know that I ever heard of him.' She felt slightly—oh, very slightly—uneasy about Daisy.

She would like her stepdaughter to keep well within sight and sound. Mr Sleuth was taking the girl to the other end of the room.

'Well, I hope you never *will* know him—not in any personal sense, Mrs Bunting.' The man chuckled. 'He's the Head Commissioner of Police—that's what Sir John Burney is. One of the gentlemen he's showing round our place is the Paris Prefect of Police, whose job is on all fours, so to speak, with Sir John's. The Frenchy has brought his daughter with him, and there are several other ladies. Ladies always like 'orrors, Mrs Bunting; that's our experience here. "Oh, take me to the Chamber of 'Orrors!"—that's what they say the minute they gets into the building.'

A group of people, all talking and laughing together, were advancing from within toward the turnstile.

Mrs Bunting stared at them nervously. She wondered which of them was the gentleman with whom Mr Hopkins had hoped she would never be brought into personal contact. She quickly picked him out. He was a tall, powerful, nice-looking gentleman with a commanding manner. Just now he was smiling down into the face of a young lady. 'Monsieur Barberoux is quite right,' he was saying; 'the English law is too kind to the criminal, especially to the murderer. If we conducted our trials in the French fashion, the place we have just left would be very much fuller than it is today! A man of whose guilt we are absolutely assured is oftener than not acquitted, and then the public taunt us with "another undiscovered crime"!'

'D'you mean, Sir John, that murderers sometimes escape scot-free? Take the man who has been committing all those awful murders this last month. Of course, I don't know much about it, for father won't let me read about it, but I can't help being interested!'

Her girlish voice rang out, and Mrs Bunting heard every word distinctly.

The party gathered round, listening eagerly to hear what the Head Commissioner would say next.

'Yes.' He spoke very deliberately. 'I think we may say—now, don't give me away to a newspaper fellow, Miss Rose—that we do know perfectly well who the murderer in question is—'

Several of those standing nearby uttered expressions of surprise and incredulity.

'Then why don't you catch him?' cried the girl indignantly.

'I didn't say we know *where* he is; I only said we know *who* he is; or, rather, perhaps I ought to say that we have a very strong suspicion of his identity.'

Sir John's French colleague looked up quickly. 'The Hamburg and Liverpool man?' he said interrogatively.

The other nodded. 'Yes; I suppose you've had the case turned up?'

Then, speaking very quickly, as if he wished to dismiss the subject from his own mind and from that of his auditors, he went on:

'Two murders of the kind were committed eight years ago—one in Hamburg, the other just afterward in Liverpool, and there were certain peculiarities connected with the crimes which made it clear they were committed by the same hand. The perpetrator was caught, fortunately for us red-handed, just as he was leaving the house of his victim, for in Liverpool the murder was committed in a house. I myself saw the unhappy man—I say unhappy, for there is no doubt at all that he was mad,'—he hesitated, and added in a lower tone—'suffering from an acute form of religious mania. I myself saw him, at some length. But now comes the really interesting point. Just a month ago this criminal lunatic, as we must regard him, made his escape from the asylum where he was confined. He arranged the whole thing with extraordinary cunning and intelligence, and we should probably have caught him long ago were it not that he managed, when on his way out of the place, to annex a considerable sum of money in gold with which the wages of the staff were about to be paid.'

The Frenchman again spoke. 'Why have you not circulated a description?' he asked.

'We did that at once,'—She John Burney smiled a little grimly,— 'but only among our own people. We dare not circulate the man's description among the general public. You see, we may be mistaken, after all.'

'That is not very probable!' The Frenchman smiled a satirical little smile.

A moment later the party were walking in Indian file through the turnstile, Sir John Burney leading the way.

Mrs Bunting looked straight before her. Even had she wished to do so, she had neither time nor power to warn her lodger of his danger.

Daisy and her companion were now coming down the room, bearing straight for the Head Commissioner of Police. In another moment Mr Sleuth and Sir John Burney would be face to face.

Suddenly Mr Sleuth swerved to one side. A terrible change came over his pale, narrow face; it became discomposed, livid with rage and terror.

But, to Mrs Bunting's relief—yes, to her inexpressible relief—Sir John Burney and his friends swept on. They passed by Mr Sleuth unconcernedly, unaware, or so it seemed to her, that there was anyone else in the room but themselves.

'Hurry up, Mrs Bunting,' said the turnstile-keeper; 'you and your friends will have the place all to yourselves.' From an official he had become a man, and it was the man in Mr Hopkins that gallantly addressed pretty Daisy Bunting. 'It seems strange that a young lady like you should want to go in and see all those 'orrible frights,' he said jestingly.

'Mrs Bunting, may I trouble you to come over here for a moment?' The words were hissed rather than spoken by Mr Sleuth's lips.

His landlady took a doubtful step forward.

'A last word with you, Mrs Bunting.' The lodger's face was still distorted with fear and passion. 'Do you think to escape the consequences of your hideous treachery? I trusted you, Mrs Bunting, and you betrayed me! But I am protected by a higher power, for I still have work to do. Your end will be bitter as wormwood and sharp as a two-edged sword. Your feet shall go down to death, and your steps take hold on hell.' Even while Mr Sleuth was uttering these strange, dreadful words, he was looking around, his eyes glancing this way and that, seeking a way of escape.

At last his eyes become fixed on a small placard placed about a curtain. 'Emergency Exit' was written there. Leaving his landlady's side, he walked over to the turnstile. He fumbled in his pocket for a moment, and then touched the man on the arm. 'I feel ill,' he said, speaking very rapidly; 'very ill indeed! It's the atmosphere of this place. I want you to let me out by the quickest way. It would be a pity for me to faint here—especially with ladies about.' His left hand shot out and placed what he had been fumbling for in his pocket on the other's bare palm. 'I see there's an emergency exit over there. Would it be possible for me to get out that way?'

'Well, yes, sir; I think so.' The man hesitated; he felt a slight, a very slight, feeling of misgiving. He looked at Daisy, flushed and smiling, happy and unconcerned, and then at Mrs Bunting. She was very pale; but surely her lodger's sudden seizure was enough to make her feel worried. Hopkins felt the half sovereign pleasantly tickling his palm. The Prefect of Police had given him only half a crown—mean, shabby foreigner!

'Yes, I can let you out that way,' he said at last, 'and perhaps when you're standing out in the air on the iron balcony you'll feel better. But then you know, sir, you'll have to come round to the front if you want to come in again, for those emergency doors only open outward.'

'Yes, yes,' said Mr Sleuth hurriedly; 'I quite understand! If I feel better I'll come in by the front way, and pay another shilling—that's only fair.'

'You needn't do that if you'll just explain what happened here.'

The man went and pulled the curtain aside, and put his shoulder against the door. It burst open, and the light for a moment blinded Mr Sleuth. He passed his hand over his eyes.

'Thank you,' he said; 'thank you. I shall get all right here.'

Five days later Bunting identified the body of a man found drowned in the Regent's Canal as that of his late lodger; and, the morning following, a gardener working in the Regent's Park found a newspaper in which were wrapped, together with a half-worn pair of rubber-soled shoes, two surgical knives. This fact was not chronicled in any newspaper; but a very pretty and picturesque paragraph went the round of the press, about the same time, concerning a small box filled with sovereigns which had been forwarded anonymously to the Governor of the Foundling Hospital.

Mr and Mrs Bunting are now in the service of an old lady, by whom they are feared as well as respected, and whom they make very comfortable.

The Last Match

Edward Fitz-Gerald Fripp

'Well, I guess we'd better be hitting for home. I don't like the smell of that wind. She's going to blizz before long, or I miss my guess.'

'By golly, I believe you're right. A dollar, fifty. That's right. Good-bye, Mr Mawson. Good-bye, Mrs Mills.'

The owner of the feed company dumped the sack of corn meal behind the seat, Mawson clicked his tongue to his horse and the cutter moved off up the one street of Sunset with a merry jingling of sleigh bells.

The little prairie town was half asleep under its mantle of snow, for it was the third winter since the slump in wheat. For three years the price of No.1 Northern had hovered round sixty cents on the Winnipeg Grain Exchange, and times were hard: harder than anyone could remember, butter being used for axle grease and eggs fed direct to the pigs for lack of a better market.

The neighbouring farmers no longer thronged into Sunset on Saturdays in their cars. One of the two garages was closed, and the other only employed one man instead of four. The cinema gave one performance a week, and the Rex Café and the Good Eats Café had an occasional customer. The stores were listless, and Ed Wilson's barber's shop and pool-room were nearly empty. This latter fact proved the severity of the depression beyond any doubt, for when the pool-room is empty, times are hard indeed. Not even the farmers themselves scanned the news of the Winnipeg Grain Exchange with greater eagerness than did the storekeepers and merchants of Sunset. Wheat was no longer king when No.1 Northern was only sixty cents a bushel.

Within a minute or two the cutter had left the little town behind, and the main street of Sunset had given place to a long straight road, stretching endlessly and always perfectly straight across the bald prairie. Behind them the grain elevator reared its white height into the air, watching over Sunset as the church spire watches over the villages of older lands.

For some time the man and woman drove in silence, wrapped in the warm buffalo robe which keeps out any draughts. The noise of the horse's hoofs was deadened by the snow, and the only sound was the jingling of the sleigh bells. Talk held no attraction for either of them; talk meant discussion of the price of wheat, and No.1 Northern was only sixty cents in Winnipeg.

At last Mawson spoke:

'Seems queer to be driving in a cutter again. Takes me back to before the war. I guess we'd all have been better off if we'd never had any cars; but once you've had one, you kind a seem lost without it. A rig seems so slow.'

'It certainly does,' she answered, and they drove on in silence.

The winter had been extraordinarily mild without one sub-zero spell. For the last two days it had been snowing with a slight south wind: a steady fall of what the prairie calls wet snow (though, even so, far drier than any which ever falls in England). The air was still full of white flakes, falling silently and yet at the same time making a gentle, almost imperceptible, patter as they settled on their hats and on the buffalo robe, which was now altogether white where it covered their knees.

The trail they had made driving into Sunset was vague and nearly obliterated. It was hard work for the horse breaking a fresh track, and progress was slow. The flakes of snow seemed to be growing smaller and falling faster, and, though they had blown into their faces during the drive into Sunset, now on the return trip they still blew slantwise against them.

'I don't like the smell of it,' Mawson muttered. 'The wind's backed to the north and that sure means something.' He raised his voice and called, 'Git on there, Pete.'

Pete shook his ears and settled his shoulders into the traces. He needed no urging, for he, too, had felt the change of wind and wanted to get back to his stable.

Gradually the gusts increased in force. On the drive in it had been pleasant to feel the south wind driving the soft flakes against their faces. They had felt almost warm as they touched the cheek.

But there was a bite in this new wind. There was no doubt now that the flakes had grown much smaller. They grew smaller every minute until they were tiny atoms blowing straight against them in a line almost parallel with the ground. The wind, coming in a sweep across hundreds of miles of barren tundra in the Arctic

Circle, without a single obstacle in the way to lessen its force, brought a wave of cold that made them shiver.

Already the mercury in thermometers on the international boundary was beginning to fall. By midnight it would be falling in the cities of the middle United States, and by midnight, twenty-four hours later, workers on cotton plantations in the Mississippi Valley, 2,000 miles to the south, would be shivering as the tail end of the storm reached them, tamed at last after its swoop across the prairies.

Presently the tiny flakes of snow began to sting their faces. As the gusts increased, the snow came in swirling clouds, rather as though someone was shaking the folds of a gigantic white carpet. During these gusts it was impossible to see more than a few yards ahead, and the sense of direction was lost as in a fog. It almost seemed that the snow was a fog, so dry it was, filtering like a fog into tiny gaps in the clothing. It crept between the top of the gloves and the sleeve of the overcoat and down the gap between the muffler and coat collar.

The wind, devoid of moisture, dried the snow which had already fallen, whirling it up into twisting spirals to join the horizontal sweep of the driven flakes. It drove the light powder against the slightest obstacles, so that each fence post was covered for a few inches on its windward side. By morning they would be nearly buried in the drifts, whose nucleus they were forming.

The man and woman sat closer together on the seat of the cutter, their heads thrust forward so that the snow would have less chance of seeping down their necks. He raised his hands to pull down his ear-flaps, and the snow fell off his mittens like powdered salt. Not a single flake had stuck to them, it was so dry.

At length Mawson indulged in the gloomy satisfaction of a prophet whose words have come true.

'I knew I could smell a blizzard coming,' he said. 'It's lucky we weren't two hours late. I guess your husband ought to be safely in the shack by now.'

She turned to answer him, and the movement allowed the wind to blow all the snow from her hat.

'Yes, he'll be all right. Reckoned he'd reach there by three.'

She bent her head to face the wind again, and they drove in silence. Her husband had left home at four o'clock that morning to drive to the bush, which began in sheltered bluffs to the north of them. The northern prairie gives way to belts of semi-stunted trees where the ground holds more moisture.

With No.1 Northern only sixty cents a bushel in Winnipeg the farmer cannot afford to buy coal, and her husband and a neighbour had gone to cut a year's supply of fuel in the poplar bluffs. Later they would have to haul it thirty miles to their homes, sitting on top of their loads as the sleighs crossed the snowy plain, the thermometer below zero and as likely as not a bitter wind numbing them in body and mind.

The cutter was approaching a house standing a little back from the road; a gaunt, unpainted, wooden house without any pretensions to adornment. It was simply an enclosed rectangle, with a front door and a back door and four rooms, and the necessary windows to admit light: a house rather than a home, a place in which to eat and sleep and take shelter from the weather, like most of the other houses on prairie farms.

It rose straight from the flat field. There was no hedge, no railings, no lawn, no flower garden, to separate it from the wheatland. Close beside it was a huge barn, dwarfing the house as the farm dwarfed the human beings who worked it.

Mawson drove up to the back door, and the woman got out, taking with her a shallow, open, wooden box which had once contained cans of condensed milk. It was now piled with brown-paper parcels, the groceries for which she had traded her butter, and underneath was her mail. The parcels were covered with a thick powder of snow which had filtered in under the buffalo robe, filling up the spaces between them till they looked like one amorphous lump.

'Thanks for driving me in,' she shouted.

'Aw, shucks, that's nothing. You're sure you'll be all right alone?'

'Yes, Jim fixed up everything before he left.'

'Have you got everything?' he asked.

'Yes,' she shouted as a gust, fiercer than any which had come before, enveloped them in swirling white.

It blew the tiny flakes into their eyes and ears and down their necks, and lifted a cloud from the box that for a minute blinded them. She had a fleeting impression that one of the top parcels had blown into the drift already forming; but when she was able to see again and looked at the box, it was once more covered white. And the snow round them looked just as it had done.

She was half frozen and wanted to gain the warmth of the house; Pete was pawing his feet, longing to be on the way to his stable, and she knew it was not wise for Mawson to linger. He had three more miles to go before he reached home, and if he did not go quickly he might be badly frostbitten, as the blizzard was increasing every minute.

She looked at her box again. It seemed just the same. She must have been mistaken in thinking that anything had been blown out of it. Even if it had, it would make no difference. She would never find it until the spring, and in any case there was plenty of food in the house.

Mawson, plainly anxious to be off, again asked: 'You're sure you're all right?'

'Yes,' she shouted, 'and thanks a lot for the lift.'

He waved his hand, and Pete seized the opportunity to dash forward. In a moment the cutter was lost to view in the driving snow, and she turned hurriedly to the door.

From the uncovered rafters of the veranda hung quantities of meat impaled on hooks, cuts of veal and pork, for her husband had lately killed a calf and a pig.

That is one good thing about the prairie winter, she thought, as she ran up the three steps. You killed a pig, simply hung up the meat and then it froze immediately, and stayed frozen until you wanted it. Pretty convenient, and they were lucky to have so much in hard times.

The snow had drifted against the back door, half hiding the washing-machine and brooms leaning against the wall. All the rest of the veranda floor was bare, every particle of dirt dried into dust and swept away by the wind; the boards looked as if they had been scrubbed.

She had no need to search for a key. You do not lock your door on the prairie when you go away for the day. She kicked the drift with a sweep of her foot, and it disappeared in a fine mist, which swirled up into her face and vanished as the wind sucked it away.

She pulled the door open quickly, and almost jumped into the kitchen in her haste to enter before another drift could accumulate and blow in after her.

What a relief to be out of that biting wind! The kitchen was almost eerie with its comparative warmth and silence after the buffeting outside. It felt curious to be there alone without her husband, even frightening with the blizzard increasing in fury. For a moment the prospect appalled her, but she was the wife of a prairie farmer and resolutely thrust off her depression.

A gust of wind, which seemed as if it would carry away the whole house, sent an icy blast under the door and through the keyhole. It was a warning not to waste time. She had to milk yet, and it would not be safe to cross the corral in the dark. A second gust roused her to action.

Lifting the lid of the stove, she saw there was a little pile of embers. She snatched two sticks of wood from the box and thrust them into the opening, pulling back the draught as she did so. The two bedrooms and the sitting-room were warmed by a box heater, but owing to the warm weather of the two previous days, she had not lighted it in her efforts to economise.

She looked hesitatingly at it, for it would be so comforting to come back to a thoroughly warm house after the frozen barn, but another roar of wind made her resist the temptation. The intensity of the storm was terrifying, and she knew both from experience and from warning that she must be back in the house before it was dark. The heater would have to wait.

She took off her good coat and hat, shook the snow off them and flung them on a chair. The loneliness of the empty room began to affect her nerves. It was more lonely than she had thought it would be, and the noises of the blizzard intensified the loneliness until she felt flustered and a little panic-stricken at the thought of the solitary vigil before her.

Her one idea now was haste—haste to get done with the milking and then to come back to the task of keeping the house warm, and its precious supply of vegetables in the cellar.

She put on her woollen blizzard-cap so that it reached halfway down her neck, and left only a tiny opening for the eyes and nose. Next she put on an old farm overcoat, fastening the collar over the lower part of her blizzard-cap so that there was no chance of her neck being frozen. Then her woollen mittens, and over them the buckskin outer mittens.

No fear of frostbite now for a little while; but she had to hurry. Every second was of importance. Should she leave the draught on in the stove to make sure of the wood catching? If she did, it would probably have burnt away by the time she came back. She could not wait to give it more time. It would soon be dark. The wood was dry and must have caught by this time, and it always burnt easily in zero weather.

Without pausing to look in her flurry, she thrust back the damper with her thumb. It closed with a clang and she hurried to the door, taking a kettle with her.

It was all she could do to open the door. The wind and cold made her gasp for breath, and a cloud of snow like the finest powder blew past her into the room. The door slammed behind her, and she picked up her milk-pail from beside the washing-machine.

For a moment she almost quailed. It was still light, but she could hardly see the huge barn although it was only fifty yards away. The air seemed to be a mass of tiny, white missiles flying towards her at the speed of an express train. They stung like needles on her eyes and nose, and she could feel them whipping past her legs. Mercifully she had put on her felt boots before going to Sunset. Her feet would have been frozen in leather ones.

She must hurry! If she let it get dark before she finished milking, she would never find the house on the way back.

The well was in a straight line between the house and the barn door, otherwise she would not have found it. She stumbled forward with her shoulders thrust in front and her head bent downward to protect her eyes from the stinging snow. Her breath came in painful gasps.

Her milk bucket knocked against the pump handle before she saw the well. She lifted the handle, and, pouring the warm water from her kettle down the pipe, pumped vigorously. Even above the wind she could hear the noise of the suction as her warm water primed the pump and drew the water upwards from the well.

She filled her milk bucket and the other bucket beside the pump. Then she lifted the handle again, and the trip action allowed the water to sink to the bottom of the well so that the pump could not freeze and burst. Her cows could only have one bucket each that night, for there was no time to go back to the house for another kettle.

With her kettle and the two buckets she staggered to the barn, buffeted by the storm and desperately afraid of spilling the water. She was gasping by the time she reached shelter. It was ecstasy to draw breath out of that wind.

There was a drift nearly three feet deep by the barn, where the snow had blown back in an eddy and come to rest in the calm. She ploughed her way through it, holding her buckets high, and the snow fell away from her boots. It was almost like going into an oven after the cold of the wind. The cows looked round from their stalls and lowed at her.

She set one bucket before the first cow, and, in spite of her urge for haste, held it while the animal drank. It would be sure to knock it over if left. Already, during the time she had walked twenty-five yards, a film of ice had formed on top of the water.

The cow sniffed and snorted and blew through its nose with exasperating deliberation before it would drink. She wanted to scream to make it hurry, but she forced herself to wait patiently. At last it thrust out an exploring tongue, and after splashing the water for a minute sucked the bucket dry without lifting its head.

When she took the bucket away the cow lowed for more. She spoke soothingly to it and watered the other cow. It drank with equally maddening deliberation, and then she ran to the pile of oat hay her husband had set in readiness for her. She placed several sheaves in the mangers, so that they should not go hungry in case she were late in the morning.

Next she took the heavy scoop shovel and prepared to clean out the gutters; but when she pushed it against the manure the handle jarred against her hands as though she had struck a granite rock. During the short time the storm had been raging the manure had frozen solid. It would take a pick-axe to move it now.

She gave up the attempt, and placed forkfuls of bedding round the cows' legs. They would need it all before the night was through.

Already tiny icicles had formed on their nostrils. She could feel the wool of her blizzard-cap as solid as a board where her own breath had caught when she gasped in the wind. It rubbed against her lip irritatingly, and made her all the more conscious of the need to hurry. She snatched the milking-stool, and, tearing off her mittens, put them in her pocket, picked up the milk bucket and hurried to the first cow, but suddenly cried out with pain.

The metal of the handle had torn all the skin from the fingers of her left hand where they had grasped it. She cried with pain and vexation at her mistake. Fool that she was! As if she did not know enough to remember that any metal would tear off the skin in zero weather!

She carried the bucket on the crook of her arm and sat down beside the cow. It was good to thrust her head into its flank and feel the warmth coming from its body.

She could not wash the udder, as she usually did, or it would be covered with icicles. With her right hand she pulled away the scraps of bedding adhering to it, and then began to milk. The skin was torn from the fingers of her left hand just where she used them to squeeze the teats, and every movement hurt excruciatingly. When she lifted them for a moment to ease them, there was a smear of blood on the teat. She felt dizzy at the sight of it, but forced herself to begin again.

Gradually she absorbed some warmth from the cow's body and felt the icy teats grow warmer under her fingers. The milk streamed into the bucket between her knees, and the homely, everyday sound of it was soothing. It encouraged her to tell herself that she would only have to do what she had to do every day when her husband was at home; but all her reasoning could not exorcise the terrors suggested by her subconscious mind. What she had to do was not the same as usual, for the simple reason that she was all alone and no one nearer to her than the Mawsons in the next house three miles away.

The sound of the milk streaming into her bucket was becoming drowned by the noise of the wind, and, though the front of her body and her hands were fairly warm, being close to the cow, her back was freezing where the draught from the door and windows struck her.

She shivered a little, and, having milked the rear teats dry, started on the front ones. With the change of position her skinned fingers hurt worse than ever, and the pain increased the tension of her nerves. It was beginning to grow dusk inside the barn. In spite of her injured fingers she milked furiously; for the idea that she must regain the house before it was dark was all the more terrifying because she knew it was justified and not a mere product of her fears. But the knowledge that it was justified made her still more highly strung.

At last! She had milked the cow dry. She gave a sigh of relief and crooked her arm under the handle of the bucket.

She could not bring herself to milk the other cow. It was going dry soon in any case. It would not hurt to be missed this once.

She pulled on her mittens, wincing as the wool pressed against her injured fingers, then unfastened the chains from the cows' necks that they might lie down against each other when they had finished eating, and so keep warm.

Now to gain the house and her own cosy kitchen once more. There were the papers to read and the letters from her husband's

English relations, whom she would never see unless wheat was worth a great deal more than sixty cents a bushel for No.1 Northern.

She felt she could not wait another minute. The chickens had a self-feeding hopper and enough to eat till morning. In any case they would be huddled shivering on their perches. She had finished! Now for a roaring fire in the stove and the heater. She would sit close to the stove and eat her supper, and read her letters and the papers, and be so comfortable that she would forget the terror of being alone. Above all, she would be warm. She would be warm even if she had to sit on top of the stove.

With the kettle and the pail of milk she hurried to the door. Cold as it was in the barn, it was far colder outside. The noise of the wind, which had been muffled inside the building, made her gasp with fear at its fury. It was not so dark, though, as she had expected, and she gave a sigh of thankfulness for this, because the house was practically invisible through the whirling maelstrom of snow. All the usual landmarks were changed, and if she had been twenty minutes late she would never have found her way.

The first two feet of ground by the barn door were still bare, but the drift had formed again where the snow blew back in the eddy. It had re-formed into a bank exactly like a wave with the crest as sharp as a knife. There was not the slightest sign of her footmarks where she had walked twenty minutes earlier.

She ploughed her way homeward, the wind at her back. It almost lifted her off her feet, the bucket of milk tugged forward at her arm, and she could hear the unceasing rustle of the snow as it rushed past her legs like an incredibly swift river. She knew she could never have walked a hundred yards against it.

It was unspeakable relief to feel her feet once more on the veranda steps. She had regained the house after all, and before her eyes floated a vision of a red-hot stove, with the kettle boiling and the teapot warming and a joint of pork sizzling in the oven. She would eat hot pork and drink boiling tea and heap the butter on her bread, and the fat would keep her warm—warm right through her shoulders and the back of her knees where the wind was cutting.

In the centre of the veranda steps the snow had drifted into a cone a foot high, but on both sides the boards were absolutely bare. Half of the veranda was still bare, but against the wall and the door there was a bank of snow. As she reached the door she glanced at the thermometer hanging on the wall. It showed twenty degrees below zero. From that she knew it would be forty below at six o'clock the next morning. Seventy-two degrees of frost! An idle fancy made her wonder how she could convey an idea of that cold to her husband's relations in England. Seventy-two degrees above freezing meant a hundred and four in the shade, hotter than it ever was in London even on the hottest day of the hottest summer. Could they imagine a temperature the same number of degrees below freezing?

At this fancy she smiled for the first time since Mawson had left her, and swept her foot at the pile of snow by the door. It was sucked up past her face and out beyond the angle of the house as if it had been a cloud of smoke from a bonfire.

With thankfulness she heard the door slam behind her. She was home. In a few minutes the stove would be roaring and red-hot, and then she would be warm. Warm! At the thought of it her tautened nerves relaxed.

She set down her bucket and ran to the stove. It did not feel as warm as it should. She took the lifter and prised off the lid, and then uttered an exclamation of vexation.

She had been in such a hurry to put in the two sticks of wood before she milked that they had jammed together at the top of the fire-box and the embers had burnt themselves out without setting them alight.

It was a mere trifle such as frequently happened when you were in a hurry, but the momentary upset to her plans for a speedy supper banished her incipient cheerfulness. Somehow it seemed to her ill-omened, and made her feel nervous again. It was different when you were all alone in a blizzard. The ordinary things were not as easy to do as when someone else was there to keep you company.

The house shook to its foundations with each gust. She could feel the cold being blown through the walls into the room as though it were something alive and menacing. The cold had taken all the moisture with which the steam from her kettles had filled the air earlier in the day, and frozen it on the inside of the windows. They were covered with an opaque thickness of ice in a formation almost like the scales of a fish.

It was nearly dark, but she was so cold that she could not wait to light the lamp. She took the two pieces of wood out of the fire-box, and, snatching a newspaper from a chair, laid her fire anew. She used plenty of kindling, for she had to have the fire in a hurry.

At last it was ready! She pulled off her mittens, hurting her skinned fingers, took the box of matches from the dresser and struck one of them. Soon she would be warm and be able to attend to her hand. She shivered nervously when she found that the match had no head.

It was a second portent of ill-omen. She glanced round the darkening room with a little quiver of fear. Everything seemed vaguely hostile in that bitter cold, and the very familiarity of the room only served to emphasise her loneliness.

There was only one more match in the box. Her hands were so numb with the cold that she could scarcely hold it, and her injured fingers were a torture. She trembled, partly from nervousness and partly from cold, as she struck it.

Just as it flared into light there was a tremendous gust of wind, which blew into the room through the crack under the door and through the very walls, where the boards had contracted from the dryness of the cold. She was afraid that the draught would put out the flame, and as soon as the edge of the paper had caught alight she slammed the door of the firebox with her elbow. She was taking good care not to touch any more metal with her fingers.

She had no fear that the fire would not go this time. Canadian stoves are far superior to an English range, and there is never any difficulty in getting the fire to go if you lay it properly, especially in zero weather. She thought no more about it, and hurried to the dresser to put some cold cream on her fingers. They were hurting so much that she felt it wiser to dress them before lighting the lamp.

The cream eased the pain a little, and she went back to the stove to see how the fire was going. Strange. There was not the roar from the stove pipe that there should have been in such a weather. Once more she felt a quiver of fear. It was positively eerie the way everything was going wrong. If only her husband had been there to chaff her for taking such a long time! At the thought of it she felt sick with loneliness.

She put on her right mitten and opened the fire-box. As she had feared, the fire had not caught. It must be bewitched, she thought, for she had laid it properly and the wood was dry enough in all conscience. There was not a vestige of moisture within hundreds of miles in that blizzard. It must be another portent of ill-omen, and in her tension she felt that the fates must indeed be against her.

She took out the sticks of wood and the kindling, and straightaway understood. The paper itself had not burnt. She held it up to the remnants of the daylight, and once more uttered an exclamation of anger. It was just possible to make out the heading, 'The Sunday Times'.

The paper which her husband's English relations sent to them every week. A good solid paper, she knew, but not the least bit of use for lighting the fire. No English papers seemed to be much good for that purpose, and from past experience she knew that the *Sunday Times* was easily the worst of the lot.

She bit her lip with vexation. It really did seem as if the fates were against her, or was it just because she was alone? Again she glanced fearfully round the room. It was horrible to be alone like that. Why on earth had she not taken a bit more care and used a Canadian paper? There were the *Winnipeg Free Press* and the *Family Herald* on the table. If only she had used them, she would have been warm by this time.

She flung the offending *Sunday Times* into the wood box, stuffed some pages of the *Family Herald* into the stove and once more set her fire. Now for another box of matches and then at last she would be warm.

But her groping fingers found no matches on their accustomed shelf. Growing more nervously excited every minute, she moved her hand over every inch of that shelf. Then over the one below it. And then over the one above it. She was gasping a little now; for though her fingers encountered cups and plates, bottles of essences and tins of salt and pepper, and all the other appliances of the kitchen, they did not close round the familiar box of matches.

She gave a little cry of alarm, for it did seem as if the place were bewitched and that something dreadful was going to happen to her. It was horrible to be so alone. Just when she thought she was going to have hysterics, she suddenly remembered, and laughed aloud from sheer relief.

Of course! What an idiot she was! It was simply absurd the way your nerves played tricks with you when you were alone.

Her husband had taken the other three boxes with him for his stay in the shack. She sighed with relief when she remembered how they had laughed over it that very morning when he put them in his pocket just before he left. How he had said it was a good thing she did not smoke, or else he could only have taken two boxes with him, and that she must not forget to buy a packet in Sunset that afternoon.

Of course, everything had a rational explanation if you did not get rattled and start thinking the house was bewitched just because you were alone. And she had bought a packet of matches in Sunset. You did not forget things like that when you only went shopping once in a blue moon and if there was enough butter made to trade with the store. She laughed once more as she stepped to the table where the box of groceries was lying. All she had to do was to open the packet, take out a box of matches, strike one and then all would be well. The stove would get red-hot, and the whole house would be warm, and she could laugh at the blizzard raging outside.

But when her hands rummaged among the paper parcels in the box, they did not feel a packet of matches. Thinking it must be because of her mittens, she took them off. She shivered as her bare fingers touched the snow between the parcels. She felt every one deliberately, expecting each time she touched one to find it was the packet she wanted.

Her heart thumped with excitement and fear when she came to the end of the box and still she had not found the packet. The house must be bewitched after all, or else she would have found it by this time. For a moment she stood in irresolution, and then, sobbing with anxiety, she turned the box upside down on the table and blew the snow away from the parcels.

It was dark and she could only see a blurred outline where they rested. She wanted to snatch at them in her search, but she knew she must be calm or she really would have hysterics. The loneliness was more terrifying than ever now, and the blizzard seemed to be threatening to carry away the whole house. She bit her lip and forced herself to stand still until she had got her nerves under control once more.

After a minute's wait she sat on a chair, put the box in her lap and methodically picked up each parcel one by one from the table and laid it in the box. Her heart began to thump again as she was nearing the end, and still she could not find that packet. At last there were no more parcels on the table, and the matches were not there!

At first she could not believe it, and moved her arms backwards and forwards over the table in ever wider sweeps, until finally she knocked two plates on the far side on to the floor. Then she was forced to believe. She was alone and she had no matches. It was dark and she would not get warm now.

It must have been the packet of matches the wind had blown away when she said good-bye to Mawson. Why, oh why, had she not stopped to look? They were past finding now. Why had she not taken more care when she set the fire? Why had she not lit the lamp first? Why…?

Her nerves got the better of her, and she screamed with terror. She was experienced enough to understand her plight. She knew that she would certainly freeze to death before morning if she went to sleep, and was more than likely to do so even if she kept herself awake. She had been on the move from two that morning, getting things ready for her husband's early start, and after that making butter to trade for their groceries, seeing to the stock, and then going to Sunset. She had eaten nothing since eleven, she was dog-tired and ravenously hungry, and above all else she was cold—cold right inside to the innermost part of her body. She did not know if she could keep awake till morning, and, even if she did, the blizzard was very unlikely to have died down.

It was hopeless to think of trying to reach her neighbours. Along the straight prairie roads she would never find her way in that maelstrom of whirling snow. And if she could find her way, she would probably die of cold before she had gone a mile. And there was nothing in the house to warm her.

Ah! She straightened with a faint hope as she thought of the barn. If she could reach it, she could snuggle between the two cows and perhaps keep life in her that way. She half started up from her chair and then sank down again despondently. There was not the slightest hope of her being able to reach the barn without a lantern.

She knew that even with lanterns, and warmed after a good meal, men had gone out in a blizzard to attend to their stock and never been seen alive again: had just set out to walk the fifty or hundred yards which they walked four times every day of their lives, and had missed their way in that bewildering fury of powdered snow. There was nothing for her to do except walk up and down the room and try to keep awake till morning came.

The loneliness, and the darkness, and the cold, weighed upon her like tangible enemies. It was so dark that she blundered into the wall at the far end of the room, and her head bumped into something. Her nerves almost made her jump from it, but when she put out her hand she felt a familiar outline, and her stifled cry turned into an exclamation of joy.

The telephone! Why had not she thought of it before? Even in that awful storm, when her plight was known, somehow or other they would form an expedition in Sunset and bring help to her.

But as she turned the handle to ring up Central, her joy gave way once more to despair, all the more bitter for the momentary ray of hope. As if she could not have remembered! The telephone had been disconnected months ago, because they could not afford the expense, and the telephone company had not bothered to take the instrument away. When No.1 Northern was only sixty cents a bushel in Winnipeg, the telephone company would not be asked to install it anywhere else. They had more disconnected instruments than they could handle as it was.

With a sigh of utter despair she pulled her overcoat closer round her shoulders and resumed her walk. Fifteen paces to the door and fifteen paces back to the telephone. Back and forward. Back and forward, and all the time her brain flayed by the tortures of Tantalus.

She was cold, and she knew that there was a great pile of wood in the box by the stove; she was hungry, and she knew that there was bread and butter and jam and pork and veal in plenty; she was afraid of the dark, and there was a lamp on the table filled with coal oil; she was lonely, and there was a telephone. But none of these things was any good to her, and as she paced slowly up and down she found herself babbling incoherently: 'Water, water everywhere, nor any drop to drink.'

Her woollen blizzard-cap was stiff against her face where her breath had frozen, and her injured fingers were throbbing. Before her eyes swam visions of a red-hot stove and a hot supper on the table and a light in the lamp, until she could stand them no longer. Even though she knew it to be useless she simply had to do something different.

If only she were not so hungry! She stumbled to the pantry and automatically caught up the bread tin. With trembling fingers she opened it and took out a loaf. She found a knife and tried to cut a slice, but it would not make the slightest impression. The loaf was frozen as hard as a stone.

'Ask for bread and ye give them a stone.' The words danced before her eyes until she knew she was nearly hysterical again. She ran her hand aimlessly along the shelf until it encountered a pat of butter. That alone, out of all her supply of food, would not be frozen like a stone. She gouged out a lump from the pat with her knife and had almost put it to her lips when she remembered her hurt fingers. If the knife touched her lips it would take all the skin off them.

She stuck the lump on her mittens and bit off a piece, but, famished as she was, it was so greasy that it nearly made her sick. She moaned with despair and idly ran her hand along the shelf again. It encountered a long, round object, and for a moment she could not think what it was. Her half-frozen fingers in their clumsy mittens could not feel, and she fidgeted with it until with a shock of surprise she saw a ray of light.

She was holding the electric torch they had bought in case they had a breakdown in their car when driving at night, and it had been put on the shelf when they could no longer afford the car. Not much good to her now, but the light was a little bit of company.

She returned to the kitchen and flashed it over the room. The walls and roof of the house cracked at intervals almost like a pistol shot as the timber contracted. She did not like the colour of the little bit of her cheek showing in the opening of her blizzard-cap. It was a dirty white and she knew she had a touch of frostbite there.

She must do something! Her despairing brain caught at the hope that there might be an odd match lying somewhere. She knew it was hopeless, but any sort of action was better than aimless pacing up and down. With the aid of her torch she searched every nook and cranny of the house, but there was no match. She turned out the drawers and all the pockets of her husband's clothes.

How she wished that she had not lectured him on his habit

of leaving loose matches in his pockets, in case they set the house on fire; and how she wished he had remained firm in his contention that there was no danger in that! If only he had gone on laughing at her, and had not conquered his habit simply to please her and turned out his pockets every time he took off his clothes!

She closed the last drawer and returned to the kitchen to resume her walk. Up and down. Back and forward. Till her brain was mesmerised and her legs ached with fatigue and cold. She was so tired that she could keep going no longer.

At any cost she must sit down and rest for a little while. She found her chair and sat down. Her head began to nod and her eyes closed, but she fought against the temptation. That way led to certain death. She began to count the minutes to help herself keep awake, but once more her eyes closed. She tried desperately to think of some possible place she might have overlooked in her search for an odd match, some possible garment of her husband's which perhaps she had missed.

Her brain swam with visions of overalls and pairs of trousers. She could not think of one she had missed, and they made her dizzy like the sheep she counted when she lay awake at night sometimes. Her head nodded again, and this time she did fall into a doze.

The electric torch slid from her nerveless fingers on to the floor, and the bang awoke her with a start. If it had not been for that torch, she would soon have been dead. Thoroughly frightened at her near escape, she picked it up and once more began her walk. But the brief period of sleep had given her subconscious mind a chance to work, and suddenly she remembered.

There was an old pair of blue denim overalls hanging on a nail on the veranda wall. They had been there for over a year. She had been meaning to cut them up for clothes to wash the milk pails with and was always forgetting. There was just one chance in a million that he left them there before he had started to turn out his pockets.

One chance in a million. There might be a match in them. Anyway she would see, and then if there was not she might just as well walk towards the barn and the warmth of the cows' bodies. She would never reach them, but it was better to die quickly attempting something than to die slowly trying to keep awake in the kitchen.

With her breath coming in sobs, she went to the door. There was a pile of snow where it had drifted through the key-hole. She caught hold of the door handle and began to turn it. But before she opened the door she glanced back and looked round the darkened room in which she had toiled and eaten and, in spite of the drudgery, been happy with her husband. She knew that it was a thousand to one she would never see it again.

With an effort she tore her eyes away and pushed open the door. It slammed behind her as the wind and snow swooped down like a million knives cutting at her body. She flashed her torch along the veranda wall. The beam of light wavered and then fastened on a tattered pair of blue overalls. There was still a chance!

She crept towards them and pulled off her right mitten with her teeth. Surely after all the misfortunes of the last few hours it was too much to expect him to have left any matches in the pockets. And if he had, supposing the pockets had holes in them. And if....

She had no more time to think, for her fingers were inside the first pocket. As she had feared, it was empty. She sobbed as she tried the second—and then the third. They, too, were empty.

She drew in her breath and paused. There was only one more pocket—the right hip-pocket—and she could not bring herself to try it. If it was empty too, then she was done for.

She could hardly move her bare fingers and knew that if she waited another minute or two they would be frost-bitten. There was nothing for it but to try, and then, if she drew a blank, that last walk to the barn. With the impatience of desperation she thrust her fingers in the pocket. They felt nothing, and with a gasp of despair she was about to withdraw them when they touched a little hard object in one corner.

It was scarcely worth trying, but she picked at it with the nail of her forefinger. It seemed to be round, and she caught her breath with excitement and fear. She was sure now that it was the head of a match, but her fingers were so cold, and she trembled so in her eagerness, that for a moment she could not move it.

Finally her reawakening hope gave her the wit to push the torch underneath the outside of the pocket. She clawed and picked at the object with her nail, and then at last she knew that it was a match, a whole match which had slipped down a tiny hole in the pocket.

Slowly and with infinite care she drew it upward with her fingernail while the torch in her left hand held the cloth steady. Higher and higher it came until at last she was able to close the other fingers of her right hand round it. She cried aloud with joy as she clutched it, and her head swam from the reaction. She stood thus trying to pull herself together, for she had yet to regain the kitchen and light the match. Her hand was almost useless from the cold, and if she was not careful she would drop the match as she took it out of the pocket.

Salvation was so near, and yet it was so fatally easy to make a mistake. With infinite caution she put her mouth against the overalls and slowly drew her lips away from the mitten she had been holding in her teeth. She pressed her cheek against the end of it to keep it against the overalls and then slowly edged her lips into the pocket.

In her excitement she almost bit the match in two as her teeth closed over it, but with a great effort she restrained herself and at last stood erect with the end of it in her mouth. Her right hand felt dead as she wriggled it into her mitten again, but the match was still between her teeth as she turned and made for the door.

She had won, and the knowledge made her calm and confident in her purpose. She knew what she had to deal with, and this time she would not fail. While she stumbled the three yards to the door her brain reviewed what she must do.

She must find the match-box she had dropped on the floor and then open the door of the fire-box, sprinkle a little coal oil from the bottle in the pantry on the wood just in case of accident; and when she had done that, and not before, she could take off her right mitten. She had just enough feeling left in her right hand to strike that one match, and after that she would have to rub snow on it to guard against frostbite. And after that on her face, and then after that light the heater and fasten up her other hand, and chop the frozen milk and water out of the buckets with the little bench axe by the wood box, and then....

With the match between her teeth she opened the door and once more stood in the kitchen. It no longer seemed hostile, and she no longer feared the loneliness, for now she had hope and something definite to do. Her head was clear and she knew that she would not fail as she switched on the torch, which was beginning to wane but ought to last until she had lighted the lamp.

The match-box was covered with snow dropped from her coat, but it was so powdery that she blew it off with one puff through her clenched teeth. Her hand did not shake until she had opened the door of the fire-box and sprinkled the coal oil over the wood.

But when she had wriggled out of her right mitten and knelt down on the floor by the fire-box, she had to work her fingers like a pianist before she could trust them to take the match from her teeth. Gingerly she transferred the match to her fingers, propped the torch up against the leg of the stove, and then took the match-box from the top, where she had laid it.

Now that the crucial moment had come she was nervous again. She was afraid to look around. Her brain told her there was no other preparation to make, but it took her a terrible, seemingly endless minute before she could bring herself to make the final move. Her life depended on that match, and if she failed....

But she would not fail. With an unconscious gesture of defiance against fate she held the match-box inside the fire-box with her left hand right up against the paper, forced her deadened right hand slowly and carefully inside the opening, and with drawn breath struck the match.

The paper, sodden with coal oil, burst into flame which scorched her left mitten and made her frozen right hand throb with pain, but she scarcely noticed it.

The fire roared up the chimney in a deafening crescendo, and she shut the door of the fire-box with a gasp of ecstasy.

Soon she would be warm.

Haunted Villages

Lt. Col. W.H. Sleeman

On the 16th, we came on nine miles to Amabae, the frontier village of the Jansee territory, bordering upon Duteea, where I had to receive the farewell visits of many members of the Jansee parties, who came on to have a quiet opportunity to assure me that whatever may be the final order of the supreme government, they will do their best for the good of the people and the state, in whose welfare I feel great interest, for I have always considered Jansee among the native states of Bundelcund as a kind of oasis in the desert—the only one in which man can accumulate property with the confidence of being permitted by its rulers freely to display and enjoy it. I had also to receive the visit of messengers from the Rajah of Duteea, at whose capital we were to encamp the next day; and finally, to take leave of my amiable little friend, the Sureemunt, who here left me on his return to Saugor, with a heavy heart I really believe.

We talked of the common belief among the agricultural classes, of villages being haunted by the spirits of ancient proprietors, whom it was thought necessary to propitiate. 'He knew,' he said, 'many instances where these spirits were so very *froward* that the present heads of the villages which they haunted, and the members of their little communities, found it almost impossible to keep them in good humour; and their cattle and children were, in consequence, always liable to serious accidents of one kind or another. Sometimes they were bitten by snakes, sometimes became possessed by devils; and at others, were thrown down and beaten most unmercifully.' Any person who falls down in an epileptic fit is supposed to be thrown down by a ghost, or possessed by a devil. They feel little of our mysterious dread of ghosts—a sound *drubbing* is what they dread from them; and he who hurts himself in one of these fits is considered to have got it. 'As for himself, whenever he found any one of the villages upon his estate haunted by the spirit of an old patel (village proprietor), he always made a point of giving him a *neat little shrine;* and having it well endowed and attended, to keep him in good humour: this he thought was a duty that every landlord owed to his tenants!' Ramchund, the pundit, said, 'That villages which had been held by old Gond (mountaineer) proprietors were more liable than any other to those kinds of visitations—that it was easy to say what village was and was not haunted; but often exceedingly difficult to discover to whom the ghost belonged! This once discovered, his nearest surviving relation was, of course, expected to take steps to put him to rest; but,' said he, 'it is wrong to suppose that the ghost of an old proprietor must be always doing mischief—he is often the best friend of the cultivators, and of the present proprietor, too, if he treats him with proper respect; for he will not allow the people of any other village to encroach upon their boundaries with impunity; and they will be saved all the expense and annoyance of a reference to the Adawlut (judicial tribunals) for the settlement of boundary disputes. It will not cost much to conciliate these spirits; and the money is generally well laid out!'

Several anecdotes were told me in illustration; and all that I could urge against the probability or possibility of such visitations appeared to them very inconclusive and unsatisfactory; they mentioned the case of the family of village proprietors in the Saugor district, who had for several generations, at every new settlement, insisted upon having the name of the spirit of the old proprietor of another tribe inserted in the lease instead of their own, and thereby secured his good graces on all occasions. Mr Fraser had before mentioned this case to me. In August, 1834, while engaged in the settlement of the land revenue of the Saugor district for twenty years, he was about to deliver the lease of the estate made out in due form to the head of the family, a very honest and respectable old gentleman, when he asked him, respectfully, in whose name it had been made out? 'In yours to be sure; have you renewed your lease for twenty years?' The old man, in a state of great alarm, begged him to have it altered immediately, or he and his family would all be destroyed—that the spirit of the ancient proprietor presided over the village community and its interests; and that all affairs of importance were transacted in his name. 'He is,' said the old man, 'a very jealous spirit; and will not admit of any living man being considered, for a moment, as a proprietor or joint proprietor of the estate! It has been held by me and my ancestors immediately under government for many generations;

but the lease deeds have always been made out in his name; and ours have been inserted merely as his managers, or bailiffs—were this good old rule, under which we have so long prospered, to be now infringed, we should all perish under his anger.' Mr Fraser found, upon inquiry, that this had really been the case; and, to relieve the old man and his family from their fears, he had the papers made out afresh, and the *ghost* inserted as the proprietor! The modes of flattering and propitiating these beings, natural and supernatural, who are supposed to have the power to do mischief, are endless.

While I was in charge of the district of Nursingpore, in the valley of the Nerbudda, in 1823, a cultivator of the village of Bedoo, about twelve miles distant from my court, was one day engaged in the cultivation of his field on the border of the village of Burkhara, which was supposed to be haunted by the spirit of an old proprietor, whose temper was so froward and violent that the lands could hardly be let for anything; for hardly any man would venture to cultivate them lest he might unintentionally incur his ghostship's displeasure. The poor cultivator, after begging his pardon in secret, ventured to drive his plough a few yards beyond the proper line of his boundary, and thus to add half an acre of the lands of Burkhara to his own little tenement, which was situated in Bedoo. That very night his only son was bitten by a snake, and his two bullocks were seized with the murrain. In terror he went off to the village temple, confessed his sin, and vowed not only to restore the half acre of land to the village of Burkhara, but to build a very handsome shrine upon the spot as a perpetual sign of his repentance. The boy and the bullocks all three recovered, and the shrine was built; and is, I believe, still to be seen as the boundary mark!

The fact was that the village stood upon an elevated piece of ground rising out of a moist plain, and a colony of snakes had taken up their abode in it. The bites of these snakes had, on many occasions, proved fatal; and such accidents were all attributed to the anger of a spirit, which was supposed to haunt the village. At one time, under the former government, no one would take a lease of the village on any terms; and it had become almost entirely deserted, though the soil was the finest in the whole district. With a view to remove the whole prejudices of the people, the governor, Goroba Pundit, took the lease himself at the rent of one thousand rupees a year; and in the month of June went from his residence, twelve miles, with ten of his own ploughs, to superintend the commencement of so *perilous* an undertaking. On reaching the middle of the village, situated on the top of the little hill, he alighted from his horse, sat down upon a carpet that had been spread for him under a large and beautiful banyan tree, and began to refresh himself with a pipe before going to work in the fields.

As he quaffed his hookah, and railed at the follies of men, 'whose absurd superstitions had made them desert so beautiful a village with so noble a tree in its centre,' his eyes fell upon an enormous black snake which had coiled round one of its branches immediately over his head, and seemed as if resolved at once to pounce down and punish him for his blasphemy! He gave his pipe to his attendant, mounted his horse, from which the saddle had not yet been taken, and never pulled rein till he got home. Nothing could ever induce him to visit this village again, though he was afterwards employed under me as a native collector; and he has often told me that he verily believed this was the spirit of the old landlord that he had unhappily neglected to propitiate before taking possession!

My predecessor in the civil charge of that district, the late Mr Lindsay, of the Bengal civil service, again tried to remove the prejudices of the people against the occupation and cultivation of this fine village. It had never been measured; and all the revenue officers, backed by all the farmers and cultivators of the neighbourhood, declared that the spirit of the old proprietor would never allow it to be so. Mr Lindsay was a good geometrician, and had long been in the habit of superintending his revenue surveys himself; and on this occasion he thought himself particularly called upon to do so. A new measuring cord was made for the occasion, and with fear and trembling all his officers attended him to the first field; but in measuring it the rope, by some accident, broke! Poor Lindsay was that morning taken ill, and obliged to return to Nursingpore, where he died soon after from fever. No man was ever more beloved by all classes of the people of his district than he was; and I believe there was not one person among them who did not believe him to have fallen a victim to the resentment of the spirit of the old proprietor. When I went to the village some years afterwards, the people in the neighbourhood all declared to me that they saw the cord with which he was measuring fly into a thousand pieces the moment the men attempted to straighten it over the first field.

A very respectable old gentleman from the Concan, or Malabar coast, told me one day that every man there protects his field of corn and his fruit tree by dedicating it to one or other of the spirits which there abound, or confiding it to his guardianship. He sticks up something in the field, or ties on something to the tree, in the name of the said spirit, who from that moment feels himself responsible for its safe keeping. If anyone, without permission from the proprietor, presumes to take either an ear of corn from the field, or fruit from the tree, he is sure to be killed outright or made extremely ill. 'No other protection is required,' said the old gentleman, 'for our fields and fruit trees in that direction, though whole armies should have to march through them. I once saw a man come to the proprietor of a jack tree, embrace his feet, and in the most piteous manner implore his protection. He asked what was the matter. 'I took,' said the man, 'a jack from your tree yonder three days ago, as I passed at night; and I have been suffering dreadful agony in my stomach ever since. The spirit of the tree is upon me, and you only can pacify him.' The proprietor took up a bit of cow-dung, moistened it, and made a mark with it upon the man's forehead *in the name of the spirit,* and put some of it into the knot of hair on the top of his head. He had no sooner done this, than the man's pains all left him, and he went off, vowing never again to give similar cause of offence to one of these guardian spirits.'

'Men,' said my old friend, 'do not die there in the same regulated spirit, with their thoughts directed exclusively towards God, as in other parts; and whether a man's spirit is to haunt the world or not after his death all depends on that.'

From *Rambles and Recollections of An Indian Official* by Lt. Col. W.H. Sleeman of the Bengal Army, Vol I.

The Vampire

Sydney Horler

Until his death, quite recently, I used to visit at least once a week a Roman Catholic priest. The fact that I am a Protestant did nothing to shake our friendship. Father R——— was one of the finest characters I have ever known; he was capable of the broadest sympathies, and was, in the best sense of that frequently-abused term, 'a man of the world'. He was good enough to take considerable interest in my work as a novelist, and I often discussed plots and situations with him.

The story I am about to relate occurred about eighteen months ago—ten months before his illness. I was then writing my novel *The Curse of Doone*. In this story I made the villain take advantage of a ghasty legend attached to an old manor-house in Devonshire and use it for his own ends.

Father R——— listened while I outlined the plot I had in mind, and then said, to my great surprise: 'Certain people may scoff because they will not allow themselves to believe that there is any credence in the vampire tradition.'

'Yes, that is so,' I parried; 'but, all the same, Bram Stoker stirred the public imagination with his "Dracula"—one of the most horrible and yet fascinating books ever written—and I am hoping that my public will extend to me the customary "author's licence".'

My friend nodded.

'Quite,' he replied. 'As a matter of fact,' he went on to say, 'I believe in vampires myself.'

'You do?' I felt the hair on the back of my neck commence to irritate. It is one thing to write about a horror, but quite another to begin to see it assume definite shape. 'Yes,' said Father R——. 'I am forced to believe in vampires for the very good but terrible reason that I have met one!'

I half-rose in my chair. There could be no questioning R——'s word, and yet——

'That, no doubt, my dear fellow,' he continued, 'may appear a very extraordinary statement to have made, and yet I assure you it is the truth. It happened many years ago and in another part of the country—exactly where I do not think I had better tell you.'

'But this is amazing—you say you actually met a vampire face to face?'

'And talked to him. Until now I have never mentioned the matter to a living soul apart from a brother priest.'

It was clearly an invitation to listen; I crammed tobacco into my pipe and leaned back in the chair on the opposite side of the crackling fire. I had heard that Truth was said to be stranger than fiction—but here I was about to have, it seemed, the strange experience of listening to my own most sensational imagining being hopelessly out-done by *fact*!

'The name of the small town does not matter' (Father R—— started); 'let it suffice it was in the West of England and was inhabited by a good many people of superior means. There was a large city seventy-five miles away and business men, when they retired, often came to——to wind up their lives. I was young and very happy there in my work until——But I am a little previous.

'I was on very friendly terms with a local doctor; he often used to come in and have a chat when he could spare the time. We used to try to thresh out many problems which later experience has convinced me are insoluble—in this world, at least.

'One night, he looked at me rather curiously I thought.

' "What do you think of that man Farington?" he asked.

'Now, it was a curious fact that he should have made that inquiry at that exact moment, for by some subconscious means I happened to be thinking of this very person myself.

'The man who called himself "Joseph Farington" was a stranger who had recently come to settle in——. That circumstance alone would have caused comment, but when I say that he had bought the largest house on the hill overlooking the town on the south side (representing the best residential quarter) and had it furnished apparently regardless of cost by one of the famous London houses, that he sought to entertain a great deal but that no one seemed anxious to go twice to "The Gables".——Well, there was "something funny" about Farington, it was whispered.

'I knew this, of course—the smallest fragment of gossip comes to a priest's ear—and so I hesitated before replying to the doctor's direct question.

' "Confess now, Father," said my companion, "you are like all the rest of us—you don't like the man! He has made me his medical attendant, but I wish to goodness he had chosen someone else. There's 'something funny' about him."

' "Something funny"—there it was again. As the doctor's words sounded in my ears I remembered Farington as I had last seen him walking up the main street with every other eye half-turned in his direction. He was a big-framed man, the essence of masculinity. He looked so robust that the thought came instinctively: This man will never die. He had a florid complexion; he walked with the elasticity of youth and his hair was jet-black. Yet from remarks he had made, the impression in —— was that Farington must be at least sixty years of age.

' "Well, there's one thing, Sanders," I replied; "if appearances are anything to go by, Farington will not be giving you much trouble. The fellow looks as strong as an ox."

' "You haven't answered my question," persisted the doctor. "Forget your cloth, Father, and tell me exactly what you think of Joseph Farington. Don't you agree that he is a man to give you the shudders?"

' "You—a doctor—talking about getting the shudders!" I gently scoffed because I did not want to give my real opinion of Joseph Farington.

' "I can't help it—I have an instinctive horror of the fellow. This afternoon I was called up to 'The Gables'. Farington, like ever so many of his ox-like kind, is really a bit of a hypochondriac. He thought there was something wrong with his heart, he said."

' "And was there?"

' "The man ought to live to a hundred! But, I tell you, Father, I hated having to be near the fellow, there's something uncanny about him. I felt frightened—yes, frightened—all the time I was in the house. I had to talk to someone about it and as you are the safest person in —— I dropped in....You haven't said anything yourself, I notice."

'"I prefer to wait," I replied. It seemed the safest answer.

'Two months after that conversation with Sanders, not only —— but the whole of the country was startled and horrified by a terrible crime. A girl of eighteen, the belle of the district, was found dead in a field. Her face, in life so beautiful, was revolting in death because of the expression of dreadful horror it held.

'The poor girl had been murdered—but in a manner which sent shudders of fear racing up and down people's spines.... There was a great hole in the throat, as though a beast of the jungle had attacked....

'It is not difficult to say how suspicion for this fiendish crime first started to fasten itself on Joseph Farington, preposterous as the statement may seem. Although he had gone out of his way to become sociable, the man had made no real friends. Sanders, although a clever doctor, was not the most tactful of men and there is no doubt that his refusal to visit Farington professionally—he had hinted as much on the night of his visit to me, you will remember—got noised about. In any case, public opinion was strongly roused; without a shred of direct evidence to go upon, people began to talk of Farington as being the actual murderer. There was some talk among the wild young spirits of setting fire to "The Gables" one night, and burning Farington in his bed.

'It was whilst this feeling was at its height that, very unwillingly, as you may imagine, I was brought into the affair. I received a note from Farington asking me to dine with him one night.

' "I have something on my mind which I wish to talk over with you; so please do not fail me."

'These were the concluding words of the letter.

'Such an appeal could not be ignored by a man of religion and so I replied accepting.

'Farington was a good host; the food was excellent; on the surface there was nothing wrong. But—and here is the curious part—from the moment I faced the man I knew there was something wrong. I had the same uneasiness as Sanders, the doctor: *I felt afraid*. The man had an aura of evil; he was possessed of some devilish force or quality which chilled me to the marrow.

'I did my best to hide my discomfiture, but when, after dinner, Farington began to speak about the murder of that poor, innocent girl, this feeling increased. And at once the terrible truth leaped into my mind: I knew it was Farington who had done this crime: the man was a monster!

'Calling upon all my strength, I challenged him.

' "You wished to see me tonight for the purpose of easing your soul of a terrible burden," I said; "you cannot deny that it was you who killed that unfortunate girl."

' "Yes," he replied slowly, "that is the truth. I killed the girl. The demon which possesses me forced me to do it. But you, as a priest, must hold this confession sacred—you must preserve it as a secret. Give me a few more hours; then I will decide myself what to do."

'I left shortly afterwards. The man would not say anything more.

'"Give me a few hours," he repeated.

'That night I had a horrible dream. I felt I was suffocating. Scarcely able to breathe, I rushed to the window, pulled it open—and then fell senseless to the floor. The next thing I remember was Dr Sanders, who had been summoned by my faithful housekeeper, bending over me.

'"What happened?" he asked. "You had a look on your face as though you had been staring into hell."

'"So I had," I replied.

'"Had it anything to do with Farington?" he asked bluntly.

'"Sanders," and I clutched him by the arm in the intensity of my feeling, "does such a monstrosity as a vampire exist nowadays? Tell me, I implore you!"

'The good fellow forced me to take another nip of brandy before he would reply.

'Then he put a question himself.

'"Why do you ask that?" he said.

'"It sounds incredible—and I hope I really dreamed it—but I fainted tonight because I saw—or imagined I saw—the man Farington flying past the window that I had just opened."

'"I am not surprised," he nodded. "Ever since I examined the mutilated body of that poor girl I came to the conclusion that she had come to her death through some terrible abnormality.

'"Although we hear practically nothing about vampirism nowadays," he continued, "that is not to say that ghoulish spirits do not still take up their abode in a living man or woman, thus conferring upon them supernatural powers. What form was the shape you thought you saw?"

'"It was like a huge bat," I replied shuddering.

'"Tomorrow," said Sanders determinedly, "I'm going to London to see Scotland Yard. They may laugh at me at first, but——"

'Scotland Yard did not laugh. But criminals with supernatural powers were rather out of their line, and, besides, as they told Sanders, they had to have proof before they could convict Farington. Even my testimony—had I dared to break my priestly pledge, which, of course, I couldn't in any circumstances do—would not have been sufficient.

'Farington solved the terrible problem by committing suicide. He was found in bed with a bullet wound in his head.

'But, according to Sanders, only the body is dead—the vile spirit is roaming free, looking for another human habitation.

'God help its luckless victim.'

The Bordeaux Diligence*

Lord Halifax

A French gentleman, who had lost his wife and was in much sadness and misery, was walking down the Rue de Bac one day when he saw three men, who looked at him very pleasantly, and pointing to a woman at the end of the street, said, 'Pardon us, sir, but would you do us a favour?'

'Certainly,' he replied.

'Would you mind asking that lady at the end of the street at what time the Bordeaux diligence starts?'

He thought the request odd, but went to the end of the street, and said to the lady, 'I beg your pardon, but could you tell me at what hour the Bordeaux diligence starts?'

She answered hurriedly, 'Don't ask me; go and ask the *gendarme*.'

So he went up to the *agent de police* and put the same question to him.

---

*A diligence was a public stage-coach.

'What?' said the man.

'At what time does the Bordeaux diligence start?'

At this, the *agent de police* turned round, arrested him, and took him to the police station, where the man was put in a cell and presently brought up before the magistrate, who asked what was his crime.

The *agent de police* replied, 'He asked at what time the Bordeaux diligence starts.'

'He asked *that*, did he?' said the magistrate. 'Put him in the dark cell.'

'But,' protested the gentleman, 'I only asked what time the Bordeaux diligence starts, to oblige some men, who asked me to ask a woman, who told me to ask the *agent de police*.'

'Put him in the dark cell,' was the only reply.

Later on, the gentleman was brought up before a judge and jury, and the judge said, 'What is this man accused of?'

The *agent de police* answered, 'He came and asked me at what time the Bordeaux diligence starts.'

'He said *that*!' exclaimed the judge. 'Gentlemen of the jury, is this prisoner guilty or not guilty?'

'Guilty!' they all cried.

'Take him away,' said the judge. 'Seven years at Cayenne.'

So the wretched man was taken out in a convict ship and kept a close prisoner at Cayenne. After a time, he struck up a friendship with the other prisoners there, and one day they decided that each should tell the reason why he came to be sent to the Island. One said one thing, another another, until it came to the turn of the latest arrival to explain why he had been sent there.

'Oh,' he said, 'I was walking down the Rue de Bac one day, when I saw three men, who asked me if I would ask a lady at the end of the street at what time the Bordeaux diligence started, just to oblige them. I went and asked her and she told me to ask the *agent de police*, but when I asked him he turned round and arrested me and I was taken to the police station, and before the magistrate, and then before a judge and jury, who sent me here.'

When he had finished speaking there was silence, and from that time forward everyone shunned him.

After a while the Governor of the prison came to investigate the crimes of the various prisoners, so that some of them might be let off with easier work. At last the gentleman was brought before the Governor, who asked him what had been the nature of his offence. He repeated his story.

'*That!*' said the Governor. 'Give him solitary confinement.'

The poor man applied for the ministrations of the chaplain, who asked him what his crime had been, but when he repeated his story the chaplain went away and left him.

So he continued in misery and agony for seven years, until at last he was allowed to return home, without money, without relations and without friends. One day, shortly after his return, he thought he would walk down the Rue de Bac once again, and as he did so he saw the same woman at the end of the street, but looking very old and horrible. He accosted her and said, 'You are the author of all my misfortunes.'

She replied, 'Don't touch me, but if you like I will tell you why I asked you to do what I did. Go to the Champs-Elysées tonight at twelve o'clock and you will find a hut. Knock at the door and go in and I will explain to you why you have suffered all this misery.'

He went to the Champs-Elysées at the time mentioned, identified the hut, knocked, entered, and found the woman inside.

'Now,' he said, 'tell me why I have suffered all this.'

'Give me a glass of cognac,' was the answer.

He took a bottle from the shelf above her head and poured out a glass of brandy, which she drank.

'Now,' he said, 'tell me.'

'Give me some more cognac,' she said.

He gave her some more and she began to speak. 'Put your ear down here,' she said. 'I am very weak and cannot speak loudly.'

He put his ear down to her and she immediately sank her teeth into it and fell back with a heavy sigh—dead.

The Doctor's Ghost

Dr Norman Macleod

A friend of mine, a medical man, once went on a fishing expedition with an old college acquaintance, an army surgeon, whom he had not met for many years, from his having been in India with his regiment. McDonald, the army surgeon, was a thorough Highlander, and slightly tinged with what is called the superstition of his countrymen, and at the time I speak of was liable to rather depressed spirits from an unsound liver. His native air was, however, rapidly renewing his youth; and when he and his old friend paced along the banks of the fishing stream in a lonely part of Argyllshire, and sent their lines like airy gossamers over the pools, and touched the water over a salmon's nose, so temptingly that the best-principled and wisest fish could not resist the bite, McDonald had apparently regained all his buoyancy of spirit.

They had been fishing together for about a week with great success, when McDonald proposed to pay a visit to a family with which he was acquainted, that would separate him from his friend for some days. But whenever he spoke of their intended separation, he sank down into his old gloomy state, at one time declaring that he felt as if they were never to meet again. My friend tried to rally him, but in vain. They parted at the trouting stream, McDonald's route being across a mountain pass, with which, however, he had been well acquainted in his youth, though the road was lonely and wild in the extreme.

The doctor returned early in the evening to his resting-place, which was a shepherd's house lying on the very outskirts of the 'settlements', and beside a foaming mountain stream. The shepherd's only attendants at the time were two herd lads and three dogs. Attached to the hut, and communicating with it by a short passage, was rather a comfortable room which 'the Laird' had fitted up to serve as a sort of lodge for himself in the midst of his shooting-ground, and which he had put for a fortnight at the disposal of my friend.

Shortly after sunset, on the day I mention, the wind began to rise suddenly to a gale, the rain descended in torrents, and the night became extremely dark. The shepherd seemed uneasy, and several times went to the door to inspect the weather. At last he roused the fears of the doctor for McDonald's safety, by expressing the *hope* that by this time he was 'owre that awfu' black moss, and across the red burn.'

Every traveller in the Highlands knows how rapidly these mountain streams rise, and how confusing the moor becomes in a dark night. The confusion of memory once a doubt is suggested, the utter mystery of places, becomes, as I know from experience, quite indescribable.

'The black moss and red burn' were words that were never after forgot by the doctor, from the strange feelings they produced when first heard that night; for there came into his mind terrible thoughts and forebodings about poor McDonald, and reproaches for never having considered his possible danger in attempting such a journey alone. In vain the shepherd assured him that he must have reached a place of safety before the darkness and the storm came on. A presentiment which he could not cast off made him so miserable that he could hardly refrain from tears. But nothing could be done to relieve the anxiety now become so painful.

The doctor at last retired to bed about midnight. For a long time he could not sleep. The raging of the stream below the small window, and the *thuds* of the storm, made him feverish and restless. But at last he fell into a sound and dreamless sleep. Out of this, however, he was suddenly roused by a peculiar noise in his room, not very loud, but utterly indescribable. He heard tap, tap, tap at the window, and he knew, from the relation which the wall of the room bore to the rock, that the glass could not be touched by human hand.

After listening for a moment, and forcing himself to smile at his nervousness, he turned round, and began again to seek repose. But now a noise began too near and loud to make sleep possible. Starting and sitting up in bed, he heard repeated in rapid succession, as if someone was spitting in anger, and close to his bed,—'Fit! fit! fit!' and then a prolonged 'whir-r-r' from another part of the room, while every chair began to move, and the table to jerk!

The doctor remained in breathless silence, with every faculty intensely acute. He frankly confessed that he heard his heart beating, for the sound was so unearthly, so horrible, and something seemed to come so near him, that he began seriously to consider whether or not he had some attack of fever which affected his brain—for, remember, he had not tasted a drop of the shepherd's small store of whisky! He felt his pulse, composed his spirits, and compelled himself to exercise a calm judgment. Straining his eyes to discover anything, he plainly saw at last a white object moving, but without sound, before him. He knew that the door was shut and the window also.

An overpowering conviction then seized him, which he could not resist, that his friend McDonald was dead! By an effort he seized a lucifer-box on a chair beside him, and struck a light. No white object could be seen. The room appeared to be as when he went to bed. The door was shut. He looked at his watch, and particularly marked that the hour was twenty-two minutes past three. But the match was hardly extinguished when, louder than ever, the same unearthly cry of 'Fit! fit! fit!' was heard, followed by the same horrible whir-r-r-r, which made his teeth chatter. Then the movement of the table and every chair in the room was resumed with increased violence, while the tapping on the window was heard above the storm. There was no bell in the room, but the doctor, on hearing all this frightful confusion of sounds again repeated, and beholding the white object moving towards him in terrible silence, began to thump the wooden partition and to shout at the top of his voice for the shepherd, and having done so, he dived his head under the blankets!

The shepherd soon made his appearance, in his night-shirt, with a small oil-lamp, or 'crusey', over his head, anxiously inquiring as he entered the room:

'What is't, doctor? What's wrang? Pity me, are ye ill?'

'Very!' cried the doctor. But before he could give any explanation a loud whir-r-r was heard, with the old cry of 'Fit!' close to the shepherd, while two chairs fell at his feet! The shepherd sprang back, with a half scream of terror the lamp was dashed to the ground, and the door violently shut.

'Come back!' shouted the doctor. 'Come back, Duncan, instantly, I command you!'

The shepherd opened the door very partially, and said, in terrified accents:

'Gude be aboot us, that was awfu'! What under heaven is't?'

'Heaven knows, Duncan,' ejaculated the doctor with agitated voice, 'but do pick up the lamp, and I shall strike a light.'

Duncan did so in no small fear; but as he made his way to the bed in the darkness to get a match from the doctor, something caught his foot; he fell; and then, amidst the same noises and tumults of chairs, which immediately filled the apartment, the 'Fit! fit! fit! fit!' was prolonged with more vehemence than ever!

The doctor sprang up, and made his way out of the room, but his feet were several times tripped by some unknown power, so that he had the greatest difficulty in reaching the door without a fall. He was followed by Duncan, and both rushed out of the room, shutting the door after them. A new light having been obtained, they both returned with extreme caution, and, it must be added, real fear, in the hope of finding some cause or other for all those terrifying signs.

Would it surprise our readers to hear that they searched the room in vain—that, after minutely examining under the table, chairs, bed, everywhere, and with the door shut, not a trace could be found of anything? Would they believe that they heard during the day how poor McDonald had staggered, half dead from fatigue, into his friend's house, and falling into a fit, had died at *twenty-two minutes past three* that morning? We do not ask anyone to accept all of this as true. But we pledge our honour to the following facts:

The doctor, after the day's fishing was over, had packed his rod so as to take it into his bedroom; but he had left a minnow attached to the hook. A white cat left in the room swallowed the minnow and was hooked. The unfortunate gourmand had vehemently protested against this intrusion into its upper lip by the violent 'Fit! fit! fit!' with which she tried to spit the hook out; the reel added the mysterious whir-r-r-r; and the disengaged line, getting entangled in the legs of the chairs and table, as the hooked cat attempted to flee from her tormentor, set the furniture in motion, and tripped up both shepherd and doctor; while an ivy branch kept tapping at the window! Will anyone doubt the existence of ghosts and a spirit-world after this?

I have only to add that the doctor's skill was employed during the night in cutting the hook out of the cat's lip, while his poor patient, yet most impatient, was held by the shepherd in a bag, the head alone of the puss, with hook and minnow, being visible. McDonald made his appearance in a day or two, rejoicing once more to see his friend, and greatly enjoying the ghost story.

All Souls'

Edith Wharton

Queer and inexplicable as the business was, on the surface it appeared fairly simple—at the time, at least; but with the passing of years, and owing to there not having been a single witness of what happened except Sara Clayburn herself, the stories about it have become so exaggerated, and often so ridiculously inaccurate, that it seems necessary that someone connected with the affair, though not actually present—I repeat that when it happened my cousin was (or thought she was) quite alone in her house—should record the few facts actually known.

In those days I was often at Whitegates (as the place had always been called)—I was there, in fact not long before, and almost immediately after, the strange happenings of those thirty-six hours; Jim Clayburn and his widow were both my cousins, and because of that, and of my intimacy with them, both families think I am more likely than anybody else to be able to get at the facts, as far as they can be called facts. So I have written down, as clearly as

I could, the gist of the various talks I had with cousin Sara, when she could be got to talk—it wasn't often—about what occurred during that mysterious weekend.

★

I read the other day in a book by a fashionable essayist that ghosts went out when electric light came in. What nonsense! The writer, though he is fond of dabbling in a literary way, in the supernatural, hasn't even reached the threshold of his subject. As between turreted castles patrolled by headless victims with clanking chains, and the comfortable suburban house with a refrigerator and central heating where you feel, as soon as you're in it, *that there's something wrong*, give me the latter for sending a chill down the spine! And, by the way, haven't you noticed that it's generally not the high-strung and imaginative who see ghosts, but the calm matter-of-fact people who don't believe in them, and are sure they wouldn't mind if they did see one? Well, that was the case with Sara Clayburn and her house. The house, in spite of its age—it was built, I believe, about 1780—was open, airy, high-ceilinged, with electricity, central heating and all the modern appliances: and its mistress was—well, very much like her house. And, anyhow, this isn't exactly a ghost story and I've dragged in the analogy only as a way of showing you what kind of woman my cousin was, and how unlikely it would have seemed that what happened at Whitegates should have happened just there—or to her.

★

When Jim Clayburn died, the family all thought that, as the couple had no children, his widow would give up Whitegates and move either to New York or Boston—for being of good Colonial stock, with many relatives and friends, she would have found a place ready for her in either. But Sally Clayburn seldom did what other people expected, and in this case she did exactly the contrary; she stayed at Whitegates.

'What, turn my back on the old house—tear up all the family roots, and go and hang myself up in a bird-cage flat in one of those new skyscrapers in Lexington Avenue, with a bunch of chickweed and a cuttlefish to replace my good Connecticut mutton? No, thank you. Here I belong, and here I stay until my executors hand the place over to Jim's next of kin—that stupid fat Presley boy … Well, don't let's talk about him. But I tell you what—I'll keep him out of here as long as I can.' And she did—for being still in the early fifties when her husband died, and a muscular, resolute figure of a woman, she was more than a match for the fat Presley boy, and attended his funeral a few years ago, in correct mourning, with a faint smile under her veil.

Whitegates was a pleasant, hospitable-looking house, on a height overlooking the stately windings of the Connecticut River; but it was five or six miles from Norrington, the nearest town, and its situation would certainly have seemed remote and lonely to modern servants. Luckily, however, Sara Clayburn had inherited from her mother-in-law two or three old stand-bys who seemed as much a part of the family tradition as the roof they lived under; and I never heard of her having any trouble in her domestic arrangements.

The house, in the Colonial days, had been foursquare, with four spacious rooms on the ground floor, an oak-floored hall dividing them, the usual kitchen extension at the back, and a good attic under the roof. But Jim's grandparents, when interest in the 'Colonial' began to revive, in the early eighties, had added two wings, at right angles to the south front, so that the old 'circle' before the front door became a grassy court, enclosed on three sides, with a big elm in the middle. Thus the house was turned into a roomy dwelling, in which the last three generations of Clayburns had exercised a large hospitality; but the architect had respected the character of the old house, and the enlargement made it more comfortable without lessening its simplicity. There was a lot of land about it, and Jim Clayburn, like his fathers before him, farmed it, not without profit, and played a considerable and respected part in state politics. The Clayburns were always spoken of as a 'good influence' in the country, and the townspeople were glad when they learned that Sara did not mean to desert the place—'though it must be lonesome, living all alone up there atop of that hill'—they remarked as the days shortened, and the first snow began to pile up under the quadruple row of elms along the common.

Well, if I've given you a sufficiently clear idea of Whitegates and the Clayburns—who shared with their old house a sort of reassuring orderliness and dignity—I'll efface myself, and tell the tale, not in my cousin's words, for they were too confused and fragmentary, but as I built it up gradually out of her half-avowals and nervous reticences. If the thing happened at all—and I must leave you to be the judge of that—I think it must have happened in this way...

★

The morning had been bitter, with a driving sleet—though it was only the last day of October—but after lunch a watery sun showed for a while through banked-up woolly clouds, and tempted Sara Clayburn out. She was an energetic walker, and given, at that season, to tramping three or four miles along the valley road, and coming back by way of Shaker's wood. She had made her usual round, and was following the main drive to the house when she overtook a plainly-dressed women walking in the same direction. If the scene had not been so lonely—the way to Whitegates at the end of an autumn day was not a frequented one—Mrs Clayburn might not have paid any attention to the woman, for she was in no way noticeable, but when she caught up with the intruder, my cousin was surprised to find that she was a stranger—for the mistress of Whitegates prided herself on knowing, at least by sight, most of her country neighbours. It was almost dark, and the woman's face was hardly visible, but Mrs Clayburn told me she recalled her as middle-aged, plain and rather pale.

Mrs Clayburn greeted her, and then added: 'You're going to the house?'

'Yes, ma'am,' the woman answered, in a voice that the Connecticut Valley in old days would have called 'foreign', but that would have been unnoticed by ears used to the modern multiplicity of tongues. 'No, I couldn't say where she came from,' Sara always said, 'What struck me as queer was that I didn't know her.'

She asked the woman politely what she wanted, and the woman answered: 'Only to see one of the girls.' The answer was natural enough, and Mrs Clayburn nodded and turned off from the drive to the lower part of the garden, so that she saw no more of the visitor then or afterwards. And, in fact, a half hour later something happened which put the stranger entirely out of her mind. The brisk and light-footed Mrs Clayburn, as she approached the house, slipped on a frozen puddle, twisted her ankle and lay suddenly helpless.

★

Price, the butler, and Agnes, the dour old Scottish maid whom Sara had inherited from her mother-in-law, of course knew exactly what to do. In no time they had their mistress stretched out on a lounge, and Dr Selgrove had been called up from Norrington. When he arrived, he ordered Mrs Clayburn to bed, did the necessary examining and bandaging, and shook his head over her ankle, which he feared was fractured. He thought, however, that if she would swear not to get up, or even shift the position of her leg, he could spare her the discomfort of putting it in plaster. Mrs Clayburn agreed, the more promptly as the doctor warned her that any rash movement would prolong her immobility. Her quick imperious nature made the prospect trying, and she was annoyed with herself for having been so clumsy. But the mischief was done, and she immediately thought what an opportunity it would be for going over her accounts and catching up with her correspondence. So she settled down resignedly in her bed.

'And you won't miss much, you know, if you have to stay there a few days. It's beginning to snow, and it looks as if we are in for a good spell of it,' the doctor remarked, glancing through the window as he gathered up his implements. 'Well, we don't often get snow here as early as this; but winter's got to begin some time,' he concluded philosophically. At the door he stopped to add: 'You don't want me to send up a nurse from Norrington? Not to nurse you, you know; there's nothing much to do until I see you again. But this is a pretty lonely place when the snow begins, and I thought maybe—'

Sara Clayburn laughed. 'Lonely? With my old servants? You forget how many winters I've spent here along with them. Two of them were with me in my mother-in-law's time.'

'That's so,' Dr Selgrove agreed. 'You're a good deal luckier than most people, that way. Well, let me see; this is Saturday. We'll have to let the inflammation go down before we can X-ray you. Monday morning, first thing, I'll be here with the X-ray man. If you want me sooner, call me up.' And he was gone.

The foot, at first, had not been very painful; but towards the small hours Mrs Clayburn began to suffer. She was a bad patient, like most healthy and active people. Not being used to pain she did not know how to bear it, and the hours of wakefulness and immobility seemed endless. Agnes, before leaving her, had made everything as comfortable as possible. She had put a jug of lemonade within reach, and had even (Mrs Clayburn thought it odd afterwards) insisted on bringing in a tray with sandwiches and a thermos of tea. 'In case you're hungry in the night, madam.'

'Thank you; but I'm never hungry in the night. And I certainly shan't be tonight—only thirsty. I think I'm feverish.'

'Well, there's the lemonade, madam.'

'That will do. Take the other things away, please.' (Sara had always hated the sight of unwanted food 'messing about' in her room.)

'Very well, madam. Only you might——'

'Please take it away,' Mrs Clayburn repeated irritably.

'Very good, madam.' But as Agnes went out, her mistress heard her set the tray down softly on a table behind the screen which shut off the door.

'Obstinate old goose!' she thought, rather touched by the old woman's insistence.

Sleep, once it had gone, would not return, and the long black hours moved more and more slowly. How late the dawn came in November! 'If only I could move my leg,' she grumbled.

She lay still and strained her ears for the first steps of the servants. Whitegates was an early house, its mistress setting the example; it would surely not be long now before one of the women came. She was tempted to ring for Agnes, but refrained. She had been up late, and this was Sunday morning, when the household was always allowed a little extra time. Mrs Clayburn reflected restlessly: 'I was a fool not to let her leave the tea beside the bed, as she wanted to. I wonder if I could get up and get it?' But she remembered the doctor's warning, and dared not move. Anything rather than risk prolonging her imprisonment...

Ah, there was the stable clock striking. How loud it sounded in the snowy stillness! One—two—three—four—five...

What? Only five? Three hours and a quarter more before she could hope to hear the door handle turned... After a while she dozed off again, uncomfortably.

Another sound aroused her. Again the stable clock. She listened. But the room was still in deep darkness, and only six strokes fell ... She thought of reciting something to put her to sleep; but she seldom read poetry, and being naturally a good sleeper, she could not remember any of the usual devices against insomnia. The whole of her leg felt like lead now. The bandages had grown terribly tight—her ankle must have swollen… She lay staring at the dark windows, watching for the first glimmer of dawn. At last she saw a pale filter of daylight through the shutters. One by one the objects between the bed and the window recovered first their outline, then their bulk, and seemed to be stealthily regrouping themselves, after secret displacements during the night. Who that has lived in an old house could possibly believe that the furniture in it stays still all night? Mrs Clayburn almost fancied she saw one little slender- legged table slipping hastily back into its place.

'It knows Agnes is coming, and it's afraid,' she thought whimsically. Her bad night must have made her imaginative for such nonsense as that about the furniture had never occurred to her before…

At length, after hours more, as it seemed, the stable clock struck eight. Only another quarter of an hour. She watched the hand moving slowly across the face of the little clock beside her bed… ten minutes…five…only five! Agnes was as punctual as destiny…in two minutes now she would come. The two minutes passed, and she did not come. Poor Agnes—she had looked pale and tired the night before. She had overslept herself, no doubt—or perhaps she felt ill, and would send the housemaid to replace her. Mrs Clayburn waited.

She waited half an hour; then she reached up to the bell at the head of the bed. Poor old Agnes—her mistress felt guilty about waking her. But Agnes did not appear—and after a considerable interval Mrs Clayburn, now with a certain impatience, rang again. She rang once; twice; three times—but still no one came.

Once more she waited; then she said to herself: 'There must be something wrong with the electricity.' Well—she could find out by switching on the bed lamp at her elbow (how admirably the room was equipped with every practical appliance!). She switched it on—but no light came. Electric current off; and it was Sunday, and nothing could be done about it until the next morning. Unless it turned out to be just a burnt-out fuse, which Price could remedy. Well, in a moment now someone would surely come to her door.

It was nine o'clock before she admitted to herself that something uncommonly strange must have happened in the house. She began to feel a nervous apprehension; but she was not a woman to encourage it. If only she had had the telephone put in her room, instead of out on the landing! She measured mentally the distance to be travelled, remembered Dr Selgrove's admonition, and wondered if her broken ankle would carry her there. She dreaded the prospect of being put in plaster, but she had to get to the telephone, whatever happened.

She wrapped herself in her dressing-gown, found a walking-stick, and, resting heavily on it, dragged herself to the door. In her bedroom the careful Agnes had closed and fastened the shutters, so that it was not much lighter there than at dawn; but outside in the corridor the cold whiteness of the snowy morning seemed almost reassuring. Mysterious things—dreadful things—were associated with darkness; and here was the wholesome prosaic daylight come again to banish them. Mrs Clayburn looked about her and listened. A deep nocturnal silence lay in that day-lit house, in which five people were presumably coming and going about their work. It was certainly strange...She looked out of the window, hoping to see someone crossing the court or coming along the drive. But no one was in sight, and the snow seemed to have the place to itself: a quiet steady snow. It was still falling, with a business-like regularity, muffling the outer world in layers on layers of thick white velvet, and intensifying the silence within. A noiseless world—were people so sure that absence of noise was what they wanted? Let them first try a lonely country house in a November snowstorm!

She dragged herself along the passage to the telephone. When she unhooked the receiver she noticed that her hand trembled.

She rang up the pantry—no answer. She rang again. Silence—more silence! It seemed to be piling itself up like the snow on the roof and in the gutters. Silence. How many people that she knew had any idea what silence was—and how loud it sounded when you really listened to it?

Again she waited: then she rang up 'Central'. No answer. She tried three times. After that she tried the pantry again... The telephone was cut off, then; like the electric current. Who was at work downstairs, isolating her thus from the world? Her heart began to hammer. Luckily there was a chair near the telephone, and she sat down to recover her strength—or was it her courage?

Agnes and the housemaid slept in the nearest wing. She would certainly get as far as that when she had pulled herself together. Had she the courage——? Yes, of course she had. She had always been regarded as a plucky woman; and had so regarded herself. But this silence——

It occurred to her that by looking from the window of a neighbouring bathroom, she could see the kitchen chimney. There ought to be smoke coming from it at that hour; and if there were, she thought, she would be less afraid to go on. She got as far as the bathroom, and looking through the window saw that no smoke came from the chimney. Her sense of loneliness grew more acute. Whatever had happened downstairs must have happened before the morning's work had begun. The cook had not had time to light the fire, the other servants had not yet begun their rounds. She sank into the nearest chair, struggling against her fears. What next would she discover if she carried on her investigations?

The pain in her ankle made progress difficult; but she was aware of it now only as an obstacle to haste. No matter what it cost her in physical suffering, she must find out what was happening downstairs—or had happened. But first she would go to the maid's room. And if that were empty—well, somehow she would have to get herself downstairs.

She limped along the passage, and on the way steadied herself by resting her hand on a radiator. It was stone-cold. Yet in that well-ordered house in winter the central heating, though damped down at night, was never allowed to go out, and by eight in the morning a mellow warmth pervaded the rooms. The icy chill of the pipes startled her. It was the chauffeur who looked after the heating— so he too was involved in the mystery, whatever it was, as well as the house-servants. But this only deepened the problem.

★

At Agnes' door Mrs Clayburn paused and knocked. She expected no answer, and there was none. She opened the door and went in. The room was dark and very cold. She went to the window and flung back the shutters; then she looked around slowly, vaguely apprehensive of what she might see. The room was empty but what frightened her was not so much its emptiness as its air of scrupulous and undisturbed order. There was no sign of anyone having lately dressed in it—or undressed the night before. And the bed had not been slept in.

Mrs Clayburn leaned against the wall for a moment; then she crossed the floor and opened the cupboard. That was where Agnes kept her dresses; and the dresses were there, neatly hanging in a row. On the shelf above were Agnes' few and unfashionable hats, rearrangements of her mistress's old ones. Mrs Clayburn, who knew them all, looked at the shelf, and saw that one was missing. And so also was the warm winter coat she had given Agnes the previous winter.

She was out, then; had gone out, no doubt, the night before, since the bed was unslept in, the dressing and washing appliances untouched. Agnes, who never set foot out of the house after dark, who despised the movies as much as she did the wireless, and could never be persuaded that a little innocent amusement was a necessary element in life, had deserted the house on a snowy winter night, while her mistress lay upstairs, suffering and helpless! Why had she gone, and where had she gone? When she was undressing Mrs Clayburn the night before, taking her orders, trying to make her more comfortable, was she already planning this mysterious nocturnal escape? Or had something—the mysterious and dreadful something, the clue of which Mrs Clayburn was still groping— occurred later in the evening, sending the maid downstairs and out of doors into the bitter night? Perhaps one of the men at the garage—where the chauffeur and gardener lived—had been suddenly taken ill, and someone had run up to the house for Agnes. Yes—that must be the explanation... Yet how much it left unexplained.

Next to Agnes's room was the linen room; beyond that was the housemaid's door. Mrs Clayburn went to it and knocked. 'Mary!' No one answered, and she went in. The room was in the same immaculate order as her maid's, and here too the bed was unslept in, and there were no signs of dressing or undressing. The two women had no doubt gone out together—gone where?

More and more the cold unanswering silence of the house weighed down on Mrs Clayburn. She had never thought of it as a big house, but now, in this snowy winter light, it seemed immense, and full of ominous corners around which one dared not look.

Beyond the housemaid's room were the back stairs. It was the nearest way down, and every step that Mrs Clayburn took was increasingly painful; but she decided to walk slowly back, the whole length of the passage, and go down by the front stairs. She did not know why she did this; but she felt that at the moment she was past reasoning, and had better obey her instinct.

More than once she had explored the ground floor alone in the small hours, in search of unwonted midnight noises; but now it was not the idea of noises that frightened her, but that inexorable and hostile silence, the sense that the house had retained in full daylight its nocturnal mystery, and was watching her as she was watching it; that in entering those empty orderly rooms she might be disturbing some unseen confabulation on which beings of flesh and blood had better not intrude.

The broad oak stairs were beautifully polished, and so slippery that she had to cling to the rail and let herself down tread by tread. And as she descended, the silence descended with her—heavier, denser, more absolute. She seemed to feel its steps just behind her, softly keeping time with hers. It had a quality she had never been aware of in any other silence, as though it were not merely an absence of sound, a thin barrier between the ear and the surging murmur of life just beyond but an impenetrable substance made out of the world-wide cessation of all life and all movement.

Yes, that was what laid a chill on her: the feeling that there was no limit to this silence, no outer margin, nothing beyond it. By this time she had reached the foot of the stairs and was limping across the hall to the drawing-room. Whatever she found there, she was sure, would be mute and lifeless; but what would it be? The bodies of her dead servants, mown down by some homicidal maniac? And what if it were her turn next—if he were waiting for her behind the heavy curtains of the room she was about to enter? Well, she must find out—she must face whatever lay in wait. Not impelled by bravery—the last drop of courage had oozed out of her—but because anything, anything was better than to remain shut up in that snow-bound house without knowing whether she was alone in it or not. 'I must find that out, I must find that out,' she repeated to herself in a sort of meaningless sing-song.

The cold outer light flooded the drawing-room. The shutters had not been closed, nor the curtains drawn. She looked about her. The room was empty, and every chair in its usual place. Her armchair was pushed up by the chimney, and the cold hearth was piled with the ashes of the fire at which she had warmed herself before starting on her ill-fated walk. Even her empty coffee cup stood on a table near the armchair. It was evident that the servant had not been in the room since she had left it the day before after luncheon. And suddenly the conviction entered into her that, as she found the drawing-room, so she would find the rest of the house—cold, orderly, and empty. She would find nothing, she would find no one. She no longer felt any dread of ordinary human danger lurking in those dumb spaces ahead of her. She knew she was utterly alone under her own roof. She sat down to rest her aching ankle, and looked slowly about her.

There were the other rooms to be visited, and she was determined to go through them all—but she knew in advance that they would give no answer to her question. She knew it, seemingly, from the quality of the silence which enveloped her. There was no break, no thinnest crack in it anywhere. It had the cold continuity of the snow which was still falling steadily outside.

She had no idea how long she waited before nerving herself to continue her inspection. She no longer felt the pain in her ankle, but was only conscious that she must not bear her weight on it, and therefore moved very slowly, supporting herself on each piece of furniture in her path. On the ground floor no shutter had been closed, no curtain drawn, and she progressed without much difficulty from room to room: the library, her morning-room, the dining-room. In each of them, every piece of furniture was in its usual place. In the dining-room, that table had been laid for the dinner of the previous evening, and the candelabra, with candles unlit, stood reflected in the dark mahogany. She was not the kind of woman to nibble a poached egg on a tray when she was alone, but always came down to the dining-room, and had what she called a civilised meal.

The back premises remained to be visited. From the dining-room she entered the pantry, and there too everything was in irreproachable order. She opened the door and looked down the back passage with its neat linoleum floor-covering. The deep silence accompanied her; she still felt it moving watchfully at her side, as though she were its prisoner and it might throw itself upon her if she attempted to escape. She limped on towards the kitchen. That of course would be empty too, and immaculate. But she must see it.

She leaned a minute in the embrasure of a window in the passage. 'It's like the *Marie Celeste*—a *Marie Celeste* on terra firma,' she thought, recalling the unsolved sea mystery of her childhood. 'No one ever knew what happened on board the *Marie Celeste*. And perhaps no one will ever know what happened here. Even I shan't know.'

At the thought her latent fear seemed to take on a new quality. It was like an icy liquid running through every vein, and lying in a pool about her heart. She understood now that she had never before known what fear was, and that most of the people she had met had probably never known it either. For this sensation was something quite different...

It absorbed her so completely that she was not aware how long she remained leaning there. But suddenly a new impulse pushed her forward, and she walked on towards the scullery. She went there first because there was a service slide in the wall, through which she might peep into the kitchen without being seen; and some indefinable instinct told her that the kitchen held the clue to the mystery. She still felt strongly that whatever had happened in the house must have its source and centre in the kitchen.

In the scullery, as she had expected, everything was clean and tidy. Whatever had happened, no one in the house appeared to have been taken by surprise; there was nowhere any sign of confusion or disorder. 'It looks as if they'd known beforehand, and put everything straight,' she thought. She glanced at the wall facing the door, and saw that the slide was open. And then, as she was approaching it, the silence was broken. A voice was speaking in the kitchen—a man's voice, low but emphatic, and which she had never heard before.

She stood still, cold with fear. But this fear was again a different one. Her previous terror had been speculative, conjectured, a ghostly emanation of the surrounding silence. This was a plain everyday dread of evil-doers. Oh, God, why had she not remembered her husband's revolver, which ever since his death had lain in a drawer in her room?

She turned to retreat across the smooth slippery floor but halfway her stick slipped from her, and crashed on the tiles. The noise seemed to echo on and on through the emptiness, and she stood still, aghast. Now that she had betrayed her presence, flight was useless. Whoever was beyond the kitchen door would be upon her in a second...

But to her astonishment the voice went on speaking. It was as though neither the speaker nor his listeners had heard her. The invisible stranger spoke so low that she could not make out what he was saying, but the tone was passionately earnest, almost threatening. The next moment she realised that he was speaking in a foreign language, a language unknown to her. Once more her terror was surmounted by the urgent desire to know what was going on, so close to her yet unseen. She crept to the slide, peered cautiously through into the kitchen, and saw that it was as orderly and empty as the other rooms. But in the middle of the carefully scoured table stood a portable wireless, and the voice she heard came out of it...

She must have fainted then, she supposed; at any rate she felt so weak and dizzy that her memory of what happened next remained indistinct. But in the course of time she groped her way back to pantry, and there found a bottle of spirits—brandy or whisky, she could not remember which. She found a glass, poured herself a stiff drink, and while it was flushing through her veins, managed, she never knew with how many shuddering delays, to drag herself through the deserted ground floor, up the stairs and down the corridor to her own room. There, apparently, she fell across the threshold, again unconscious...

When she came to, she remembered her first care had been to lock herself in; then to recover her husband's revolver. It was not loaded, but she found some cartridges, and succeeded in loading it. Then she remembered that Agnes, on leaving her the evening before, had refused to carry away the tray with the tea and sandwiches, and she fell on them with a sudden hunger. She recalled also noticing that a flask of brandy had been put beside the thermos, and being vaguely surprised. Agnes's departure, then, had been deliberately planned, and she had known that her mistress, who never touched spirits, might have need of a stimulant before she returned. Mrs Clayburn poured some of the brandy into her tea, and swallowed it greedily.

After that (she told me later) she remembered that she had managed to start a fire in her grate, and after warming herself, had got back into her bed, piling on it all the coverings she could find. The afternoon passed in a haze of pain, out of which there emerged now and then a dim shape of fear—the fear that she might lie there alone and untended until she died of cold, and of the terror of her solitude. For she was sure by this time that the house was empty—completely empty, from garret to cellar. She knew it was so, she could not tell why; but again she felt that it must be because of the peculiar quality of the silence—the silence which had dogged her steps wherever she went, and was now folded down on her like a pall. She was sure that the nearness of any other human being, however dumb and secret, would have made a faint crack in the texture of that silence, flawed it as a sheet of glass is flawed by a pebble thrown against it...

★

'Is that easier?' the doctor asked, lifting himself from bending over her ankle. He shook his head disapprovingly. 'Looks to me as if you'd disobeyed orders—eh? Been moving about, haven't you? And I guess Dr Selgrove told you to keep quiet until he saw you again, didn't he?'

The speaker was a stranger, whom Mrs Clayburn knew only by name. Her own doctor had been called away that morning to the bedside of an old patient in Baltimore, and had asked this young man, who was beginning to be known at Norrington, to replace him. The newcomer was shy, and somewhat familiar, as the shy often are, and Mrs Clayburn decided that she did not much like him. But before she could convey this by the tone of her reply, she heard Agnes speaking—yes, Agnes, the same, the usual Agnes, standing behind the doctor, neat and stern-looking as ever. 'Mrs Clayburn must have got up and walked about in the night instead of ringing for me, as she'd ought to.' Agnes intervened severely.

This was too much! In spite of the pain, which was now exquisite, Mrs Clayburn laughed. 'Ringing for you? How could I, with the electricity cut off?'

'The electricity cut off?' Agnes's surprise was masterly. 'Why, when was it cut off?' She pressed her finger on the bell beside the bed, and the call tinkled through the quiet room. 'I tried that bell before I left you last night, madam, because if there'd been anything wrong with it I'd have come and slept in the dressing-room sooner than leave you here alone.'

Mrs Clayburn lay speechless, staring up at her. 'Last night? But last night I was all alone in the house.'

Agnes's firm features did not alter. She folded her hands resignedly across her trim apron. 'Perhaps the pain's made you a little confused, madam.' She looked at the doctor, who nodded.

'The pain in your foot must have been pretty bad,' he said.

'It was,' Mrs Clayburn replied. 'But it was nothing compared to the horror of being left alone in this empty house since the day before yesterday, with the heat and the electricity cut off, and the telephone not working.'

The doctor was looking at her in evident wonder. Agnes's sallow face flushed slightly, but only as if in indignation at an unjust charge. 'But, madam, I made up your fire with my own hands last night—and look, it's smouldering still. I was getting ready to start it again just now, when the doctor came.'

'That's so. She was down on her knees before it,' the doctor corroborated.

Again Mrs Clayburn laughed. Ingeniously as the tissue of lies was being woven about her, she felt she could still break through it. 'I made up the fire myself yesterday—there was no one else to do it,' she said, addressing the doctor, but keeping her eyes on her maid. 'I got up twice to put on more coal, because the house was like a sepulchre. The central heating must have been out since Saturday afternoon.'

At this incredible statement Agnes's face expressed only a polite distress; but the new doctor was evidently embarrassed at being drawn into an unintelligible controversy with which he had no time to deal. He said he had brought the X-ray photographer with him, but the ankle was much too swollen to be photographed at present. He asked Mrs Clayburn to excuse his haste, as he had all Dr Selgrove's patients to visit besides his own, and promised to come back that evening to decide whether she could be X-rayed then, and whether, as he evidently feared, the ankle would have to be put in plaster. Then, handing his prescriptions to Agnes, he departed.

Mrs Clayburn spent a feverish and suffering day. She did not feel well enough to carry on the discussion with Agnes; she did not ask to see the other servants. She grew drowsy, and understood that her mind was confused with fever. Agnes and the housemaid waited on her as attentively as usual, and by the time the doctor returned in the evening her temperature had fallen; but she decided not to speak of what was on her mind until Dr Selgrove reappeared. He was to be back the following evening, and the new doctor preferred to wait for him before deciding to put the ankle in plaster—though he feared this was now inevitable.

★

That afternoon Mrs Clayburn had me summoned by telephone, and I arrived at Whitegates the following day. My cousin, who looked pale and nervous, merely pointed to her foot, which had been put in plaster, and thanked me for coming to keep her company. She explained that Dr Selgrove had been taken suddenly ill in Baltimore, and would not be back for several days, but that the young man who replaced him seemed fairly competent. She made no allusion to the strange incidents I have set down, but I felt at once that she had received a shock which her accident, however painful, could not explain.

Finally, one evening, she told me the story of her strange weekend, as it had presented itself to her unusually clear and accurate mind, and as I have recorded it above. She did not tell me this until several weeks after my arrival; but she was still upstairs at the time, and obliged to divide her days between her bed and a lounge. During those endless intervening weeks, she told me she had thought the whole matter over: and though the events of the mysterious thirty-six hours were still vivid to her, they had already lost something of their haunting terror, and she had finally decided not to reopen the question with Agnes, or to touch on it in speaking to the other servants. Dr Selgrove's illness had been not only serious but prolonged. He had not yet returned, and it was reported that as soon as he was well enough he would go on a West Indian cruise, and not resume his practice at Norrington until the spring. Dr Selgrove, as my cousin was perfectly aware, was the only person who could prove that thirty-six hours had elapsed between his visit and that of his successor; and the latter, a shy young man, burdened by the heavy additional practice suddenly thrown on his shoulders, told me (when I risked a little private talk with him) that in the haste of Dr Selgrove's departure the only instructions he had given Mrs Clayton were summed up in the brief memorandum: 'Broken ankle. Have X-rayed.'

Knowing my cousin's authoritative character, I was surprised at her decision not to speak to the servants of what had happened; but on thinking it over I concluded she was right. They were all exactly as they had been before that unexplained episode: efficient, devoted, respectful and respectable. She was dependent on them and felt at home with them, and she evidently preferred to put the whole matter out of her mind, as far as she could. She was absolutely certain that something strange had happened in her house, and I was more than ever convinced that she had received a shock which the accident of a broken ankle was not sufficient to account for; but in the end I agreed that nothing was to be gained by cross-questioning the servants or the new doctor.

I was at Whitegates off and on that winter and during the following summer, and when I went home to New York for good early in October I left my cousin in her old health and spirits. Dr Selgrove had been ordered to Switzerland for the summer, and this further postponement of his return to his practice seemed to have put the happenings of the strange weekend out of her mind. Her life was going on as peacefully and normally as usual, and I left her without anxiety, and indeed without a thought of the mystery, which was now nearly a year old.

I was living then in a small flat in New York by myself, and I had hardly settled into it when, very late one evening—on the last day of October—I heard my bell ring. As it was my maid's evening out, and I was alone, I went to the door myself, and on the threshold, to my amazement, I saw Sara Clayburn. She was wrapped in a fur cloak, with a hat drawn down over her forehead, and a face so pale and haggard that I saw something dreadful must have happened to her. 'Sara,' I gasped, not knowing what I was saying, 'where in the world have you come from at this hour?'

'From Whitegates. I missed the last train and came by car.' She came in and sat on the bench near the door. I saw that she could hardly stand, and sat down beside her, putting my arm about her. 'For heaven's sake, tell me what happened.'

She looked at me without seeming to see me. 'I telephoned Nixon's and hired a car. It took me five hours and a quarter to get here.' She looked about her. 'Can you take me in for the night? I've left my luggage downstairs.'

'For as many nights as you like. But you look so ill——'

She shook her head. 'No; I'm not ill. I'm only frightened—deathly frightened,' she repeated in a whisper.

Her voice was so strange, and the hands I was pressing between mine were so cold, that I drew her to her feet and led her straight to my little guest-room. My flat was in an old-fashioned building, not many stories high, and I was on more human terms with the staff than is possible in one of the modern Babels. I telephoned down to have my cousin's bags brought up, and meanwhile I filled a hot water bottle, warmed the bed, and got her into it as quickly as I could. I had never seen her as unquestioning and submissive, and that alarmed me even more than her pallor. She was not a woman to let herself be undressed and put to bed like a baby; but she submitted without a word, as though aware that she had reached the end of her tether.

'It's good to be here,' she said in a quieter tone, as I tucked her up and smoothed the pillows. 'Don't leave me yet, will you—not just yet.'

'I'm not going to leave you for more than a minute—just to get you a cup of tea,' I reassured her; and she lay still. I left the door open, so that she could hear me stirring about in the little pantry across the passage, and when I brought her the tea she swallowed it gratefully, and a little colour came into her face. I sat with her in silence for some time; but at last she began: 'You see it's exactly a year——'

I should have preferred to have her put off until the next morning whatever she had to tell me; but I saw from her burning eyes that she was determined to rid her mind of what was burdening it, and that until she had done so it would be useless to proffer the sleeping draft I had ready.

'A year since what?' I asked stupidly, not yet associating her precipitate arrival with the mysterious occurrences of the previous year at Whitegates.

She looked at me in surprise. 'A year since I met that woman. Don't you remember—the strange woman who was coming up the drive the afternoon when I broke my ankle? I didn't think of it at the time, but it was on All Souls' eve that I met her.'

Yes, I said, I remembered that it was.

'Well—this is All Souls' eve, isn't it? I'm not as good as you are on Church dates, but I thought it was.'

'Yes. This is All Souls' eve.'

'I thought so ... Well, this afternoon I went out for my usual walk, I'd been writing letters, and paying bills, and didn't start until late; not until it was nearly dusk. But it was a lovely, clear evening. And as I got near the gate, there was the woman coming in—the same woman ... going towards the house...'

I pressed my cousin's hand, which was hot and feverish now. 'If it was dusk, could you be perfectly sure it was the same woman?' I asked.

'Oh, perfectly sure, the evening was so clear. I knew her and she knew me; and I could see she was angry at meeting me. I stopped her and asked: "Where are you going?" just as I had asked her last year. And she said, in the same queer, half-foreign voice. "Only to see one of the girls", as she had before. Then I felt angry all of a sudden, and I said: "You shan't set foot in my house again. Do you hear me? I order you to leave." And she laughed: yes, she laughed—very low, but distinctly. By that time it had got quite dark, as if a sudden storm was sweeping up over the sky, so that though she was so near me, I could hardly see her. We were standing by the clump of hemlocks at the turn of the drive, and as I went up to her, furious at her impertinence, she passed behind the hemlocks, and when I followed her she wasn't there ... No; I swear to you she wasn't there ... And in the darkness I hurried back to the house, afraid that she would slip by me and get there first. And the queer thing was that as I reached the door the black cloud vanished, and there was the transparent twilight again. In the house everything seemed as usual, and the servants were busy about their work; but I couldn't get it out of my head that the woman, under the shadow of that cloud, had somehow got there before me.' She paused for breath, and began again. 'In the hall I stopped at the telephone and rang up Nixon, and told him to send me a car at once to go to New York, with a man he knew to drive me. And Nixon came with the car himself...'

Her head sank back on the pillow and she looked at me like a frightened child. 'It was good of Nixon,' she said.

'Yes; it was very good of him. But when they saw you leaving—the servants, I mean...'

'Yes. Well, when I got upstairs to my room I rang for Agnes. She came, looking just as cool and quiet as usual. And when I told her I was starting for New York in half an hour—I said it was on account of a sudden business call—well, then her presence of mind failed her for the first time. She forgot to look surprised, she even forgot to make an objection—and you know what an objector Agnes is. And as I watched her I could see a little secret spark of relief in her eyes, though she was so on her guard. And she just said: "Very well, madam," and asked me what I wanted to take with me. Just as if I were in the habit of dashing off to New York after dark on an autumn night to meet a business engagement! No, she made a mistake not to show any surprise—and not even to ask me why I didn't take my own car. And her losing her head in that way frightened me more than anything else. For I saw she was so thankful I was going that she hardly dared speak, for fear she should betray herself, or I should change my mind.

After that Mrs Clayburn lay a long while silent, breathing less unrestfully; and at last she closed her eyes, as though she felt more at ease now that she had spoken, and wanted to sleep. As I got up quietly to leave her, she turned her head a little and murmured: 'I shall never go back to Whitegates again.' Then she shut her eyes and I saw that she was falling asleep.

I have set down above, I hope without omitting anything essential, the record of my cousin's strange experience as she told it to me. Of what happened at Whitegates that is all I can personally vouch for. The rest—and of course there is a rest—is pure conjecture; and I give it only as such.

My cousin's maid, Agnes, was from the Isle of Skye, and the Hebrides, as everyone knows, are full of the supernatural—whether in the shape of ghostly presences, or the almost ghostlier sense of unseen watchers peopling the long nights of those stormy solitudes. My cousin, at any rate, always regarded Agnes as the—perhaps unconscious, at any rate irresponsible—channel through which communications from the other side of the veil reached the submissive household at Whitegates. Though Agnes had been with Mrs Clayburn for a long time without any peculiar incident revealing this affinity with the unknown forces, the power to communicate with them may all the while have been latent in her, only awaiting a kindred touch; and that touch may have been given by the unknown visitor whom my cousin, two years in succession, had met coming up the drive at Whitegates on the eve of All Souls'. Certainly the date bears out my hypothesis; for I suppose that, even in this unimaginative age, a few people still remember that All Souls' eve is the night when the dead can walk—and when, by the same token, other spirits, piteous or malevolent, are also freed from the restrictions which secure the earth to the living on the other days of the year.

If the recurrence of this date is more than a coincidence—and for my part I think it is—then I take it that the strange woman who twice came up the drive at Whitegates on All Souls' eve was either a 'fetch', or else, more probably, and more alarmingly, a living woman inhabited by a witch. The history of witchcraft, as is well known, abounds in such cases, and such a messenger might well have been delegated by the powers who rule in these matters to summon Agnes and her fellow servants to a midnight 'Coven' in some neighbouring solitude. To learn what happens at Covens, and the reason of the irresistible fascination they exercise over the timorous and superstitious, one need only address oneself to the immense body of literature dealing with these mysterious rites. Anyone who has once felt the faintest curiosity to assist at a Coven apparently soon finds the curiosity increase to desire, the desire to an uncontrollable longing, which, when the opportunity presents itself, breaks down all inhibitions; for those who have once taken part in a Coven will move heaven and earth to take part again.

★

Such is my—conjectural—explanation of the strange happenings at Whitegates. My cousin always said she could not believe that incidents which might fit into the desolate landscape of the Hebrides could occur in the cheerful and populous Connecticut Valley; but if she did not believe, she at least feared—such moral paradoxes are not uncommon—and though she insisted that there must be some natural explanation of the mystery, she never returned to investigate it.

'No, no,' she said with a little shiver, whenever I touched on the subject of her going back to Whitegates, 'I don't want ever to risk seeing that woman again…' And she never went back.

The Phantom 'Rickshaw

Rudyard Kipling

> May no ill dreams disturb my rest,
> Nor Powers of Darkness me molest.
> Evening Hymn

One of the few advantages that India has over England is a great knowability. After five years' service a man is directly or indirectly acquainted with the two or three hundred Civilians in his Province, all the Messes of ten or twelve Regiments and Batteries, and some fifteen hundred other people of the non-official caste. In ten years his knowledge should be doubled, and at the end of twenty he knows, or knows something about, every Englishman in the Empire, and may travel anywhere and everywhere without paying hotel-bills.

Globe-trotters who expect entertainment as a right have, even within my memory, blunted this open-heartedness, but nonetheless to-day, if you belong to the Inner Circle and are neither a Bear nor a Black Sheep, all houses are open to you, and our small world is very, very kind and helpful.

Rickett of Kamartha stayed with Polder of Kumaon some fifteen years ago. He meant to stay two nights, but was knocked down by rheumatic fever, and for six weeks disorganised Polder's establishment, stopped Polder's work, and nearly died in Polder's bedroom. Polder behaves as though he had been placed under eternal obligation by Rickett, and yearly sends the little Ricketts a box of presents and toys. It is the same everywhere. The men who do not take the trouble to conceal from you their opinion that you are an incompetent ass, and the women who blacken your character and misunderstand your wife's amusements, will work themselves to the bone in your behalf if you fall sick or into serious trouble.

Heatherlegh, the Doctor, kept, in addition to his regular practice, a hospital on his private account—an arrangement of loose boxes for Incurables, his friend called it—but it was really a sort of fitting-up shed for craft that had been damaged by the stress of weather. The weather in India is often sultry, and since the tale of bricks is always a fixed quantity, and the only liberty allowed is permission to work overtime and get no thanks, men occasionally break down and become as mixed as the metaphors in this sentence.

Heatherlegh is the dearest doctor that ever was, and his invariable prescription to all his patients is, 'Lie low, go slow, and keep cool.' He says that more men are killed by overwork than the importance of this world justifies. He maintains that overwork slew Pansay, who died under his hands about three years ago. He has, of course, the right to speak authoritatively, and he laughs at my theory that there was a crack in Pansay's head and a little bit of the Dark World came through and pressed him to death. 'Pansay went off the handle,' says Heatherlegh, 'after the stimulus of long leave at Home. He may or he may not have behaved like a blackguard to Mrs Keith-Wessington. My notion is that the work of the Katabundi Settlement ran him off his legs, and that he took to brooding and making much of an ordinary P. & O. flirtation. He certainly was engaged to Miss Mannering, and she certainly broke off the engagement. Then he took a feverish chill and all that nonsense about ghosts developed. Overwork started his illness, kept it alight, and killed him, poor devil. Write him off to the System that uses one man to do the work of two and a half men.'

I do not believe this. I use to sit up with Pansay sometimes when Heatherlegh was called out to patients and I happened to be within claim. The man would make me most unhappy by describing in a low, even voice, the procession that was always passing at the bottom of the bed. He had a sick man's command of language. When he recovered I suggested that he should write out the whole affair from beginning to end, knowing that ink might assist him to ease his mind.

He was in a high fever while he was writing, and the blood-and-thunder Magazine diction he adopted did not calm him. Two months afterwards he was reported fit for duty, but, in spite of the fact that he was urgently needed to help an undermanned Commission stagger through a deficit, he preferred to die; vowing at the last that he was hag-ridden. I got his manuscript before he died, and this is his version of the affair, dated 1885, exactly as he wrote it:—

My doctor tells me that I need rest and change of air. It is not improbable that I shall get both ere long—rest that neither the red-coated messenger nor the mid-day gun can break, and change of air far beyond that which any homeward-bound steamer can give me. In the meantime I am resolved to stay where I am; and, in flat defiance of my doctor's orders, to take all the world into my confidence. You shall learn for yourselves the precise nature of my malady, and shall, too, judge for yourselves whether any man born of woman on this weary earth was ever so tormented as I.

Speaking now as a condemned criminal might speak ere the drop-bolts are drawn, my story, wild and hideously improbable as it may appear, demands at least attention. That it will ever receive credence I utterly disbelieve. Two months ago I should have scouted as mad or drunk the man who had dared tell me the like. Two months ago I was the happiest man in India. To-day, from Peshawar to the sea there is no one more wretched. My doctor and I are the only two who know this. His explanation is, that my brain, digestion, and eyesight are all slightly affected; giving rise to my frequent and persistent 'delusions'. Delusions, indeed I call him a fool; but he attends me still with the same unwearied smile, the same bland professional manner, the same neatly-trimmed red whiskers, till I begin to suspect that I am an ungrateful, evil-tempered invalid. But you shall judge for yourselves.

Three years ago it was my fortune—my great misfortune—to sail from Gravesend to Bombay, on return from a long leave, with one Agnes Keith-Wessington, wife of an officer on the Bombay side. It does not in the least concern you to know what manner of woman she was. Be content with the knowledge that, ere the voyage had ended, both she and I were desperately and unreasoningly in love with one another. Heaven knows that I can make the admission now without one particle of vanity. In matters of this sort there is always one who gives and another who accepts. From the first day of our ill-omened attachment, I was conscious that Agnes's passion was a stronger, a more dominant, and—if I may use the expression—a purer sentiment than mine. Whether she recognised the fact then, I do not know. Afterwards it was bitterly plain to both of us.

Arrived at Bombay in the spring of the year, we went our respective ways, to meet no more for the next three or four months, when my leave and her love took us both to Simla. There we spent the season together; and there my fire of straw burnt itself out to a pitiful end with the closing year. I attempt no excuse. I make no apology. Mrs Wessington had given up much for my sake, and was prepared to give up all. From my own lips, in August 1882, she learnt that I was sick of her presence, tired of her company, and weary of the sound of her voice. Ninety-nine women out of a hundred would have wearied of me as I wearied of them; seventy-five of that number would have promptly avenged themselves by active and obtrusive flirtation with other men. Mrs Wessington was the hundredth. On her neither my openly-expressed aversion nor the cutting brutalities with which I garnished our interviews had the least effect.

'Jack, darling!' was her one eternal cuckoo cry: 'I'm sure it's all a mistake—a hideous mistake; and we'll be good friends again some day. *Please* forgive me, Jack, dear.'

I was the offender, and I knew it. That knowledge transformed my pity into passive endurance, and, eventually, into blind hate—the same instinct, I suppose, which prompts a man to savagely stamp on the spider he has but half killed. And with this hate in my bosom the season of 1882 came to an end.

Next year we met again at Simla—she with her monotonous face and timid attempts at reconciliation, and I with loathing of her in every fibre of my frame. Several times I could not avoid meeting her alone; and on each occasion her words were identically the same. Still the unreasoning wail that it was all a 'mistake'; and still the hope of eventually 'making friends'. I might have seen, had I cared to look, that that hope only was keeping her alive. She grew more wan and thin month by month. You will agree with me, at least, that such conduct would have driven any one to despair. It was uncalled for; childish; unwomanly. I maintain that she was much to blame. And again, sometimes, in the black, fever-stricken night-watches, I have begun to think that I might have been a little kinder to her. But that really *is* a 'delusion'. I could not have continued pretending to love her when I didn't; could I? It would have been unfair to us both.

Last year we met again—on the same terms as before. The same weary appeals, and the same curt answers from my lips. At least I would make her see how wholly wrong and hopeless were her attempts at resuming the old relationship. As the season wore on, we fell apart—that is to say, she found it difficult to meet me, for I had other and more absorbing interests to attend to. When I think it over quietly in my sickroom, the season of 1884 seems a confused nightmare wherein light and shade were fantastically intermingled—my courtship of little Kitty Mannering; my hopes, doubts, and fears; our long rides together; my trembling avowal of attachment; her reply; and now and again a vision of a white face flitting by in the 'rickshaw with the black and white liveries I once watched for so earnestly; the wave of Mrs Wessington's gloved hand; and, when she met me alone, which was but seldom, the irksome monotony of her appeal. I loved Kitty Mannering; honestly, heartily loved her, and with my love for her grew my hatred for Agnes. In August, Kitty and I were engaged. The next day I met those accursed 'magpie' *jhampanies* at the back of Jakko, and, moved by some passing sentiment of pity, stopped to tell Mrs Wessington everything. She knew it already.

'So I hear you're engaged, Jack dear.' Then, without a moment's pause: 'I'm sure it's all a mistake—a hideous mistake. We shall be as good friends some day, Jack, as we ever were.'

My answer might have made even a man wince. It cut the dying woman before me like the blow of a whip. 'Please forgive me, Jack; I didn't mean to make you angry; but it's true, it's true!'

And Mrs Wessington broke down completely. I turned away and left her to finish her journey in peace, feeling, but only for a moment or two, that I had been an unutterably mean hound. I looked back, and saw that she had turned her 'rickshaw with the idea, I suppose, of overtaking me.

The scene and its surroundings were photographed on my memory. The rain-swept sky (we were at the end of the wet weather), the sodden, dingy pines, the muddy road, and the black powder-riven cliffs formed a gloomy background against which the black and white liveries of the *jhampanies*, the yellow-panelled 'rickshaw and Mrs Wessington's down-bowed golden head stood out clearly. She was holding her handkerchief in her left hand and was leaning back exhausted against the 'rickshaw cushions. I turned my horse up a bypath near the Sanjowlie Reservoir and literally ran away. Once I fancied I heard a faint call of 'Jack!'. This may have been imagination. I never stopped to verify it. Ten minutes later I came across Kitty on horseback; and, in the delight of a long ride with her, forgot all about the interview.

A week later Mrs Wessington died, and the inexpressible burden of her existence was removed from my life. I went Plainsward perfectly happy. Before three months were over I had forgotten all about her, except that at times the discovery of some of her old letters reminded me unpleasantly of our bygone relationship. By January I had disinterred what was left of our correspondence from among my scattered belongings and had burnt it. At the beginning of April of this year, 1885, I was at Simla—semi-deserted Simla—once more, and was deep in lover's talks and walks with Kitty. It was decided that we should be married at the end of June. You will understand, therefore, that, loving Kitty as I did, I am not saying too much when I pronounce myself to have been, at that time, the happiest man in India.

Fourteen delightful days passed almost before I noticed their flight. Then, aroused to the sense of what was proper among mortals, circumstanced as we were, I pointed out to Kitty that an engagement ring was the outward and visible sign of her dignity as an engaged girl; and that she must forthwith come to Hamilton's to be measured for one. Up to that moment, I give you my word, we had completely forgotten so trivial a matter. To Hamilton's we accordingly went on the 15th of April 1885. Remember that—whatever my doctor may say to the contrary—I was then in perfect health, enjoying a well-balanced mind and an *absolutely* tranquil spirit. Kitty and I entered Hamilton's shop together, and there, regardless of the order of affairs, I measured Kitty for the ring in the presence of the amused assistant. The ring was a sapphire with two diamonds. We men rode out down the slope that leads to the Combermere Bridge and Peliti's shop.

While my Waler was cautiously feeling his way over the loose shale, and Kitty was laughing and chattering at my side-while all Simla, that is to say as much of it as had then come from the Plains, was grouped round the Reading-room and Peliti's veranda, I was aware that someone, apparently at a vast distance, was calling me by my Christian name. It struck me that I had heard the voice before, but when and where I could not at once determine. In the short space it took to cover the road between the path from Hamilton's shop and the first plank of the Combermere Bridge I had thought over half a dozen people who might have committed such a solecism, and had eventually decided that it must have been some singing in my ears. Immediately opposite Peliti's shop my eye was arrested by the sight of four *jhampanies* in 'magpie' livery, pulling a yellow-panelled, cheap, bazar 'rickshaw. In a moment my mind flew back to the previous season and Mrs Wessington, with a sense of irritation and disgust. Was it not enough that the woman was dead and done with, without her black and white servitors reappearing to spoil the day's happiness? Whoever employed them now, I thought I would call upon, and ask as a personal favour to change her *jhampanies'* livery. I would hire the men myself, and, if necessary, buy their coats from off their backs. It is impossible to say here what a flood of undesirable memories their presence evoked.

'Kitty,' I cried, 'there are poor Mrs Wessington's *jhampanies* turned up again! I wonder who has them now?'

Kitty had known Mrs Wessington slightly last season, and had always been interested in the sickly woman.

'What? Where?' she asked. 'I can't see them anywhere.'

Even as she spoke, her horse, swerving from a laden mule, threw himself directly in front of the advancing 'rickshaw. I had scarcely time to utter a word of warning when, to my unutterable horror, horse and rider passed *through* men and carriage as if they had been thin air.

'What's the matter?' cried Kitty; 'what made you call out so foolishly, Jack? If I *am* engaged I don't want all creation to know about it. There was lots of space between the mule and the veranda; and, if you think I can't ride—— There!'

Whereupon the wilful Kitty set off, her dainty little head in the air, at a hand-gallop in the direction of the Band-stand; fully expecting, as she herself afterwards told me, that I should follow her. What was the matter? Nothing indeed. Either that I was mad or drunk, or that Simla was haunted with devils. I reined in my impatient cob, and turned round. The 'rickshaw had turned too, and now stood immediately facing me, near the left railing of the Combermere Bridge.

'Jack! Jack, darling!' (There was no mistake about the words this time: they rang through my brain as if they had been shouted in my ear.) 'It's some hideous mistake, I'm sure. *Please* forgive me, Jack, and lets' be friends again.'

The 'rickshaw-hood had fallen back, and inside, as I hope and pray daily for the death I dread by night, sat Mrs Keith-

Wessington, handkerchief in hand, and golden head bowed on her breast.

How long I stared motionless I do not know. Finally, I was aroused by my syce taking the Waler's bridle and asking whether I was ill. From the horrible to the commonplace is but a step. I tumbled off my horse and dashed, half fainting, into Peliti's for a glass of cherry-brandy. There two or three couples were gathered round the coffee-tables discussing the gossip of the day. Their trivialities were more comforting to me just then than the consolations of religion could have been. I plunged into the midst of the conversation at once; chatted, laughed, and jested with a face (when I caught a glimpse of it in a mirror) as white and drawn as that of a corpse. Three or four men noticed my condition; and, evidently setting it down to the results of over-many pegs, charitably endeavoured to draw me apart from the rest of the loungers. But I refused to be led away. I wanted the company of my kind—as a child rushes into the midst of the dinner-party after a fright in the dark. I must have talked for about ten minutes or so, though it seemed an eternity to me, when I heard Kitty's clear voice outside enquiring for me. In another minute she had entered the shop, prepared to upbraid me for failing so signally in my duties. Something in my face stopped her.

'Why, Jack,' she cried, 'what *have* you been doing? What *has* happened? Are you ill?' Thus driven into a direct lie, I said that the sun had been a little too much for me. it was close upon five o'clock of a cloudy April afternoon, and the sun had been hidden all day. I saw my mistake as soon as the words were out of my mouth: attempted to recover it; blundered hopelessly and followed

Kitty, in a regal rage, out of doors, amid the smiles of my acquaintances. I made some excuse (I have forgotten what) on the score of my feeling faint; and cantered away to my hotel, leaving Kitty to finish the ride by herself.

In my room I sat down and tried calmly to reason out the matter. Here was I, Theobald Jack Pansay, a well-educated Bengal Civilian in the year of grace, 1885, presumably sane, certainly healthy, driven in terror from my sweetheart's side by the apparition of a woman who had been dead and buried eight months ago. These were facts that I could not blink. Nothing was further from my thought than any memory of Mrs Wessington when Kitty and I left Hamilton's shop. Nothing was more utterly commonplace than the stretch of wall opposite Peliti's. It was broad daylight. The road was full of people; and yet here, look you, in defiance of every law of probability, in direct outrage of Nature's ordinance, there had appeared to me a face from the grave.

Kitty's Arab had gone *through* the 'rickshaw: so that my first hope that some woman marvellously like Mrs Wessington had hired the carriage and the coolies with their old livery was lost. Again and again I went round this treadmill of thought; and again and again gave up baffled and in despair. The voice was as inexplicable as the apparition. I had originally some wild notion of confiding it all to Kitty; of begging her to marry me at once; and in her arms defying the ghostly occupant of the 'rickshaw. 'After all,' I argued, 'the presence of the 'rickshaw is in itself enough to prove the existence of a spectral illusion. One may see ghosts of men and women, but surely never coolies and carriages. The whole thing is absurd. Fancy the ghost of a hillman!'

Next morning I sent a penitent note to Kitty, imploring her to overlook my strange conduct of the previous afternoon. My Divinity was still very wroth, and a personal apology was necessary. I explained, with a fluency born of night-long pondering over a falsehood, that I had been attacked with a sudden palpitation of the heart—the result of indigestion. This eminently practical solution had its effect: and Kitty and I rode out that afternoon with the shadow of my first lie dividing us.

Nothing would please her save a canter round Jakko. With my nerves still unstrung from the previous night I feebly protested against the notion, suggesting Observatory Hill, Jutogh, the Boileaugunge road—anything rather than the Jakko round. Kitty was angry and a little hurt; so I yielded from fear of provoking further misunderstanding, and we set out together towards Chota Simla. We walked a greater part of the way, and, according to our custom, cantered from a mile or so below the Convent to the stretch of level road by the Sanjowlie Reservoir. The wretched horses appeared to fly, and my heart beat quicker and quicker as we neared the crest of the ascent. My mind had been full of Mrs Wessington all the afternoon; and every inch of the Jakko road bore witness to our old-time walks and talks. The bowlders were full of it; the pines sang it aloud overhead; the rain-fed torrents giggled and chuckled unseen over the shameful story; and the wind in my ears chanted the iniquity aloud.

As a fitting climax, in the middle of the level men call the Ladies' Mile the horror was awaiting me. No other 'rickshaw was in sight—only the four black and white *jhampanies,* the yellow-panelled carriage, and the golden head of the woman within—all apparently just as I had left them eight months and one fortnight ago! For an instant I fancied that Kitty *must* see what I saw—we were so marvellously sympathetic in all things. Her next words undeceived me—'Not a soul in sight! Come along, Jack, and I'll race you to the Reservoir buildings!' Her wiry little Arab was off like a bird, my Waler following close behind, and in this order we dashed under the cliffs. Half a minute brought us within fifty yards of the 'rickshaw. I pulled my Waler and fell back a little. The 'rickshaw was directly in the middle of the road; and once more the Arab passed through it, my horse following. 'Jack! Jack dear! *Please* forgive me,' rang with a wail in my ears, and, after an interval: 'It's all a mistake, a hideous mistake!'

I spurred my horse like a man possessed. When I turned my head at the Reservoir works, the black and white liveries were still waiting—patiently waiting—under the gray hillside, and the wind brought me a mocking echo of the words I had just heard. Kitty bantered me a good deal on my silence throughout the remainder of the ride. I had been talking up till then wildly and at random. To save my life I could not speak afterwards, naturally, and from Sanjowlie to the Church wisely held my tongue.

I was to dine with the Mannerings that night, and had barely time to canter home to dress. On the road to Elysium Hill I overheard two men talking together in the dusk—'It's a curious thing,' said one, 'how completely all trace of it disappeared. You know my wife was insanely fond of the woman (never could see anything in her myself), and wanted me to pick up her old 'rickshaw and coolies if they were to be got for love or money. Morbid sort of fancy I call it; but I've got to do what the Memsahib tells me.

Would you believe that the man she hired it from tells me that all four of the men—they were brothers—died of cholera on the way to Hardwar, poor devils; and the 'rickshaw has been broken up by the man himself. Told me he never used a dead Memsahib's 'rickshaw. Spoilt his luck. Queer notion, wasn't it? Fancy poor little Mrs Wessington spoiling any one's luck except her own!' I laughed aloud at this point; and my laugh jarred on me as I uttered it. So there *were* ghosts of 'rickshaws after all, and ghostly employments in the other world! How much did Mrs Wessington give her men? What were their hours? Where did they go?

And for visible answer to my last question I saw the infernal Thing blocking my path in the twilight. The dead travel fast, and by short cuts unknown to ordinary coolies. I laughed aloud a second time and checked my laughter suddenly, for I was afraid I was going mad. Mad to a certain extent I must have been, for I recollect that I reined in my horse at the head of the 'rickshaw, and politely wished Mrs Wessington 'Good-evening'. Her answer was one I knew only too well. I listened to the end; and replied that I had heard it all before, but should be delighted if she had anything further to say; some malignant devil stronger than I must have entered into me that evening, for I have a dim recollection of talking the commonplaces of the day for five minutes to the Thing in front of me.

'Mad as a hatter, poor devil—or drunk. Max, try and get him to come home.'

Surely *that* was not Mrs Wessington's voice! The two men had overheard me speaking to the empty air, and had returned to look after me. They were very kind and considerate, and from their words evidently gathered that I was extremely drunk. I thanked them confusedly and cantered away to my hotel, there changed, and arrived at the Mannerings' ten minutes late. I pleaded the darkness of the night as an excuse; was rebuked by Kitty for my unlover-like tardiness; and sat down.

The conversation had already become general; and under cover of it, I was addressing some tender small talk to my sweetheart when I was aware that at the further end of the table a short red-whiskered man was describing, with much broidery, his encounter with a mad unknown that evening.

A few sentences convinced me that he was repeating the incident of half an hour ago. In the middle of the story he looked around for applause, as professional story-tellers do, caught my eye, and straightway collapsed. There was a moment's awkward silence, and the red-whiskered man muttered something to the effect that he had 'forgotten the rest', thereby sacrificing a reputation as a good story-teller which he had built up for six seasons past. I blessed him from the bottom of my heart, and—went on with my fish.

In the fullness of time that dinner came to an end; and with genuine regret I tore myself away from Kitty—as certain as I was of my own existence that it would be waiting for me outside the door. The red-whiskered man, who had been introduced to me as Dr Heatherlegh of Simla, volunteered to bear me company as far as our roads lay together. I accepted his offer with gratitude.

My instinct had not deceived me. It lay in readiness in the Mall, and, in what seemed devilish mockery of our ways, with a lighted head lamp. The red-whiskered man went to the point at once, in a manner that showed he had been thinking over it all dinner-time.

'I say, Pansay, what the deuce was the matter with you this evening on the Elysium Road?' The suddenness of the question wrenched an answer from me before I was aware.

'That!' said I, pointing to it.

'*That* may be either D.T or Eyes for aught I know. Now you don't liquor. I saw as much at dinner, so it can't be D.T. There's nothing whatever where you're pointing, though you're sweating and trembling with fright, like a scared pony. Therefore, I conclude that it's Eyes. And I ought to understand all about them. Come along home with me. I'm on the Blessington lower road.'

To my intense delight the 'rickshaw instead of waiting for us kept about twenty yards ahead—and this, too, whether we walked, trotted, or cantered. In the course of that long night ride I had told my companion almost as much as I have told you here.

'Well, you've spoilt one of the best tales I've ever laid tongue to,' said he, 'but I'll forgive you for the sake of what you've gone through, Now come home and do what I tell you; and when I've cured you, young man, let this be a lesson to you to steer clear of women and indigestible food till the day of your death.'

The 'rickshaw kept steady in front; and my red-whiskered friend seemed to derive great pleasure from my account of its exact whereabouts.

'Eyes, Pansay—all Eyes, Brain, and Stomach. And the greatest of these three is Stomach. You've too much conceited Brain, too little Stomach, and thoroughly unhealthy Eyes. Get your Stomach straight and the rest follows. And all that's French for a liver pill. I'll take sole medical charge of you from this hour! For you're too interesting a phenomenon to be passed over.'

By this time we were deep in the shadow of the Blessington lower road and the 'rickshaw came to a dead stop under a pine-clad, overhanging shale cliff. Instinctively I halted too, giving my reason, Heatherlegh rapped out an oath.

'Now, if you think I'm going to spend a cold night on the hillside for the sake of a Stomach-cum-Brain-cum-Eye illusion——Lord, ha' mercy! What's that?'

There was a muffled report, a blinding smother of dust just in front of us, a crack, the noise of rent boughs, and about ten yards of the cliff-side—pines, undergrowth, and all—slid down into the road below, completely blocking it up. The uprooted trees swayed and tottered for a moment like drunken giants in the gloom, and then fell prone among their fellows with a thunderous crash. Our two horses stood motionless and sweating with fear. As soon as the rattle of falling earth and stone had subsided, my companion muttered: 'Man, if we'd gone forward we should have been ten feet deep in our graves by now. "There are more things in heaven and earth" ... Come home, Pansay, and thank God. I want a peg badly.'

We retraced our way over the Church Ridge, and I arrived at Dr Heatherlegh's house shortly after midnight.

His attempts towards my cure commenced almost immediately, and for a week I never left his sight. Many a time in the course of that week did I bless the good fortune which had thrown me in contact with Simla's best and kindest doctor. Day by day my spirits grew lighter and more equable. Day by day, too, I became more and more inclined to fall in with Heatherlegh's 'spectral illusion' theory, implicating the eyes, brain, and stomach. I wrote to Kitty, telling her that a slight sprain caused by a fall from my horse kept me indoors for a few days; and that I should be recovered before she had time to regret my absence.

Heatherlegh's treatment was simple to a degree. It consisted of liver pills, cold-water baths, and strong exercise, taken in the dusk or at early dawn—for, as he sagely observed: 'A man with a sprained ankle doesn't walk a dozen miles a day, and your young woman might be wondering if she saw you.'

At the end of the week, after much examination of pupil and pulse, and strict injunctions as to diet and pedestrianism, Heatherlegh dismissed me as brusquely as he had taken charge of me. Here is his parting benediction: 'Man, I certify to your mental cure, and that's as much as to say I've cured most of your bodily ailments. Now, get your traps out of this as soon as you can; and be off to make love to Miss Kitty.'

I was endeavouring to express my thanks for his kindness. He cut me short.

'Don't think I did this because I like you. I gather that you've behaved like a blackguard all through. But, all the same, you're a phenomenon, and as queer a phenomenon as you are a blackguard, No!'—checking me a second time— 'not a rupee, please. Go out and see if you can find the eyes-brain-and-stomach business again. I'll give you a lakh for each time you see it.'

Half an hour later I was in the Mannerings' drawing-room with Kitty—drunk with the intoxication of the present happiness and the foreknowledge that I should never more be troubled with its hideous presence. Strong in the sense of my new-found security, I proposed a ride at once; and, by preference, a canter round Jakko.

Never had I felt so well, so overladen with vitality and mere animal spirits, as I did on the afternoon of the 30th of April. Kitty was delighted at the change in my appearance, and complimented me on it in her delightfully frank and outspoken manner. We left the Mannerings' house together, laughing and talking, and cantered along the Chota Simla road as of old.

I was in haste to reach the Sanjowlie Reservoir and there make my assurance doubly sure. The horses did their best, but seemed all too slow to my impatient mind. Kitty was astonished at my boisterousness. 'Why, Jack!' she cried at last, 'you are behaving like a child. What are you doing?'

We were just below the Convent, and from sheer wantonness I was making my Waler plunge and curvet across the road as I tickled it with the loop of my riding-whip.

'Doing?' I answered; 'nothing, dear. That's just it. If you'd been doing nothing for a week except lie up, you'd be as riotous as I.

> 'Singing and murmuring in your feastful mirth,
>   Joying to feel yourself alive;
> Lord over Nature, Lord of the visible Earth,
>   Lord of the senses five.'

My quotation was hardly out of my lips before we had rounded the corner above the Convent; and a few yards further on could see across to Sanjowlie. In the centre of the level road stood the black and white liveries, the yellow-panelled 'rickshaw, and Mrs Keith-Wessington. I pulled up, looked, rubbed my eyes, and, I believe, must have said something. The next thing I knew was that I was lying face downward on the road, with Kitty kneeling above me in tears.

'Has it gone, child?' I gasped. Kitty only wept more bitterly.

'Has what gone, Jack dear? What does it all mean? There must be a mistake somewhere, Jack. A hideous mistake.' Her last words brought me to my feet—mad—raving for the time being.

'Yes, there *is* a mistake somewhere,' I repeated, 'a hideous mistake. Come and look at It.'

I have an indistinct idea that I dragged Kitty by the wrist along the road up to where It stood, and implored her for pity's sake to speak to It; to tell It that we were betrothed; that neither Death nor Hell could break the tie between us: and Kitty only knows how much more to the same effect. Now and again I appealed passionately to the Terror in the 'rickshaw to bear witness to all I had said, and to release me from a torture that was killing me. As I talked I suppose I must have told Kitty of my old relations with Mrs Wessington, for I saw her listen intently with a white face and blazing eyes.

'Thank you, Mr Pansay,' she said, 'that's *quite* enough. Syce, *ghora lao.*'

The syces, impassive as Orientals always are, had come up with the recaptured horses; and as Kitty sprang into her saddle I caught hold of her bridle, entreating her to hear me out and forgive. My answer was the cut of her riding-whip across my face from mouth to eye, and a word or two of farewell that even now I cannot write down. So I judged and judged rightly, that Kitty knew all; and I staggered back to the side of the 'rickshaw. My face was cut and bleeding, and the blow of the riding-whip had raised a livid blue wheal on it. I had no self-respect. Just then, Heatherlegh, who must have been following Kitty and me at a distance, cantered up.

'Doctor,' I said, pointing to my face, 'here's Miss Mannering's signature to my order of dismissal and—— I'll thank you for that lakh as soon as convenient.'

Heatherlegh's face, even in my abject miser, moved me to laughter.

'I'll stake my professional reputation——' he began.

'Don't be a fool,' I whispered. 'I've lost my life's happiness and you'd better take me home.'

As I spoke the 'rickshaw was gone. Then I lost all knowledge of what was passing. The crest of Jakko seemed to heave and roll like the crest of a cloud and fall in upon me.

Seven days later (on the 7th of May, that is to say) I was aware that I was lying in Heatherlegh's room as weak as a little child. Heatherlegh was watching me intently from behind the papers on his writing-table. His first words were not encouraging; but I was too far spent to be much moved by them.

'Here's Miss Kitty has sent back your letters. You corresponded a good deal, you young people. Here's a packet that looks like a ring and a cheerful sort of a note from Mannering Papa, which I've taken the liberty of reading and burning. The old gendeman's not pleased with you.'

'And Kitty?' I asked dully.

'Rather more drawn than her father from what she says. By the same token you must have been letting out any number of queer reminiscences just before I met you. Says that a man who would have behaved to a woman as you did to Mrs Wessington ought to kill himself out of sheer pity for his kind. She's a hot-headed little virago, your mash. Will have it too that you were suffering from

D.T. when that row on the Jakko road turned up. Says she'll die before she ever speaks to you again.'

I groaned and turned over on the other side.

'Now you've got your choice, my friend. This engagement has to be broken off; and the Mannerings don't want to be too hard on you. Was it broken through D.T. or epileptic fits? Sorry I can't offer you a better exchange unless you'd prefer hereditary insanity. Say the word and I'll tell 'em it's fits. All Simla knows about that scene on the Ladies' Mile. Come! I'll give you five minutes to think over it.'

During those five minutes I believe that I explored thoroughly the lowest circles of the Inferno which man is permitted to tread on earth. And at the same time I was watching myself faltering through the dark labyrinths of doubt, misery, and utter despair. I wondered, as Heatherlegh in his chair might have wondered, which dreadful alternative I should adopt. Presently I heard myself answering in a voice that I hardly recognised—

'They're confoundedly particular about morality in these parts. Give 'em fits, Heatherlegh, and my love. Now let me sleep a bit longer.'

Then my two selves joined, and it was only I (half-crazed, devil-driven I) that tossed in my bed tracing step by step the history of the past month.

'But I am in Simla,' I kept repeating to myself. 'I, Jack Pansay am in Simla, and there are no ghosts here. It's unreasonable of that woman to pretend there are. Why couldn't Agnes have left me alone? I never did her any harm. It might just as well have been me as Agnes. Only I'd never have come back on purpose to kill *her*. Why can't I be left alone—left alone and happy?'

It was high noon when I first awoke: and the sun was low in the sky before I slept—slept as the tortured criminal sleeps on his rack, too worn to feel further pain.

Next day I could not leave my bed. Heatherlegh told me in the morning that he had received an answer from Mr Mannering, and that, thanks to his (Heatherlegh's) friendly offices, the story of my affliction had travelled through the length and breadth of Simla, where I was on all sides much pitied.

'And that's rather more than you deserve,' he concluded pleasantly, 'though the Lord knows you've been going through a pretty severe mill. Never mind; we'll cure you yet, you perverse phenomenon.'

I declined firmly to be cured. 'You've been much too good to me already, old man,' said I; 'but I don't think I need trouble you further.'

In my heart I knew that nothing Heatherlegh could do would lighten the burden that had been laid upon me.

With that knowledge came also a sense of hopeless, impotent rebellion against the unreasonableness of it all. There were scores of men no better than I whose punishments had at least been reserved for another world; and I felt that it was bitterly, cruelly unfair that I alone should have been singled out for so hideous a fate. This mood would in time give place to another where it seemed that the 'rickshaw and I were the only realities in a world of shadows; that Kitty was a ghost; that Mannering, Heatherlegh, and all the other men and women I knew were all ghosts; and the great, gray hills themselves but vain shadows devised to torture me. From mood to mood I tossed backwards and forwards for seven weary days; my body growing daily stronger and stronger, until the bedroom looking-glass told me that I had returned to everyday life, and was as other men once more. Curiously enough my face showed no signs of the struggle I had gone through. It was pale indeed, but as expressionless and commonplace as ever. I had expected some permanent alteration— visible evidence of the disease that was eating me away. I found nothing.

On the 15th of May I left Heatherlegh's house at eleven o'clock in the morning; and the instinct of the bachelor drove me to the Club. There I found that every man knew my story as told by Heatherlegh, and was, in clumsy fashion, abnormally kind and attentive. Nevertheless, I recognised that for the rest of my natural life I should be among but not of my fellows; and I envied very bitterly indeed the laughing coolies on the Mall below. I lunched at the Club, and at four o'clock wandered aimlessly down the Mall in the vague hope of meeting Kitty. Close to the Band-stand the black and white liveries joined me; and I heard Mrs Wessington's old appeal at my side. I had been expecting this ever since I came out; and was only surprised at her delay. The phantom 'rickshaw and I went side by side along the Chota Simla road in silence. Close to the bazar, Kitty and a man on horseback overtook and passed us. For any sign she gave I might have been a dog in the road. She did not even pay me the compliment of quickening her pace; though the rainy afternoon had served for an excuse.

So Kitty and her companion, and I and my ghostly Light-o'-Love, crept round Jakko in couples. The road was streaming with water; the pines dripped like roof-pipes on the rocks below, and the air was full of fine, driving rain. Two or three times I found myself saying to myself almost aloud: 'I'm Jack Pansay on leave at Simla—*at Simla!* Everyday, ordinary Simla. I mustn't forget that—I mustn't forget that.' Then I would try to recollect some of the gossip I had heard at the Club: the prices of so-and-so's horses—anything, in fact, that related to the work-a-day Anglo-Indian world I knew so well. I even repeated the multiplication-table rapidly to myself, to make quite sure that I was not taking leave of my senses. It gave me much comfort; and must have prevented my hearing Mrs Wessington for a time.

Once more I wearily climbed the Convent slope and entered the level road. Here Kitty and the man started off at a canter, and I was left alone with Mrs Wessington. 'Agnes,' said I, 'will you put back your hood and tell me what it all means?' The hood dropped noiselessly, and I was face to face with my dead and buried mistress. She was wearing the dress in which I had last seen her alive; carried the same tiny handkerchief in her right hand; and the same card-case in her left. (A woman eight months dead with a card-case!) I had to pin myself down to the multiplication-table, and to set both hands on the stone parapet of the road, to assure myself that that at least was real.

'Agnes,' I repeated, 'for pity's sake tell me what it all means.' Mrs Wessington leaned forward, with that odd, quick turn of the head I used to know so well, and spoke.

If my story had not already so madly overleaped the bounds of all human belief I should apologise to you now. As I know that no one—no, not even Kitty, for whom it is written as some sort of justification of my conduct—will believe me, I will go on. Mrs Wessington spoke and I walked with her from the Sanjowlie road to the turning below the Commander-in-Chief's house as I might walk by the side of any living woman's 'rickshaw, deep in conversation. The second and most tormenting of my moods of sickness had suddenly laid hold upon me, and like the prince in Tennyson's poem, 'I seemed to move amid a world of ghosts'. There had been a garden-party at the Commander-in-Chief's, and we two joined the crowd of homeward-bound folk. As I saw them it seemed that *they* were the shadows—impalpable fantastic shadows—that divided for Mrs Wessington's 'rickshaw to pass through. What we said during the course of that weird interview I cannot—indeed, I dare not—tell. Heatherlegh's comment would have been a short laugh and a remark that I had been 'mashing a brain-eye-and-stomach chimera'. It was a ghastly and, yet in some indefinable way, a marvellously dear experience. Could it be possible, I wondered, that I was in this life to woo a second time the woman I had killed by my own neglect and cruelty?

I met Kitty on the homeward road—a shadow among shadows. If I were to describe all the incidents of the next fortnight in their order, my story would never come to an end; and your patience would be exhausted. Morning after morning and evening after evening the ghostly 'rickshaw and I used to wander through Simla together. Wherever I went the four black and white liveries followed me and bore me company to and from my hotel. At the Theatre I found them amid the crowd of yelling *jhampanies;* outside the Club veranda, after a long evening of whist; at the Birthday Ball, waiting patiently for my reappearance; and in broad daylight when I went calling. Save that it cast no shadow, the 'rickshaw was in every respect as real to look upon as one of wood and iron. More than once, indeed, I have had to check myself from warning some hard-riding friend against cantering over it. More than once I have walked down the Mall deep in conversation with Mrs Wessington to the unspeakable amazement of the passers-by.

Before I had been out and about a week I learned that the 'fit' theory had been discarded in favour of insanity. However, I made no change in my mode of life. I called, rode, and dined out as freely as ever. I had a passion for the society of my kind which I had never felt before; I hungered to be among the realities of life; and at the same time I felt vaguely unhappy when I had been separated too long from my ghostly companion. It would be almost impossible to describe my varying moods from the 15th of May up to to-day.

The presence of the 'rickshaw filled me by turns with horror, blind fear, a dim sort of pleasure, and utter despair. I dared not leave Simla; and I knew that my stay there was killing me. I knew, moreover, that it was my destiny to die slowly and a little every day. My only anxiety was to get the penance over as quietly as might be. Alternately, I hungered for a sight of Kitty, and watched her outrageous flirtations with my successor—to speak more accurately, my successors—with amused interest. She was as much out of my life as I was out of hers. By day I wandered with Mrs Wessington almost content. By night I implored Heaven to let me return to the world as I used to know it. Above all these varying moods lay the sensation of dull, numbing wonder that the seen and the unseen should mingle so strangely on this earth to hound one poor soul to its grave.

★

August 27—Heatherlegh has been indefatigable in his attendance on me; and only yesterday told me that I ought to send in an application for sick leave. An application to escape the company of a phantom! A request that the Government would graciously permit me to get rid of five ghosts and an airy 'rickshaw by going to England! Heatherlegh's proposition moved me to almost hysterical laughter. I told him that I should await the end quietly at Simla; and I am sure that the end is not far off. Believe me that I dread its advent more than any word can say; and I torture myself nightly with a thousand speculations as to the manner of my death.

Shall I die in my bed decently and as an English gentleman should die; or, in one last walk on the Mall, will my soul be wrenched from me to take its place for ever and ever by the side of that ghastly phantasm? Shall I return to my old lost allegiance in the next world, or shall I meet Agnes loathing her and bound to her side through all eternity? Shall we two hover over the scene of our lives till the end of Time? As the day of my death draws nearer, the intense horror that all living flesh feels toward escaped spirits from beyond the grave grows more and more powerful. It is an awful thing to go down quick among the dead with scarcely one-half of our life completed. It is a thousand times more awful to wait as I do in your midst, for I know not what unimaginable terror. Pity me, at least on the score of my 'delusion', for I know you will never believe what I have written here. Yet as surely as ever a man was done to death by the Powers of Darkness, I am that man. In justice, too, pity her. For as surely as ever a woman was killed by a man, I killed Mrs Wessington. And the last portion of my punishment is even now upon me.